SEARCHING FOR HOME

After losing their parents in a freak war-time plane crash, Amelia and her fiercely angry older sister Mattie try to leave the past behind, but the past will not let them go. Searching for a place to call home, they are rescued by their aunt Lucy, and their grandparents, a wonderfully eccentric British couple from colonial India, who are also scarred by the war. As they grow up and move from 1940s Ireland, through post-war England, to golden Malta and London in the 1960s and 1970s, they accidentally uncover the cruellest secret of all...

SEARCHING FOR HOME

SEARCHING FOR HOME

by

Mary Stanley

Magna Large Print Books
Long Preston, North Yorkshire,
BD23 4ND, England.

British Library Cataloguing in Publication Data.

Stanley, Mary
    Searching for home.

    A catalogue record of this book is
    available from the British Library

    ISBN   0-7505-2385-9

First published in Great Britain 2005 by Headline Book Publishing

Copyright © 2005 Mary Stanley

Cover illustration © David Grogan by arrangement with
Headline Book Publishing Ltd.

The right of Mary Stanley to be identified as the author of this work
has been asserted by her in accordance with the Copyright, Designs
and Patents Act, 1988

Published in Large Print 2005 by arrangement with
Headline Book Publishing Ltd.

Magna Large Print is an imprint of Library Magna Books Ltd.

Printed and bound in Great Britain by
T.J. (International) Ltd., Cornwall, PL28 8RW

For Zanna Hornby and Patrick Grant,
who were there

Acknowledgements

I thank all who helped me, whether they meant to or not.

My vibrant and colourful friends in Malta for great times, wonderful memories and affection.

Carole Blake, agent and confidante, whose 'advice' I invariably take.

Dr Martin Brady for his classical knowledge when I got lost in the islands of the Mediterranean.

Corinne Gerada for the winds of Malta.

Zanna Hornby for advice on blowing up a lab, which has proved indispensable.

Ingrid Nachstern for being uniquely herself.

The one and only Flora Rees, brilliant editor and my friend.

Lorie Scicluna, for her friendship, farmhouse, the laughing afternoons and all the tiny details.

Lucy Stanley for reading and reading.

Tacchi for making me laugh.

Dr Justin Corfield for his philosophical knowledge, clarity of thought, continuous support, inspiration and for just being there.

The ultimate value of life depends upon awareness, and the power of contemplation rather than upon mere survival.

Aristotle, *384–322 BC*

PROLOGUE

I remember my father picking a wasp from his gin and tonic, believing that it had drowned.

It had not. It was merely drunk on the fermented juniper berries, unable to believe its luck, rescued by a lemon on which it momentarily rested until my father's long fingers plucked it from his glass, and placed it on the palm of his hand for my sister Mattie to admire.

'See its beauty,' he said. 'See the perfection of its stripes, the frailty yet strength of its wings.'

My sister Mattie obediently looked at the insect, which at that moment recovered from its bout of drunkenness, woke up and stung my father in the palm of his hand.

My mother, who was recently given to inappropriate fits of laughter, broke into peals of giggles and almost fell off her chair. My sister looked from one parent to the other, trying to decide with whom she should identify. The large eyes in her four-year-old face did not blink, nor did her head move as she observed both parents. Finally she chose my father, who had liberally cursed, and she said, 'Bugger the wasp,' in a momentary lapse from her customary silence.

This stopped both my parents in their tracks, as it was the first time Mattie had ever contributed a comment that was not a question. She looked hopefully from one adult to the other again, wondering if she had managed to bring about a truce. She had not.

Instead, my mother said irritably, 'Now look what you've gone and done.'

'How do you mean?' asked my father, peering at his hand before shaking it up and down, wincing in pain.

'The child's words,' said my mother, with exaggerated horror on her face.

'Could have been worse,' my father said.

And, indeed, it could have been worse.

Mattie was dressed in white. White dress, white stockings, and white shoes with tiny buttons along the sides accentuated the whiteness of her appearance. Her dark hair was curly and fell loose on her shoulders, with a small white bow adorning the top of her head, slightly to one side, attached to a hair clip, which held a front lock off her forehead. Her chubby little hands were folded on her lap. Mattie's expression was completely blank again and she sat with her lips tightly closed, her eyes turning from one parent to the other. Her white sunhat was lying on the table.

The lawn was the brightest green. My father regularly stuck a fork into it to help it both breathe and drink. The rest of the gardening he left to Feilim. Feilim was the handyman. He milked the cows, cut the hedges, replaced tiles on the roof, drank large cups of tea and always wore Wellingtons. Even in the height of summer.

Feilim was gormless. Or so my father said. 'Gorm' was the Irish for blue, but this did not mean that Feilim was blueless, rather that he was lacking in intelligence. My father said he couldn't help it. My mother said that he was only gormless when it suited him. My mother mispronounced the word and made the 'gorm' part sound like 'worm', rather than having it rhyme with 'norm'.

My mother's English was, as my father said, unique. Her name was Hilary. Before she was married she had been Hilary Entwhistle. She was brought up in colonial India and had been lovingly known as Hilarymem. My father said that he had rescued her from her fate. My mother neither reacted nor responded when he made this claim, as he often did.

'Time to teach the child croquet,' my father said. This was one of his many non-sequiturs.

'The mallets are too long for her,' my mother replied, smiling at him and the movement of his mind, which she alone seemed to follow.

Mattie sat very still, her eyes quickly moving from one parent to the other.

'We'll see about that,' my father said, taking to his feet and heading for the garage or a shed or somewhere closer to the house – I am not sure where exactly.

He returned with a mallet and a saw.

He told Mattie to stand and to hold the mallet in front of her while he gauged where he should make the cut. Obediently she climbed down from

15

the chair, and stood. Her white dress came to her calves, and now I could see that she had a white satin ribbon around her waist, tied at the back. She took the mallet in her hands and stood with it resting on the ground. The handle reached well above her head. My father marked it with a pen, and then, taking it from her, he laid it on the garden table and sawed most of the handle off.

He passed it back to her and said, 'Now, my girl. I'll teach you how to play.'

Mattie followed him down the grass to where the croquet hoops were laid out. He had them on the slope, which made it extremely hard work to get the ball through the hoops, because he always insisted that the game was played uphill.

The top of the handle was slightly chipped from the sawing, but my father said that he would sand it down later.

He never did.

Mattie tried to take a swing at the ball but nearly fell over from the weight of the head of the mallet.

'Champion,' my father pronounced.

My mother returned to her gin and tonic and sat staring down the lawn to where they stood swinging their mallets, or, in my sister's case, kicking the ball when my father was not looking.

The sea was remarkably blue that day. Every colour seemed accentuated. Red and orange flowers stood proudly in the borders, and the white lilac glistened in the sun as if it had been sprayed with silver.

My mother slowly swivelled her wedding ring around on her finger and stared at it with vacant eyes. She was finding the summer long and hot and difficult to deal with. And there was something exceptional about that particular day. It was not merely hot, it was sweltering, and there was a dull heaviness in the air making any kind of movement difficult.

My mother, pregnant for the third time – eight months into her cycle – and completely bored by circumstance, toyed with that gin and tonic for over an hour before pouring it out on to my father's perfect lawn. The war irritated her. So did pregnancy. Added to that, her sense of belonging – of being part of this home and this country – seemed distanced.

My father, on the other hand, belonged to that distinct social class of Ireland, which meant that he was as Irish if not more so than the Irish, and yet his accent, his English public schooling, and his very appearance differentiated him from most of our neighbours. He had thick dark curly hair and his slight upwards tilt of the chin might have given him an air of arrogance, but was belied by the wildness of his dark eyes and his loud and cheery laugh.

His country tweeds, his shirts from Jermyn Street, his boaters and his old school ties might have made him an alien in his homeland, but his ease with people, his neverending wit, his enthusiasm for his country life gave him an odd sense of compatibility.

He was liked.

No. It was more than that. His friends and neighbours enjoyed him, as an eccentric and endearing man.

My mother was tall with blonde curly hair and a propensity for wearing thin chiffon scarves that accentuated her long swan-like neck, and added to her general air of elegance. This elegance was maintained in her posture even while sitting there in the last stages of pregnancy, with the sun beating down on her, her slim ankles crossed and a look of composed withdrawal on her features.

The way she was sitting brought her own mother to mind and she could see her clearly in a deckchair on the terraced gardens of their Indian home, gin fizz in hand and at least two servants hovering nearby. Looking around, my mother winced. Staff in Ireland were not so easy to come by, and those they had appeared to have personalities that were larger than life. It was not what Hilary had been brought up to expect.

In a sense my parents came from different continents although they seemed to think they were of a similar culture. My mother's childhood was spent in Kashmir as the elder of Colonel Entwhistle's two daughters. Hilary mem and Lucy mem, names that soon rolled into Hilary-mem and Lucymem and somehow stuck as a joke between them, were seven years apart.

My father's family name was Cholmondesley, pronounced Chumley, and my mother sometimes called him Chum, just as his schoolmates and friends did. My father's home was Ithaca, residence of generations of Cholmondesleys, and there they lived with portraits of his ancestors in the hall and corridors, staring down.

Theirs was a very large house, the lawns of which sloped gently towards the dunes and on

18

down to the sea. My father had come into his inheritance on his twenty-first birthday, his parents having died in the sinking of the *Lusitania* while he was little more than an infant. His interests were varied, including hunting, shooting, farming, and the power of the elements, in particular fire and water. These latter pastimes may have reflected in some way his feelings towards the untimely demise of his parents. However, as he never spoke of them, it was difficult to know.

He refused to have fencing at the end of the garden, which kept my mother in a high state of alert with two very young children on the loose. His beach bonfires were well known in the neighbourhood – and, indeed, that was where our garden fence had ended up. He gathered driftwood and had in the past burned old furniture in these bonfires – often to my mother's consternation.

'I was very fond of that chest of drawers,' she was, from time to time, heard to mutter when she entered one of the spare bedrooms and bemoaned its emptiness.

Mattie, however, enjoyed his pastime and was known to help him by gathering pine cones and twigs from the trees around, bringing them lovingly to him, and gazing with delight when his fires took off, the flames leaping high into the sky, and the dry wood sparking outwards, bringing to the fore Hilary's maternal fears.

The war had put paid to his bonfires for the time being, as lighting fires on the beach at night was against the law in case it attracted German attention from across the sea.

My sister Georgina was having a nap on that afternoon, and my father had plans for the evening that he had not yet shared with Hilarymem.

'Matthew,' my mother called, as he and Mattie struggled uphill with their mallets and balls, 'one of us really ought to go and waken Georgina.'

'Let her sleep,' he shouted, knowing that he would have to attend to her when woken. It was a Sunday afternoon and the staff, such as they were, were absent on Sundays. Cook, maid and handyman all had their day off.

'Bugger Georgina,' Mattie said, clearly attracted to the new word she had learned, and giving her mallet an extremely hard swing for one so small. The mallet flew from her hand and landed quite some distance away.

'Did you see that?' my father called. 'It's cricket I should be teaching you. You'll be a fast bowler if that throw is anything to go by.'

My mother sighed. His enthusiasms were far-reaching, but as long as they did not involve her she usually managed to ignore them. However, at the moment everything he or the children did managed to exasperate her on some level.

'This terrible war,' my mother said aloud, with a vague effort to communicate some deeper emotion. These feelings of despair encompassed her mother in India, her sister in England and her father in the Far East. But she also hated the trouble it put her to and the worries and fears it evoked. At the weekends she had to close the curtains herself, although my father did check that there was no light showing from any window. The war had curtailed her and while she still carried out what she saw as her social obligations, she felt reined in by what my father referred to as the curfew.

'Curfew, curfew,' he would shout, and then he would set off about the house from room to room, even those unoccupied, as if on a nightly supervision of his property.

'I should be fighting,' he said in fury from time to time.

My mother held her peace. She feared saying anything in case he took himself off to the war. He and her children were her only consolation. With all her worries for the rest of her family, at least she had those nearest to her close.

'We'll hit the mountains tonight,' he announced.

'Oh, no, Chum, not that again,' she moaned, although she knew it was in vain.

Papa, as I always think of him, smiled boyishly at her. 'You need not come,' he announced, knowing full well that there was no way she would not accompany him.

If she found being in the house irksome, it was nothing to what she felt if she were left there alone.

My mother did not lack maternal instincts. She loved her daughters and coped with the difficulties of parenting as best she could. However, her mothering skills, such as they were, had been inherited from her mother, and they involved passing the children from ayah to ayah, although in Mother's case there were no ayahs in Ireland. She had plans on that front, though, and had written to her mother asking if one could be sent.

My grandmother, the Colonel's wife, known as the Colonel Memsahib in her now-native India, where, if truth be told, she was more at home than she had ever been in London or in Paris, had received this letter earlier in the year and contemplated its contents before putting her own plans into action.

Lucy, her second daughter, had finished her schooling in England, but due to the war could not return to Kashmir. My grandmother wrote to her and suggested that she go to stay with Hilary in Ireland until such time as she could return to the fold. My grandmother's suggestions were invariably taken as orders so Lucy simply pretended she had never received the letter in question. The thought of Ireland at that time was too off-putting for words and my aunt Lucy had other plans.

Lucy had not escaped the constraints of boarding school, and the far-reaching hand of her mother, to find herself incarcerated in the Cholmondesley home on the east coast of Ireland with her wings clipped. London was where Lucy dwelled, and where Lucy intended to stay, where her adrenalin flowed as she moved her way between air raids, shelters, work and parties with the ever-persistent sirens wailing in the distance. Her sister's home in County Wicklow across the Irish Sea had no lure for her, despite her strong sororial feelings. And mingled with that love was a sense of relief that her sister and her sister's family were safely away from the storm of war.

And so, without the help of Lucy or an ayah, and despite Mattie's persistent attempts to get them to rouse Georgina, whom she adored, my parents left the child to sleep for another two hours and when she woke the blackout was in place, curtains drawn and only a low light on in the kitchen where my mother lifted a salad from the fridge and added several slices of ham to it. From the breadbin, white soda bread was taken, which my mother briefly thought of claiming to have made, but good sense got the better of her as it occurred to her that Papa might ask her to bake another some time in the future.

Georgina banged a spoon on the table in anticipation but was easily distracted by Mattie, who removed the implement, scooped a piece of ham from her own plate and carried it to her sister's mouth.

Mattie, glancing conspiratorially at her sister, said, 'Bugger the ham,' and my mother winced.

'Ignore,' my father mouthed in an effort at solicitude.

They ate their meal and read for a while, before my father said, 'The mountains,' and my mother flinched again.

If there was one thing she hated it was his late-night mountain drives, which were becoming more frequent. They were always similar, but despite the tedium she went too.

He had been doing them sporadically since the war started, but ever since April of 1941, when one hundred and eighty German bombers attacked Belfast, he had been going up more regularly. A clear night, a cloudy night, it made no difference. After dark, when the mood took him, he would happily lift the sleeping children from their beds, always exclaiming how much better they would sleep in the mountain air.

He bundled the girls into the back of the car, and my mother climbed in beside him. He cranked the engine, and they were away.

The drive should have been slow as he could not turn on the car lights, but so used was he to the road that lack of lighting did not deter him from driving at full speed. There were no other cars out this particular night, and it was only at the foot of the mountains that they passed a woman walking alone.

'Slow down,' my mother said as they tore past her. 'You nearly hit her.'

'Hit whom?' my father asked. 'I saw no one.'

My mother did not reply. She saw no point.

On arriving at his destination, my mother, despite the heat, wrapped herself in a rug from the boot, while he woke the two girls and got them out of the car. Carrying Georgina, he started the climb further up the mountain with Mattie. He liked to look across the night over the sea and contemplate England, somehow hoping that he was offering moral support to friends, relatives and the general inhabitants across the water, who were undergoing the air raids. These air raids had earlier been nightly and very heavy before becoming sporadic and intermittent over the years, but none of this deterred him from his need to look across the sea.

What had started as a clear enough night with sufficient moon for him to drive without lights up into the hills – not that a lack of moon would have discouraged him – deteriorated very quickly, and the storm, which had been brewing in the heat of the day, finally erupted.

My mother, in the car, thought of getting out to call him to return and to bring them all safely home, but the wind whipped up and storm clouds gathered from the south, rolling in at an unusual speed, so she stayed where she was in the uncommon warmth and waited.

He, however, climbed higher than usual, with Georgina in his arms, and Mattie stoically following on her short legs. He was torn between returning to the car and staying to watch in silence as he imagined the damage being done in England and Wales that night.

The weather was freakish in the extreme, and it was with amazement he realised that the noise he could hear was not merely thunder but something more than that. He released Georgina from his arms as he listened into the wind. Then he became aware of a plane coming up from the southeast.

He started to shout, 'Get back, you Jerry bastards,' with Mattie trailing behind him, now clasping Georgina's hand and calling, 'Bugger the bastards' in mutual support.

They were quickly drenched to the skin but the drone of distant engines kept him rooted to the spot as the German plane, completely disorientated, headed straight for the mountains.

We lost them there that night, my father, one of my sisters and the pilot, when the plane plunged directly into the hillside. Down below where the car was parked, the rain on the window seriously impaired my mother's vision, and she sat there in the darkness, silently cursing his eccentricities and longing to get home to bed.

I was born that night in 1944, and while I have been told that it is impossible for the unborn child to see and to hear, it is my belief that I did hear and could somehow sense all that happened that day. Certainly no one told me about it – or at least I do not think that they did. But I recall the heat of the afternoon, the game of croquet, the ham and salad tea in the kitchen, and then the long drive up the mountains as some mute observer. I have no memory of the ball of fire, which must have occurred as the plane crashed straight into the mountainside, drowning out the furious roars of my father telling them to get back to Germany.

With the sound of the crash, it dawned on my mother very quickly what had happened. She went into labour immediately, and was so smitten by the pain that she was unable to get out of the car. Gasping and panting between contractions, she clutched the door handle in terror as the sound from the exploding aircraft faded to a dull and horrific silence before the roll of thunder overtook the night.

The emergency services, dispatched to the mountain on account of the terrible accident, discovered they had more than dead Germans to deal with. They tried to get my mother to release her hand from the nearest door so they could open it, but with all her strength she held on, just as she was holding on to me inside her. Initially her fear had been in giving birth alone there on the mountain in my father's car. Now that help had arrived, her fear seemed to have evolved so that she was just afraid of giving birth at all.

I like to think that she wanted to spare me the distress of being born in such a place, with the echo of the explosion and the pallor of death heavy in the air. But she may just have wanted to spare me being born at all on a night like that. They reached her through the driver's door, and delivered her right there on the front seat. They were bewildered as to what she was doing in a car on a mountainside, alone on a night like that. She tried to explain how my father used to go regularly up there to give moral support to the British across the Irish Sea, but the man who was trying to interview her between her labour pains, kept saying, 'What?' in such utter disbelief that she soon subsided in her efforts to say that her husband and daughters were somewhere up on the mountainside and she wanted them back, and she just screamed at God, the war and my father as I was being born.

Bring your desires down to your present means. Increase them only when your increased means permit.

Aristotle

CHAPTER ONE

Before the war, at the time of Lucy Entwhistle's last journey back to school in England from her home in Kashmir, she had felt, while saying goodbye to her parents, that she was, in some strange and as yet unidentified way, saying goodbye to her childhood.

On that last morning, wakening early and sitting up for a moment looking through the gauze netting around her bed, she had wondered when, if ever, she would return to India.

The bright light coming in the window lit up the pale smooth walls of her room and it was with a sense of both sadness and expectation that she slipped from her bed in Eden House for the last time. She twirled lightly on the wooden floor, catching sight of herself in the mirror and smiling while the sun caught the golden strands of her hair as they lifted around her head. Over at the window she looked down to the courtyard where she could see her mother, Harriet Entwhistle, and Mrs Patel deep in conversation. Mrs Patel was undoubtedly trying to convince her mother to buy some commodity with that persistence and perseverance that was uniquely hers – seemingly oblivious to the fact that to endeavour to push anything on Lucy's mother was a waste of time and energy.

Lucy smiled. She knew that she would miss those moments – those repetitive moments, which often irked because of their pointlessness, but which later became something that was part of a unique experience and whose absence would mean loss. She had experienced this in the past on other journeys back to school, when fleeting moments of nostalgia rose in her and she longed for sounds to remind her of home – such as her mother's voice commanding immediate obedience, or the clicking of the mah jong tiles falling on the table. There were nights in school when she would remember the jasmine petals strewn on the ground as their season ended, and the chattering of the monkeys in the empty ruins of the temple down by the gardens beyond the bridge.

Now, on the voyage back to England and with lazy days passing peacefully, the immediacy of being in India was fading, and she could feel herself in many senses turning westwards.

The journey by boat had brought some surprises with it.

Lucy knew that her mother had envisaged a safe return for her, and to that end all dates and times had been tied up carefully so that she was being accompanied by her older sister, Hilary, and Hilary's new husband, Matthew Cholmondesley. The timing of this marriage had been fixed so that Hilary and Matthew would have three days in the hills as a honeymoon, before leaving India and travelling with Lucy back to her school, and then on to Ireland.

Her mother, the Colonel Memsahib, left no stone unturned in her organisation and arrangements, and had believed that three days of honeymoon would suffice Matthew's male needs and would mean that he and Hilary would have plenty of time to spend with Lucy on board.

Lucy had rather thought the same, and was quite surprised when Hilary and Matthew took to rising late, rarely appearing more than twenty minutes before luncheon, and even then only just in time for a quick pre-prandial drink.

By day two it was clear that a pattern was forming. Hilary and Matthew danced all night, stayed in bed all morning, rising for lunch, and then returning to their cabin for most of the afternoon.

At first, Lucy naïvely thought that they were exhausted from the wedding preparations, the wedding itself, and then the trip up to the hills, but on day three, looking at her sister across the table, it occurred to her that exhaustion was not the cause of their cabin confinement.

Her sister was glowing. Hilary was literally radiating health and happiness. She and Matthew touched at every opportunity. Their glances were lingering. Hilary's eyes had developed a habit of changing from fiery excitement to a sultriness, which Lucy started to recognise. When this sultry, come-hither look appeared on her sister's face, Matthew invariably excused them both, and they disappeared for hours at a time.

And so the days passed. Lucy found herself increasingly alone, despite the activity on board ship and the vast number of ex-pats returning home.

She sat on deck thinking about this. Her book was abandoned in the heat, and even her hat seemed to wilt. She felt lonely. She knew many of the other passengers, including some girls returning to her school in England, but they did not interest her. She wanted her sister's companionship. She did not understand what was going on, but felt if she could not have inclusion with Hilary, she was not prepared to make an effort with other people on board.

Lucy had been a late developer, but she already carried her mother and her sister's elegance. Long and lean of limb, slim ankles crossed as she sat on her deck chair, one elbow propped on the arm rest, she looked older than she was while she was wearing her sunhat. With the hat off, her girlishness became apparent, with her fair hair, parted in the centre, neatly braided into plaits. She carried a childish element about her, totally belied by the reality. As the boat docked in Alexandria, she sauntered to the rail to look down at the bustle below.

That was when she first spotted Reinhold Kobaldt. And he spotted her.

He was standing on the quayside with his head held high and his legs apart. Dressed in khakis, with a hat, he carried his rifle slung across both shoulders, and held it in position by resting his wrists over it. From above he appeared tall, and was standing with his head slightly inclined to the left.

She watched him as she leaned on the railing. And he, looking up, saw a slender girl in a loose low-belted lemon dress, staring down.

Raising one hand from his rifle he lifted his hat off and stared up at her.

He had not been home for five years. The African sun had tanned his skin, his fair hair bleached blond by it, his mind slaked by too much time in Kenya. That had been followed by a long year further north, and the last few months had left him tired.

There was something hauntingly youthful and innocent about the girl on deck looking down with the possibility of a smile on her pretty face, and he waved up to her.

She waved back, and then immediately admonished herself, and pulled back from the rail lest he think her forward. But when she moved back again to look, he was still standing there staring up. It was difficult to be sure because of the distance down, but he looked as if he was smiling at her. The midday sun, burning down on her head – the sunhat now lying on the deck chair recently abandoned – appeared to him like a halo, and he was caught within its rays.

She thought about him during that afternoon. He had disappeared in the throngs both leaving and boarding the ship, and she wondered if he had been there to meet someone who was disembarking, or if possibly, just possibly, he might appear on deck.

The afternoon passed and before dinner she

knocked on her sister's cabin door.

Matthew appeared with a towel around his waist.

'Come in, come in,' he said enthusiastically.

Lucy, glancing past him at the tousled bed and her naked sister sprawled across it, opened and then closed her mouth.

'What is it?' Hilary called.

'It's young Lucymem, and she won't come in,' Matthew replied. He ran a hand through his thick curly black hair, and looked backwards and forwards between the two sisters as if unsure what to do.

Hilary rolled over quickly in the bed, pulling at the sheet to cover herself.

'Is anything the matter?' she asked.

'No,' Lucy answered. 'I just wanted some help dressing for dinner,' she added, a little wistfully.

She was torn between wanting to enter, to explore further, and the need to go and get herself ready. The smell in the room was tantalising. It reminded her of a particular flower in India, which gave off a similar musky spicy odour as it died. Hilary's long naked legs hinted at something beyond her imagination. Paralysed for a moment she gazed at her sister. Then she stepped back from the cabin door and slowly turned away.

'Are you sure?' Matthew said.

'Sure?' She turned back and looked at him, her mouth slightly open.

'That you won't come in?'

'No, thank you. No. I've to dress for dinner,' she said.

Half an hour later, she was brushing her hair when Hilary appeared at her door.

'Sorry, I've been ignoring you,' Hilary said. 'Not deliberately, though. Just been busy,' she giggled.

'What's it like?' Lucy asked, looking at her older sister, at the clear complexion of her skin, and the smile on her face.

'It? Well,' Hilary hesitated. Her smile extended. 'You're too young to understand,' she said.

'No, I'm not. Tell me. Please.'

'It's brilliant,' Hilary said. The smile turned into a laugh. 'Absolutely wonderful.'

Lucy was intrigued. This was not quite what their mother had implied. She had referred to it as one's duty. She had said that if all else failed one could think of England, or indeed that at least when it was over one would still be alive. Lucy could remember her mother taking her aside one afternoon and giving her a 'talk' on several matters, one of which was marital duty.

'Never forget,' the Colonel's wife had said with customary firmness. 'Never forget that men are basically animals. They have not evolved as far as women on the evolutionary scale. Their instincts are primal. Do you understand?' she asked.

'Yes, Mother,' Lucy had said, albeit a little doubtfully, as she was quite unsure to what her mother might be referring.

'Never, ever marry for love,' the Colonel Mem-sahib continued. 'Love is a mere diversion in the course of life.'

'Oh,' said Lucy with more than a little surprise. She had never questioned before if her parents loved each other. Was her mother implying

34

otherwise? Lucy's mind raced as she pondered this quickly before deciding that Harriet was giving her rules in general, but not necessarily rules to which she herself had adhered.

'You marry a man who will satisfy your needs,' continued her mother, now getting into her stride. 'And the needs of a woman are fairly straightforward. We need a home and a life that suit us. And a man whose head is not too big. Do you understand?'

Lucy tried to nod, but found she was shaking her head. A man whose head was not too big did not fit any of the equations she might heretofore have contemplated.

'A large head on a man may mean a large head on his child, and that would be very difficult. Am I making myself clear?'

Lucy imagined large-headed children wandering around and wondered why she had never seen any.

'They are difficult to give birth to,' her mother said firmly. 'Now, am I making myself clear?'

'Yes, Mother,' Lucy said, thinking about her father's head. It had always seemed quite normal to her but now she wondered if her mother was talking from personal experience.

Hilary brushed Lucy's hair for her, and even lent her a pink silk shawl embroidered with gold and black thread to wear over her white dress.

'What's this all about?' Hilary asked at one point. 'You dressing up so carefully, I mean.'

'I don't know,' Lucy said, looking at her sister in the mirror. 'I just wanted some time with you,'

35

she continued.

'Well, here I am,' Hilary said, glancing surreptitiously at her watch. She had left Matthew in his bath, and she still had to get herself ready.

'You look happy,' Lucy said, trying not to notice Hilary checking the time.

'I am happy.'

'Is Matthew mad?' Lucy asked.

'Mad? What do you mean? Mad as in angry? Like the Americans say?'

'No, not angry. Oh, just something Mummy said. I think she meant crazy.'

'She said Matthew was crazy?' Hilary paused, holding the hairbrush in one hand and stepping back so that she could see her sister's face better.

'I didn't mean mad,' Lucy said, trying to backtrack. 'I can't remember what she said. It was something to do with his attitude. Towards us, I mean. About us being British and our role in India. I think.'

Hilary looked surprised. 'I don't understand,' she said.

'Remember,' Lucy tried again. 'That evening, at dinner with Mummy and Daddy, when Matthew said something about people should be in their own countries, or something like that.'

'Oh, that,' Hilary snorted. 'It's an historical thing. He doesn't believe in colonialism. He says there will be a price to pay for it. Maybe not now. But sometime later.'

Lucy thought about that. 'Hilary, do you ever wonder about us? About who we are. Who we really are, I mean.'

Now Hilary looked even more surprised. 'No, I

36

don't. I know exactly who I am. I'm Hilary Cholmondesley. Matthew's wife.'

'And is that it? Is that all there is? You once were an Entwhistle. So you were Mummy and Daddy's. And now you belong to Matthew?'

'Yes, I belong to Matthew now, but I'm still me,' Hilary said. 'I am who I am.'

But Lucy, looking at her in the mirror, wondered if Hilary had understood.

'I don't want to just be an Entwhistle, and then someone's wife,' she said. 'I don't want to belong to anyone.'

'Don't you want to get married? Isn't that what it's all about?' Hilary asked.

'But there must be more,' Lucy said. 'There has to be. Otherwise, what's the point? That's like saying we're just born to get married and have babies. Like we've been pre-destined to do that.'

'But we have choice,' Hilary explained. 'Like I chose Matthew.'

'But didn't he choose you?'

'Well, we chose each other. But it was my choice. It wasn't like Mummy wanted me to marry him.'

Lucy smiled. She knew that initially her mother had not been at all enthusiastic. 'Mummy says that Matthew grows on you,' she said helpfully.

'She likes him now,' Hilary informed her firmly. 'And I love him. And that is what counts.'

'But now,' Lucy said. 'What now? You go to live in Ireland with him and you won't belong there either.'

'What on earth are you talking about? I belong wherever I live.'

'I wonder if we belong anywhere,' Lucy said

thoughtfully. 'I mean, here we are having been brought up between India and England. I don't know if I belong in either place. Or if, indeed, I belong anywhere.' There was a sense of question in her voice, a hopefulness that Hilary might reassure her.

'You think too much,' Hilary said. 'Mummy has always said that. She says that it's easier if you just do your duty and get on with things. That's what makes the world go round.'

Lucy laughed. 'Like thinking of England and being careful to find a man with a head that is not too large?'

Now Hilary laughed too. 'Did Mummy tell you that as well? Pay no attention whatsoever. That was just Mummy trying to be reassuring.'

'Reassuring? It was the most disturbing thing she has ever said.'

'Don't think about it. I can assure you that it's wonderful, and there's no time to think of England or large heads, or indeed anything – anything but the moment.'

Lucy looked up at her in delight – it was definitely the most intimate they had been in a long time. As Hilary continued to brush her hair, she looked back through the mirror and they caught each other's eye and they grinned.

The seven-year age difference did inhibit all kinds of conversation, but Lucy loved it when Hilary included her. Sometimes she wondered if that was all she wanted – just to be included and to have Hilary make her feel that she had some importance.

Hilary said she would come back and collect

Lucy on her way up to dinner. She put the hairbrush down on the dressing table and, leaning forward, she kissed her on her forehead. Lucy sat there after she had gone and basked in the moments they had just shared, feeling how close they were and how nothing and nobody could impinge on their relationship.

However, when Matthew and Hilary returned shortly afterwards to fetch her, and Lucy walked with them up the stairs, she was excluded again as they seemed totally absorbed in each other. Matthew held Hilary's elbow as they entered the dining room and Lucy felt once again that she was trailing behind them. They constantly exchanged glances during dinner, and their eyes met over their glasses every time they drank, turning to each other as though in a conspiracy. Lucy felt untold things were being said, and she thought of her sister lying face down on the bed and Matthew with a towel around his waist and she had to look away because she knew that she was blushing.

After dinner, Matthew and Hilary got up to dance and Lucy sat there slowly twirling her glass of wine in her fingers and wondering what to do. Gradually she became aware of someone sitting directly behind her and, turning, she found herself looking straight at the man from the quayside.

He was wearing a dinner jacket and his blond head looked a perfectly normal shape and size. He had blue eyes and the nicest mouth, a straight nose and a firm chin. He looked at her slightly quizzically and she could see that his eyes were taking her in just as she had stared at him.

'Good evening,' he said, a smile on his lips, half-rising to his feet, and bowing his head slightly.

'I didn't think you were on board,' she replied quickly. Too quickly, she knew, making it apparent that she had been watching out for him. She could feel her face light up.

Close to, she could see that he was older than she had first thought. Maybe even a little older than Matthew. Matthew was twenty-six.

'I knew you were sitting there,' the man said. 'Although at first I didn't recognise you with your hair down,' he added.

She laughed. 'I just didn't know you were here,' she said. She had looked around for him but only fleetingly. Even though she had dressed in the hope that he might appear on board, she had not really believed that it was likely. It certainly never occurred to her that he might be at the very next table. She glanced around his table, taking in several dinner-jacketed men, and two women, their hair perfectly coiffed, wearing long gloves up and past their elbows, with cigarettes in holders. Their lips so red. The smoke drifting upwards and around them. There was a mixture of aloofness and intensity at the table that Lucy identified as sophistication. Then she realised they were speaking in German. She looked back at him in surprise.

'You're German?' she asked.

'In a manner of speaking,' he said. 'Allow me to introduce myself. I'm Reinhold Kobaldt. Call me Rhino. Everyone does.'

'Rhino?' she repeated.

'A single-horned animal with a tough hide,' he

40

said with a laugh. His eyes never left hers.

She wondered for a moment what he meant, and then as it dawned on her, she blushed. She did not know what to say.

'You're thinking perhaps, don't rhinos have two horns?' he suggested.

'No. In India they have one horn,' she said quickly, trying to pretend she had not understood some half-hinted innuendo.

He laughed. His eyes were both kindly and amused. 'And your name?'

'I'm Lucy. Lucy Entwhistle. I'm here with my sister and her husband,' she added.

'I thought she must be your sister,' he said. 'You look alike.'

She was pleased. Everyone always said how beautiful Hilary was.

'My sister just got married,' Lucy said, looking across the floor to where Matthew and Hilary were waltzing. Her sister's long back was bare and as they danced Matthew drew one of his fingers down it, and Hilary moved closer to him. It was intensely erotic, and, glancing back at Rhino, Lucy knew that he had seen it too.

'One moment,' he excused himself to her. Then turning to the man sitting beside him at the table he put two fingers on his forearm and spoke quietly into his ear.

The man turned and looked at Lucy. He was younger than Rhino, also with blond hair but ice-blue eyes. A youthful face with high cheekbones and eyes so cold Lucy almost shivered. His long hands – slender and powerful – rested on the table.

'Friedrich Arnheim,' Rhino said to Lucy. 'Miss Lucy Entwhistle,' he said to his friend.

The young man stood and bowed his head to her. 'Enchanted,' he said, taking her hand and bringing it to his lips.

'Now,' Rhino interrupted them. 'Will you dance with me?' he asked Lucy.

He held her with one hand firmly in the small of her back so that she was almost carried by him as they moved. She was taken aback at how well he danced. She was used to something more formal, more obligatory, while this was remarkably sensual and very adept. They spoke briefly only, as he seemed very involved in the sound and the rhythm of the music, and she felt a sense of abandonment like none she had felt before.

A surge of sensuality rushed through her and the touch of his hand on her bare shoulder aroused her. They danced and danced, and the music played on as other couples came and left the ballroom floor, and Rhino kept her locked between his hands, playing her like a marionette, twirling and releasing her, knowing she would spin back to his arms.

'This is like learning how to ride a bicycle,' she said to him. 'Once you've learned you can then go wherever you want.'

He laughed, and she knew that he was laughing at her words rather than at her meaning, and she did not understand. She felt caught between child and adult, girl and woman, wanting and needing, aspiring but not comprehending. It was as if she were not quite old enough to get the joke.

'Where are you really from?' she asked him.

'Really from? I'm German,' he said. 'A German who has been living in Africa. And you?'

It made her think of her conversation about home earlier with Hilary. People from one place living in another, unsure of their roots, although Rhino sounded certain enough – as if it made sense to him. Maybe everyone else was like that, she thought.

'I'm English. We live in India. I was born there, and I'm on my way...' she was about to say, to school, but she cut the sentence short as she didn't want him to know that she was still at school.

'On your way back to school? Is that what you were going to say?' he asked.

She dropped her head and then said yes. There was little point in denying it.

'I liked you with your hair in plaits,' he said.

It was unspoken, but it was there. She knew that he recalled as clearly as she did that first look between them when she had been on deck and he on the docks.

Matthew cut in then and started dancing with her.

'Why did you do that?' she asked.

'He's far too old to be dancing with you,' he said.

'He's not much older than you, and you're dancing with me.'

'That's not the point, and you know it.'

'That's not fair,' she said. 'You don't dance with me. You're so busy with Hilarymem. What am I supposed to do?'

'Dancing with him once or twice is fine, but you've been at it for far too long,' he admonished. 'And he's German.'

'So what? You're Irish,' she said.

'Now, now,' he laughed. 'Next thing you'll be telling me there is something wrong with being Irish.'

'No more nor less than being German,' she said.

'There's going to be war,' Matthew said reprovingly to her. 'Don't forget that.'

'I want to sit down,' Lucy said. She felt cross, but as they walked to the table she saw that Rhino had moved his chair back, detaching himself from his table and was now talking to Hilary.

'Mr Kobaldt—' Hilary started to say.

'Oh, please call me Rhino,' he said, as he took out a silver cigarette case and offered it around. 'Everyone does.'

'Rhino,' Hilary tried again, this time addressing Matthew, 'is only on the boat until tomorrow. He is disembarking in Malta.'

Lucy could feel how Hilary was filling Matthew in, and how Matthew immediately relaxed as he realised that that would be the end of Reinhold Kobaldt and that he need not worry about her after that.

This made Lucy determined to thwart her brother-in-law. He had ignored her ever since the wedding, had stolen Hilary from her, and only paid her any attention because some man wanted to dance with her. And added to that, Hilary was helping him.

'So may I dance with your sister now?' Lucy suddenly heard Rhino asking Hilary, and Hilary laughed.

'If she wants to dance with you ... she may.'

He did not ask her. He stood up and put his

44

hand out for hers and she took it. She was aware of the silence at his table as his companions watched her being led back to the dance.

This time he talked as he moved her with ease across the floor.

'The interesting thing about being brought up in different places or just in living in different places,' Rhino said to her, 'is that you end up knowing all kinds of things that other people don't know.'

'How do you mean?' Lucy asked.

'What you know is unique,' he explained.

'It's not really,' she tried. 'I always feel that I know less than other girls at school.'

'They may know more about one place or one thing, but the sum total of what you know is wider.'

'I only know little bits about lots of things.'

'Exactly.'

'And my mother and sister probably know way more about the same things.'

'Yes, but they won't have your perspective,' he said.

She thought about that as he moved her backwards across the floor. The sum total of her knowledge she felt, was how to obey, to sit with a very straight back while sipping a long cold drink, to aspire to being like her sister ... and yet there was more, there must be more, the need to find out who she was and what she really wanted, the desire not to be constrained but having no idea how to accomplish an objective as yet unclear. She wondered what things he knew about, and realised how very different his experiences must be to hers.

Ta-ra-ra-ra went the trumpeter, and Rhino

swirled her around and back into his arms.

'Where were you living?' she asked him.

'I was in Kenya. My family was in coffee. Still is, in fact. But I've been in Egypt and Sudan for the last year or so.'

'What were you doing?'

'Oh, I was learning to fly a plane,' he said.

'How exciting.'

And it was exciting. She imagined landscapes that stretched forever against a horizon that was unlike any she knew, beneath a sky that was a different colour blue. She imagined lion and elephant moving across distant neverending plains, the smell of coffee in a plantation, different noises and different sunsets. She felt Africa must have a different sound from the babbling and the chattering in the markets in India, and to the coldness of her boarding school in England, which was all that she had to look forward to.

At some point the ship left its berth – Lucy did not know when, so engrossed was she in her thoughts about this German who had crossed her path. And the following day it docked in Malta for a brief five hours.

Before going to bed the previous night, she had asked Hilary about going ashore, but her sister had refused permission.

'You just want to spend the afternoon in bed,' Lucy said crossly.

'What I want to do is neither here nor there,' Hilary said. 'We're not here for long enough, and what if the ship leaves without you?'

The prospect of that was enough to cause Lucy

to acquiesce out loud, but internally to decide that she was getting off in Malta.

She found Rhino that morning at breakfast. He was sitting at his table with Friedrich Arnheim.

'*Guten Tag*,' she said to them.

'Oh, and has the young English *Mädchen* learned German overnight?' Rhino asked.

Both men rose to their feet.

Lucy smiled but ignored the question.

'Are you leaving today?' she asked.

'And why does Fräulein Entwhistle want to know?' he asked in response.

She scuffed her shoe on the ground beside his chair, wondering how blatant she dared to be.

'It's a long way to England,' she tried. 'I just thought it would be nice to find my land legs again. Even briefly.'

'Well, you're in luck,' he said. 'I am getting off here. We both are – Friedrich and I. But our boat for Italy does not leave until tomorrow morning. So, would you like a short trip into Valletta?'

She nodded with pleasure.

'I'll see you later, Fritz,' Rhino said to his companion. 'Please excuse me.'

She was aware of the coldness of Friedrich's eyes as Rhino got up from his chair. She knew those eyes were boring into her back as Rhino now sat at her table, and asked a waiter to bring him over his coffee. She made herself not turn her head around but she felt slightly uneasy at the intensity of the other German's gaze.

'Did you have other plans for today?' Lucy asked him, aware that she had intruded, but not wanting to withdraw.

'My plans include a walk into Valletta, and a visit to my favourite place. I would like to show it to you.'

She said not a word to Hilary and Matthew. Instead, when the ship docked beneath the bastions, she and Rhino disembarked together, and she stood looking up at the walls that surrounded the capital.

'Amazing, are they not?' he said to her. 'Built for protection – fortification. Once the island was ruled from Mdina, a city in the centre, but then they moved to here.'

They wandered together up through the narrow cobbled streets, the morning sun already high in the sky, its heat burning down on them. They both wore hats, and he took her elbow as they walked uphill. The front door of the terraced houses opened straight on to the streets. Up above, on the first floor, their bay windows stuck out over the narrow pavements. Children were playing on the street, mothers calling across the roads to each other. It all seemed slightly dusty and enchanting.

'The winds from the south carry desert sand from the Sahara,' Rhino said. 'There are many different winds, though, that circle this island.'

'It's lovely,' she said. 'I'm so glad to be off the ship, even for a little while.'

'I'm going to show you what is probably one of the most beautiful churches in the world,' he said to her.

'You've been here before?'

'Yes,' he said. 'Several times, in fact. It has been one of my ports of call.' He sounded both worldly wise and well travelled, adding to his intrigue and drawing her closer in.

He took her to St John's Co-Cathedral.

Lucy was moved beyond words, both at the cathedral and at the fact that Rhino clearly loved it and knew all about it.

He explained the side chapels to her, each one belonging to a different langue of the Order of the Knights.

'Beneath the floor,' he explained, 'each of the knights is individually buried in his own crypt.' She looked down and thought of them, knight by knight, buried long ago, one by one in their own space, silent and alone.

'The original cathedral is in Mdina – also known as the Silent City,' he explained. 'This one was built in fifteen seventy-eight, and I suppose you could say it was co-opted as a second cathedral a couple of hundred years later. Next time we come here,' he said, 'I will take you to St Paul's Cathedral. That's the one in Mdina.'

And Lucy rejoiced in the fact that Rhino had said this as if it would happen. As if there were no doubt.

One day she and he would come back here again.

'There was an Italian painter,' Rhino continued. 'His name was Mattia Preti and he worked here for twenty years. This is really his,' gesticulating with his hand. 'The carving, the gilt, the marble – all is his work, or work that he supervised. This is baroque at its best – for me.'

She was struck by his feelings and awareness at their surroundings. And in turn, she too became absorbed. She was also taken by his eloquence when he explained the ceiling, with its life of St John adorning it. She turned to glance at this man who had kept her awake in the night with her thoughts of dancing with him. She wondered why he wanted even to talk to her, as she knew she was still little more than a child, but a bit of her did not care. It was as though she had been given the chance to seize these moments as she passed this stranger on a boat.

And so she seized them.

They kneeled together in one of the side chapels. She was unsure if he was praying or not, but she prayed briefly. She prayed that she would see him again.

'Man's gift to God,' he said as they got up to leave, and she knew he was referring to the church.

Outside in the heat of the day he bought her coffee before bringing her back to the ship.

'Where do you go from here?' she asked.

'I leave in the morning for Palermo,' he said. 'And then Rome before going home.'

'And home is...?'

He hesitated. 'I don't know,' he eventually said. 'Home is yet unclear. Dresden, possibly – my sister lives there.' He laughed at himself. 'But I want to live here. Here in Malta. I thought that the first time I came here. I would like to make here – this island – home. But it won't be now. Nor for sometime.'

'Matthew says there is going to be war. Daddy says the same,' she said.

'Yes. There will be war. And you and I and

50

other civilised people will be on different sides. Never abandon hope, Lucy,' he said. 'No matter what happens.'

They were looking down on the harbour and she could see the submarines lying like gigantic steel fish slightly outside the inlets. She thought that if Matthew had said that to her, she would have found it patronising. But because it was Rhino, she did not.

He interrupted her thoughts. 'Do you know what day it is?' he asked her.

'Yes, it's Friday,' she said.

'I mean the date.'

'Yes,' she said. 'August the eighteenth.'

'That's right. Don't forget it. That's the best I can do. Don't forget the date. Promise.'

She looked at him, puzzled both by his meaning and his intensity.

He took from his pocket what looked like a stone. 'It's amber. We call it *Bernstein* in German,' he said. 'It's between thirty and ninety million years old. I want you to have it. I bought it in a market in Alexandria. It symbolises everything.'

He put it into her hand and she looked at it carefully.

'The insects caught in the amber – they are like us. Caught in a moment in time. Trapped by it. Like we are now.'

'It's beautiful,' she said to him.

'Yes. It is the fossilised resin of ancient trees, and trapped in the resin are feathers, leaves, debris, and insects – whatever was there in that instant. Holding this in your hand makes you feel you are holding one precious second in the aeons of time.'

It started to feel hot to her touch as though her own heat was entering into it.

'When you think about today, think of it as something beautiful, like this stone,' he said.

She looked up at him and she felt the intensity of his gaze as he looked down into her open face.

'I would like to kiss you,' he said.

She wanted him to but she did not know how to say it. She lifted her chin higher, looking hopefully at him, and then he brought his lips down to hers. He kissed her on the side of her mouth.

'I promise I will kiss you again,' he said. 'When you are older.'

She held those words in her head, wanting more but knowing there was no more to be given or taken. The kiss and the stone, the hours in Valletta, the dancing on board – those were to be her treasures, her memories locked in her heart as they walked back down the streets to the dock.

He brought her back to the ship, and as she went aboard he called up to her, 'Don't forget the date.'

He waved once and then he walked away, pushing himself through the crowds. She suddenly saw Friedrich Arnheim appear from nowhere, carrying a rifle, which he handed to Rhino. Rhino stood for a moment, his wrists resting on the length of the gun, just as she had seen him in Alexandria. The two men stood clearly talking, and then they strode away.

Lucy went back to her cabin with her piece of amber in her hands, and she kissed it, as she would have liked him to kiss her.

All human actions have one or more of these seven causes: chance, nature, compulsions, habit, reason, passion, desire.

Aristotle

CHAPTER TWO

The ship sailed into Southampton less than a week later, and Lucy accompanied Hilary and Matthew to the Entwhistles' London house. Hilary spent the next three days helping Lucy pack for school, buying last-minute requisites and taking her to get her hair cut. Lucy had longed before for time alone with her sister, but now Hilary's presence was a distraction.

She kept her visit to Valletta a secret, and the piece of amber she carried in her bag, vowing to keep it with her always. There were moments when Hilary was speaking and Lucy would find she had only heard one or two words because her mind was wandering down cobbled streets, with Rhino's hand taking hers as she stepped off the pavement, or touching her forearm to point out the light coming through the stained-glass window in the cathedral or the painting on the ceiling.

Light played a role in her memory.

One moment she was dancing in the dimness of the dance floor, then she was looking through the flame of Friedrich Arnheim's lighter as he leaned towards the cigarette of one of his dinner companions, and she could feel Rhino's eyes watching her as she took it all in. Under the Maltese sky the brightness of the light almost blinded her and she would find herself turning away from Hilary and blinking in surprise as she realised they were walking on the streets of London and that Rhino was not there. And not only that, but he would not be there.

She knew it was unlikely that they would meet again, and yet she hoped. She could not bear the idea of him being gone from her life for ever and that her image of him striding away from the ship would be her last. She imagined sometimes that he had turned back, had come running back along the quayside, and she looking down would hear him calling to her.

She woke in the night with the music throbbing in her blood and her body racked with desire, a sensation that she only barely understood but knew that it was in some way interlinked with that momentary glance she had had of her naked sister on the tousled bedclothes, and Matthew with the white towel wrapped around his waist. She wanted to be on that bed in that cabin, with Rhino towel-draped like her brother-in-law and she turning slowly over on the bed as he approached, feeling the heat of his body before he even touched her.

'You're very quiet again,' Hilary said. They were in the dining room of the Entwhistles' home in North London.

Lucy pulled herself back from the bedroom in

her mind and looked up from her half-finished dinner. Closing her knife and fork she tried smiling at Hilary.

'What are you thinking about?' Hilary asked. 'Are you all right?'

'Does going back to school bother you?' Matthew asked.

He was playing the role of big brother-in-law and that slightly amused her now. She felt that he and her sister had their secrets, but that was no longer a source of jealousy for her, because she too had a secret to sustain her. She no longer resented him and his possession of Hilary.

'No, not really,' she said.

'It's not so bad as schools go,' Hilary said kindly.

Because of the age difference they had never been there at the same time, but she had accompanied Lucy on a number of occasions when their mother had not been free to come back from India.

There was a single candle on the dining-room table and Lucy wondered what it would be like to look through its flame into Rhino's eyes.

'School is not bad at all,' Lucy replied, suddenly thinking of St John's Co-Cathedral in Valletta with its knights in their crypts frozen for ever in time. And she knew that if she could not be with Rhino Kobaldt, then school was the next best thing that was on offer at that moment.

'We're not so far away,' Matthew said. 'And you'll come to us for the holidays this year.'

Lucy nodded. She was curious to see Hilary's home and wondered how her sister would cope with a new way of life in Ireland – a life she knew little or nothing about.

'You'll come for Christmas,' Hilary said.

Again Lucy nodded. She was miles away inside her head, thinking of Rhino walking away. Walking into what?

'I wonder what that German was really up to?' Matthew suddenly remarked, as if reading her thoughts.

'How do you mean?' Lucy asked defensively, thinking he was referring to what Rhino had been up to with her.

'Well...' Matthew hesitated, 'there was something odd about the way he talked about what he had been doing. He was vague about it.'

'No, he wasn't,' Lucy said firmly. 'He told me about Sudan and Egypt. He was learning to fly a plane there.'

'I thought he had come from Kenya,' Hilary said.

'No, he had been living in Kenya. That's where his family live,' Lucy informed them. 'Then he had spent some time in Sudan and then in Egypt. Meeting people. I think...' Her voice trailed away. Having started her explanation with enthusiasm, if not with pride, self-doubt and the knowledge of her own naïvety entered her consciousness.

'And counting submarines in Malta,' Matthew said. 'Clearly he was a spy.'

'A spy?' Lucy looked up in shock. 'Of course he wasn't a spy,' she said, but suddenly she was not quite so sure.

'Anyway, I don't think he was much of a threat to you,' Matthew said.

'What? What do you mean?' Lucy was puzzled. She caught Hilary shaking her head at Matthew and glaring. 'What are you talking about?' Lucy asked.

'Not to put too fine a point on it, I think he wears his trilby indoors, so to speak,' Matthew said with a smile.

'Matthew,' Hilary hissed.

'What do you mean?' Lucy asked.

'Nothing,' Matthew replied, and would not be drawn further on the subject.

Lucy thought about it when she was alone in her room. Had Matthew been referring to the fact that Rhino was no longer around and therefore they, Matthew and Hilary, need not feel him as a threat to her? It made no sense.

She took the piece of amber from her bag, sat down on her bed and held it between her hands. She stared vacantly at the window where darkness had already fallen. The light in her bedroom seemed dim. The family home had been bought long ago by her father's parents and had been kept on by the Entwhistles after they had moved to India some twenty years earlier. The terraced house, with its bay windows, stood on a quiet road, three steps leading up to the hall door, which was separated from the street by a small area of shrubs with black railings. Their father had continually said they should sell it and buy somewhere in the country. He fancied a house in a field with trees and a kitchen garden, but their mother had said this home made more sense until retirement. They could decide then where they wanted to live. She undoubtedly wanted to live in the city when that day came, and so it would not be sold, but their father lived in hope.

The house was in need of redecoration but that had been postponed, as no one was ever there for long enough to organise and to supervise the venture. Lucy's room still had the wallpaper from her early years on it – intertwined roses, which stood in slight relief on a fading pink background. The carpets throughout the house were still in good condition through lack of use, although the paintwork could have done with a new coat. Lucy ran her finger over the yellowing windowsill.

She feared that Matthew had been right in what he had suggested over dinner about Rhino being a spy. The fear was not for her or for the secrets Rhino might have uncovered in his time in North Africa, but rather for Rhino and what those secrets might mean for him.

She thought about his face, his bronzed skin, his blue eyes, the broadness of his shoulders, the loose way he walked, how his hand had held her in the small of her back while they danced, how his fingers had felt and how his eyes had looked as he had drawn closer to her to kiss her on her lips. She knew she was consumed by him and she tried to close her mind to the thoughts as she unpacked her travel clothes and hung them in the wardrobe, removing her school uniform from its box where it had been neatly placed before her last trip to India.

She put the piece of amber under her pillow and the incredible happiness she felt earlier was suffused with sadness. She wondered where Rhino was now, and how he had travelled from Sicily to Rome and whom he had met there and why.

She wanted to tell Hilary what had happened and how he had made her feel, but she did not know how to bridge the gap with her sister on such a subject. She knew that Hilary saw her as a child and that Hilary would not understand.

Hilary and Matthew were still downstairs. They had asked her to join them in a game of rummy, and while she had said that she ought to unpack the new items they had bought and sort her things for school, she now regretted that.

Putting on a dressing gown and slippers over her flannel pyjamas she went back downstairs.

They looked up from the card table, and seemed pleased to see her.

'Come and join us,' Matthew said. 'Will you have a little port?' he asked.

She shook her head. He had only offered her the port to create some kind of bond between them, and she was not interested now in that kind of connection, although weeks, even days earlier, she would have latched on to it. She would have latched on to anything that would have made her feel closer to Hilary and more a part of the adult world that Hilary inhabited.

'No, thank you.'

'I'll make you cocoa,' Hilary said to her.

Matthew shuffled and dealt the cards while she and Hilary went out to the kitchen.

'Are you all right, Lucymem?' Hilary asked.

'Of course I am.'

'If I were Mother, I'd say you were sickening for something,' Hilary said.

59

'I'm fine really,' Lucy replied. 'It's just the whole thing. You know. Home in India. Then this home. Then school. Then the whole cycle starts over again. Sometimes you don't know where you are or who you are.'

'Oh, not that again,' Hilary laughed. 'We had this conversation. You are Lucy Entwhistle, good little daughter of the Colonel and the Colonel Mem. And you're on your way back to school. And one day the world will be your oyster.'

'Like the way it is your oyster?' Lucy asked, watching her sister's face carefully.

'Just like it is my oyster,' Hilary confirmed with satisfaction in her voice.

'Aren't you afraid of your new life at all?' Lucy asked her.

'With Matthew? In his lovely home? In a green land...? No, I am not afraid at all.' Hilary turned from the cupboard with the cocoa jar in her hand. She unscrewed the lid and sniffed it before continuing. 'Are you afraid, little Lucymem?' she asked.

Lucy shook her head. 'Not afraid,' she said. 'It's just there is so much unknown. So many things and I don't know anything about any of them.'

'Well, like we said, you'll come and stay with Matthew and me at Christmas and then you'll know all about Ireland and our life there and that should answer some of your questions,' Hilary said.

'But the war,' Lucy began hesitantly.

'What about it?'

'Aren't you afraid of it?'

'No,' Hilary said. 'Matthew said we'll be safe in

Ireland. And if it does break out, you can come to us, so you'll be safe too. And Mother said that she would be fine holding the fort at home. I'm afraid for Daddy,' she added thoughtfully. 'Soldiers are the unknown quantity in a war. But Mother said Daddy is a survivor and he will be fine.'

And that is that, thought Lucy. Hilary thinks all will be well.

Was Hilary being naïve, or was she just trying to protect her little sister? These were questions that haunted Lucy both then and later that night in bed. It seemed unlikely that Hilary was naïve. She was her mother's daughter, well-travelled, well-educated, well-read. Naïvety did not really enter into her personality. She came from a family of women who were anything but naïve. They were certainly pragmatists, women with their feet firmly on the ground, and the ground they walked was solid, and they walked it with confidence. They were women who had a grip on duty and responsibility. If, Lucy thought, you are brought up with pragmatists, then that is what you become. She wrote that in her diary that very night. Her journal was at times boring and bored her, but at other times was full of insight. Until that trip home via Malta, there were no references to the oncoming war, other than a concern about when she would see her parents again. But, of course, both Hilary and Lucy, because of their home being in India and their school in England, were used to there being long periods of time between seeing their parents.

61

Until now, Lucy had shown very little interest in politics but she suddenly became conscious of what was happening after her meeting with Rhino Kobaldt. Her diary entries changed and they began to refer to what was going on around her. She wrote of the civilian evacuation of London, which had already begun when they got there that August. She wrote of the sense of urgency in the city, of men in uniform, of advertisements in the newspaper – morale-boosting advertisements and ones for enlisting.

Matthew and Hilary drove Lucy to her boarding school in Kent, and when they were leaving her, Hilary put her arms around her and hugged her.

'You will be safe here,' she said.

It was those words that somehow suddenly chilled Lucy to the bone. The concept of being safe in her school implied the opposite outside, of the danger for those who were not in safe places. Her father's kindly face came to mind and she clung to Hilary as fear washed through her.

They said goodbye in her dormitory and they left her there unpacking. It was only then that she allowed herself to think of Rhino and, kissing the piece of amber, she placed it under her pillow, knowing she would hold it in her hands as she went to sleep that night.

The girls whose beds were on either side of hers were calling across her to each other. Lucy felt distanced from them as though she had moved on into a more adult world. They appeared not to be aware of what was about to happen and were talking of holidays at the sea, the excitement of all the men in uniform, a summer romance, things that seemed trivial to Lucy as she put her clothing in her narrow cupboard and her hairbrush on her cabinet. She wanted the others to stop talking so that she could concentrate but she was not sure what it was she wanted to think about. All thoughts seemed too frightening.

On 1 September, the Nazis invaded Poland. And on the third, Britain, France, Australia and New Zealand declared war on Germany.

Lucy did go to stay with Matthew and Hilary, but not for Christmas as had been planned – plans that were scuppered due to rules in the school and the difficulty in travelling. It was not easy to keep abreast of what was happening outside, as the girls were allowed only one hour a day last thing in the evening to listen to the crackling wireless in their common room.

Lucy spent that hour as close to the radio as she could get, listening to it intently, trying to get a feel for what was happening in the world outside. In November an assassination attempt on Hitler failed, and shortly afterwards the Soviets attacked Finland. Lucy wondered at the American stance on neutrality. None of it made sense. It was as if the whole world outside their orderly school had gone mad. There was talk of impending rationing and some of the girls speculated as to whether the fees would be reduced. Lucy wondered if she had lost her sense of humour or if it was just that every other girl was juvenile. She felt detached from school and almost desperate to get information

63

from the outside world. Her plans for going to university seemed redundant as she became more and more aware of the impending sense of doom outside. There was a need for ambulance drivers and fire wardens in the cities and she toyed with the idea of joining the services.

How Hilary could be writing from Ireland about hunts and parties puzzled Lucy. Hilary spoke of 'the Emergency', and it was some time later before Lucy discovered this was the Irish term for a world war. Hilary's letters became increasingly vague, and while Lucy devoured them, she gleaned nothing from them other than what the weather was like and what book Hilary was reading.

It was summertime before Lucy was allowed to go to Ireland. School was finished and she made the long and lonely journey by train and boat, torn between wanting to go to London and spending time with her sister. The school encouraged her to go to Ireland.

She took the boat from Holyhead and Matthew met her in Dublin. He looked exactly the same, with his thick dark hair and his cheery demeanour.

'Good timing,' he said jovially to her, having given her a hug.

First hug I've had in ten months, she thought as they drove down from Dublin along the coast to his home.

'We've a surprise,' he told her.

'A surprise?' she asked. 'For me?'

'For all of us,' he laughed.

And indeed there was a surprise, several of them.

The first was the house itself. Hilary's few letters had been vague on details, referring to people whom Lucy had never met, giving her no inkling about the size of their home.

The road separated the front of the property from meadowland beyond – field after field that stretched upwards towards the hills. The drive-way, with a large pillared gateway with 'Ithaca' carved on one side, had an entrance and an exit sweeping round in a large semi-circle in front of the hall door. The house appeared to be L-shaped, with the front part of the L extending into small cottages and outhouses.

'Goodness,' Lucy said. It was larger than she had imagined. 'Is this all yours?'

'Well, we just live in the house,' Matthew said vaguely. 'Cook lives in the connection, with her son and daughter. Plenty of room for us all,' he added, as if that had been in question.

The hallway extended in all directions, and portraits of Matthew's ancestors hung in gilt-edged frames, staring down at the surprised Lucy. In one letter Hilary had referred to 'the eyes that watch' and Lucy had presumed she was referring to the neighbours or maybe even to the sheep or cattle, which sometimes featured in her sister's lengthy but vague epistles. Now it was clear what Hilary meant because the eyes indeed were watching. They followed her down the hall. Many of the portraits had a look of Matthew about them with his slightly square head and dark curly hair. There too was a portrait of Hilary looking very aristocratic, with her long slender neck, and an expression of detachment in her beautiful face. Beside it hung a reproduction of Rembrandt's painting of Aristotle and Homer. In it the philosopher stood surveying a bust of the poet. Lucy found herself drawn back to it. It seemed to have more meaning than the family portraits. She recognised it because her father had a similar print in his study.

The next surprise was her sister.

Hilary was nine months pregnant, and Lucy arrived to find her ensconced on a sofa, almost incapable of moving she was so large.

'You never said,' she said to Hilary. 'Why did you not say?'

'State secret,' Matthew said. 'Hilary did not want your mother worrying, so we said nothing to anyone. She's due this week,' he added. 'Time enough to tell the Memsahib then that we have a son and heir.'

There was something remarkably Henry the Eighth about this, and Lucy eyed them both with interest.

'How do you know it is going to be a boy?' she asked.

'The first Cholmondesley child has always been a boy,' Matthew said, pouring himself a drink.

Lucy looked at Hilary to see her reaction. Hilary shrugged. 'Cook says it's a boy,' she volunteered.

'How does Cook know?' Lucy asked.

'She held a piece of string above me with a stone attached to it, and it spun to the right. Or maybe it was the left. I don't remember. She says it's a boy.'

Lucy was very surprised to hear Hilary talking like this. She did not recall her having any time for what she had called 'Indian superstition'.

It soon became clear that Hilary pregnant was not the same as Hilary used to be.

Lucy leaned to give her sister a kiss.

'Don't touch me,' Hilary said.

'She doesn't like being touched,' Matthew said with a resigned air. Lucy had already gathered that. She looked in surprise at her sister, remembering how she and Matthew had seemed incapable of keeping their hands off each other. Gone were the sultry looks of passion, and instead her sister's eyes seemed both remote and tired.

'Pour me a drink too,' Hilary said to her husband.

'You won't drink it,' he said, but poured her a drink as well, before turning to Lucy and asking her what she would like.

Something had changed between Matthew and Hilary, and Lucy felt it immediately. She wondered at first if it was to do with Matthew showing himself in his real colours, which was something their mother said would happen. 'It isn't until you live with someone that you really know them,' was one of her sayings. 'And of course,' she always added, 'you cannot live with them until you are married. So you need to be very sure.' The difficulty in the logic of this comment had bothered Lucy. On the one hand it appeared that the sooner you got married the sooner you could work on the other person's true colours. Whereas on the other, Lucy suspected it implied that you better not get married, as you could never be sure what the outcome might be. Like many of their mother's observations it was unclear if this was something Harriet had personal experience of, or if it was one of her wilder surmisings.

Hilary's letters had complained of Matthew's enthusiasm for hunting and fishing, something he hadn't really revealed in India. Perhaps Matthew's true nature was now coming through and he had settled back into his old habits and hobbies as if he were still a bachelor.

But it became apparent that Matthew was not the problem. Certainly he was engaged outside the house, but there was no doubt that his home was the love of his life, and that Hilary in it was part of what he embraced. So Lucy turned her attention to her sister, but it was difficult to assess what was happening. Her pregnancy appeared to have stultified her. She lay looking at the ceiling, waiting for the hours to pass.

'It is so slow,' she said to Lucy. And Lucy wondered if she meant her pregnancy or her life.

Lucy, looking around her at the luxury within which Hilary lived, could see that materially her sister was lacking nothing, and so she concluded that it was the long waiting time of pregnancy that was reducing her sister to the almost inanimate object she appeared to have become.

'It's so beautiful,' Lucy said to Hilary the morning after she arrived, having tried to encourage her to walk on the beach.

'What is?' Hilary asked from her place on the couch.

'The sky, the sea, the dunes, the air – everything. It's like living in a clean dream,' Lucy replied.

Hilary turned her head to look out the window and then turned it back again so that she was gazing once more at the ceiling.

'Come on, Hilarymem,' Lucy encouraged her. 'Take me down to the beach. I want to go back again. Just a short walk.'

'I can't,' Hilary said. 'Maudge will be in shortly and I need to tell her what to do.'

'Maudge?'

'Cook's daughter. She cleans for us. There's also Feilim. He's gormless. Don't ask. You wouldn't believe the set-up. I don't know what Mother would make of it.'

Lucy met them in due course. Cook was a large rotund woman with a red face, who was very good in the kitchen. She rustled up chicken broth for Hilary to get her on her feet, as she put it.

'That girl is pining for something,' she said to Lucy. 'It's not right that she lies there like that. Look at my Maudge, up and at it no matter what.'

When Maudge appeared Lucy realised what Cook had meant. Clearly Maudge had been up and at it and was nearly as pregnant as Hilary. She bustled around the place, dusting and beating rugs as if there were no tomorrow.

'Is Maudge married?' Lucy asked her sister over dinner.

'I don't think so,' Hilary said. 'She's got awfully slow around the place. I don't know what's wrong with her.'

Lucy looked at Matthew, who was peering into the soup tureen.

'Well, she is about seven months pregnant, if you're anything to go by,' Lucy said, wondering how Hilary could be so unfeeling. 'No wonder she's got a bit slow.'

'Pregnant?' Hilary expressed surprise. 'Don't be ridiculous. Maudge isn't pregnant.'

Now Matthew looked up in surprise. 'Pregnant? Of course. It never occurred to me. I thought she looked a bit ... heavier.'

Lucy, looking at the pair of them, wondered how they could not have noticed. Hilary clearly did not believe either of them, and it wasn't until Cook brought in the lamb and vegetables and Hilary asked her in a roundabout way if there was anything Cook would like to tell them that she finally realised that Maudge had, as Cook put it, 'a bun in the oven'.

'But whose is it?' Hilary asked. 'She's not married, is she? Did she get married and nobody told us?' She looked from Matthew to Cook and back in disbelief.

'She met a fella,' Cook said. 'And fellas will be fellas.' And turning on her heel she went back to the kitchen.

'What do we do?' Hilary said.

'What do you mean?' Matthew asked.

Lucy helped herself to the vegetables.

'Is this acceptable?' Hilary asked.

'Nothing much we can do about it,' Matthew said. 'It'll be a playmate for our son. We're going to call him Matthew,' he told Lucy. 'After my father.'

'They're all called Matthew,' Hilary said. 'Every last one of them.' Her voice betrayed no emotion even though the words might have contained an element of bitterness.

Lucy wondered what their mother would say about the new playmate. Harriet Entwhistle was known for her beliefs. It was one of the reasons that India suited her. All Indians, in her view, aspired to return in future existences, rising up and up the social order, until they too, one day, would be either Colonel Sahib or Colonel Memsahib. Lucy was quite sure that Cook's daughter's child would not be considered suitable as a playfellow for any Entwhistle or Cholmondesley offspring. She said nothing.

Neither did Hilary, and Lucy had no idea what Hilary was thinking.

'Hilarymem,' she said to her later, 'what are you thinking?'

'About what?' Hilary asked. She had returned to her view of the ceiling.

'About anything,' Lucy said, exasperated.

'I'm trying not to think about anything,' came the reply.

More than that, Lucy could not get from her.

The Cholmondesley residence boasted a library – a good one, which contained books on a great variety of subjects. Matthew took Lucy in and guided her through the various sections.

'I don't know how well read you are,' he said thoughtfully, 'but this place certainly lends itself to reading – that and hunting and fishing, of course.'

'Have you read all of these?' Lucy said as she

walked the length of the room, peering at different shelves.

'God, no,' Matthew said. 'But one day I will. My problem is that I started with A for Aristotle and I'm still there.'

'Daddy reads Aristotle,' Lucy informed him.

'There's a painting of him in the hall,' Matthew said. 'My father bought it, I think.'

'I saw it,' she replied. 'Beside the portrait of Hilary. When was that done?'

'I got it done for Christmas, as a present for myself,' he smiled.

He seemed glad of her company and hovered with her in the library as she browsed among the books.

She wanted to ask him about her sister and her lethargy, but broaching the subject felt like a betrayal of Hilary. Then it occurred to her that he might feel the same, so she asked somewhat tentatively if Hilary was always so tired.

'Just of late,' he said.

The next day Lucy spent most of her time alone on the beach walking, or sitting with her back to the dunes reading. Everyone seemed to be waiting for the time to pass, with Hilary lying on her sofa, and Matthew pacing in and out of the house and up and down the garden. Lucy had always been under the impression that such behaviour did not begin until the onset of labour, but Matthew appeared nervous and apprehensive already.

The following night Hilary finally went into labour. Cook, who claimed experience in these matters, was called. As was the doctor.

Harry O'Dowd, roused at four o'clock in the morning, came over to take a look at the situation. Encouraged by Cook, who seemed to think that a brandy for everyone would be a good idea, Matthew had downed several in an effort to calm his nerves, as, indeed, had Cook.

'You've time to drive her up to Dublin if you want,' the doctor suggested.

By now Matthew did not trust himself to drive.

'I'll drive,' Lucy said, but Hilary, lying on her bed, refused to get off it. Harry O'Dowd sent for the midwife and the midwife sent for tea.

Hours later, Lucy, carrying a small tray, met Matthew on the landing. The last she had seen of him was through the bedroom window when he had headed off at about six thirty in the morning with his shotgun. He had now returned with the gun under his arm.

'You're back,' she said. It was as much a statement as a question.

'I couldn't concentrate,' he said. 'Is Hilary all right?'

'Of course she is.' Lucy tried to sound reassuring.

The truth was Lucy was completely out of her depth. Nothing had prepared her for this, and she rather wished she were not there. Hilary held her hand too tightly and cursed in the most surprising and unbecoming way, using words that Lucy had actually never heard before.

When Hilary took to blaspheming some eight hours later, loudly calling on the Good Lord and shouting what she would like to do to him, Lucy said, in an effort to calm her, 'I wish Mother was here.' This was as much for her own sake as for Hilary's, as she would have preferred her mother to be there in her place.

As the pain briefly subsided Hilary said, 'That bloody woman. Why didn't she tell me what this was like? I'd never, ever, ever...'

What she would never ever have done was never to be uttered as she gave the most gut-wrenching of screams.

'Push,' said the midwife.

Hilary pushed and Mattie was born.

'A girl?' Matthew was disbelieving. 'Are you sure?'

'Of course I'm sure,' Lucy said to him.

Matthew was amazed. He had quite genuinely never imagined for one instant that the baby could be anything other than a boy. He took a pot shot out of the landing window and ran exultant into the bedroom. Lucy was momentarily concerned because he took the shotgun with him, but his joy was evident.

'She is beautiful,' his voice came, jubilant and triumphant through the open door. 'We can still call her Matthew.'

'You can't call her Matthew,' the midwife said. 'She's a girl.'

'What's wrong with Matthew for a girl?' he asked.

Lucy was now glad that her mother was not there because she could imagine what her parent would say.

'It'd be better to find a pretty girl's name for her,' the midwife said, handing the baby to Hilary

74

in the bed. 'You must have thought of a nice name in case it was a girl.'

They had not. They had thought of no name whatsoever to cover that particular eventuality.

Hilary, holding the baby bundle in her arms, was shaking her head in bewilderment. 'I had no idea,' she kept saying. 'No idea...'

'No idea about what?' Lucy asked her.

'About this. That it could feel like this ... that I could feel like this. Isn't she the most beautiful baby in the world?'

The distance Hilary had displayed since Lucy arrived was gone. Hilary's vacant gaze was replaced by a look of such tenderness and love that made Lucy think of paintings of the Virgin and Child.

Sometime in the next half-hour, Mathilde was named and immediately shortened to Mattie. A priest was called and she was baptised in the bedroom with the summer sun shining in on her.

Lucy, down on the beach a while later, walking furiously to rid herself of the memories of the long night and the even longer birth, marvelled at how a tiny baby could already so clearly resemble one of its parents. Mattie had a squarish face just like her father, and tiny sprigs of dark curly hair, and her eyes already looked like those in the portraits in the hall. Lucy was not altogether sure how appealing these features would be in a girl. She was not altogether sure how appealing they were in a man, although as a composite whole Matthew was acceptable.

Her mind turned to Rhino Kobaldt, who was

75

still her ideal of the perfect male, and she wondered for a brief moment if he was flying his plane somewhere over Europe, if he was still alive, and if he ever thought of her.

She closed her mind to the thoughts. She knew that they could only eat into her. As her mother had often said, 'You can have dreams. But always remember that is what they are. If they take over, you lose stability.'

On that walk, Lucy decided that she definitely wanted to return to London. The house was empty and awaiting her. She would work as an ambulance driver and university would wait. The one thing she did not want was to stay in this home of her sister's. It was too like her own childhood, with an excess of domesticity, and yet she felt detached. She contemplated what she thought was ideal and realised that she didn't know, but that she did know that she just did not want to be part of this family atmosphere. Matthew was excited, but not like her father had been. Matthew was more exuberant, more emotional. Her father was a mixture of kindness and aloofness. Hilary, who had been petulant, was now absorbed in the baby. For Lucy, this was not the right time to be part of family circumstances. She felt too young for it, too remote, too removed, and she wanted to distance herself from it physically as quickly as possible.

She wanted to get back and be part of what was happening in England. She wanted time to grow up and to taste freedom. She had turned eighteen, her schooldays were over, and for the first time in her life she had freedom of choice.

'I'm going back to London,' she said to Hilary a few days later. She expected disapproval, maybe even for Hilary expressly to forbid her. But instead, Hilary looked at her and smiled.

'I'm not surprised,' she said.

'Aren't you? Why not, Hilarymem?' Lucy asked.

'This isn't for you.'

'What isn't?'

'This ... babies, the quiet home life. Not yet. Not now, anyway. Go and have fun, but please, please be careful. I don't want Mother blaming me if something goes wrong.'

Plenty could have gone wrong, but it did not. Lucy made her way back to London, and walking up the road to their house, she met the man from next door. His parents, who owned the house he was living in, had recently moved north, but he stayed on and some of his friends rented from him and shared it.

'Hello,' he said to Lucy. 'Remember me? I'm Roger – Roger Farrington – from next door.'

'Hello,' Lucy responded. She was pleased he remembered her as he was older and they had not seen each other in several years. He told her he was in the War Office and asked her if she'd like to come to a dance the following evening.

It seemed a great start to her new venture and she readily agreed. With that the sirens started and he made her leave her case under a bush in the front garden as they headed towards the shelters.

There was something both terrifying and wonderful about being back there, and Lucy felt it was where she belonged. As they ran down the street, she thought momentarily of the beach, of waves washing on to the shore and the distant screech of a seagull, but the thought was not with any longing. And in the shelter, a woman gave birth and an old man sang a song.

Lucy, sitting beside her neighbour, felt her heart pounding. There was a sense of intense excitement – the mingling of fear and adrenalin. She had arrived back in London just in time for the start of the German air raids.

Coming out from that first attack, shocked into complete silence, shaken to her core, she walked with Roger slowly looking at the damage. A fireman asked them to assist him to lift some rubble from someone trapped beneath.

It was Roger who helped Lucy find her way into the ambulance service; it was he who often collected her at the end of a shift, taking her for a drink on their way home, or to a dance when she was not on duty on a Saturday night.

Anybody can become angry – that is easy, but to be angry with the right person and to the right degree and at the right time and for the right purpose, and in the right way – that is not within everybody's power and is not easy.

Aristotle

CHAPTER THREE

For more than four long years the events of the war unfolded, with Lucy living alone in the house in North London with Roger Farrington next door. She made friends with hospital staff, ambulance colleagues, fire wardens, and firemen. She sat and drank coffee with the girls from the crew. They followed the invasion and fall of cities all over Europe. They lived on the very knife-edge of existence with the wireless, newspapers, rumour and chat as their link to the world events. She saw life and death coming and going as London burned. She closed her mind on memory and lived in the immediacy of the moment.

Roger took her out regularly – always gentlemanly, always solicitous. She fell into bed tired at night and clasped the amber stone in one hand as she fell asleep. When her thoughts went to Rhino, they were distant now. The immediate ache was long over. She thought of him as the ultimate – a perfect man in a perfect moment when their paths had crossed. No one and nothing could live up to that ideal. She was invited out on dates, and sometimes she went and sometimes she declined.

Roger said to her, 'Lucy, is there someone else?'

He had been giving her a good night kiss on the cheek and had paused, looking into her eyes, outside their houses.

And she said, 'Yes ... no ... yes...'

And he said, 'I see.' After a pause, he added, 'Do you want to tell me?'

But she shook her head. There was nothing to tell. She knew that. She had met a man for a few hours years ago and he, like she, had been swept away by the war. She no longer prayed that he was alive, only that whatever his fate had been that it was easy, and if by any chance he was still out there, that he was safe.

She worked for a while in Roger's office when the air raids eased – it seemed that the war would never end, even when they said that the tide was turning. And then the telegram arrived.

It was Cook who found Lucy's address in Hilary's desk and assisted in the wording of the message. Cook who wisely thought it better not to mention the children, missing presumed dead.

The telegram arrived as Lucy came home from her day at the War Office: 'Plane crash. Matthew dead. Hilary very ill. Come immediately.'

Cold with shock, Lucy read it twice, trying to take it in. It was Roger she turned to, and he, listening to the wording of the telegram, wondered for a moment if this news was connected with the German bomber that had hit the Wicklow Mountains and which had been reported that morning. He helped her pack a small bag, and took her to the station to start the journey to Ireland. He held her on the platform, checking that she had her tickets, holding her for a farewell hug and wishing her well.

'I'm here if you need me,' he said.

'You'll mind the house?'

'You know I will.'

It took two days to get to Ithaca, two long days of travelling and waiting between train and boat, standing with soldiers on platforms, in a state of fear and disorientation, not knowing what nightmare was going to be at the other end, only then to find that she had to travel back to Dublin where Hilary was lying close to death in hospital. The baby, Amelia, was doing fine.

'Amelia?' Lucy said, taking the little blanketed bundle from the nurse.

'Mrs Cholmondesley said it means beloved,' the nurse explained.

'A lovely name,' Lucy said, taking in the beauty of the tiny baby. Amelia was a combination of daintiness and prettiness with the elegant Entwhistle features somehow already present. Lucy held her close, touching her tiny limbs, and trying to both give and receive comfort.

Hilary died that night with a look of profound grief on her face, believing that Matthew and both her daughters had perished on the mountain. Lucy, sitting by her bed, looked down at the slender hand still lying in hers, unable to comprehend what had happened.

That same day, when the emergency services went back yet again to the site of the crash to sift through the now cooled debris to search for the dead, they found a little girl in a very dirty dress, with matted dark hair and glazed eyes, crouching beside the remnants of the shattered plane.

'Who are you?' she was asked.

At first she did not answer, but then, continuing to stare at the wreck, she whispered, 'Papa.'

Puzzled men looked at each other. Papa was not a word that was used by Irish children to address their parents, and the child's husky dried voice sounded distinctly foreign. How could a German child be there on the mountainside? How could she know that her father was flying that plane?'

Mattie's throat was parched and her voice almost non-existent, both from shock and from thirst.

'Does anyone speak any German?' one of the men called.

No one did.

Could she have been on the plane, they wondered. But no one could have survived the crash and they knew that.

With difficulty they tried to encourage her away from the plane, enticing her with hot tea and bread and cheese, and in the end one of the men picked her up and carried her down the mountain.

She was taken to the local police station, and the German Embassy was contacted.

'*Wie heisst du?*' she was asked by a dark-suited diplomat.

Mattie, having no understanding of what she

was being asked, sat silently and, having perused his face, looked at his shoes.

She had by now spent two nights on the hill, alone, shocked and thirsty. She had hidden behind rocks in a hollowed-out pit when the crash took place, having run as fast as she was able. That she had not caught pneumonia was in itself an achievement; in the damp and cold that night after the storm, she had slept curled up in the pit. As the temperature soared again the next day, she woke briefly but, unable to deal with the shock and anguish, soon escaped back into sleep. When she woke again she crawled towards the plane's wreckage to look for her papa, and was still there when the rescuers returned.

In hospital her mother was dying. The people who had come on the night of the crash and who had listened in disbelief to Hilary's story of Matthew's night-time journeys to shout across to Britain were now off duty, and as both the Cholmondesley girls were missing, presumed dead, no one realised that this silent forlorn child could be one of them.

'*Wo kommst du her?*' Mattie was asked.

'*Bist du Deutscherin?*'

'*Komm mal, sprech mit mir.*'

This might have continued had not a local garda, coming into the station to check on something and hearing what was going on in the back room, said, 'And are you sure she isn't one of the missing children?'

Being asked in English if she was a Cholmondesley, Mattie nodded her head, and then closed her eyes.

A doctor was called and she was taken to hospital.

Lucy, sitting in a different hospital in Dublin, holding the baby Amelia in her arms, was trying to take in everything that had happened. She still did not know that her eldest niece had been found. Her sister had just died, and the grief she was feeling was like a cloak around her, within which she held the tiny baby girl. She found she could not cry. There was a numbness that held her completely still, and her mind, while grief-stricken, was already busy with practicalities.

In some ways she knew she was reacting as she had done when dealing with emergencies in London, when she had closed down her mind so that she would not have to handle the emotions she was feeling, but at the same time could deal with the immediate needs of the situation. But she also knew this was different. It was not that she was deliberately shutting herself off. It was quite simply that she was in shock.

The nurse who was sitting with her was called out, and when she came back some ten minutes later she sat back down and suggested that she took the baby because she wanted to talk to Lucy. She had something to tell her.

'What is it?' Lucy looked up, distracted from her thoughts.

'Pass me the baby,' the nurse said again.

Lucy detached the sleeping baby's tiny hand, which was clasping one of her fingers, and obediently handed Amelia over.

Another nurse came in with a cup of tea for Lucy. 'We have something to tell you,' she said.

'Yes?' Lucy could not imagine what could be added to the events of the past few days.

'They think they've found one of your nieces,' she was told.

'Oh.'

'Alive and well.'

It took Lucy long moments to digest this.

'Which one? Who have they found?' Her voice sounded desperate although she knew it made no difference which child had been found. It would be one child or the other child. One child alive and one child dead – one saved, one lost, and Hilary was dead too and would never know.

'She's three or four years old, with dark hair,' one of the nurses told Lucy.

'That's Mattie,' she said. She still thought of her niece as she had last seen her when she was little older than Amelia was right then. She had been just a tiny baby, squawking her way into life.

Mattie was asleep when Lucy arrived at the Children's Hospital. When she woke her face had a dull blankness to it that concerned not just Lucy, but also the doctors and the nurses.

'She needs time,' Lucy was told.

'Time?' She could not imagine what they meant.

She tried holding Mattie, telling her that it was all going to be all right, that she would stay with her and mind her, that she had a baby sister and it was all going to be fine, although at that time she could not think what fine could mean.

Mattie's little body remained still and un-

85

responsive in Lucy's arms, and her confused mind understood only that her sister was safe – her sister Georgina.

Days passed as in a slow paralysing dream for Lucy. She waited in Dublin until Mattie was released from the Children's Hospital. Mattie still had not spoken.

'She will,' they said. 'When she is ready.'

Lucy took her niece by the hand and introduced her to her baby sister. Mattie looked from Amelia to Lucy and back again, but made no other reaction.

Lucy took both girls home, Mattie silent, Amelia gurgling in blissful baby ignorance.

With Cook and Maudge's help, Lucy put into practice what she remembered from Mattie's birth, bottle-feeding the baby, and trying to communicate with the older child.

A few days later, coming into the nursery to lift Amelia, Lucy found Mattie standing beside the crib, staring at the tiny baby.

'That isn't Georgina,' Mattie said to her when Lucy joined her beside the cot.

'No,' Lucy said to her gently. 'That's not Georgina. That's Amelia. The new baby. Your new baby sister. Amelia means beloved. She is a beloved baby. Mummy chose her name.'

'Georgina's gone,' Mattie said, and Lucy was unsure if that was a question or a statement, and she was equally uncertain what was the best response. The truth was that no trace of Georgina whatsoever had been found, and very little of Matthew had been taken from the scene of the crash.

'Mummy called Georgina her angel,' Mattie contributed, and Lucy forced herself again and again not to think about her own grief and not to cry, but to put herself in the shoes of this forsaken child. She kneeled down to put her arms around her, but Mattie stood there stolidly and did not yield. All Lucy could do was feel relief that at least the barrier of silence had been broken.

Mattie continued staring at the cot, her face pursed in concentration, clearly trying to understand how on that night, out of that ball of fire, which had lit up the mountain, another baby had been born.

The funerals took place in the tiny church down the lane, with Cook and Maudge minding the girls at home, while Lucy kneeled in the front pew, trying to handle the upsurge of anguish and sadness that overtook her.

'Dust to dust,' the vicar proclaimed in the churchyard over the open grave and the three coffins, and Lucy, looking at Matthew's coffin, tried hard not to think what little lay within it. The tiny white coffin was empty.

She tried over the following weeks and months to involve Mattie with the baby, but Mattie showed little overt interest other than occasionally to look at Amelia in puzzlement. Lucy wrote to her mother in India, telling her of the accident on the mountain and filling her in on the subsequent tragedy. It was difficult to find the words to explain the present situation.

Amelia, the baby, is easy to handle. She is happy

to be fed and cuddled. She sleeps well. Mattie is a more difficult proposition. She doesn't say much and doesn't like to be touched, although I am working on that. There is a little boy called Sean – our cook's grandson – he is Mattie's age. He dotes on Amelia. It is sweet to watch him guarding Amelia on her rug when we are sitting on the beach or on the lawn. It's comforting I suppose…

Lucy knew that, like Hilary, she did not have great mothering skills, and she was drawing on her memories of her ayah and the relationship she had had with her but none of that could be put in the letter, as it would sound like an indictment of her mother. Instead she told her how Mattie liked to be read to, and that she spent hours every day reading the various children's books in the house and was having more sent down from Dublin. She tried to describe the house and their daily routine, and the help she got from Cook and Maudge, both of whom were now the mainstays in her life.

But the truth was they were difficult times as she found herself plunged into a role she had never expected, and for which she was totally unprepared.

Mattie battled against everything when she was paying attention; the rest of the time she lived as in a dream world, staring vacantly at the fire in winter or in bewilderment at Amelia.

Amelia grew and gave her first smile to Mattie, although Mattie appeared not to notice. She gave her second smile to Lucy.

Lucy did her best with both girls. While she

cuddled and hugged one, she read to the other. She became absorbed in her time with them. Amelia was crawling as she began to teach Mattie to read, and Sean kept an eye on the baby while Lucy spent endless hours with Mattie and her books. At first she had them in separate bedrooms so that Amelia would not disturb her sister, but later she talked to Mattie about sharing a room, explaining to her that Amelia needed a roommate.

It was an attempt to make Mattie more aware of her sibling. Lucy did not assume that it would work and all it really did was to make Amelia even more aware of Mattie, whom she appeared to love regardless of how much she was ignored.

Lucy drifted through their early childhood, aware that she had no idea how to deal with her truculent elder niece, but she tried so hard with endless patience – patience that she did not know she possessed.

She thought how once she had envied Hilary her passivity, her approach to life, and indeed her life itself. And now she felt she had in some sense grown into her older sister. There she was, in Hilary's house, playing the role of mother, spending her days as she assumed Hilary had done, with two little girls who were dependent on her for everything. The role in which she found herself evolved, and absorbed her completely.

Had she known that this was what would happen to her, that this was what her life would become, she would have balked, just as she once had done when she had been told by her mother to go to Ireland to help Hilary. If she had regrets, they were for her sister's death and nothing more. Having seen so much death and destruction in London, and watched people picking up the shattered pieces of their lives during the air raids, she knew that her lot could have been worse. And she no longer viewed her life in terms of 'her lot'. Instead she just got on with things.

'Ruth among the corn in an alien land,' she read in a book, and she admonished herself for equating herself in any way with Ruth. She was not enslaved, even though she had nowhere to escape to. In the early days there was no time to think, and later, when she did have time to think, she was so ensconced in Ithaca and so involved in the children's lives that she could no longer imagine a different way of living. In the material sense they lacked for nothing, and so with her Entwhistle pragmatism and stoicism, she accepted her life and made the most of it.

This acceptance had been reinforced when Matthew's will was read and she discovered that in the event of both his and Hilary's deaths, she was legal guardian of their heirs.

Over the next few years she sometimes thought of Hilary – Hilary in love, Hilary happy, Hilary holding Mattie the day she was born – and realised that one day during that period, her sister and Matthew must have gone to a solicitor for just this eventuality. And she grieved again for her Hilary's short life.

She bought Homer's *Odyssey* and told the girls the story of Odysseus and his journey, the battles he fought, the fights he won, and his ultimate

90

return to Ithaca.

'To here?' Amelia asked.

'No, to a different Ithaca,' Lucy said. 'To his Ithaca.'

She read the philosophy books in the library and then bought more to devour at night when the girls were asleep.

'What is life?' she asked them, always interested and amazed at their replies.

'Life is a dream,' Amelia replied. 'It's running on the beach and seeing a bird in the sky.'

'Life is a nightmare,' Mattie snapped. 'It is waiting for what you cannot have.' They were not the exact words of the two children, but they summed them up.

But Lucy did not want to see life in terms of waiting – she had done that for long enough in her dreams of Rhino Kobaldt, in that last year of school when she thought about him ceaselessly, so that he absorbed too much of her waking moments. The death she had seen in London had made her aware of the pointlessness of waiting for things that might not happen – that life itself was so intangible that if she did not seize the moments as they were, then they could pass her by. And for what? Within the blinking of an eyelid the moments could be over for ever. As indeed her time in London seemed gone for ever. And so Lucy read her philosophy at night and spent her daytime with the girls.

'What is God?' she asked them.

'He minds Mummy and Daddy,' Amelia said.

'He is a ball of fire,' Mattie said.

There were no real answers.

Happiness depends upon ourselves.
Aristotle

CHAPTER FOUR

Grandmother Entwhistle arrived in the summer of 1947 when Amelia was three years old. The war was over and the billowing darkness that had swept Europe for so many years was lifted.

It had been different in India. There, in Eden House, where Harriet had lived for many years, her life continued as it had before, except that her husband and daughters had departed. She kept a close eye on the regiment and was involved in the socialising that continued, despite world events. She shopped in the markets, occasionally drank tea on a houseboat with friends, attended church on Sundays, visited the returning men in the hospital and most of all she waited.

She waited for news from the outside world. Communication was limited. There was nothing from the Far East where Edward, her husband, seemed to have disappeared. There were rumours of prison camps and she could but hope that he was alive and safe in one and would eventually emerge from Burma.

During this time her first two granddaughters were born in Ireland and she could only imagine what was happening there as letters rarely got through. She worried about Lucy in London, being, as she was, quite aware of the destruction that was taking place in the home country, and she knew that North London had taken many hits.

When the news came of Hilary's death, Harriet sat alone in her garden, gazing dimly down the pathways, unable to believe that her beautiful daughter was gone. And not just Hilary and Matthew, but also her little granddaughter Georgina.

She did not even have a photograph of Georgina – nothing but a description of her in Hilary's elegant hand. Hilary was elegance, she thought. Hilary was beauty. And of course she had thought that Hilary was safe. Where could be safer than a neutral country?

It was Lucy she had worried about – Lucy in London in an ambulance. She had been disbelieving when she first heard about Lucy's venture into the ambulance service. She had even sent a telegram ordering her daughter to get over to Ireland at once, or at the very least, to stay indoors. But Lucy had stubbornly stuck to her guns. As time went on Harriet, despite her fears, felt pride in Lucy and the part she was playing.

Then when Hilary died, Harriet was frustrated that she could not be there for Mattie and the baby, but there was relief that Lucy was close by and that Lucy left everything to go to the children. In her initial distress Harriet wanted to try making her way back across Europe, but friends talked her out of it, pointing out that she was needed in India, that the situation in Ireland was under control – tragic and all as that was – and that the Colonel might reappear and it would

93

be Harriet he would need.

And all of this was true. The Colonel did indeed reappear. A pale and shaken shadow of his former self. He was little more than skin and bone and his eyes had the look of a man who had died.

Harriet nursed him in the hospital. She spent all day and most of the night there. She held his hand when he slept and was there when he woke. She feared he would die, but as one of her friends observed to another, he would be afraid to die with Harriet at his side ordering him to live.

Harriet brooked no nonsense. She was used to obedience. And the Colonel recovered. He had always been a man of contemplation – but he was more so now. He sat silently a lot of the time, engrossed in his own thoughts, jumping only when the dogs barked outside and a look of uncertainty would cross his face.

Harriet was there. She donned the cloak of Colonel Memsahib. She protected him from intrusion and supported him, often in an unusual but pragmatic silence. She was a mighty woman in many respects. Her belief in herself, her family and her position in life had given her a confidence that other people, both men and women, only aspired to. She had been known, in a conversation with members of the clergy in India, outside church on her way to some diplomatic or military bash, to announce forthrightly, tapping her ample bosom, 'But for these, I could have been Pope.' This had brought a startled silence while the onlookers took in her words and her gesture.

'What about me?' her husband had said gently.

'Edward, you would never have made Pope, dear,' she said, completely misunderstanding him and the fact that he had never had any idea that she might have had such aspirations, and that that was what he was querying.

'I meant, that we are married,' he said.

'And I meant, that had I not been born a woman, I could have been the one explaining doctrine and enlightening these good men,' she said, including all of the clergymen in a sweep of her head. 'What the Church needs is enlightenment,' she added. 'Women at the helm – a lot of the world's problems would be immediately sorted.'

'What problems?' she was asked.

She cast a cold eye on the enquirer – a local politician, who wilted somewhat under her gaze.

'Like war,' Harriet replied resolutely. 'With women at the helm there would be no war. What woman would send her husband or children out to kill other women's husbands and children and to die themselves?'

It was she who said to her husband some weeks after he returned from hospital and appeared to be recovered, that they should go to Ireland. It was he who said that she was right but they would not come back to India. She did not argue. She carried out the move single-handedly while the Colonel read Aristotle.

'What are you reading?' she asked him on board ship on the long journey home, Eden House having finally been closed.

'I'm reading about virtue,' he replied.

95

Harriet did not have much time for philosophy. She had her own and that was all that counted. But in her efforts to indulge and encourage the Colonel in his new and somewhat fragile state, she asked him was this relevant.

'The thing about Aristotle,' Edward replied, 'is that he, of course, unlike modern philosophers, has no notion of evolution.'

'Evolution?' said Harriet, as if hitting on a distasteful word. 'The implication that my fore-bears were monkeys?'

The Colonel pondered her words. Then he shook his head. 'Don't worry, dear,' he said gently, returning to his book.

Harriet wrote in advance that they were coming to stay, but the letter declaring her imminent arrival had gone astray. And so she swept in, both unexpected and unannounced.

Until then the house had been very peaceful with its regular routine. The children's world appeared quite simple.

They spent their summer days on the beach. Mattie, Sean and Amelia. Sean ran barefoot, his little breeches held up with a cut-down pair of braces, resewn to fit. The width of the elastic in the braces covered most of his collarbone. He had spiky dark hair and sallow skin. He bore no resemblance to the maternal side of his family. His father, a local boy, had left with four others to find work in England and had never come back.

Sean loved Amelia with a passion that was reciprocated.

The day of Harriet's unexpected arrival in Ireland found the children on the beach, and Lucy sitting reading on the dunes. Beside Lucy, on the sand, lay a golf club and a croquet mallet. There was a morning routine to their trip down the garden to the sea. Lucy took the golf club to decapitate any unsuspecting dandelions, aided by Amelia, who used the mallet that her father had cut to size three years earlier.

Mattie refused to touch the mallet. She had never played croquet since that last day of her childhood as she had known it, and she had little interest in anything other than reading and fire. The summer days lay long and hard on her, as the fire was never lit in the grates in either the drawing room or the day room. She longed for winter when she could sit and stare at the flames, whiling away hour after hour, gazing in silence.

Grandmother Entwhistle, in the past few weeks since she left India, had taken to wearing turbans made from silk she had bought in the markets of Rampur. Glorious affairs they were, wound carefully up and around her head, in wonderful shades of raspberry, sky blue, the deepest of yellows or, as she called it, 'maharajah red'.

Her appearance on the beach, approaching from the lawn behind the house, was as dramatic as if she had arrived by elephant.

She stood at the top of the dunes, taking in the white-topped waves on the sea, the golden stretch of sand, three small children, two of whom were playing with a ball, and one who appeared to be doing something with a magnifying glass and a piece of paper. She looked straight down and there below her, nestled with her back into the dunes, was Lucy, golf club and a croquet mallet beside her, reading a novel.

For their part, one by one the children stopped what they were doing and looked up at the grass-topped dune, and saw, standing there with her arms raised to the sky, her legs slightly apart to assist her balance at the top of the drop, a tall person with brightly coloured headgear, standing like a colossus looking down.

'Lucy,' she barked.

In disbelief, Lucy dropped her book and jumped to her feet. Despite the fact that she had not seen her mother for eight years, she reacted just as she had always done to that call in the past. Her guilty reaction was enhanced by the look of total surprise on her face.

'Mother,' she shouted, looking around her.

The height of the dunes and the light breeze had thrown her mother's voice so that it did not occur to her that her mother was directly above her.

The children, though, standing motionless staring upwards, positioned her parent for her and convinced her that she was not dreaming.

'Who is that?' asked Sean of the two girls.

'I don't know,' said Amelia Cholmondesley.

'I think that might be Grandmother,' Mattie said, slipping her magnifying glass into her pocket, and kicking some sand over the paper, leaving just an edge sticking up for easy recovery later when she would return to her experiment. Mattie's earlier preoccupation with watching fire had moved to an obsession with creating it.

'Oh.' Sean looked with interest, as Lucy scrambled up the dune into the arms of her mother.

The arrival of Grandmother Entwhistle would have been enough to frighten most children, but Amelia had never known any reason to be afraid before. And Mattie, who had been through trial by fire, feared nothing either.

Lucy and her mother held each other for long moments before the Colonel Memsahib stepped back and held her at arm's length and surveyed her face.

'It's all right,' she said to her daughter. 'I'm here now.'

Harriet Entwhistle's arrival anywhere usually changed the status quo. And until then, life had been drifting along nicely. Lucy loved the summers best, and sitting on the beach with the children was probably the highlight of those long days and nights, now that she had neither toddler nor baby on her hands. And for the children, scantily clad, just in their vests and with cotton skirts tucked into their knickers, the days were easy.

It was an emotional moment for both mother and daughter. In a new and very real way, her mother was forced to face Hilary's death in those seconds in which she and Lucy held each other and then looked into each other's faces. And any hopes that Harriet might have had that there had been some terrible mistake and that these things could not have happened were wiped away by the reality of the two little girls on the beach and the wrong daughter minding them.

Up the beach the children came, Sean hanging back and watching, as the sisters climbed the dune and stood before their grandmother as if for inspection.

Seven years of absentee grandmother's love and affection in the case of Mattie, and three in the case of Amelia came pouring out in the moments after surveying the children. But Harriet Entwhistle was a wise enough women to release both girls as soon as she had given them an initial hug. She had felt Amelia's compliance as the little girl had let herself be enveloped in her grandmother's embrace. She had equally felt the rigidity in Mattie's sturdy body.

'Girls,' she said, 'I've brought you presents.' And up to the house they went.

Amelia, looking back to see where Sean was, found he had disappeared.

Grandmother's cases were unpacked in her room, and the girls watched in excitement as a set of elephants carved from rosewood, complete with ivory tusks, was unwrapped. These elephants were followed by jasmine petals in a carved box inlaid with more ivory; coloured hanging bells, which tinkled magically against each other when Mattie held them aloft; jewellery boxes with various stones, some already made into pendants or bracelets.

'Mother,' Lucy said aghast, looking in the jewellery boxes, 'you can't give them these. They're too young.'

'They can be put away for them,' her mother replied.

'But we can look at them sometimes, can't we?' Mattie said. Her eyes were lit up in anticipation as the gifts were unpacked.

Neither child had ever seen such an abundance of the unknown before. The smell of jasmine and incense filled the air. They looked at each other in wonder and laughed in delight.

'Oh, Grandmother,' Mattie said. 'Thank you.'

Lucy bit back any further comment because she had seen the excitement in Mattie's face and she rejoiced that the child was capable of such emotion.

Later, when Grandmother and Lucy were sitting sipping sherry in the drawing room, Amelia hid behind the long sofa. She wondered where Mattie was and then, out of the corner of her eye, she saw Mattie's foot and knew that Mattie too had ensconced herself behind one of the armchairs, between the mahogany bookcase and the wall. Both girls were listening carefully to the ongoing discussion.

'Where is Father?' Lucy asked.

'He's in the Shelbourne Hotel,' her mother said. 'He'll come down and join us now.'

'Why didn't he come with you?'

'I thought it better if I checked the lie of the land before his arrival,' her mother replied. Harriet Entwhistle had not been married to a soldier for thirty-five years for nothing.

'Is he all right?' Lucy asked.

Her mother nodded her assent. 'Under the

circumstances he's doing very well,' she said briskly.

These words worried Lucy. They held the implication that he was not doing very well at all. 'What do you mean?' she asked.

Her mother took another sip of sherry before replying. 'Two years in a prison camp doesn't do anyone any good,' she said thoughtfully. 'He's regaining his health. I hardly recognised him when he arrived back, but he is looking well again. Quite well. He was badly treated,' she added.

Lucy stayed silent. The thought of her father being badly treated – he who had only ever treated those around him with respect – was appalling.

'So many of his men did not come back,' her mother continued. 'That takes its toll on anyone. He would have given his life for those men. Almost did, in fact.

'Now, to the girls,' she went on, changing the subject abruptly. 'I should take them back with me, to London.'

'What?' Lucy looked at her in bewilderment.

'You can't care for them properly here,' her mother said.

'But I *have* cared for them properly here,' Lucy retorted. 'They're happy and healthy. I did what Hilary wanted me to do.'

'I don't doubt that for a moment,' her mother said. 'But you're entitled to a life of your own. Aren't you, dear?'

'What are you saying, Mother?' Lucy asked, distressed. 'That I have not cared for them as they should be cared for?'

'No. Of course not, dear. That's not what I'm saying at all. I think you've done a wonderful job, all things considered.'

'What do you mean, "all things considered"? What more could I have done? What do you think they are lacking?' Lucy was really startled. 'You can't take them away.'

Behind the sofa, Amelia shifted uncomfortably, and was aware that Mattie's foot had disappeared as she too changed position, both craning forwards to listen better.

'We need to sort out the details before your father arrives. He should not be bothered with minutiae,' her mother said firmly.

'You can't take them away from me,' Lucy said. 'I'm all they know. For heaven's sake, Mother, I am like a mother to them. Amelia has never known any other arrangement, and Mattie ... well, Mattie ... I'm the one who gives her stability.'

'Don't speak to me like that, Lucy,' Harriet Entwhistle said firmly, in that voice that brooked no defiance. 'I know what is best for my granddaughters.'

'Mother,' Lucy said, 'I beg to differ. You don't know your granddaughters. Granted–' she got no further.

'I came as soon as I could,' her mother interrupted. 'Don't think I haven't been worried sick for the last three years. Don't think I haven't grieved for my Hilary, and worried about her two little girls. But now is the time that I can do something.'

'Then help me,' Lucy said. 'But don't talk about taking them away. I am their guardian in every sense of the word. And with me they will stay.'

'But you're entitled to a life,' her mother said. 'You've had your youth snatched away from you.'

'Mother,' Lucy said, and all of a sudden her tone of voice was remarkably similar to her mother's, 'I am the first to admit that this was not what I had planned or hoped for. I never imagined that my sister would die – with me beside her. I held her hand as she died, don't you dare forget that ... and I still have nightmares about it. But those girls need me. And it is what Hilary wanted. I think she believed ... I think she thought that both Mattie and Georgina were dead when she died. She gave me Amelia in trust. The fact that Mattie survived only adds to the trust that she placed in me.'

This was the first time that either Amelia or Mattie had heard Lucy speak like this. Any reference to their mother from Lucy up until then had been to do with how much Hilarymem had loved them, and how Hilarymem had danced with their father, stories of happiness that Lucy thought would enrich both the children.

Amelia had heard little if anything about Georgina, and it wasn't until now that she realised that Georgina had actually been a real person.

Cook had once said something about how like Georgina Amelia looked. And when Amelia had asked who Georgina was, Cook put her hand to her mouth and said, 'Don't mind me, Amelia. I'm mixing everything up these days.'

Amelia had wondered if Cook had meant to say Mattie when she used the name Georgina, but later, looking at herself and her sister in the mirror, she did not think it very likely that Cook would have said that she resembled Mattie. Mattie was tall and she was small. Mattie's hair was very dark, whereas Amelia's hair was still very fair, although already beginning to darken too.

Lucy had said to her that she looked like her mother, Hilarymem. In her mind Amelia had worked out that Hilarymem and Mummy were the same person, and that that person was dead. She knew of Mummy from Mattie. Not that Mattie talked about Mummy, but in her sleep she sometimes called out, 'Mummy, Mummy,' as she tossed and turned and wet the bed.

Amelia knew the word dead, because often after church on Sunday they walked around to the little cemetery behind, and there was a large stone with beautiful writing on it, and she and Mattie placed little bundles of flowers in front of the stone. Sometimes Amelia would try to take Mattie's hand so that they could share these precious moments, but Mattie always withdrew.

Amelia knew what was written on the stone. Lucy had read the words to her until they were embedded in her mind, beautiful words that described her parents and their position in her universe.

Here lies Matthew Cholmondesley
His beloved wife Hilary
Together for ever with their angel Georgina
Requiescat in Pace

105

There were other stones in the cemetery and Amelia had learned what was written on them all. There was William O'Shaughnessy, who died in his eighty-seventh year; and little Breda Mangan, who died when she was two; and Mary Driscoll, whom God took when she was twenty. They all requiescated in pace.

Lucy had told her that *pace* meant peace, and that it was a wonderful way to be. Amelia had thought that Georgina was the name of Mummy's special angel, and when she prayed at night with Mattie and Lucy before going to sleep, and Lucy said,

'There are four corners on my bed
There are four angels at my head
Matthew, Mark, Luke and John,'

one night Amelia said, '*and* Georgina,' because she thought that Georgina was one of those special angels.

She only said it the once because Mattie reached out and hit her with a balled-up fist, and said, 'Not Georgina.'

The prayer disintegrated as Amelia started to cry. Her crying set off Mattie, and Lucy held them each in her arms, close to her chest and kissed them both.

'It doesn't hurt if Amelia says Georgina too, does it, Mattie?' she asked.

'Not Georgina,' Mattie repeated and, slipping away from Lucy, she clambered into her bed and pulled the covers over her head.

Having tucked Amelia into bed and soothed her tears, Lucy tried to entice Mattie downstairs with her, but Mattie refused to move or even to acknowledge that Lucy was speaking to her.

'What more could I have done?' Lucy said.

'But don't you want time for yourself?' her mother continued. 'Don't you want parties and fun and maybe love?' she added tentatively.

'The war changed things for everyone,' Lucy said. 'They are my girls now, and with me they will stay.'

'I'm only trying to make things better for you,' Harriet Entwhistle said. 'You're still young enough to get married.'

'I don't need marriage right now,' Lucy said. 'This is my life.'

'You're twenty-five,' her mother said. 'You don't want to end up on the shelf.'

'What are you suggesting? That I abandon the girls and go off and find myself a husband? I would never ever do that. I love these girls like they are my own. In fact, they are my own,' Lucy said.

Behind the sofa, Amelia felt a surge of love flood through her. She knew that Lucy would never leave them. She tried to restrain herself, but she could not, and she rushed out from her hiding place and threw herself into Aunt Lucymem's arms.

'I love you, Lucymem,' she said. 'I just love you and love you.'

And Lucy, holding the little bundle in her arms, looked across the top of her head at her mother, who, sitting there, took in the scene and said nothing.

Over the next days Amelia and Mattie found hiding places in every room where they could listen in on the adult conversations. They also crouched outside open windows, side by side, craning to hear. Some of these hiding places they shared, with Mattie reluctantly moving up to accommodate Amelia. There seemed a silent admittance that she actually needed her younger sister. There was occasional eye contact between them as they huddled behind the sofa.

Their grandfather arrived, and Lucy, coming out on to the front drive to greet him, rushed forwards. As she opened the car door for him, they both paused and looked carefully at each other before he climbed out and took her in his arms. He was a tall and very thin mustachioed military man, always serious and focused, but in that moment she was aware of how much weight he had lost and also that he held her in a way he never had before. She knew that his embrace encompassed Hilary and it included all the lost years. He released her and held her by her shoulders, looking into her eyes.

Neither spoke. There were long moments during which he kissed her on both cheeks and then looked into her eyes again. She could feel tears burning behind her lids and slowly appearing from her eyes and trickling down her cheeks. She cried not just for him, but for all the loss and the senseless waste of life. He wiped her tears away with a large white handkerchief and then he released her and turned to his two grand-daughters.

He had kindly eyes with smile lines at the sides, but sometimes now his eyes seemed to drift away. Amelia was sitting on his lap, fiddling with his moustache, the first time she noticed this. He had been smiling at her, his big hands holding her firmly so that she could not fall, and suddenly his smile seemed to freeze and he looked through hers and beyond to some other place.

'Come back to me, Grandfather,' she said, looking up at him and hopefully waving a tiny hand in front of his face, and he, blinking, seemed to recall where he was. The look in his eyes made her think of the look she sometimes saw in Mattie's eyes. Full of pain and secrets. As if she had gone to some other place, a place she would rather not be, but could not escape from.

In their various hiding places the girls heard all kinds of things being discussed.

Grandfather and Grandmother were not return-ing to India. 'Our day there is done,' Grandfather said. 'There is no place for us in India now.'

'Will you live in London?' Lucy asked.

This became unclear, as Grandmother wanted to settle in London, whereas Grandfather wanted somewhere quieter.

'Whatever we do,' her mother said, 'we'll keep the house. It will be a base for us all in the city.'

Her father said nothing. He did not really mind what they did with the London house as long as he could live somewhere quiet, where he would be woken in the morning by the sound of birds singing, and the most he would have to worry about would be if a mole was burrowing its way through his garden. He quite liked the idea of a mole under the grass and found himself thinking about this from time to time and wondering if he could get a book on the subject. He also wondered if you could assist the mole's passageway underground by putting air holes in the grass, or if perhaps by doing that he would be interfering with the natural plans of the mole and the mole might go and burrow elsewhere deep beneath the earth.

The idea of being buried alive disturbed him greatly, and with good reason. He had lost more than a few of his men through such torture while in Burma. He realised now on one level that there was nothing he could do about those men and he hoped he would never find himself in the position again in life where he would have to watch such cruelty – the cruelty of man to man, of captor to victim, of prison guards to his men, his boys – chaps he had known for years. He had known and loved his soldiers as companions and as sons. Their lives were ended, and it was only in his nightmares that he struggled with hard dry clay, scrabbling at it with his fingers, trying to release them from their vertical hellholes, while the raw steel of bayonets slipped along the back of his neck. He had given up on them in daylight hours, but he could perhaps assist the life's-work of moles.

His two granddaughters worried him. He was drawn to them because of Hilary – beloved Hilary – in her grave in the church cemetery, but he feared for them too. He was disturbed by the knowledge of what life might throw at them with all their optimism and energy. One scrambled on to his lap for a hug and to play with his moustache, the other stood at the doorway watching him balefully, and both hid behind chairs and sofas to listen in on adult conversation.

He was always aware who was in the room and where they might be hidden, but he said nothing. He just enjoyed their proximity and rejoiced in the fact that they were alive.

He was aware of the juxtaposition of life and death within the house of Ithaca. Here one of his daughters lived with two of his granddaughters. And down the road by the little parish church another of his daughters lay with yet another granddaughter. The plot in the churchyard held such terrible tragedy that he could not bear to think of its contents. The idea of his elder daughter and the bits of his son-in-law and his missing granddaughter lying there, disintegrating and disintegrated, was anguish for him. On their first visit to the churchyard he had stood there beside his wife, and when he felt her body sigh in its grief, he had held one of her elbows and briefly said, 'At least they are in coffins.'

Harriet stroked his fingers on her elbow and bowed her head. She did not need to ask to what he referred, so she held her peace, and hoped that Lucy had not heard, not to mention Mattie and Amelia.

Mattie, who had heard, looked up at her grandfather and then back to the grave. Her eyes then travelled across the fields and up towards the hills before she closed them tightly. She stood there on her short stocky legs, dressed in a sailor suit with her summer straw hat perched on her head and held in place by elastic under her chin. In matching outfit, Amelia wanted to show her grandparents how well she could read. She also hoped that by mentioning the angel Georgina, she might acquire a little information on who or what Georgina was exactly. But Mattie was listening, so she started on some of the nearby tombstones. She knew the words on every tombstone by heart because she always got Lucy to read them to her.

'Look, Grandmother,' she said. 'Here lies Breda Mangan aged two. And here lies William O'Shaughnessy in his eighty-seventh year. And here lies Mary McBride whose magnanimity will never be forgotten.' She struggled with the word magnanimity and had to be helped.

'And look, Grandmother,' she said, pointing with a small finger at the tombstone. '"Together for ever with their angel Georgina."'

Mattie opened her eyes and glared at her.

Grandmother said, 'Yes, dear. '"Together for ever with their angel Georgina."'

'Cook says I look like Georgina,' Amelia tried hopefully, while holding her Grandfather's hand as they walked back up the road.

'Do you indeed, m'dear?' he said. 'Did she have hair like yours? Was it not darker? More like Mattie's. But it was curly, like yours and Mattie's.

112

I'm right, I think. Harriet,' he said loudly so that his wife could hear.

Harriet was walking behind with Lucy and Mattie.

'Harriet, did Georgina have wavy hair? She did, didn't she? I'm sure I recall that from a letter of Hilary's. I wish she had sent us photographs.'

Mattie broke free from her grandmother's hand and ran down the road so fast and so carelessly, that she tripped just at the corner and cut both knees, and Amelia's opportunity passed in a scream of pain from her sister, and the following half-hour of bathing and removing gravel from her sister's knees.

While Mattie sat on the kitchen table, and Lucy worked with a bowl of hot water, disinfectant and cotton wool, Amelia came to watch how proceedings were developing.

Every so often she would look up at Mattie's face to see how her sister was handling the pain. It occurred to her that the look Mattie was giving her was unfriendly in the extreme, so eventually she ran off to find her grandfather.

He was sitting on a rug at the end of the lawn overlooking the sea. His posture, even in repose, could only have been that of a man in control. Straight-backed, almost to the point of rigidity, he sat staring out across the sea.

Amelia slipped down beside him on to the rug. She slid a small hand into one of his, and they sat there together in silence.

Harriet, watching them from a landing window, wondered what was the best thing for everyone.

113

It had become clearer and clearer that Lucy was not going to give up the children, and their grandfather, much as he enjoyed them, felt that their rightful place was with their aunt, who had been, as he pointed out to his wife, 'their substitute mother for all these years.'

The argument over the custody of the children had gone back and forth for days, with Harriet, unusually, weakening little by little as she felt the ground she stood on was not as firm as she had assumed.

'But we need time with them too,' she said to Lucy. 'We both do. Your father and I.'

She was moved by the girls' behaviour, particularly with their grandfather, as both had taken to him, and he to them. He had come more out of himself and had started playing cricket on the beach with them and with the little boy from the adjoining cottage.

Sean made him laugh. He raced against Mattie but often let her win in an attempt to cheer her up, and his kindness to Amelia was remarked on. In some way he was a link across the blank space between the two girls, happy to join in when he felt he was not in the way, always ready to play when he was called upon.

'You're a good lad,' Grandfather said to him.

Mattie's knees now cleaned and bandaged, Lucy joined her mother on the landing. Looking down on the garden and seeing Amelia and her father on the rug hand in hand, she turned to her mother.

'I would not mean to deprive either of you of your granddaughters. You must know that. But their place is with me.'

'You will come and visit regularly?' Harriet asked.

'Without any doubt,' Lucy replied, knowing that the battle was over and that they would now move on.

Fear is pain arising from the anticipation of evil.
Aristotle

CHAPTER FIVE

And so the Colonel and Harriet returned to London, with a promise from Lucy that she and the girls would visit as soon as they were settled. Even Mattie hugged both her grandparents with an affection that had hitherto not been displayed.

Back in England they were a while finding a place in Kent that satisfied them both. It was the following spring before they bought a country house not far from Tunbridge Wells with a garden the size of a football pitch.

Like some cultures pray for rain, the Colonel prayed for moles. He insisted on keeping more than half the garden in a wild state in the hope that this would appear as a more habitable and natural environment for the animals he was sure would soon move in.

Harriet, on the other hand, encouraged his ramblings among the overgrowth and insisted only on a lawn close to the house where she could have garden parties and play croquet. She was used to a busy social life and had no doubt such would continue, with the return to England of so many of their friends from India. Although she decided that for now she would proceed with caution because she did not want the Colonel to feel swamped with visitors.

Watching him sitting at the far end of the garden contemplating she knew not what, she did feel a sense of dismay. She decided for the moment to limit her invitations to family and so she wrote to her brother's son, inviting him and his family to visit.

'And what are you planning on doing with the other half of the garden?' her brother's son, Jupe, asked on his first visit.

'At the moment we are enjoying the wilderness,' she announced. 'So different to India – a different type of wilderness,' she added.

She remained blissfully unaware of what was going on in the Colonel's mind. Had she known, she would have been very perturbed, and would have been quick to point out that wild animals that burrow would not keep to one end of the garden, an observation that the Colonel appeared not to have considered.

In London he asked in a pet shop if he could buy a mole or maybe two, but was told that they were not considered pets and were not purchasable.

Harriet, with her customary zeal, laid out a small vegetable garden and planted lettuce at much the same time as the Colonel gave up on the moles and brought home two rabbits, which he released into the garden and which duly demolished Harriet's tiny crop.

Harriet and the Colonel were sitting at breakfast one morning and she was bemoaning the destruction of her work, when looking out the kitchen window she saw some fifteen or more

117

tiny rabbits playing on the grass.

'My God,' she muttered.

'The girls will love them,' the Colonel said.

He had wired off the vegetable garden but the burrowing rabbits had found their way in from beneath.

'Edward, do you think I am going to continue growing foodstuffs just for those furry-back rats to eat?' Harriet asked.

The Colonel looked mildly uncomfortable, but felt relieved that he had never mentioned the moles to her.

'Perhaps if you tried fruit instead,' he suggested. 'I could put up canes for raspberries.'

Somewhat mollified by his acceptance of her complaint, Harriet agreed, and was indeed buoyant when he promised to buy her a variety of fruit trees. He went straight out and bought her a pear tree and a partridge for dinner that evening. She made gravy with a dash of his best brandy, and he opened a bottle of Nuits-Saint-George and they talked about their grandchildren and Lucy.

Retiring to the drawing room after dinner, Harriet poured him a whisky.

'Edward,' she said. 'I wonder if you would read to me?'

He looked at her in surprise. 'I would be delighted,' he replied.

It was many, many years since he had suggested that, or she had asked. He searched the bookshelves for something he felt she would like.

She sat by the fire, ankles crossed, watching him as he searched for a book of poetry. The look on her face was soft.

He was a good reader, and she listened in silence.

'We are not now that strength which in old days
Moved earth and heaven, that which we are, we
   are, –
One equal temper of heroic hearts,
Made weak by time and fate, but strong in will
To strive, to seek, to find, and not to yield.'

'What is that, Edward?' she asked.

'Tennyson ... "Ulysses".'

'Hmm,' she said thoughtfully. 'I think I can still move earth and heaven if need be.'

He smiled.

In Ireland plans were afoot for the children's first trip abroad. There was a sense of excitement tinged with disappointment because they would not be putting up a Christmas tree. The bags were packed and Lucy reassured both girls that there would be a tree in their grandparents'.

Lucy arrived with Mattie and Amelia three days before Christmas, making the first of what would become a regular journey across the Irish Sea, and taking the train to London where Harriet met them at Euston Station. Harriet's driving skills, which the girls had encountered in Ireland when their grandmother had taken them out, amused them but terrified Lucy. Lucy, like her mother, had learned to drive in India, but while Lucy had adapted to the rules of the road in the British Isles, Harriet had not.

'Shall I drive, Mother?' she asked her parent.

Amelia clasped her aunt's hand while Mattie stood apart and watched the proceedings.

'I think not,' her mother replied. 'You're far too young to drive.'

Mattie and Amelia exchanged glances.

'Mother, I've been driving since I was sixteen. I learned on the hills around Eden House, don't you remember?'

'You were far too young then,' her mother said, her logic apparent only to herself.

'Mother, I drove an ambulance in the Blitz,' Lucy protested.

'Don't remind me,' Harriet said.

'Mother...' Lucy objected again.

Mattie and Amelia exchanged small smiles. It was a momentary and rare connection between the two of them. There was something amusing about Lucymem in this role.

They got into the car and Lucy clutched the door handle tightly.

'Drive on the left, Mother,' Lucy said nervously as they swung out of their parking space. 'The left, Mother, the left,' she shouted.

'Don't shout, dear. I know exactly what I'm doing,' her mother replied as she drove down the centre of the road.

In the back of the car the girls were now grinning at each other. This inclusive moment had now happened twice within minutes, but Mattie looked away while Amelia continued to gaze at her with affection.

Far from their friend Sean and their own surroundings for the first time, they found themselves in a new situation. Usually Mattie and Sean made a silent journey on foot to the local school, while at home Sean and Amelia played endlessly together. Now, without his presence and in the absence of his influence, they found themselves thrust into each other's company in a new way. The experiment of having them share a bedroom at home had not lasted long, but now they were back together, sharing a room in their grandparents' country home. Twin beds with linen sheets, thick blankets and eiderdowns awaited them in the little room under the eaves.

'I bags the window bed,' Mattie said.

Amelia said nothing. She longed to have the bed that overlooked the garden, but instead she clambered on to the bed near the door and bounced up and down on it. She would wait until Mattie was elsewhere before climbing on to her bed and lying on it to see what it felt like to stretch out in that part of the room. Floral wallpaper, chintzy cushions on the chair, a tall dark chest of drawers and pretty curtains adorned the room. On the dressing table there was a photograph of their mother, Hilarymem, standing beside a horse somewhere in the hills above Pankot.

Peering at the photograph, Amelia said to Mattie, 'You look like Mama.'

There was a momentary silence and then Mattie got up off her bed to come and take a look.

'Do I?' she asked. Amelia could hear the pleasure in her voice. 'Really?'

'Yes,' she replied.

And it was true. Mattie was elongating. Her

121

limbs were now extending and gangly, a far cry from the stocky figure she had been. Her face was longer too. She still had her father's eyes and his dark curly hair, but the face was definitely her mother's.

'Grandfather said there are rabbits in the garden,' Amelia said hopefully to Mattie. She was trying to create a conversation although she was unsure how to do it.

Mattie went back and looked out the window. 'I think it's too cold for rabbits to be out there,' she said. 'I bet they're asleep somewhere.'

'Grandfather said he had built a hutch at the end of the garden.'

'Let's go and look,' Mattie said. She pulled on an extra jumper to counteract the winter chill. At the doorway she glanced back at Amelia. 'Are you coming?' she asked, and then she raced down the stairs.

Delighted at being included, Amelia ran down after her.

'Gently,' their grandmother called from the kitchen as their footsteps clattered down the wooden stairs.

'We're going to look for the rabbits,' Amelia announced as they arrived in the kitchen.

The kitchen was large, with a long scrubbed pine table in the centre. Grandmother was sitting reading the newspaper with a cup of tea beside her. The room was painted a bright yellow, and white net curtains were gathered with ribbon against the leaded window panes. There was a fire burning in the grate and the atmosphere was cosy. Amelia went running back to the hall and into the drawing room where her grandfather was reading.

'I will come with you,' he said.

But the momentary connection between the two girls was dispelled once they were outside in the garden.

'Grandfather,' Amelia called, 'I'm going to find the rabbits' home.' She ran down the garden, disappearing between the trees and getting lost in the long grass of the section now known as the Wilderness.

'Grandfather, I'm lost,' she called.

Her grandfather had gone to fetch his coat, and it was Mattie who heard her plaintive cry, and Mattie who promptly turned on her heel and went back into the house, forestalling her grandfather's exit and delaying him by getting him to tie her shoelace and then saying she was cold and could they have a hot drink.

'Where is Amelia?' her grandmother asked as Mattie and the Colonel returned to the kitchen.

'Getting ready,' Mattie replied.

'I thought she went outside,' the Colonel said. 'I'd better go and see.'

He found her crying in the Wilderness.

'I got losted,' she sobbed. 'I got completely losted.' Her vocabulary had disintegrated in her distress.

He held her close and told her that she was now found and that she wouldn't get lost again because he was going to give her his compass and show her how to use it.

They spent the next half-hour with him patiently explaining the positioning on the compass and how, no matter where she went in the garden, the house was always to the north.

'You set the hand on the N, and then you just go in that direction,' he said. 'And home you will come.'

'No matter where I am?'

'No matter where you are. As long as you are in the garden, of course,' he added.

'But what if I get lost at night and can't see the compass?' Amelia said.

'Well, if you're planning on nighttime expeditions,' he said, 'then I'm going to have to teach you how to read the stars.'

From the crisscross panes of the kitchen window, Mattie watched them and she glowered with fury. She did not know what it was she wanted. Her anger did not go in any particular direction. She was pleased to see her grandparents again and excited about the house and garden. She had enjoyed the shared glee with Amelia over their grandmother's driving but had immediately felt the need to re-establish her independence when they arrived in the house. Her need to diminish Amelia was predominant and she was frustrated that her attempts to have her sister feel isolated in the garden had failed. She wanted her grandfather to show her how to use a compass and yet somehow she had managed to create a situation in which Amelia was the centre of his attention, and it was Amelia who now carried his compass on a chain around her neck.

Lucy returned from an expedition to town, with

presents for Christmas for everyone and a big smile on her face.

'You look so pretty, Lucymem,' Amelia said.

And she did. Her face was glowing from the cold. She looked smart in a new coat with its tight waist and slightly swirling skirt.

'You look lovely, my dear,' her father said to her, putting an arm around her.

'I want you out more,' her mother said. 'This is your holiday. Your father and I will mind the girls and you can look up old schoolmates and make new friends while you're here.'

Amelia started up in distress. 'But you won't leave us, Lucymem, sure you won't. Promise.'

Lucy lifted her up off the ground and twirled her around. 'Do I look like the kind of aunt who would leave her favourite nieces?' she asked.

'You don't have any other ones,' Mattie pointed out. 'Anyway, my father and my mother did not look like the kind of people who would leave their children.' She turned and went out the door.

The earlier moment of happiness Amelia had felt when her older sister briefly related to her was followed by much anguish when Mattie's anger became apparent and she lashed out, hurting whoever was in her path.

'I think you should send Mattie to boarding school,' Harriet said to Lucy. 'I think it would be better for her.'

'She is in pain,' the Colonel said.

They were sipping port in the drawing room after dinner, believing both girls to be tucked up asleep in bed.

In her customary hiding place behind the curtains Amelia listened to this in consternation. She didn't want Mattie to be in pain, and she didn't want her to be sent away.

'She would find out in boarding school that she is not the only child to have lost a parent,' her grandmother said. 'Neither her grief nor her situation is unique, and she should learn that. She's the right age to go away. It would do her good. At her age you and Hilary were away in school. It didn't do you any harm.'

'But wasn't that different?' Lucy asked. 'Wasn't that because of circumstances? Because we lived in India, because of the army, because of events? Isn't that why we went away to school?'

'No,' her mother replied. 'Even if we had been living here, we'd have sent you off to school. It's part of growing up. That's what it is. And I think Mattie would benefit from it. If you sent her to school here, she would have your father and me to visit her, and she could come to us for the shorter holidays. It would be better.'

Lucy had never seen boarding school as an option for the girls, and had always believed that she had been sent there only because there was no choice. In this moment she felt distanced from her mother and in some way disappointed. Her mother seemed to be saying they would never have had that close mother-daughter relationship that Lucy had thought was denied her for geographical reasons.

Behind the curtain the window and the window-ledge were getting colder and colder. Amelia

126

started to shiver. She could hear the intensity of the words and knew there were changes afoot. It was like the summer when Grandmother had come to Ithaca, and she knew that Grandmother had plans that Lucy did not like. She did not want Mattie to depart from her life, and she had understood that Mattie had a pain. When Amelia had had a pain in her head and throat the previous year, Lucymem had kept her in bed and had cared for her. But this was different. This was Mattie being sent away. Amelia wondered how Mattie would feel about that. She looked through the window into the night and thought of Mattie wandering outside in the dark. She was trapped behind the curtain until the adults went to bed. She heard a thud outside in the dark and for a moment could not place the sound and then it dawned on her. Mattie was playing croquet.

She would have loved to go out and play with her sister. In Ireland there was a cut-down mallet she could use. Mattie always glowered when she saw Amelia pick it up. Slipping from the windowledge on to the floor, still hidden behind the curtains, she curled up in a ball and fell asleep. In her sleep she heard her grandmother's voice encouraging Lucymem to sell the house in Ireland and to move to London. In her sleep she was afraid. She feared the loss of Mattie and of their home. It was all she needed. Home. Aunt Lucymem, of course. Mattie. Grandpa, and she supposed Grandmother. There was always a hesitancy in her thoughts about her grandmother. It was Grandmother who was always trying to change things, always adding momentum to calm enough situations. Grandmother who wanted them to leave Ithaca, and send Mattie away.

She woke to Mattie's voice shouting, 'Amelia is gone. She's run away. I woke up and she was gone.' Mattie's voice did not sound perturbed, more gleeful or triumphant.

There was consternation. At first Amelia did not know if she was dreaming or was awake. And then the curtain was pulled back, and Grandfather was lifting her from the floor.

'I should have known,' he said. 'I should have known. Hush, hush. It's all right now.' And she was crying in his arms, saying, 'Don't sell our home, and don't send Mattie away.'

This brought tears of fury from Mattie, and both children were cradled in adult arms until they fell asleep and were carried up to bed.

She woke in the morning to Mattie prodding her with the pole that was used to open the window.

'I was so glad when you were gone,' Mattie said. 'We were perfectly happy until you came along. I don't know why you came, anyway. You're useless. You don't play like Georgina played with me.'

'But I will play with you,' Amelia said. 'I'll play any game you like.'

Aunt Lucymem came into the room and found both children crying again.

'It's Christmas Day tomorrow,' she said. 'Come now, girls. We've to get up and help put up the tree. Your grandparents usually put it up earlier than this but they kept it for you. Grandpa's gone to get the turkey, and when he comes back he is going to take you out. And your grandmother is getting down the box with the decorations. We've a very busy day ahead, and we mustn't have any fighting or Santa won't come.'

'He won't come anyway,' Mattie said. 'Or if he does come, he won't bring the right presents. He never does.'

'I thought he always did,' Lucy said as she pulled out clean clothes from the chest of drawers.

'Well, he doesn't,' Mattie said sulkily. 'He never brought back Daddy and Mummy.'

And Amelia lay there trying to bite back more tears and she thought about how she had never thought of asking Santa to bring her back either her mother or her father. 'We have each other,' she said hopefully to both Mattie and Lucy.

'It's not enough,' Mattie said.

'Well, it's all you've got,' Grandmother said with typical pragmatism, as she entered the room. 'And I think you're going to have to make the best of it.'

That seemed reasonable to Amelia. It was enough. But then she had never known anything more. Christmas in England was more fun than at home. She thought it was because there were more of them, and then there was the added bonus of Grandmother's nephew and his family. They learned that he was called Uncle Jupe, and the family were referred to as the Jupes. Uncle Jupe was very tall. He wore tweed jackets and sometimes smoked a pipe. Grandmother made a face when Amelia asked her if Jupe was a nickname and Amelia knew that she didn't approve of it. Grandmother said that Jupe was called after Jupiter, who was the Roman top god. Uncle Jupe had a sister called Titania, queen of the fairies, but Amelia and Mattie had never met her. She lived in Scotland with grouse and heather, Grandmother said. Uncle Jupe's children, who were ten and eight years old, were Mars and Ophelia. And Uncle Jupe's wife was Anne. 'A good solid name,' Harriet said.

They came for Christmas dinner, a party that started well, with even the children being allowed a sip of champagne. Uncle Jupe had brought it back from France at the end of the war and had kept it for a special occasion.

'And this is that occasion,' he said, smiling at his cousin Lucy. 'Not only have Uncle Edward and Aunt Harriet finally returned from India, but my favourite cousin has emerged with two of the loveliest little girls in the world.'

There was a small squeak from his own daughter, but he swung her up in the air and said, 'You're not being excluded, Ophelia. You're not a little girl. You're *my* little girl.'

Mattie glowered and Amelia knew that her sister was somehow feeling excluded. But Amelia did not feel that exclusion because she knew that Lucy would say that about her and Mattie, because they belonged to Lucy. She went over to her aunt and hugged her.

Dinner was a success, with crackers being pulled and paper hats on everyone's heads. Grandmother said she would read the children a story while Lucy and Aunt Anne cleared away. Grandfather and Uncle Jupe settled into the port.

Grandmother read them the story of Boadicea, and when she had finished, Amelia said, 'When I grow up and have a daughter, I'm going to call her Boadicea.'

'Over my dead body,' said Grandmother firmly.

'Well, it would be over your dead body,' Mattie said. 'By the time Amelia is old enough to have a child named Boadicea, you'll be pushing up the daisies.'

'I beg your pardon,' Grandmother said in a tone of voice that did not sound very Christmassy at all.

Mattie was sent to her room for rudeness.

'I'm not sure you were fair there, Harriet dear,' Grandfather said. There was laughter in his voice. 'It's an expression she learned from you, you know. What I like about that girl is that she speaks it as she sees it.'

A few years later the rabbits died. Myxomatosis had not yet arrived in England, so no one knew what they died from. Grandfather was devastated, and Grandmother was furious.

Lucy, Mattie and Amelia were back for their fourth Christmas in Kent. Now eleven and seven years old, the relationship between them still fluctuated up and down. Mattie's occasional connection with Amelia invariably became cruelly undermined with Amelia hanging on every word of her older sister.

'Why is Grandmother so cross?' Amelia asked. The death of the rabbits seemed to her to be very sad rather than something that would make you angry.

'She's cross because now she can't make rabbit stew,' Mattie said. She sounded cross too.

'Why would she want to make rabbit stew?' Amelia asked.

'That's what we've been eating every couple of days since we came here,' Mattie said.

'No, we haven't,' Amelia said, puzzled. 'We've had chicken and–'

'We haven't had chicken,' Mattie said. 'We've had Belinda, Grey-ears, and Mopsy.'

Amelia howled in horror, and Grandfather had to take her outside and tell her over and over that Belinda, Grey-ears and Mopsy had not been eaten, but that they had in fact died of this mysterious disease and that they were gone to rabbit heaven where they would lop up and down all day under blue skies, roll on green grass and eat endless lettuce. This was definitely a better option than that they were rolling around in her tummy.

Grandfather missed his rabbits. Granted they had not been very active in winter, and he had had to bring them down food to the multiple open-doored shelters that he had built them. But he loved doing that. And while Amelia really loved the rabbits and missed them, she was sorrier for Grandfather. Much sorrier.

The explanation for Grandmother's annoyance remained unclear to Amelia. At least now she could fill up the rabbit holes in the grass, safe in the knowledge that they would not reappear.

'Why are you so cross, Grandmother?' Amelia

asked her tentatively. She was still trying to reassure herself that it was not because of the lack of rabbit pie.

'Because your grandfather doted on them,' Grandmother said. 'And while I didn't particularly like them because they ate everything in my vegetable garden, the truth is, your grandfather did. They made him happy. And for that reason, and that reason alone, I'm really sorry they died.'

Amelia liked that. She thought about it afterwards when Grandmother was bustling around the kitchen. It seemed to her to be the most loving comment she had ever heard from Grandmother.

Harriet was carefully wiping the kitchen table and asked Amelia to lift her arms off it while she swept the cloth across the surface.

The staff had been downsized from what she was used to in India. Now she had a woman who 'did' for them every day. But it was Christmas Eve and Mrs Trotter was busy with her own family.

Grandfather took both girls into town on that Christmas Eve. He wanted them each to choose a special bauble for the tree, which they duly did. Amelia's was pink with silvery glitter on it, pointed at the bottom and hanging from a piece of thread. Mattie's was red. Red was her favourite colour. They asked Grandfather if they could look in the sweetshop next door. Even though there were no sweets in it because of rationing, it was still known as the Sweetshop. Mattie wanted to buy a box of matches. She didn't tell Grandfather about the matches, but Amelia knew that was what she wanted. Amelia had no particular opinion on this as Mattie was a law unto herself, and anyway she wanted to go to the shop on the other side of the street because she had had a wonderful idea.

Grandfather said he would meet them in the sweetshop in about ten minutes and that they weren't to wander off.

'How old does he think we are?' Mattie snarled as they went out on to the street.

'I'm only seven,' Amelia murmured. She hated when Mattie said unpleasant things about him, but at the same time she knew it was safer for her not to sound too forceful in her response.

'Yes, but I'm eleven,' she replied. 'Old enough for both of us.' And with that she went into the newsagents and left Amelia on the street.

Amelia went straight to the pet shop on the other side of the road, and bought a puppy. A black, beautiful, silken-eared puppy with the most enormous paws she had ever seen. He cost all her money, and even then she knew they had given him to her at less than what he should have been. But then it was Christmas Eve.

She just wanted to sit down on the ground and hold him and play with him, but she thought she had better get back across the road, before Grandfather found she was missing, and Mattie got cross.

She carried the puppy close to her, holding him with both arms. His baby-puppy smell was in her nose, and she kept kissing the top of his head. She thought Mattie would be really impressed with him. How could she not be?

Well, she was not, as Amelia soon discovered. Grandfather had just got to the sweetshop and they were looking for her.

'What is that brute you've got there?' Mattie said with a snarl.

'He's a present for Grandfather,' Amelia replied. She had hoped for help to keep him hidden until the following day. She did not know how they could have done that anyway, but had both thought and believed that Mattie could do anything she wanted. Grandfather was looking surprised, but Amelia knew he was delighted.

'How wonderful,' he said. 'How truly wonderful. For me? Really?'

'He's for tomorrow,' she said. 'He's for *you* for tomorrow. For Christmas Day. I wanted to keep him as a surprise.'

'He is a surprise,' Grandfather reassured her. 'He's the best surprise I've had in years. What was that you called him, Mattie? Bruce? Wonderful name. Bruce he is.'

'I said Brute,' Mattie said, but Grandfather did not respond.

He took the puppy from Amelia and cradled him in his arms. Bruce was reacting perfectly. He took to Grandfather just like he had taken to Amelia. His tail was wagging so hard that she could hardly see it, and he licked Grandfather's hand all the time.

She could see that Grandfather was terribly pleased, even when he said that he wasn't sure what the Memsahib was likely to say.

'She'll love him,' Amelia said. It was her turn to

reassure him.

He didn't look terribly sure about that, but he said that they would cross the bridge when they came to it. She didn't know what bridge he was referring to, but he was gaining confidence by the moment.

'The rabbits are all gone,' he said. 'He'll have the whole garden to play in.'

So Bruce went home with them, and Grandmother was not too keen, or so they thought. She pursed her lips and Lucy waited for her to throw a fit, as she would have done ten years earlier. Dogs for her were anathema. They were creatures that howled in the night in the distance outside the compound in Kashmir, baying at a moon that seemed a bit too close to the planet.

Lucy watched her mother as Harriet looked around at the expectant faces. Lucy saw her taking in her father's pleasure as he held the puppy in his arms, and then suddenly Harriet rallied round.

'We need extra milk,' she said. 'Someone will have to go over to the farm and get it.'

She asked Mattie to get an old blanket from the cupboard in the girls' bedroom. Mattie said they needed all the blankets they had because it was going to get colder.

'Nonsense,' said Harriet. 'We have to make a bed for Bruce.'

And a bed of sorts was made in the kitchen with a box and a cut-up blanket that had a hole in it.

'That's my favourite blanket,' Mattie hissed.

'Mattie,' Harriet said to her, 'it's partially moth-eaten. You've never used it before. And I don't want to hear another word about it.'

Her grandmother's voice was more than firm, and Mattie wisely decided to hold her peace. When her grandmother suggested they stuff an old sock with newspaper for Bruce to play with, Mattie ran upstairs to find one before Amelia could, but having brought it back down she did nothing more. She sat at the kitchen table and watched Amelia and her grandmother crumple up paper and make Bruce a toy.

Later in the day, after the tree had been put up, Lucy went into the kitchen and Mattie was standing there looking at Bruce. He was on the floor in front of her, wagging his tail.

'Why don't you pet him?' Lucy asked her.

'Because he'll go and die,' Mattie said.

Lucy thought about that for a moment. 'I don't think he is going to die,' she said to her. 'He's just a puppy. He's going to live for years and wouldn't it be nice to be friends with him?'

Mattie scowled and went out of the room. Lucy wanted to tell her mother about it, but she knew the response would be 'send that child to boarding school', and she was not sure that was the best answer. Her mother suggested it time and again, and Lucy always resisted.

Amelia came into the kitchen. She wanted to take Bruce in to show him the tree. He loved it. He piddled just underneath it. Fortunately her grandmother wasn't looking.

In what was beginning to become an annual routine, Uncle Jupe and Aunt Anne came with

Mars and Ophelia the following morning. Amelia had liked Mars in previous years and had assumed these feelings would continue this time. Both he and Ophelia had grown. He had straight dark hair, and Ophelia was fair, and they often held hands or he tickled his sister unabatedly, and Amelia envied them their sibling relationship. However, this time they were in the house a mere half an hour when her feelings towards him underwent a serious change.

Mars and Ophelia took to Bruce and actually loved him so much that they wanted to bring him home. Having initially felt very important because she was the one who had brought Bruce into the family, Amelia began to panic because Mars could be very persistent.

'When Mattie and Amelia return to Ireland,' he said, 'poor Bruce won't have any children to play with. I think he would be much better off with us.' Amelia was unsure if his logic would prevail, but it was Grandmother who stopped him in his tracks.

'Mattie may be going to boarding school here in England,' she said. 'Just like you, Mars. So in fact you wouldn't be at home to entertain Bruce anyway. And it will be nice for Mattie during holidays to come here and know that Bruce is waiting for her. And also nice for Amelia to know exactly where he is.'

'And anyway,' Amelia piped up, 'Bruce is Grandfather's, and no one is going to take him away. Are they, Grandfather?'

Grandfather was suitably reassuring.

'If you gave me a present, Grandfather,' Amelia

continued, 'I wouldn't go and give it away.'

'I know you wouldn't,' he said. 'And Bruce is here to stay. Aren't you, Bruce?'

Bruce wagged his tail. As Grandmother said, he knew which side his bones were buttered.

Mattie had made no comment when Grandmother said she might be going to boarding school but Amelia heard her saying later to Lucy that the only reason she had said nothing was to stop Mars thinking he could have Bruce.

This surprised Amelia because she thought that Mattie didn't like the dog and so she did not know what was meant. Could it be that Mattie did like Bruce? Or that Mattie didn't want Mars to get his way? She could not work it out.

Grandmother had mentioned boarding school the day before and there had been the usual reaction from Lucy and a sullen silence from Mattie, but the way Grandmother had brought it up in front of the Jupes had implied a foregone conclusion. Amelia felt that she had missed something – had boarding school been agreed, or was it still being discussed?

Then, when no one was looking, Bruce ate a whole box of chocolates that someone had given to Mars as a present.

'I'm going to eat that dog at dinner tomorrow instead of the leftover turkey,' Mars said. He sounded really cross and very serious.

'You can't,' Amelia screamed.

At that point Bruce threw up the chocolates all over the floor and over Mars' shoes. Chocolate was still a precious commodity, not easily come by in post-war England, and there was an awareness of waste as well as of carelessness.

'If you want your chocolates back so much,' Mattie said, 'why don't you just eat the vomit?'

Amelia really liked Mattie for saying that, even though she got into trouble for being disgusting, but Amelia felt she was in the right. There were the chocolates on the floor in a different consistency.

Ophelia said that Mattie was horrible and Mattie said that Mars was a bollawalla. Amelia did not know what a bollawalla was meant to be, nor did anyone else, but it sounded wonderfully insulting, and she said that Mattie was her best friend and that if she was being sent to her room for being vulgar she was going too because she thought that Mattie was in the right.

Grandmother sighed and said blood was thicker than water. Amelia didn't know what she meant either because Bruce had thrown up neither blood nor water.

Mattie and she, in a moment's solidarity, went up to their room together and sat on their beds looking at the gifts in their Christmas stockings, while Mars was made to clean up the mess downstairs because, as Grandmother pointed out, he had been told not to leave the chocolates anywhere low down because of Bruce.

'Honour satisfied,' murmured Mattie.

Again Amelia didn't know what that meant, but Mattie seemed happier and that was all that mattered.

Mattie, sitting on her bed, with Amelia smiling hopefully at her, looked at her presents and was glad that Amelia had come upstairs with her. She felt a moment's gratitude towards her sister, liking her for her loyalty, and yet there lingered in her mind the knowledge that there should have been a different Christmas. A Christmas with her own mother and her own father... And somewhere in the depths of her mind the memory of a child called Georgina, and her own guilt for letting Georgina's hand go before the ball of fire descended.

Without friends no one would choose to live, though he had all other goods.

Aristotle

CHAPTER SIX

From the day she got the telegram to say that Matthew was dead and Hilary ill, Lucy lost her freedom. Every waking moment seemed full to capacity, and her stolen time at night she used for reading.

Time became a commodity she lusted after but could not have. If she had had time to think she knew that she would have regretted leaving her London life to go to Ireland to be with Hilary, but she never saw it like that. Later, in quiet moments, she missed the buzz of the city, the feeling of togetherness that they, who were there, actually had. She missed her ambulance, she missed the tiredness when her day ended, and she missed her friends. What she had built up for herself within the context of the war evaporated overnight.

And instead of that hectic life, where she used to fall exhausted into bed in the Entwhistles' London house in the city late at night, she found herself caught up in her sister's tragedy.

The look on Hilary's face as she died haunted Lucy. It was a look of such sadness and despair. Lucy wished that she could have that time over, and that she could tell Hilary that all was not as it seemed. That she could reassure her that all was not lost, that Mattie, who had disappeared with Georgina on the mountain, had in fact returned; that Amelia was the most beautiful of children, kind and good-natured. But time was relentless. It moved in one direction only and Lucy could only look back in sadness. Hilary's life, in those moments after her death, seemed to have been thoroughly wasted. Lucy kept thinking about the joy she had once seen on her sister's face and how it had ended like this, tragically, bereft, in a hospital bed.

Lucy had not seen Mattie since shortly after her birth, and so when she was brought to the Children's Hospital, she did not know if this was the real child. By that she did not mean whether or not she was actually Mattie, because of course she was Mattie. She meant that she did not know how identifiable she really was as the essence of the original Mattie.

This child's eyes were blank, traumatised by what she had witnessed. Like Mattie, Lucy had seen things that she preferred not to think about. Death ... death in many guises ... in this case, by fire. It made Lucy think on the one hand of India, where isolated cases of suttee still continued, and on the other of the Blitz and blazing buildings.

Once in her ambulance days they had been called to a scene where a house had come down and she had held the hand of a woman – she couldn't see her, but she held her hand, a lone hand that emerged from dirt and stone and clutched hers for a while. She was covered with rubble, and the men were trying to dig her out, brick by brick without dislodging an iron girder. She remembered when the hand went limp. She felt a hand sometimes in her dreams and, wakening, was unsure if it was Hilary's hand or the woman's under the rubble. She knew that her father had seen things one shouldn't see. But for Mattie it was worse. She had been only little at the time. And what she had seen left her an orphan. And so Lucy tried to give her love and show her that she still had family.

But it was very hard.

She had written briefly to her mother that Amelia was such a passive baby and an adorable child – loving and giving and so easy to interact with. But she realised that of course that could be because she had known her since her birth and to some extent was her parent. Whereas with Mattie, she did not know what was going on. Mattie watched everything and glowered and was excessively secretive.

Lucy had once asked Harry O'Dowd, their doctor in Ireland, about her, and he had said, 'Ah, sure, she'll be grand, so she will.' There was something rather dismissive if friendly about the utterance, and so Lucy had not pursued the matter.

But when Harriet had arrived in Ireland, Lucy knew that her mother saw that there was something wrong. Harriet could be remarkably astute when it suited her. This was apparent in her handling of the Colonel, as though she intuitively knew when to leave him alone and when to intrude and jolly him along. Sometimes in the kitchen in the house in Kent, Lucy and her mother would look down the garden and see her father sitting looking at the earth and she knew her mother must have been at least a little worried. But Harriet seemed to cope with a combination of stoicism, pragmatism and good humour.

And so when Harriet brought up the subject of Mattie and boarding school, which she did from time to time, Lucy, although adamant that she did not want one of her girls to go away, also felt forced to listen to her mother. There was always the possibility that her mother was seeing things clearer than she was. And yet she was unsure if her mother was taking into account the full horror of the experience on the mountain from Mattie's perspective.

Sometimes when Lucy thought of Mattie's re-emergence on the mountains, she could believe there was the possibility of Reinhold Kobaldt reappearing in her life. That out of death there could be life. Momentary hopes that she pushed away because with them came the pain of reality.

Their visits to England brought back many memories for Lucy. Of course her life was not the same as during the war years. She had neither the space nor the freedom. But while Harriet encouraged her to foray out alone, she found it difficult. Her days had changed from being at the centre of fear and excitement, living on the very edge of life and death, to the years at Ithaca, where time lay quietly and moved slowly, and the only real difficulty she had to deal with was Mattie. Mattie brooding, Mattie squabbling, Mattie skulking...

She made the effort and tried to contact some of her old friends. But the girls who had worked the ambulance shifts with her had moved away. She could only trace two, one of whom now lived in Yorkshire and the other in Wales. Sometimes she stayed up in the house in North London, and while there she was invited in to the Farringtons' next door.

Roger, who had once dined and danced with her, run with her to the air-raid shelter, gently kissed her good night in the dark outside their houses, had now married, and had children of his own. Lucy liked his wife and always felt welcome in their home, but somehow watching their happiness made her feel more isolated, and it was with relief that she would return to Kent, to the girls and her parents.

She sometimes felt that not just her life had changed, but that she had too. Her aspirations were different, her needs much simpler, her worries were just for the girls. And so when Mattie made the comment about Bruce dying, Lucy needed to tell someone and in due course, later that day, she took her mother aside.

'I would like to tell you what Mattie said,' she said. It had been preying on her mind to such an extent that she had to discuss it.

'Tell me,' her mother said.

And Lucy told her about Mattie's observation about the pointlessness of loving Bruce, because he would just go and die.

When she had finished, her mother said, 'I know you don't want to do it, Lucy. And, God knows, I've respected your wishes all along – but I really believe that child would be better off in a boarding school. Companions her own age. The realisation that the whole world does not revolve around her. That there are other children who lost as much – indeed more.'

It was a conversation that repeatedly came up. Lucy was torn in her emotions. She could not imagine that Hilary would have wanted to send either or both of the girls away, and yet ... and yet... She knew she was making no inroads with Mattie. In fact nothing seemed to improve. Mattie's anger was always just below the surface. She was always a little too quick at lashing out, and her broody silences were very difficult to handle.

'It would give you extra time for Amelia,' her mother said, 'and it would give you time for yourself.'

This was one of her mother's themes. Lucy knew that her mother wanted her to have a social life, and the reality was that she had no social life whatsoever. Lucy knew that her mother feared that she was on the shelf. She thought about it sometimes, wondering if she saw it that way, or whether the tide of events had swept her up to such an extent that it did not matter. She concluded that there was no time to miss what might have been, and yet she harboured something, a yearning for a moment that was caught in her memory, when the sun had shone on her back and she had looked down over the side of the ship and seen a man with a rifle, standing with his legs apart, gazing up at her. More than any other moment within that rendezvous before the war, it was that one that stood out in her mind and captured her imagination. His kiss had faded – she could only remember the feeling as his face approached hers, and then there was a blank. She remembered looking down from the bastions in Valletta and how the light hit the water and submarines below. She remembered his friend, Friedrich Arnheim, with his aristocratic face and his cold eyes. She wondered if he had survived.

She no longer kept the amber under her pillow. Now it was in a drawer and occasionally she took it out and looked at it, and she tried to recall what Rhino had said about creatures caught in time, trapped because of where they were at a particular instant. It was a terribly real observation in the light of the plane crash on the mountain and the tragedy that had evolved from it.

Looking at her amber stone she was torn by a wave of sadness, aware that she would never know if Rhino had died, and where or how.

But Lucy was essentially a pragmatist like her mother, and after that Christmas, during a morning up in London without the girls but with her mother, as they sat in Lyons' Teahouse, she finally acquiesced and agreed that Mattie might be better in boarding school.

'There are good ones in Ireland,' she said to her mother. 'I just need to start looking.'

'I think that one here makes more sense,' her mother said. 'It would mean that your father and I could visit her.'

'But I could visit her if she were in Ireland,'

Lucy replied.

That was not part of Harriet's plan, a plan that included having Lucy and Amelia in England and Lucy hopefully finding a social life. So with clever words her logic prevailed and it was somehow decided that Mattie would attend Hilary and Lucy's old school.

'It will be nice for her to be where her mother and you were schooled,' Harriet said to her daughter. 'She will grow up with the same values, and will have the same outlook on life. This will give her a more positive approach, and hopefully will make her less selfish.'

Lucy had not thought of Mattie as being selfish.

'I think she is just troubled,' she said.

'Well, it will untrouble her,' her mother replied in her best Colonel's wife voice. 'I'll contact the school tomorrow, and see if they will take her when term restarts in two weeks' time.'

'I was thinking more about next September,' Lucy said.

'Strike while the iron is blisteringly hot,' her mother replied.

And so the school was contacted and Mattie, eyes flashing with fury, equipped with a trunk of school clothing, books and general requisites, was sent to school, a mere forty miles away. Unbeknownst to the adults, stashed in her bag was a box of matches. It was the one item that gave her comfort as she departed.

They returned to Ireland, Lucy and Amelia,

149

where they had to deal with Cook's consternation at Mattie's absence. In the past Mattie had been the bane of Cook's life, constantly hovering in the kitchen doorway and watching the wood fire in the stove. Now she was suddenly 'that poor wee lamb', which added to Lucy's lack of certainty at the decision she had made.

The house seemed larger now, and emptier. The portraits in the hall had less to stare down upon, and Lucy looked at the possibility of selling the Cholmondesley home. Harriet had encouraged her to think about it. Cook mentioned that some foreigners had come and asked if the house was occupied while Lucy was in England. It was a coincidence that Lucy pondered, wondering if they were really interested in buying it and, if so, how she could possibly contact them.

While she was still thinking about this, they returned.

First an estate agent contacted Lucy. He sent a letter and then he came to see her. He asked Lucy if she would like to meet the family who were interested in buying. The following day the German family called. The man gave Lucy a card with his name on it – Gerhardt Schmitz. He introduced his family.

He had a wife named Elsa and two children, a blond boy and an equally blonde girl – Ulrich and Karla – the boy had green eyes, the girl's were grey-blue. Herr Schmitz had had a twin brother who had died in the war. The boy was his brother's son, and he had adopted him. The girl was adopted too. She had been in the same orphanage as Ulrich when the war ended.

'The Red Cross found Ulrich for us,' the German explained.

'This place would suit us,' he told Lucy. 'You may not be thinking of selling, but if you are, we would be most pleased if you would let us know.'

Amelia, hovering in the doorway, was asked if she would take the children down on to the beach.

Amelia repeated the children's names in her head – Ulrich and Karla – names she had never heard before. She brought them down to the sea where they met up with Sean. If Sean had been surprised or disappointed at Mattie not returning that Christmas, he did not show it. It was Amelia he had always seen as his friend, his face lighting up whenever she appeared. He smiled shyly at Ulrich and Karla as they threw stones from the water's edge, trying to make them bounce on the waves, and when that was unsuccessful, competing to see who could throw them the furthest. And Amelia, looking up at the house beyond the dunes, wondered what was happening. Lucy had talked to her about the possibility of living in England, of seeing more of her grandparents and Bruce, and it seemed like an adventure. She did not really understand that she would be saying goodbye to Ithaca.

'I need time to think,' Lucy said to Gerhardt Schmitz. 'It has been on my mind, but I need to be sure that this is the right time.'

Running back into the drawing room, the three children came to an abrupt halt as they realised a

151

very serious conversation was taking place. They looked from one to the other silently as Lucy explained to the Schmitzes that Mattie and Amelia had been orphaned, and that quite simply she needed to think carefully before doing anything as definite as selling the house.

'I have been thinking about it,' Lucy admitted. Then, seeing the children in the doorway, she called to them, 'Come on in.'

Amelia came over to her and sat close to her on the sofa, while Ulrich and Karla joined their parents.

'You said the children had been orphaned? Like my nephew who is now my son? Like little Karla? It is the story of this war, is it not?'

Lucy nodded in agreement. She felt Amelia moving closer to her and she slipped her arm around her.

'The orphanages are still full,' Gerhardt Schmitz said, taking Karla on his knee. The child, with her huge grey-blue eyes, looked at him and put her arms around his neck, burying her face in his shoulder.

There was a long silence, a silence that contained a deep sense of awareness and of meaning.

Then they left the moment and talked about the land that came with the house, and Herr Schmitz seemed very enthusiastic about keeping things just as they were, with Cook, Maudge, Sean and Feilim the Gormless living in the cottages, their work remaining the same. He even suggested keeping the paintings hanging on the walls, when Lucy said that she had nowhere to take them and would have to consider selling them.

152

'We lost everything,' he said to her by way of explanation. 'Our family portraits are gone, I know not where.'

'Why here?' Lucy asked curiously. 'Why have you come to Ireland?'

'I want a new start for my family,' he replied. 'And we have links here – I have personal ones. I would like to root here.'

Amelia liked the word 'root'. It reminded her of the pear tree Grandfather had told her he'd planted for Grandmother, and Grandmother saying after the puppy's arrival, 'I hope to the holy heavens that Bruce doesn't dig that tree up now that it is rooted.'

Amelia wondered if she had roots.

She wasn't sure that she had.

Lucy contacted her parents and told them about the offer that had been made on the house. She was uncertain what her parents would think because of the nationality of the potential buyers.

'If needs must,' her mother said in a letter. 'So what if they're Germans? It's not as if you are going to be living with them.'

'We are all human beings,' her father said.

'We're going to go and live in London,' Lucy said to Amelia. 'It will be wonderful, I promise.'

'And we'll see more of Mattie?' Amelia asked.

'You miss her, don't you?' Lucy said. 'Yes, it will be easier. She won't have to make the journey over here, and we'll all be close to your grand-parents.'

'And to Bruce,' Amelia said with satisfaction.

Lucy wrote to Mattie and explained they were

selling the home. Mattie insisted on coming back for Easter just as they were packing up the contents. Lucy went up to Dublin to fetch her from the boat and whatever good humour she might have had on arriving back in Ireland had certainly dissipated by the time they got home.

'What do you mean, Germans are buying the house?' Mattie asked Amelia. 'Why didn't you tell me that, Lucymem?' she asked her aunt.

'I didn't think of it,' Lucy said. 'We've sold the house. It doesn't really matter to whom, does it?'

'Of course it does,' Mattie said.

'They're human beings,' Lucy said to her. 'My father once said to me that war is like a gigantic machine and it scoops up human beings so that they do things they would never normally do. The Schmitzes are a family quite like us.'

'Well, they're not quite like us,' Mattie said, her anger apparent in her voice.

'Aren't they?' Aunt Lucymem asked her.

'They're a real family,' Mattie said. 'A father and a mother and two children. They are real. The way they are supposed to be.'

'They lost family in the war,' Aunt Lucymem said. 'Both children are adopted. And they lost their home and all their possessions.'

'So now they're going to take ours instead?' Mattie snorted.

'They're buying the house,' Lucy explained for the hundredth time. 'And they have said that they will keep the portraits for you and Amelia, and later in life, if you want them, or if you just want to see them, you can come back here and look at them.'

'They're ever so nice,' Amelia tried reassuring Mattie, but her sister cut her short.

Mattie did not calm down and Amelia was aware of the pent-up anger that consumed her. Nothing deterred Amelia from her hero-worship of her sister, loving her because she was older and more able, and because she was the link with the past, with a real father and mother and another sister. But she was also afraid of her, afraid of threats that Mattie had once made about setting fire to her on the beach, and afraid because Mattie sometimes gave her a hard punch or pushed her away when Amelia was trying to get her attention.

Lucy was busy with arrangements and there was an air of expectancy in the house, with trunks being packed and old clothing sorted and thrown out. Mattie, Amelia and Sean spent some time on the beach still dressed in winter woollies, as spring was late. There was a sense of sadness as something was coming to an end, something that Sean and Mattie were more aware of than Amelia. She was now excited about the future, about the house in London and the new life that Lucy had painted in such enticing colours – with a school down the road, a park around the corner and lots and lots of children. If Amelia was afraid of anything it was that Mattie seemed more withdrawn, and she felt her sister was hatching some plan but she could not see what it might be. She still tried to get her attention, wanting her affection and friendship, but nothing was forthcoming.

The contracts were signed and money and deeds handed over. Two days later Mattie and Amelia said goodbye to their old home. Sean said he would miss them and that they were to come back to visit. Maudge hugged them both, Amelia yielding to her embrace, Mattie withdrawing. Feilim the Gormless said to think of him milking the cows on a summer's evening. Amelia said she would. Cook waved her tea towel from the kitchen window and turned away to dry her eyes.

Just as they were leaving, Mattie ran back into the house because she said she thought she had left something in her room.

They sat in the car, Lucymem, and Amelia, who wondered what Mattie was really doing, as there was nothing left in her room at all.

When she came down she seemed in an awful hurry, and she kept telling her aunt to hurry up or they would miss the boat.

'We won't miss the boat,' Lucymem said. 'Calm down, Mattie. All is well.'

All was not well and Amelia knew it but she didn't know what to do about it. There was a look on Mattie's face and she knew what that look was. It was a look of satisfaction, a look she had seen when Mattie had successfully made fire with a magnifying glass and compass, or when she stole a box of matches from the fireplace and patted her pocket.

Sean was at the gate to wave them farewell.

Amelia asked Lucymem to stop the car, saying she wanted to say goodbye to him.

'You've said goodbye already,' Mattie complained. 'Come on, Aunt Lucymem, drive.'

But Aunt Lucymem stopped the car, saying that they had held up their departure to suit Mattie, and they would now do the same for Amelia.

Amelia got out of the car and she hugged Sean again, whispering to him to go and check the house because she feared what Mattie had done. He pulled back from her and looked at her face and then he ran hell for leather back up the driveway.

Aunt Lucymem looked at Amelia as she stood there beside the car. Amelia wanted Lucy to go and help Sean but, fearing Mattie, she said nothing.

'All well?' Lucy asked.

She nodded miserably. Lucy must have thought that her feelings were to do with leaving the house because she told her to hop in and they would be away.

They started up the road but Amelia could not keep it to herself.

'We have to go back,' she said to her aunt from the back of the car.

'Drive, drive,' Mattie said.

'Why?' Aunt Lucymem asked.

'We just have to,' Amelia said.

She turned to Mattie. 'It's Maudge and Feilim the Gormless's home. It is Sean's home. Cook... You can't... I can't...'

Lucy stopped the car. She looked around at the two girls in the back. Amelia was almost in tears. Then she looked at Mattie.

She got out of the car and looked back at the

house. There was a glow from one of the upstairs windows.

And then she got into the car, turned it round and went back at full speed.

There was a blank in Amelia's memory at this point. Shivering and crying, she stayed in the car while Lucy ran up the driveway. Mattie had disappeared; Amelia did not know where. She huddled down on the back seat. She had never been so afraid in the whole of her short life. She knew Aunt Lucymem was going to be justifiably furious and while she had never seen her furious, she had a feeling that there were going to be shades of Grandmother appearing.

Mattie had been practising fire since Amelia first became aware of her. She had perfected the art of fire-making at an early age. Magnifying glass and kindling of one sort or another – she had even shaved fur off Sean's cat to assist this art – flint and steel, and finally matches. These were Mattie's favourite toys, but ones she had kept secret from the various adults in their lives. Amelia knew about them, both because she had seen her in action on the beach or in fields, and because, like any little sister, she knew every hiding place that Mattie had.

She also knew that Mattie might set fire to her for betraying her in front of Aunt Lucymem.

Lucy, having run at full speed back into the house, shouting for Cook and Maudge to come and help, found Sean in Mattie's bedroom with a bucket he had taken from the airing cupboard and filled in the bathroom. They put the fire out, the four of them, with the damage confined to the one room, helped by the fact that because the room was empty there was nothing that could really work as fuel. The floorboards and the windowframe were partially destroyed, but at least the fire had been contained. Lucy congratulated Sean on his bravery, while shaking in terror at what had happened and how it had come about.

She found Mattie in the churchyard, staring stubbornly at the grave.

'Why?' she shouted at Mattie. 'For God's sake, tell me why you did that?'

In fury she slapped her across the face, which so startled Mattie that she blurted out, 'You're selling the house to Germans. *To Germans.* Of all the people in all of the world, why do you have to sell it to Germans? I hate them.'

'They're human beings just like us,' Aunt Lucymem said. 'They're living breathing sentient human beings.'

'I don't know what sentient means,' Mattie said. 'And I don't want to know. They shouldn't be here. This is our place. They killed my family.'

But Lucy had lived with other people and other cultures. She knew of oppression and had seen the Blitz. She had her own views.

'They didn't kill your family. And don't forget they were my family too.'

'You never came here before. You didn't know them. You know nothing about us,' Mattie shouted.

'I knew your mother for all of my life,' her aunt

said. 'And I loved her with all my heart. She was my only sister. I miss her too, you know. And I did come here – I was here for your birth. And this family who are coming here – they are victims too. Victims of a war which devastated Europe – and not just Europe,' she added, thinking of her father and the changed man he had become with his years in prison far away – years that had changed him beyond recognition. 'They are human beings whose lives were destroyed and, like us, they are trying to pick up the pieces.'

She took Mattie by the arm and dragged her back up the lane to the road and across to the house. She took her upstairs and showed her the damage she had caused. She shook her in fury before releasing her in despair.

'You are so selfish,' she said. 'So terribly, terribly selfish. Just look what you've done to their home.'

'I bet he was in the army,' Mattie said.

'Mr Schmitz? I'm sure he was. Everyone was caught up in the war in some way or another. He lost his twin brother. Think what that must be like.'

'I lost my sister – the angel,' Mattie said in fury.

'Then you must know what he feels like,' Aunt Lucymem said.

Their journey back to England was delayed for nearly a week, a week in which Lucy contacted the Schmitzes and received permission to hold the keys for the house. She got in workmen to repair the damage and to hand the house over in reasonable order to the Schmitz family. While this was being done, she and the girls stayed in a hotel in Wicklow.

Lucy invited Herr and Frau Schmitz over to Ithaca to explain what had happened and why Mattie had done it. She told them of the plane crash and the deaths of Matthew and Hilary and the angel Georgina. Herr Schmitz, who had been standing at the start of the explanation, sat down heavily and put his head in his hands.

'*Mein Gott*,' he said. '*Mein lieber Gott.* The poor child.'

Aunt Lucymem was quite relieved when he added 'the poor child' comment, because until then she could not quite work out what line he was taking. As she said to her parents later, she feared he would want to withdraw from the whole deal and she could hardly blame him. To be semi-burned out of his home before he moved into it because someone did not like his nationality was not the greatest start to the new life he was trying to build for his family.

'May I talk to her?' Gerhardt Schmitz asked.

'She won't talk to you,' Lucy said. 'She won't even see you.'

'You're the little sister, are you not?' he said to Amelia, who was standing in the doorway, watching the proceedings. 'Well, some day will you tell your older sister that we will look after the Cholmondesley home the same way you did. I said to you before that we would care for your pictures until such time as you want them. And I meant that. We will keep your pictures on the walls – your family portraits, and the painting of

161

Homer and Aristotle. They will be there for you. We will farm the land as your family did. And when you grow up, if you would like to come back to visit, you and your sister will be more than welcome.'

Amelia thought this was very generous of him.

'And you'll be friends with Maudge, Feilim and Sean, just like we were?' Amelia suggested.

'We will.'

'And you'll keep Cook?'

'Of course we will. We need Cook. Indeed,' he replied, 'and I won't do anything that might destroy their home.'

Amelia supposed this was a way of pointing out that had Mattie succeeded in her pyromaniac actions, Cook, Maudge, Feilim and Sean would have been homeless.

They left a week later and made a silent journey by car to London where Aunt Lucymem, Mattie and Amelia were going to live in the old Entwhistle home. Mattie refused to speak to Amelia. She directed her comments either straight up into the air or else through one of the adults in their lives.

Grandmother said that Mattie should be sent to a borstal and not back to boarding school. She and Grandfather had come up to London to open the house for them. During term time Lucy and Amelia would live in the London house, but holidays would be spent with their grandparents.

Back in England Grandmother endeavoured to encourage Grandfather to give Mattie the hiding

162

that she said was long overdue. Grandfather's response was quite simple.

'I could never strike another human being,' he remarked thoughtfully.

'I hope that doesn't mean you'd hit an animal,' Amelia said.

He laughed at her in his kindly way. 'Do you think I'd hurt anyone, Amelia darling?'

She shook her head. She knew he wouldn't. That was the anomaly of war. That was what Aunt Lucymem wanted them to understand. She knew that war brought out things in people that should never be brought out. And also that people do things in war because they are under instruction to obey. It's why war was evil. Grandfather had said that once to them: 'War is evil.'

Sullenly, Mattie returned to boarding school and Amelia took to city life. Having been used to the silence of their home and the sound of waves on the beach, or the wind whistling in the trees, the noise came as a shock. The clippety-clop of the milkman's horse early in the morning took her to the window to watch their pint of milk being delivered. Both in Ireland and in their grandparents' home, the milk had come in a pail or jug from the farm. There was traffic on the street – cars and buses, trams and lorries – in Ithaca it was a rare event for a bicycle to ever pass by the gates. In the park children played on the swings or jumped with skipping ropes, they fed the ducks and kicked a ball. Lucy took her there with the Farrington boys from next door. It was the

Farrington parents who helped Lucy find the local school and made the necessary introductions, and Roger Farrington who walked there with both Lucy and Amelia on her first day.

'It reminds me of walking you places long ago,' he said to Lucy, and she smiled.

'Long ago,' she said.

Most weekends they went down to Kent straight from school on Friday, Amelia still neatly dressed in gymslip, blouse and tie, and when in the country she was always busy with Grandfather in the garden. There were endless fruit trees now, and she was chief harvester of their crop. She played ceaselessly with Bruce, who had grown into the largest dog in England, or so Grandmother said. He had shiny black hair and paws that were almost the size of grandfather's feet, and if he accidentally stood on someone it really hurt.

'Get off,' Amelia shouted at him as he stood with one paw carelessly on her foot. He had huge sad eyes and he looked at her with concern, having no idea that he had pinned her in position.

He loved being tickled, and would roll on his back on the grass while she tickled him under his arms and on his tummy. He loved Grandfather as his chief companion, and Grandmother as his source of food. And Amelia decided he loved her because he thought she was a dog too. And surprisingly he loved Mattie. When Mattie was there he lay on the ground looking at her, having greeted her effusively, which greeting she always ignored. Sometimes, though, when Mattie

164

thought no one was looking she would pet his head and he would drool lovingly all over her shoes.

A further year passed with a routine set in place. When Lucy and Amelia went to Kent for the weekend, they usually stayed until early on the Monday morning and Lucy would drive back up in time for school. Some weekends they stayed in London, did some shopping, and went to the pictures – but those weekends were rare. Mattie came home from school for the holidays, but she still did not speak to Amelia. Occasionally she would appear to forget and would ask or say something, but then she would remember and the veneer of coldness would reappear. By now, Amelia had got used to it, and while both grandparents and Lucy had tried talking to Mattie to make her see Amelia's role in the fire was that of a victim, Mattie held to her silence, and Amelia kept out of her way.

Somehow it came to Amelia's awareness that Grandmother and Aunt Lucymem were going on a trip. It further evolved that this trip was going to last some six weeks and that she was not going with them.

She had never been away from Aunt Lucymem before and she had a problem in believing that she would want to go away without her.

It was Grandmother who talked to her about it.

'Your aunt Lucy needs a rest,' she said. 'All that business of selling the house and then the fire. And repairing the damage and all the worry attached to that. Then settling back into London and driving up and down to us nearly every weekend for the last year – she needs to get away for a while. It'll help her. You want that for her, don't you, Amelia?' she asked, using the tone of voice which meant that 'yes' was the only answer.

'She might like me to come with her to look after her,' Amelia suggested. She was absolutely sure Lucymem would want her to come with her.

'Not this time,' Grandmother said. 'I'm going to accompany her.' Amelia wanted to say, don't leave me behind, but there were things you could not say in the face of such arrangements, and she knew at that moment that this was all organised and that there was nothing she could do about it.

'You'll stay here with your grandfather,' she said to her. 'Your Uncle Jupe will come down now and again, and for one of the weeks you will go and stay with him. Mars will be at a summer school up in Scotland, and Mattie will stay on at her boarding school. But you will have Ophelia as a playmate. It will be perfect.'

Perfect for Grandmother maybe, but Amelia didn't think perfect for her. She loved Grandfather and Bruce and knew they would be happy together but she wanted to know all the details of the arrangements.

'What about school?' she asked.

'You're going to go to the village school here for that period,' Grandmother announced. 'It's all arranged. And when you go up to Uncle Jupe's it will be holiday time at that point.'

'But what about Mattie?' Amelia enquired carefully, as Grandmother sometimes thought one

166

was giving cheek when one was not.

But Amelia was just concerned, Harriet supposed, about being alone with Mattie. Mattie still had shown no signs of forgiveness.

Grandmother said, 'Don't you worry,' which meant that she had seen through the question and had some idea of the depth of her fears. 'Mattie,' she continued, 'will be staying on in school for a couple of weeks and then your Uncle Jupe is going to have her to stay. It will be some time after the week you stay with the Jupes. He will collect her from school and will come by here to leave her school things and to pick up her holiday clothes. Don't worry, Uncle Jupe and Aunt Anne know the whole story. It will be fine.'

Amelia thought about that. She couldn't imagine that Mattie would be too pleased at staying on in school.

'Will other girls be staying on too?' she asked. 'I mean in school.'

'Apparently there will be a few. There are some girls from abroad and they don't get home every year.'

Amelia had not thought of that. That was a relief. It meant that Mattie had company and there was less likelihood of her razing the place to the ground, which was something neither Grandmother nor Aunt Lucymem appeared to have taken into account.

Lucy was excited and she talked the plans through carefully with Amelia.

'It's so nice of my mother to want to take me away for a holiday,' she said. 'I'm not deserting

167

you, you know. I will send you a postcard from every place we visit, and I will bring you back presents.'

'And for Mattie too?' Amelia asked.

Lucy hugged her. 'Yes, for Mattie too.'

An atlas was found and a route was planned. Different countries, different cities, culture mixed with a modicum of relaxation as her grandmother appeared determined to take Europe by storm.

'Look,' Lucy said to her, pointing to a tiny island. 'That is Malta. We're going to go there. A long time ago I spent a day there, one of the happiest days of my life. And I'm going to go back and see it again. And if it's as nice as I remember, I will take you there when you are older.'

As she spoke of Malta, she thought of the amber. It had been some time since she had looked at it closely. She no longer carried it with her from one home to the next, instead she kept it in the house in London.

The following evening, having returned to the city to sort and pack her clothes for travelling, she took it out and as the last rays of the dying sun came through her bedroom window, the stone seemed almost on fire, the black debris trapped in its depths of colour, and she allowed herself to think of that day long ago when she had walked in Valletta. She sat silently on the edge of her bed for long moments before wrapping it in a handkerchief and replacing it among her clothing.

In due course Aunt Lucymem and Grandmother departed, and Grandfather, Bruce and Amelia sat underneath the heavily laden plum trees and Amelia drank lemonade, and he iced tea, and they planned their weeks off the leash, as Grandfather put it.

Mrs Trotter came in every day, cleaned the house, tidied up and prepared their dinner, and then left them to heat it in the evening.

Their first dinner alone together, Grandfather asked her would she like to sit in Grandmother's place at the end of the dining-room table, or to stay in her usual seat. Amelia considered this carefully, unsure if she wanted to sit so far down the table, but then she thought it might be a good idea, and so she took her grandmother's place and insisted on clearing the plates out to the kitchen and washing them herself, even though Grandfather said he would help.

He promised to take her for fish and chips in the village some four miles away and to take her to the seaside for a couple of days.

He was reading a book called *Across the River and into the Trees*. He told her it was about the war, and Amelia hoped it wouldn't make him sad because Grandmother had said that the war had changed him.

His vines were doing well and they planned an autumn harvest of the grapes, and he promised she could dance on them barefoot in a bucket.

The ideal man bears the accidents of life with dignity and grace, making the best of circumstances.

Aristotle

CHAPTER SEVEN

Back in her role as the retired Colonel's wife, Harriet took Lucy to Paris and on to Montreux. From there they crossed into Italy where Lucy threw coins into the Trevi Fountain. Harriet said, what a waste of money, but none the less threw in a coin as well.

'Are you sure you want to go on down to Malta, dear?' she asked her daughter. 'It's going to be very hot.'

But there was no dissuading Lucy. 'Part of this trip for me is a reminder of my journeys to and from school.'

'I don't recall you ever stopping in Malta,' her mother said.

'We did on a couple of occasions. Including the last trip. The trip with Hilary,' Lucy said, hoping that would bring about an end to the conversation. 'It's fourteen years ago,' she added.

'Do you have any idea how hot it is going to be?' her mother asked.

'Nearly as hot as it was in India,' Lucy said with a smile. 'We handled that. We can handle this.'

And on south they went by train, the heat increasing by the hour.

'It makes me wonder how we used to cope,' her mother said, waving her fan rapidly before her face.

Lucy laughed. 'I recall the extraordinary feeling of leaving the heat in India and knowing that within two weeks I'd be missing it. And then I always got chilblains in school. Hilary did too – I remember her telling me. Damp mittens that would never properly dry, and classrooms that weren't warm enough. What a contrast.'

They sailed into the Grand Harbour in Valletta early on the morning of 18 August and transferred by taxi to their hotel. It was eleven o'clock before Lucy managed to escape, leaving her mother drinking some slightly alcoholic fizzy drink.

'I know it's early in the day, dear, but it will kill or cure.' She had not slept well on board ship, but would not hear of Lucy staying behind with her. The heat was intense.

'I will be ready for activity later in the day,' she said. 'Go on without me.'

Memories of Valletta, which had been so very clear in her head while in England, had faded and blurred now, and Lucy found herself lost on the narrow cobbled streets, unsure which way to turn.

By continually asking directions she eventually found herself on St John's Street, standing before the cathedral that embodied her memories of the past and the love that she carried in her mind for Rhino Kobaldt, a man whom she no longer knew was alive or dead.

Why had she come here? She asked herself that repeatedly. In some part of her intellect she wanted to bury the past, to let go the tentacles of that day so long ago. But she also knew that those memories had sustained her. She had precisely planned the day she would arrive here so that it would coincide with the day she had last seen him, and the date he had told her to retain in her memory. And that in itself implied that she did not want to let those memories go. She also knew that when something, like her memories, like her hopes, sustained one for so long, that to give them up with not a thing to replace them was nothing short of foolish.

And so Lucy entered St John's Co-Cathedral, leaving the bright light and heat outside and going into the comfort of the shade. She walked slowly up the aisle, her heels clicking on the marbled slabs beneath which the knights lay, each in his silent vault. She passed the side chapels and approached the main altar where she kneeled and prayed. Now and again she was aware of movement somewhere in the body of the church behind her, but she was engrossed in her contact with her own spirituality. She did not believe in the word 'God'. She believed in concepts, taken from different religions, which she had used to form and enhance her own faith. Her strongest belief was in *ahimsa* – the notion of refraining from hurting any other living being, which doctrine she had absorbed rather than deliberately learned from both Hindus and Buddhists in her childhood. She felt that it was incompatible with Christianity as it was practised, but that the world would be a better

172

place if it were universally accepted. And when she prayed it was to the embodiment of enlightenment rather than to an enlightened god. God to her meant clarity and involved all the best aspects of different faiths. She knew that her notion of 'best aspects' might not coincide with the rest of the human race's, but she believed in compassion, *ahimsa*, and the importance of selflessness.

It was that selflessness that had assisted her through the years of rearing Hilary's children and putting herself in their shoes rather than bemoaning the lot that had come her way by Hilary's death.

She prayed to Hilarymem, as she thought of her sister, and she thought briefly of Matthew Cholmondesley. She prayed for the angel Georgina and she thought of the empty white coffin in the churchyard in Wicklow. She prayed for the amber stone that lay in a drawer in her home in London, and she prayed for the insects caught in their final paralysing moment. Then she prayed for herself, for peace of mind and the pleasure of memory. And when she stood up to walk back down the aisle, Reinhold Kobaldt was sitting on a chair about ten rows behind her, lost in thought.

The light coming through the stained-glass window behind her shone directly down on Rhino's face and he, looking up, became suddenly aware of movement in the rows ahead of him. Lucy paused in incredulity as she stared at him. He had aged, but not disagreeably. He was tanned just as she remembered him to be. There were lines from the sun around his eyes, and his mouth was set firmly above his strong chin, and his eyes widened in both surprise and disbelief as he looked up into the face he had not seen in more than a decade.

They stared at each other in complete amazement, before she brought her hand to her throat in a gesture that displayed an inability to move in any other way. She appeared to sway slightly on her feet, and then he was by her side, holding her arm and leading her down the aisle.

In a neighbouring café he ordered both coffee and cognac, and he kept her hand in his, neither uttering a word.

'It was a stillness,' Lucy later wrote in her diary, the first real entry she had written in a long while, 'and I would that it had lasted for ever.' It encompassed all the energy and passion of fourteen long years, and reflected the silence that had held them all that period of time.

It was broken only when he finally addressed her.

'Drink your cognac,' he said.

As she sipped it, colour returned to her cheeks and he finally released her hand.

'You are more beautiful,' he said.

'More beautiful than what?' she laughed shyly.

'Than I remember.'

They still stared at each other, unashamedly taking the other in, and Lucy wondered if his thoughts were like hers, wondering if each really had held the other as dear, wondering if the other had remained true, wondering how the other recalled that day before the war started and they had shared what she recalled as the ultimate in romance.

It took an hour or more for them to put certain things together, for him to find out that Lucy was here with her mother, for her to realise that he actually lived here in Malta, but not in Valletta. His home was on the other side of the island on the edge of a tiny village.

'I come here always on this day,' he said.

'Always?'

'Since I came to live here, nearly three years ago. I have always hoped, always wondered.'

'I too,' she said.

'I did not know if you were alive. Did not know how to find out. I lived on my hopes,' he said.

'I too,' she repeated.

She wanted to ask him about the war, about those missing years, where he had been, what he had done. But these things seemed too much to ask about so early. And he seemed to feel the same.

He spoke about his life on the island, about his farmhouse, the building construction he was involved in, the company he had set up.

'The heat...' she said, leaving the observation open.

'A more clement climate than many I have endured,' he said. 'An easy winter, a beautiful spring, a very hot summer and then the bliss of an autumn that is like a second spring.'

She held on to his words as pictures formed in her head.

'And you, where do you live?' he asked.

'In London part of the time, and in the country with my parents the rest of it,' she said. Images of the children were foremost in her mind as she explained what sounded like an easy life to her own ears – London and the country.

'Did you marry?' he asked. His voice was more urgent now.

'No.' She shook her head. 'There was no time for such things. Do you remember my sister? You met her on the boat?'

'Hilarymem, you called her,' he said. 'Yes, of course I remember her. Nearly but not quite as beautiful as you. And her husband, the bulldog.'

Lucy laughed and then sighed. 'They died,' she said. 'And I look after their children. Mattie and Amelia.'

'My sister died too,' he told her, squeezing her hand. 'I'm sorry. I understand.'

And she knew that he did. To have experienced that sense of loss and to live on, she knew they shared an incredible grief. There was silence between these pooled memories.

'I too have a child now,' he said, momentarily startling her. 'My sister's son. He lives with me.'

'And his father?'

'He disappeared on the Russian front. So even if he survived that, he would be dead by now,' he said. 'No one is coming back from the Russian prisons.'

'There is so much to say,' she said.

'I know,' he replied, and they sat in silence again, unsure what of so many things should be said, not wanting to start new topics and long explanations and so to waste time.

'How long?' he asked.

'How long?' she repeated puzzled.

'How long are you here for? How long do we have?'

She looked at her watch and realised how much time had passed.

'I have to get back to the hotel,' she said. 'My mother...'

'What do you mean, you met a man?' her mother asked. She had been lying on her bed with a damp flannel over her face, but Lucy's announcement had brought her to an upright position and the flannel was now on the floor.

'It's a long story,' Lucy said.

'You got out for a couple of hours and you come back and say you have met a man,' her mother repeated in disbelief. 'Well, what's he like? Does he have a big head?'

Lucy laughed. 'His head is fine,' she said. 'It seems to me to be the right size.'

'You may laugh,' her mother said, 'but I was always worried about Matthew's head. And,' she continued, 'I was right to worry. Look what happened.'

Lucy didn't answer. If her mother chose to believe that Matthew's head had killed both himself and Hilary, well then, maybe she was right. It had been Matthew's strong-headedness that had brought them out to the mountains on that fateful night. Lucy could not argue with that.

'You'll meet him later,' she said to her mother. 'We're going to have dinner tonight.'

This galvanised Harriet into action, and finally

got her to unpack and to sort her clothing.

'We can go out in a horse-drawn carriage and look around,' Lucy suggested, trying to keep her mother from asking further questions. But her mother said that was a good idea, as they could have a good talk while driving around.

'After all these years,' her mother said as the carriage took them down by the seafront. 'Imagine that.'

Lucy could not tell from her tone of voice what she was actually thinking. 'I don't know what you are really feeling,' she said tentatively.

'I was thinking that you don't know him. Not at all. But I don't want to prejudge this.'

Under the circumstances it was as good as Lucy could have hoped for.

'I know that he's kind,' she said. 'I know that not a day has gone by that I have not thought about him. I know that those thoughts are very special ones...' Her voice filtered away into silence.

'It's been a long time since you met him,' her mother said. She was aware that what Lucy had told her was probably the most intimate they had ever been and she held her words carefully. 'Just go slowly, Lucy,' she said.

These were words that Lucy couldn't hear.

'Sometimes things aren't as they seem,' her mother said. 'Just go slowly,' she repeated.

But what is slowness, what is quickness when your heart has done somersaults and your mind is full of love and passion, the culmination of years and years of holding a few precious memories and an amber stone? The light on the sea was never so dazzling, the sky never so clear and there was magic in the air for Lucy.

They met him in the Phoenicia Hotel for dinner. He was waiting in the foyer, smartly dressed in a suit and tie, leaping to his feet when they appeared, his face open and smiling in greeting.

'I can see where Lucy gets her beauty,' he said as he escorted them to the dining room.

'I thought you'd have a German accent,' Harriet commented.

'I told you Rhino lived in Africa most of his life,' Lucy said, momentarily embarrassed. She had not realised what her mother might have been expecting.

'There is nothing wrong with a German accent,' her mother said. 'Germans can't help it.'

He laughed. 'I agree,' he said. 'There is nothing wrong with any accent. It is the person who is relevant.'

He spoke about his life up until the war. Of the years in Africa and his parents' coffee plantation, of learning to fly a plane, of overseeing workers in the fields, of drought and heat and wild animals.

'You have more in common with Lucy than I might have expected,' her mother said.

'I don't know much about overseeing workers in fields or flying planes,' Lucy said.

'That is not what I meant,' her mother said. 'I was talking about growing up in a foreign place and making it your own.'

'Heat and dust,' Rhino contributed. 'And the smell in the markets, and the sounds of another world, drums in the distance, the drone of insects.'

'Belonging but not belonging,' Lucy said. 'That's what I felt.' She was unsure if she said it aloud because she was storing all his words in her mind as the images that unfolded gave her access to his past, to the expanse of the plains that had been his home, and to the life of a German boy growing up in a distant place.

'Your parents?' her mother asked.

His hand was steady as he reached for the wine glass. His voice betrayed little emotion.

'My mother died of malaria,' he said. 'I was eighteen. My sister went to live in Dresden where she married, and Lucy may have told you that she died towards the end of the war. Her daughter, my niece, died in the fires in Dresden as well. She was never found. My father was in the army, he died in Alexandria.'

'I'm sorry,' Harriet said to him. 'I know that my husband would say that we share the bond of the war no matter what side we were on.'

Lucy was grateful for her magnanimity because she felt that her mother did not quite see it like that.

There was a hush in the dining room as Rhino raised his glass and said, 'A toast to beauty and to my Indian rose.'

'She's English,' Harriet responded firmly.

'When I toasted beauty I toasted you both,' he replied. 'And, to me, Lucy has all the exotica of an Indian rose.'

'I don't recall any roses in India – native ones I mean.'

'There is only one,' he said. 'It's how I've remembered Lucy from when we first met. A golden rose.'

'You have a way with words,' Harriet said.

Lucy was blushing.

'Tomorrow may I invite you to my place?' Rhino asked. 'I would like you to meet Thomas, my nephew. And I would like you to see my home.'

'He has a way with words,' Harriet repeated when they were back in their room.

'But you like him, don't you?' Lucy pleaded.

'Yes,' Harriet said, looking at her hopeful face. 'Yes. He has charm and he knows how to use it. He appears quite perfect,' she added. Lucy did not hear the emphasis on the word *appears*.

'And you'll come tomorrow?' Lucy asked, unsure if she really wanted her mother to come or not.

'Oh, yes. I'll be there,' her mother replied. 'I'll be there all right.'

He arrived in a black Ford Prefect.

'That's a nice car,' Harriet said. 'It looks new.'

'It's a 1950 model,' he explained. 'Thomas – my nephew – washed it for me this morning, but the dust is already beginning to settle on it.'

'It's a very dusty island,' Harriet said.

'Even heaven must have a fault,' he replied.

'Do you think there is dust in heaven?' she asked.

'That is not what I meant. But Malta is my heaven and there is dust.'

181

Lucy smiled. His suavity impressed her. It swept her along. He opened and closed doors for them; he helped them into the car. He talked about the roads and how poor they were. He kept a conversation going all the way across the island, pointing out various landmarks and villages.

Lucy, in the back of the car, took in the stone walls and small fields, the parched landscape, the cacti and the prickly pears, the yellow stone of the buildings, the quietness of the country roads...

They arrived at their destination, which appeared to be yet one more dusty laneway with high walls and old doors leading through them.

Rhino, having parked, helped them to climb down and Lucy stood for a moment on the dirt track and savoured the silence while her mother fanned herself and looked around with slightly pursed lips. But behind one door in the wall a different sight greeted them. A stone archway laden with grapevines led them along a path to a large stone farmhouse. Bougainvillaea nodded over shuttered windows.

Thomas, the nephew, greeted them in the first room that doubled as hall and dining room. He was a gangly youth of some fourteen years, with fair hair and grey-blue eyes, who bore little or no resemblance to Rhino other than in height. He appeared shy and kept looking to Rhino for reassurance.

'Thomas and I live here alone,' Rhino explained. 'Thomas started in the local village school, but now I drive him over to Valletta to school every day.'

'The other side of the island?' Harriet asked in surprise.

'It's a very small island,' Rhino said. 'It doesn't take long. The only problem is the quality of the roads.'

Lucy took Thomas in carefully while pretending to look around. 'Know the father, know the child,' her mother used to say. She would never know the real father, but Rhino *in loco parentis* was as good as she would get. She wondered if Rhino had been like Thomas when he was a child. She thought of Mattie and her surly awkwardness, and Amelia with her serious but light touch. But the youth in front of her was different again. He seemed remote in some way that perhaps reminded her of Mattie, but he was deferential to his uncle and at ease with making them tea and bringing it into the garden where they sat in the shade on wicker chairs.

In some ways the day was a blur for Lucy except that she recalled later the need she had felt to reach out and communicate with the boy, knowing what had happened to him and knowing that she could identify with it. She wanted to tell him what had happened to her sister and how Mattie had survived the night but that Georgina had not. She could not bring herself to say it because of the German connection.

'You have a lovely place,' Harriet remarked. 'And beautifully kept, I must say.'

'We're all right here, aren't we, Thomas?' Rhino said. 'We have good friends.'

They were in the middle of lunch when there was

the sound of a key turning in the front door and a man appeared.

'You have visitors?' he said as he glanced around at them. He was tall and blond, with one blue eye and a black leather eye patch over the other. Slim and well-dressed in casual but expensive clothing, he approached the table.

'Allow me to introduce Friedrich Arnheim,' Rhino said. 'Fritz, please meet Mrs Entwhistle, and her daughter, my friend Lucy.'

Lucy and Friedrich looked at each other in surprise as recognition dawned.

'We met before,' he said, coming round the table and taking her hand. His mouth was smiling but she was not sure if his eye was. 'How very lovely to meet you again.'

He turned to Harriet. 'My pleasure, Mrs Entwhistle,' he said, taking her hand and kissing it.

'You know each other?' Harriet said, looking from him to Lucy and back again.

'We met on the ship,' Lucy said. 'When I first met Rhino.'

'I had forgotten,' Rhino said. 'Of course you did. Join us, Fritz,' he added, gesturing to a chair.

Thomas, having looked up briefly, returned to the cheese on his plate.

'Hello, Thomas,' Friedrich said. His voice was suddenly hard and clipped, unlike the way he had addressed Lucy and her mother. Lucy wondered what had happened to his eye. From under the eye patch, coming down his cheek in a jagged line was a thin scar. She had to force herself not to look at it.

'Good afternoon,' Thomas replied, his voice

devoid of intonation.

'I'll join you for coffee,' he said.

'I was about to make some.' Rhino got up from the table and went into the kitchen and Friedrich seated himself at the table, crossing his legs and smiling at Lucy. He reached down and removed a speck of dust from his cream shoes. This movement brought attention both to his hand and his feet, and the word 'elegant' sprang to Lucy's mind. His presence seemed to dominate the room. And for some reason she could not determine, Lucy felt inadequate.

'When you let yourself in,' Harriet said, 'I wondered who on earth you could be. Where we come from it is unusual to have the key of someone else's house and to let oneself in without knocking.'

Friedrich smiled at her but said nothing.

In the silence that followed, Harriet eyed the house key, which was now lying on the table.

Lucy would have cringed with embarrassment had she not been so interested in finding out what was going on, and in a sense she admired her mother for her directness, although she was unsure what Harriet was thinking.

'I'm a very good friend, am I not, Thomas?' Friedrich addressed the youth, as if those words explained his having a key to the house.

'If you say so,' Thomas replied.

'That is extremely rude,' Friedrich announced. His voice was ice cold.

'I don't think he meant it the way it sounded,' Rhino said, coming back in from the kitchen. 'A direct translation from the German, I would

185

think,' he continued agreeably. 'Which you your-self should recognise, Fritz. It merely confirms agreement with what you said.' Putting the cups down on the table he ruffled Thomas's hair.

'I think his English is excellent,' Harriet said.

'Thank you, Mrs Entwhistle,' Thomas said, suddenly smiling at her.

'I think it needs quite a lot of work,' Friedrich said, sounding irritated.

'Thomas has only been here for a year,' Rhino explained to Harriet and Lucy.

'Your English is really very good,' Lucy said to him.

Again he thanked her and said that it was becoming easier not to miss intonation and nuance.

'Imagine even knowing those words,' Lucy said. 'I think you're marvellous.' She hoped she did not sound too effusive but she was embar-rassed at the way Rhino's friend tried to diminish the boy.

'Clear the plates away, Thomas,' Friedrich said to him.

Obligingly, he got up and took the plates out to the kitchen.

'I ought to get back to the hotel,' Harriet said in due course. 'Would you be kind enough to drive me?' she asked Friedrich, who looked more than a little surprised. 'It would be nice for Reinhold and my daughter to have some more time together. They have a lot to catch up on.'

In a sense Harriet said this simply to annoy the other visitor as she herself was unsure if she wanted her daughter to have more time with

Rhino. But at the same time she was aware that that was what Lucy would have liked and she wanted her to be happy. Friedrich appeared momentarily uncertain, looking from Rhino to Lucy, and then standing up abruptly, he addressed Harriet.

'Allow me to escort you home,' he said, holding out his hand for her to take.

And so, against her better judgement, Harriet bought Lucy time with Rhino.

Later that day, when Lucy and Rhino were alone, they went out for dinner. On the way back, they stopped on the Dingli Cliffs where he parked the car, and they walked towards the edge. He held her hand as they looked out at the moonlit sea and the steep drop down below.

'Out there, beyond the horizon,' he said to her, 'is Libya. There is nothing between North Africa and us.'

The wind lifted her hair. It was a night breeze that brought relief from the heat of the day, and he reached out and brushed stray strands back from her face.

'You and I are connected by the sea,' he said, and she smiled gently in the dark. 'Remember, we came from North Africa to here.'

'I often think of standing on the bastions and looking down at the harbour,' Lucy said slowly.

He said nothing. He might have moved slightly closer because she was suddenly aware of the heat from his arm as if it were barely touching her.

'Let's go back to the house,' he suggested.

She wondered if she should suggest going back to the hotel, but she did not want to. She wanted to prolong time with him, so she made no such suggestion.

When they got back to his house, he poured them each a brandy and then started up the gramophone.

They had become quieter over the previous hour or so, as if there was less to say, and yet Lucy felt there really was much more to say, but it was as if she did not know how to break through. As they walked from the dining room through the open door to the courtyard with the garden beyond, she could hear the first few bars of the music and then a shiver went up her spine as she recognised it.

Ta-ra-ra went the trumpeter and she looked up at Rhino. He put their drinks down on a table and he reached for her hand, pulling her to him. They danced as they had danced long ago on the ship. He drew her in close, and led her around the flagstones, and Lucy's heart melted. Gone were the years of war, the agony of loss, the acceptance of her changed lot in life, and she was back on the ship as it cut through the Mediterranean, and the beat of the music aroused the spirit she had felt as a teenage girl in his arms.

'Lucymem,' he murmured.

Their eyes met as they had done before, with lust and fascination, and he guided her into a waltz.

'That's our music,' Lucy said.

'That's why I bought it,' Rhino said, his hand in the small of her back, her feet moving with his as

188

they swirled around on the stone slabs.

'I don't want to lose you again,' he said.

'You never lost me,' she replied.

He kissed her then in the moonlight.

And she kissed him back with all the passion of the lost years in her lips. Slow and sensuously at first, and then harder as his mouth closed on hers. His hand slipped under the arm of her short-sleeved blouse and he ran his fingers across her shoulder.

'In times of difficulty,' he whispered, 'I thought of doing this to you. And this,' he added, as he kissed her throat. His fingers fiddled with the buttons on her blouse, undoing them one by one, and he stepped back a little, turning her so that the moonlight caught her face and her chest. 'I shall take this off,' he said, slipping the blouse easily off her arms and tossing it on to the garden chair. The garment slipped and landed on the ground. She made a movement as if she would go and pick it up, and he said, 'Leave it, Lucy. Just leave it there.'

They danced again and he caressed her, before pulling her close so that she could feel the heat of his body under the soft cotton of his shirt as her breasts rubbed against him.

'Let's go upstairs,' he murmured gently.

'Thomas?' she said enquiringly.

'He will be asleep,' Rhino said. 'Don't worry about Thomas.'

He led her up the stone stairs to his room, and he lit a candle by the bed, and then he undressed her slowly. She felt waves of desire, as she stood there naked before him. He undressed quickly and guided her back on to the bed.

She had had no idea what this would be like, no real preconceptions – only vague memories of the scent in Hilary's cabin and her sister's eyes. Her wildest and most intimate imaginings had not included the prying of his fingers, the ease with which he slipped his hand around her body as though it was something he was well used to doing, while she gasped in a mixture of lust and hunger as his fingers slid between her legs, finding what he was looking for and then slipping away again to caress the contours of her body.

She found herself raising her hips, hoping for those fingers to find their way again, and at the same time twisting slightly in his arms to give him greater ease of movement with his hands.

'I want you,' he said.

Oh, I want you too, she thought. I want you and want you.

He took her firmly, finding his way until he filled her and then they moved together as the moon shone in on the white-sheeted bed. For a fleeting moment she thought of Hilary again and what she and Matthew had been doing all day and all night long on that journey back to England, thinking they had the opportunity to do it for ever, and at the same time utilising every minute that they had. She briefly thought how glad she was now for Hilary that her sister had at least had that time before it was taken away from her.

She let the thoughts drift from her mind as she felt herself sucked against his body and they moved as one.

Back in the hotel, Harriet Entwhistle sat on her bed reading the telegram that had just arrived. She folded it up, closing her eyes, before opening it out again to reread it. Then she got up and started to pack. When she had finished she read the telegram one more time before sitting in the armchair in the corner of the room, where she sat with her legs neatly crossed at her ankles and she waited.

All virtue is summed up in dealing justly.

Aristotle

CHAPTER EIGHT

The days had slipped by after the departure of Grandmother and Lucymem. Amelia had hated their leaving. Never having been away from her aunt before, she could not imagine what it was going to be like. She bit back tears when they left, not wanting Grandfather to feel that he was not enough for her, but at the same time staring down the long hours, days and weeks until Lucy would return.

However, Grandfather had plans that would keep her occupied.

Grandfather had recently taken up painting and they sat for hours in the garden, he with a palette and easel, and she imitating his work as best she could, painting the trees and the flowers. She liked painting Bruce and some of her efforts were really quite good. Bruce lay as if he knew he was supposed to be posing and Grandfather said her pictures were excellent and should be in the National Gallery, but she thought he was saying that just to encourage her. She didn't need much encouragement, though, because she loved sitting on the ground with a small wooden board on her lap and her paper pinned on to it and just think-ing about the object she was painting. She followed her grandfather around just like Bruce did, needing his company, wanting his protection and his attention. Her initial desperate longing for Lucymem eased a little, and while she thought about her every day, she stopped being consumed by the sense of loss in her absence.

Then there were days at the sea when Grandfather drove them to Brighton, with Amelia in the back because he said it was safer, and Bruce in the passenger seat with his head out the window. They stayed in a hotel that catered for Bruce, who slept in a kennel in a small yard behind the hotel, but spent all day with Grandfather and Amelia.

Bruce and she took to swimming in the summer's heat wave and even Grandfather joined them once in what he called 'the icy waters of England'. Amelia played on the beach with Bruce, while Grandfather read, and they spent hours in the sea until Grandfather called them to shore, concerned about them freezing to death.

They walked on the pier and it was there Amelia saw her first Punch and Judy show. She was holding an ice cream in one hand, standing beside Grandfather with Bruce on his lead, lying on the ground waiting while they watched.

Amelia didn't like the show. She found it vicious and cruel, and she could not bear how they hit and punched each other. They beat each other to death and everyone shouted and cheered and yelled out names. She wanted to tell Grandfather that she did not like it, but she was afraid of hurting his feelings, because after all he had brought her there.

As they turned away to leave, she thought she saw Mattie – Mattie dressed in a blue cotton skirt and a white blouse with little puffed-up sleeves. She had never seen her sister dressed like that before.

She stepped away from Grandfather and was about to call out Mattie's name when it suddenly occurred to her that Mattie was supposed to be safely locked up in boarding school. She looked back at Grandfather, who had reached down to stroke Bruce. She was about to draw his attention to Mattie and then she decided not to. If Mattie had somehow escaped from school, she would not want attention brought to herself, and anyway, Amelia knew that she would not speak to her, so there was no point. She went back to her grandfather and took his hand. Looking back she saw Mattie again with another girl and a woman and she concluded that Mattie had been taken out for the day. If Mattie saw her, she gave no sign of recognition and, rejected but also relieved that Mattie was not alone, Amelia turned away. She thought about it all that day and the next – what Mattie was feeling, if she were back in school or had been allowed to stay with a friend, whether she had enjoyed the Punch and Judy show, if her sister had indeed seen her and had decided to ignore her. Were Mattie's clothes borrowed from her friend, and if not, where had she got them?

She hoped Mattie had had fun, and that she would have forgiven her when they next met.

A few days after they returned from Brighton, Uncle Jupe collected Amelia and she spent a week with him, Aunt Anne and Ophelia. Amelia felt a little lost, as Ophelia did not want to play with her. Friends of Ophelia invited them out but they did not talk to Amelia and she was isolated when she was with them. She found herself trailing along behind them, and she knew that Ophelia could not be bothered with her.

The Jupes had a house full of books. So did Grandfather and Grandmother, but these were different books. She found them more exciting and they became her salvation during the lonely days.

She worked her way through Ophelia's collection. There were myths and legends from every country. Amelia loved the god Thor with his roll of thunder, and Pegasus, the horse with wings. She was absorbed by the goblins from northern Europe and the images of dark and sunless days with children lost in thick forests. And, oh, her mind soared on its journey to the past where Hercules pushed a rock up a mountain, and Lorelei sang on the River Rhine, luring sailors to their deaths. She worshipped the other world of Mount Olympus with its host of gods, and back came memories of Lucy reading to her in the nursery, memories that comforted her now as she lay in bed late at night, trying to sleep, memories that included the story of Odysseus and his long journey home to Ithaca.

And then she found a book on Malta, and pleasure was now mixed with curiosity. No one knew where the name Malta originated, she discovered. It could have been from the Greek for honey, which is meli, or it could be from the Greek for bee, which is melitta, or from the Phoenician for harbour, which is mala. She envisaged honeybees everywhere and harbours and bays at every angle. She learned about Aeolus, who was the father of the winds in Greek mythology. He lived in islands in the Mediterranean. There were many islands and Malta was part of the Maltese Archipelago. That's where Aunt Lucymem was – she had told Amelia before she left that she was going back to a place where she had once been terribly happy. Aeolus kept the winds in bags on the islands and set them free when he felt like it. Amelia wondered if her aunt knew. She hoped Lucy wouldn't be blown away. She longed to tell Grandfather, but he was at home alone painting in the garden while she was staying with Uncle Jupe.

Once upon a time Poseidon, God of the Sea, was really angry when Odysseus blinded his son Cyclops, and he sent a storm that stranded Odysseus on the island of Malta. Amelia hoped that Lucy would not be stranded there. Aeolus came to Odysseus' rescue and gave him all the winds except for Zephyr, because Zephyr would have brought him straight to Ithaca, which is where he wanted to go, and Amelia, contemplating that, supposed there would have been no story if he had gone straight home to Ithaca. It also made her think about Ithaca, her Ithaca, her home where she had played in the garden, and run in the house, chasing Sean, looking at the portraits in the hall, and in her memory those were the happiest days ever. Back then maybe

Mattie had liked her – back then, before Mattie set fire to the house and refused to speak to her again. She was not sure that Mattie had liked her, but she thought that it must have been better than it was now.

While they were journeying back to Ithaca, not knowing they didn't have the right wind to get there, Odysseus' companions opened the bag and let out all the winds and they were blown back to Malta. Aeolus would not help them again because he was so cross with their carelessness. There was another island beside Malta called Gozo, although the Greeks had called it Oxygia. There lived a nymph named Calypso and there Odysseus stayed after he was shipwrecked later in the story, and after all his companions had died. Eight years he was trapped until the gods decided that he had been punished enough, and he built a raft and was allowed to leave. Oh, how Amelia hoped Aunt Lucymem would come back safely. Eight years seemed a very long time. Beside it, the concept of six weeks paled to virtually nothing, and three weeks had almost passed already. She was nearly halfway there. Six weeks was time that she now knew she could endure in Lucy's absence.

Ophelia was not much interested in her myths and legends, and Uncle Jupe allowed Amelia to bring six of the books home with her when the week was up.

Back she went to Grandfather with great relief. She had been looking forward to being with Ophelia but her cousin had been moody and sulky and rather like Mattie, which Amelia had not expected. Ophelia had not liked sharing her room, and while there were plenty of other rooms she could have been put in, her Aunt Anne thought it would be nice for the girls to be together. Amelia felt that Ophelia was just too used to having her own way and that sharing anything was beyond her imagination. It was with great relief that she returned to her grandfather and Bruce, and settled back into a routine with them.

Grandfather made fresh lemonade every few days, with Amelia watching him carefully as he cut and squeezed the lemons. They sat in the garden companionably together. At night Amelia slept in Mattie's bed, so that she was closer to the window. She kept the curtains open and, looking out, she could see the rising moon, waxing night by night as she fell asleep.

There were still two weeks until Lucymem and Grandmother were due home. By now Grandfather and Amelia had developed a very companionable routine. There were the odd days up in London, when they stayed in the London house and went to art galleries, or there were trips to the sea, walks in the woods, and plenty of time in the garden with paints and books.

In the evenings they listened to the wireless, or Grandfather read her poetry and Amelia pored over her grandparents' photograph albums. Grandfather often offered a running commentary, which she really enjoyed.

One evening, having taken out yet another

album, she settled herself beside him and she started looking at pictures of India. Grandfather, who had been reading from Tennyson's 'Ulysses', and had just read 'I am a part of all that I have met;' put down his book and looked at the album with her.

'Your grandmother took these,' he said, turning the leaf.

On the next page there were pictures of him in his army clothing with a group of men.

'My men,' he said thoughtfully. 'Must have been taken on the day we left, I think.'

'The day you came back to England?'

'No, the day we went to the East.'

'Where are they now?' Amelia asked him.

He was silent as he stared at the page.

'My men,' he repeated. 'They're gone now,' he said, returning to her after a long pause. 'All gone. Every last one of them.'

'They look nice,' she said, hoping he would tell her more.

'Yes.'

Silence settled between them and it lengthened beyond what she felt comfortable with. She was unsure whether to turn the page, as Grandfather, although not speaking, seemed to be looking very closely at the pictures.

'I was older than them all,' he finally said. 'And I outlived them all. That is my punishment.'

'Your punishment?' she asked. 'What do you mean? What did you do?' she asked quickly, afraid that he would stop.

'I did nothing,' he said. 'I could do nothing. I couldn't stop what happened.'

'Why is that a punishment?'

He shook his head. 'I watched them die,' he said. 'That was their punishment. Death. And mine was that I had to live.'

Amelia didn't know what to say. She didn't know what he meant. He looked so terribly sad as he peered at the photos.

'Sometimes in life we have choice. I had none,' he continued. 'I had no choice. That is what is so unbearable. It's better to have choice and maybe choose the wrong option. It's the thing about being an adult – I suppose it is the thing about being a human being. We are given choice all the time. We do our best when we make that choice. We choose with our conscience and our intelligence...' his voice trailed off. 'When you take freedom of choice away from human beings, there is nothing left,' he suddenly continued.

Amelia waited hopefully. She felt he was telling her something very important, something that she could use as she grew up, but she didn't know what it was.

'Were they good men?' she eventually asked him.

'Yes. Every last one of them. I loved them all. And they are all gone.'

'But you have Grandmother, and Aunt Lucy-mem, Mattie and me,' she said. 'We love you. And you love us, don't you, Grandfather?'

He seemed to come back to her then and, closing the album, he said, 'You are absolutely right, Amelia. I have been a lucky man. A good family and good men. I am a lucky man.'

'And I'm lucky too, aren't I, Grandfather?' she asked.

'Yes, my pet,' he said. 'You're a lucky little girl.'
But his voice was sad. She did not know why.

While they were in the kitchen the following day, Mrs Trotter let herself in.

'I'm terribly sorry, Colonel,' she said, putting her head around the door. 'My sister has been taken ill, and I have to go and care for her and the family for a few days. I'll be back in a week. Will you manage all right?'

The Colonel was concerned for her, reassuring her that they would cope splendidly.

'Fish and chips tonight in town,' he said to Amelia with a wink when Mrs Trotter was gone.

'What will we do this afternoon?' Amelia asked him.

He was looking in the pantry. 'We're out of lemons,' he said. 'We'll go and get some tomorrow. I'm going to teach you the joys of iced tea. How about that? There is tea in the pot left over from breakfast and we'll just add water to it, and then we'll make it taste perfect.'

'Do we need sugar, Grandfather?' she asked him.

'We definitely do,' he said.

She put in two spoons of sugar and they stirred the tea before bringing it out to the garden on a tray. He went to the herb garden and plucked two leaves of mint, which he placed on top of each glass and told her to smell it before she drank. She settled herself on the rug and he on the deck chair beside her, and he handed her a glass.

'Smell adds to the taste,' he said.

She loved the smell, probably because he had

201

suggested that she would, and she loved everything he liked. He was her hero. He had been to war and had come back, and he was the best grandfather in the world. He knew how to care for her, and there was nothing lovelier than being in this garden with him, with the ivy growing up the walls and the raspberry canes in their neat rows.

He painted for a while and she tried to paint her toenails with his watercolours, but the paint went into little blobs like it did on the palette and she ended up wiping them off on the rug when he wasn't looking. Bruce watched her with interest. Bruce watched everyone and everything with curiosity. She petted his head and then lay down on the rug beside Grandfather's chair with the intention of reading.

Grandfather, having abandoned his painting was now reading too, and Bruce, crouching down on his hunkers, was guarding them both. Amelia could feel her book slipping from her hands as the heat of the afternoon washed over her and she couldn't keep her eyes open any more, and she slipped into a doze.

She dreamed a vivid dream of colours and light, and she could smell mint, fresh and clear. Then, suddenly, there was the sound of steel clashing on steel and she could hear footsteps far away. She saw that she was looking into a long black tunnel and halfway down the tunnel Grandfather was walking towards the light at the other end. She thought the voices she could hear were shouting at him, and then she realised that they were calling to him. 'Colonel, Colonel,' she could hear them clearly. They were men's voices.

Grandfather stopped for a moment as though listening, and then he turned back to her. He looked at her straight in the face down the length of the tunnel but said nothing for a long moment.

'No, Grandfather,' she called. 'No.'

But she knew he could not hear her, because all he said was, 'I have to leave you now. You will be all right. Just stay here.'

And then he walked on down the tunnel to the light and she wanted to scream, no, no, no, but she made no sound. She just watched him as he walked away until he disappeared into the light at the end. For a moment he appeared illuminated and then he was gone and there was just the darkness of the tunnel.

She woke shivering. Bruce was looking at Grandfather in his chair and gradually the expression on Bruce's face changed and then he howled. It was the longest heaviest deepest howl she had ever heard from an animal and her blood went even colder.

She looked at Grandfather. His book was resting on his lap, and his head had dropped forward. She hoped he was asleep. She thought he must be.

Yes, she was almost sure he was asleep.

She sat up on the rug and waited a while, as she didn't like to waken him.

Eventually Bruce settled down on the ground right up against Grandfather's feet and she picked up her book, not wanting to acknowledge that there could be anything wrong. She tried reading, but found she was rereading the same sentence over and over again as if she could not take in its content.

Eventually she said, 'Grandfather,' in a very small voice.

He didn't answer.

Bruce, keeping his head firmly on Grandfather's feet, turned his eyes towards her, but other than that he didn't move.

'Grandfather, would you like some more iced tea?' she asked.

Grandfather did not reply. His hand was strangely cold when she touched it.

She got up and went into the house and went to the bathroom. She knew something was terribly wrong and she thought she knew what it was, but didn't know what to do. She wished they had a telephone. Uncle Jupiter had a telephone, she thought, and she could have phoned him.

It was a good four miles to the village and she was not allowed to go there by herself anyway. She looked out the front door.

There were some soldiers on the road, walking down in twos and threes. There were soldiers everywhere in those days. Grandfather had said that it was because of National Service. She thought of calling to them, but didn't like to. She was afraid.

Back inside she made jam sandwiches for Grandfather and herself because she couldn't think what else to do. He didn't eat his. Bruce did. Amelia ate hers and sat there waiting as the sun went down, and then she got Grandfather a blanket from the house and she wrapped it around him. She put on a jumper and rolled herself up in the rug and slept there in the garden beside him, with Bruce standing guard.

But in the morning there was no change and she could not imagine what to do next. Mid-morning she went inside to watch for the postman through the drawing-room window, but he never came. In fact no one came down the road past the house at all that day, at least not during the time she sat in the front room looking out the window.

Bruce whined a lot during the day and refused to leave Grandfather for more than a few minutes. He wouldn't eat his lunch but he did eat the jam sandwiches Amelia made on and off during the day. She brought his bowl of water outside for him, and he drank from it drearily, before settling back down beside Grandfather. Amelia painted a bit and then she read. She kept hoping Aunt Lucymem and Grandmother would come back soon. It was a very long day, and so was the next one. The stars were beautiful at night, and she lay wrapped in the rug and looked up and back into the heavens. There were wonderful constellations to be seen. She knew about them from the books of legends. Grandfather had said that if everyone looked up at night into the sky they would all see the same things but in different ways. She hoped that Aunt Lucymem was looking up at the sky and maybe she would know that it would be better if she came home.

She found a tin of Spam in the pantry, but in prising the lid off with a knife, it slipped in her hand and the jagged edge cut her deeply across her palm and around the ball of her thumb. She wrapped it in a tea towel but she could not get it to stop bleeding.

Bruce was restless. He had come into the kitchen when he heard her cry out, and now he stood watching her. He whined and whined and she wanted to cry, but she couldn't remember how.

The day after that there was a ring at the hall door while she was in the kitchen. The bread had mould on it, and she didn't know what to do. There didn't seem to be anything to eat. There was butter in the larder and jam in the cupboard. There were a few tins, but her hand hurt too much to actually hold one in order to open it. Bruce came with her when the bell went and she held his collar while opening the door. It was Uncle Jupe and Mattie.

Uncle Jupe took one look at her and he said, 'Amelia, what's happened?'

She hadn't spoken in nearly four days and she couldn't find any words to tell him. She did not think she knew what had happened. She just looked at him and at Mattie.

'Cut my hand,' she tried. Her voice didn't really sound like hers at all. It was sort of hoarse and the words came out in a whisper.

Uncle Jupe picked her up and carried her into the drawing room. 'Where's your grandfather?' he asked.

'I don't know where he's gone,' she said.

'Stay with her, Mattie,' Uncle Jupe said, and Mattie surprisingly tried to open the tea towel and she looked at her with as much kindness as

Amelia had ever seen in her sister's face and she said, 'That looks very sore.'

Amelia nodded. In fact it wasn't sore. She couldn't feel anything.

Uncle Jupe came back into the room. 'When did this happen, Amelia?' he asked.

She thought he was talking about her hand. She said that she thought it had just happened but that she was not sure. It might have been the previous day.

'Does anyone have a phone around here?' he asked Mattie.

She looked puzzled. 'No one lives around here,' she replied. 'They have a phone at the farm, but there isn't anyone else around for miles.'

'The two of you had better get into the car and come with me,' he said.

Amelia got to her feet but her knees felt wobbly as if the bones were gone in her legs. Uncle Jupe carried her out to the car, having shut Bruce in the kitchen.

He spoke to Mattie but Amelia couldn't hear what he was saying. Then she heard the words, 'I need you to be brave, Mattie. I need you to hold Amelia while we go for help.'

Amelia wondered what had happened.

The rest of the day was a blur, between Mrs Bradey, the farmer's wife, washing her hand and then saying that she ought to have a bath, and Uncle Jupe using the telephone and asking could he leave the girls with her while he dealt with things.

Mattie sat in Mrs Bradey's kitchen and stared

at the stone floor.

'Mattie, look at me,' Uncle Jupe said to her. 'I need you to help Mrs Bradey with Amelia. It's going to be all right. I'll be back for you both just as soon as I can.'

Amelia sat in the Bradeys' bath, motionless in the hot water, trying to cover herself up.

'Don't be ashamed,' Mrs Bradey said to her. She was a big heavy woman with a kind face, and she wiped Amelia's face with a flannel that smelled of a mixture of disinfectant and soap. Not soap like Grandmother and Aunt Lucymem used. Something else. It had a strong smell but was not as nice. Amelia wanted to go home to her own bath. She wanted Aunt Lucymem there.

'I have grown children of my own,' Mrs Bradey continued, 'and I've bathed them all. None of us are any different,' as she scoured her body with the evil-smelling flannel and Amelia winced.

'I want Aunt Lucymem,' Amelia whinged. She could hear her own voice. She knew Grandmother wouldn't like her to talk like that, so she stopped and then said nothing.

'Who did this?' Mattie suddenly asked. Her voice was angry. She took Amelia's other hand. 'Who did this?' she repeated.

'I did,' she whispered. 'I was trying to open a tin of Spam. I was hungry.'

'Poor child,' Mrs Bradey said.

'I don't mean your hand, silly,' Mattie said. 'I mean Grandfather.'

'There were soldiers on the road,' Amelia tried. She was really trying to be helpful, but did not know what was wanted of her.

'Soldiers?' Mattie said, aghast. 'Germans?'

Amelia hadn't thought they might be Germans. That was something that had never occurred to her. She didn't think they were. She couldn't see how they could be. They were dressed in standard military uniform. She had been sure they were British.

'Germans?' she repeated. It was meant as a question, not as a statement.

'I knew it,' Mattie said viciously.

Mrs Bradey had gone to get towels, having washed Amelia's hair, which felt very knotted and Amelia knew it was going to hurt when it was brushed out.

Mattie brushed it out for her, and it did hurt, but not as much as she thought it would because Mattie was trying to be gentle. Or maybe Mattie wasn't trying to be gentle. Maybe it was just because Amelia couldn't feel anything really at all.

Uncle Jupe came back later in the day and Amelia heard Mrs Bradey saying to him that she thought the doctor should be called. Mattie said that the police needed to be called, as she wanted the soldiers found.

'What soldiers?' Uncle Jupe asked in surprise.

'Amelia said they were German,' she said.

Uncle Jupiter looked even more surprised. 'What are you talking about?' he asked.

'Amelia said that German soldiers killed Grand-father,' Mattie said. 'They kill everyone. All my family.' She stood there, all thirteen years of her, shouting at Uncle Jupiter, who was clearly as startled as Amelia was. Amelia knew that he had a terrible problem ahead of him, because it was impossible to change Mattie's opinion on anything.

'The doctor said that your grandfather died very peacefully,' he said to Mattie.

She looked at Amelia. 'You said the Germans shot him,' she said angrily.

Amelia didn't think she had said that. In fact she couldn't remember even hinting at such a suggestion. She tried shaking her head, but she really felt very strange – sort of disorientated – and she kept wondering what was real and what was not.

'That child needs bed and a doctor,' Mrs Bradey said to Uncle Jupiter. 'She has been through the wars.'

'She doesn't even remember the war,' Mattie shouted. 'I was the one who was there.'

The strange hallucinatory feeling that Amelia seemed to have been encountering on and off over the past few days caught up and completely overwhelmed her and she fell asleep sitting there upright on Mrs Bradey's bed with her hair all wet and half brushed out.

When she woke up she was in her own bed and the doctor was bandaging her hand.

'How long were you alone here?' he asked her as though he were just continuing a conversation. Having no recollection of anything that might have been said before that, Amelia obliged none the less by trying to answer the question.

'I wasn't alone,' she said. 'Grandfather and

Bruce were here.'

'Bruce is the family dog,' Uncle Jupe said.

Amelia had not realised he was in the room.

'It's certainly four or five days,' the doctor said to Uncle Jupe. She hadn't realised it was that long. She knew now that Grandfather was dead.

'He went to the soldiers,' she tried explaining.

'What soldiers?' the doctor asked.

'There were these soldiers calling him. I couldn't see them. They're the ones in the photograph.'

The album was brought in, and she showed him the picture of the soldiers. She hadn't seen them but she knew that they were the ones who had called him from the other end of the tunnel.

'I have sent a telegram to her grandmother and my cousin Lucy. They should be on their way home,' Uncle Jupe said.

'It's a long time for a little girl to be alone,' the doctor said. 'But you'll be fine now.' He said something about hallucinating to Uncle Jupe. 'That wound is a couple of days old,' he said, putting a poultice on it. 'It's badly infected but she'll be all right. She needs sleep.'

He gave her something to drink and then she did not remember anything else.

She slept heavily and then woke and slept again and when she finally woke up properly Aunt Lucymem was sitting beside her on the bed, and then she cried and cried and she couldn't stop.

Grandmother came in and she held her hand. Amelia thought she would be angry with her because she had not managed to stop Grandfather going down the tunnel, but Grandmother did not seem to see it that way, even when Amelia explained to her what had happened.

'All of life comes to an end at some time or another,' she said. 'It was time for your grand-father to make that journey. It's all right, Amelia. These things happen. It was just the right time for him – and the wrong time for us, because we weren't here. Did he say anything?'

Amelia remembered their conversation from when they had been looking at the photographs the evening before he died.

'He said he loved you and Lucymem, Mattie and me,' she said to her grandmother.

It must have been the right thing to say, because Grandmother looked really pleased and she said, 'Did he, darling, did he indeed? Isn't that nice?'

And Aunt Lucymem, holding her other hand, dropped her head, but Amelia could see that she was crying too.

We make war that we may live in peace.

Aristotle

CHAPTER NINE

Reinhold Kobaldt arrived about a week later –
Uncle Rhino, as they were encouraged to call
him. He had a nephew who lived with him, Aunt
Lucymem told them before he came.

'And I suppose the nephew's name is Hippo,'
Mattie said evilly.

Grandmother laughed, but Lucy, taking the
comment seriously – and indeed it may have
been a serious comment as one could never be
quite sure with Mattie – said, 'No, his name is
Thomas. He's a bit older than you, Mattie. He's
a nice boy. Like you, he survived the war.'

'Another lucky bastard,' Mattie said.

Grandmother was shocked. 'Don't you dare
use that language with me,' she said to Mattie.

'I wasn't talking to you,' Mattie said rudely.

'Don't you use that language in this house,'
Grandmother said, her amusement over Mattie's
earlier comments about Hippo quickly evaporating. Grandmother's voice was icily furious.
'And don't use that tone with me.'

'Thomas was lucky,' Aunt Lucymem said to
Mattie, ignoring the confrontation. 'He was very
lucky. He lost both his parents and his little sister
in the war and survived the most terrible fire

bombing in Dresden. Dresden was destroyed, but Thomas survived. And after the war was over, his Uncle Rhino found him through the Red Cross and now Thomas lives with him in Malta.'

Malta – Amelia's heart lifted for the first time in days and days. Land of honey and bees and harbours. A place of happiness and safety. A place where Aunt Lucymem had been terribly happy once long ago.

Mattie was not interested in Malta but she suddenly became interested in Thomas. 'What does he look like?' she wanted to know.

'He's going to be tall like Rhino,' Aunt Lucymem said. 'But Rhino has blond curly hair and Thomas has straight hair.'

'Blond?' asked Mattie.

'Yes. Very. As blond as you are dark,' Aunt Lucymem said.

Mattie's hair tumbled in dark curls on to her shoulders and down her back. Amelia's hair, that had once been almost white in its fairness, was dark now too, and like Mattie's it had grown into curls and she wore it the same way as her sister, or at least she would when it grew back. Someone had taken the scissors to it while she had been sick with her sore hand. She supposed because it had been so knotted. She realised she must have forgotten to brush it during those days when Bruce and she were in the garden with Grandfather.

'Does he have any brothers or sisters?' Mattie wanted to know, even though Lucy had just said that he had had a sister.

'He had one sister, younger than him,' Aunt

214

Lucymem replied patiently. 'Rhino never said if there were others, and I didn't think to ask. I'm sure there weren't, or he would have said.'

Amelia thought it would be nice if he had a sister her age, an open happy girl whom she could talk to – not like Ophelia, who was grumpy, and not like Mattie, whom she loved but who was really very difficult at times. But as it turned out there was no other sister, only the one who had died. Now there was just Thomas and his Uncle Rhino, and if Rhino had not found him in the orphanage he would have been alone for ever. Thomas had stayed in the farmhouse in Malta when Rhino made the journey to England to visit.

Aunt Lucymem was engaged to be married. They did not know this at first because she didn't have a ring on her finger, and she didn't tell them until after the funeral. Rhino had asked her to marry him that night as he brought her back to Harriet in the hotel, and her joy had turned to grief as she read the telegram.

'You don't have a ring,' Mattie said. 'Is he too mean or too poor to buy you one?'

'No. Neither,' Aunt Lucymem said. Her patience was endless. 'We had no time. When we got the telegram from your uncle Jupiter, we came straight back here – there was no time for anything else.'

Her voice seemed resigned in some way and Amelia wanted Mattie to stop trying to upset her. Amelia had lost her grandfather, but she had only known him for a few years; Aunt Lucymem had lost her father, whom she had known for

215

more than five times longer than they had. Amelia felt she must have been feeling very sad.

She said that to Mattie when they were going to bed that night.

'What do you mean?' Mattie asked, clearly not understanding.

'I don't know,' Amelia said. 'I think I meant poor Aunt Lucymem. She's lost her father. You must know what that means, Mattie. You know what that feels like. It's not like me. I never really knew Papa.'

'You didn't know Papa at all,' Mattie said. 'So don't try to compare this with me losing my father. I was the one out on the mountain. I was the one who couldn't keep up with him ... me and Georgina.'

Her voice was really angry, so Amelia put her head under the bedclothes and she thought about Aeolus instead and the winds that swept Malta.

Amelia initially liked Rhino. Greeting the girls both with courtesy and interest, he smiled at them both. Mattie did not smile at him although she did let him shake her hand. She stared at him and said nothing.

He seemed a pleasant man, who tried to please them all, especially Aunt Lucymem. Even though Lucy was very sad because of Grandfather, she smiled all the time when Rhino was staying with them, and she hung on his every word. Mattie said he was well named because he was just like the rhinoceros in London Zoo, which didn't even notice when a bird was sitting on top of its head. Rhino didn't notice when Grandmother said things like, 'I hope no one else will have a key to your house after you are married,' or, 'This is happening very fast. Lucy needs time to grieve as well as to think.'

Aunt Lucymem was not behaving like someone who needed time for anything. All she wanted was to be with Rhino and to live happily ever after, but Amelia thought maybe that was how one reacted when one's father died. It saddened her because she had never felt that, nor would she ever. But the grief she felt swamped her and she worried for her grandmother, because Grandmother had known him, had loved him, had been with him for most of her life. And although Grandmother bustled around the place, organising everything for Uncle Rhino's visit Amelia could see the sadness in her eyes.

There followed strange days – days of both loss and uncertainty, as the structure on which Amelia's life had been built appeared to change again. People who had been at the bedrock of her existence had come and gone – people like Cook and Maudge, Sean and Feilim and now Grand-father.

Amelia wanted Lucymem around more because she had missed her and was so relieved that she was back, but Lucy's mind was elsewhere – absorbed in Rhino and her joy at refinding him, combined with an acute sense of loss.

Lucy and Rhino spent a large amount of their time going up and down to London, and staying over in the London house. Grandmother, Mattie and Amelia spent the end of the summer in the garden. Initially Amelia felt uncertain about going back outside. She was unsure if Grandfather was still there, as nothing had really been explained to her. It did not really seem likely that he might be, and yet when she thought about the garden, she could see his deck chair so clearly and always envisaged him in it.

It was Mattie who went out with her the first time after she recovered from the infection in her hand. Grandmother had washed the rug that Amelia had sat and slept on and she could see it hanging on the line in the sun as a strange reminder of her days living on it.

It was Mattie, too, who took it down from the line and said that it was dry and why did they not go and lie in the sun in the last days of summer. Amelia wondered if Grandmother or Aunt Lucymem had suggested this to Mattie, but that did not seem likely. Mattie had never responded well to encouragement, and Amelia felt a sense of inclusion that Mattie would want her in the garden with her.

There were days of late when Mattie was almost kind to her, and there was no mention of anything to do with the fire at Ithaca, nor any blame thrown at Amelia. It was as if Mattie had somehow forgiven her, or maybe even felt a sense of affection towards her, and she talked to her now in a new and different way.

Grandmother sat in the deck chair, lying back in the sun, while Amelia read and Mattie perused the other books of myths and legends with a certain amount of interest. Uncle Jupe brought more to her when he came down at the weekends.

'I'm going to write legends when I grow up,' Amelia told him one Saturday.

'You can't write legends,' Mattie said scornfully. 'They've already been written.'

Amelia had not thought of that. She liked the idea of sitting in a study writing away, using Grandfather's fountain pen, which Grandmother had just given her.

'I can,' she said. 'I can write them differently. I can tell the same stories but using different words.'

'No one would want to read them,' Mattie said.

'What are you going to do when you grow up?' Uncle Jupe asked her, in an effort to distract her from Amelia.

'I'm thinking of joining the fire brigade,' Mattie replied, undaunted.

More like starting a fire to give the fire services something to do, Amelia thought, but she didn't voice this aloud.

'How interesting,' Uncle Jupe said.

Uncle Jupe encouraged everyone in his or her ideas. Amelia had noticed that when she was staying with the Jupes.

Amelia had already started to rewrite Odysseus' journey. In it he was a very brave man and he had a large dog called Brucius. She thought Brucius was the kind of name Odysseus might have given his dog. In the evening, when Mattie was outside banging a tennis ball off the wall – a rather worn and chewed tennis ball, as it was the one

Grandfather had used for playing with Bruce – she sat in the drawing room on the windowledge.

She used her painting board for support, and wrote in a notebook. She made line drawings to illustrate her story. Odysseus looked like Grandfather. He was a good man and had been punished for something he did not do. She did not know what that thing was, and neither did he. And in her story, as he travelled from island to island in the Mediterranean Sea, one by one his men were killed. That was their punishment. And his was that he had to live and see them die. And as time wore on, this Odysseus became more and more tired. By now he had no men left, just a little girl called Calypso whom he had met on one of the islands, and one day he said to Calypso and to Brucius that he had to go on to Ithaca alone.

And that became Calypso's punishment. She hadn't done anything and yet she was being punished by being left to live on, all alone, on the island with Brucius.

Amelia looked out the window. Bruce was watching Mattie play against the wall. He couldn't take his eyes off the ball and his head was going from side to side as he watched it. So involved was she in her game, hitting the ball harder and harder, that Mattie was completely unaware of Bruce's fascination. He was almost salivating, and Amelia knew that he hoped she would throw the ball for him.

She could hear Uncle Jupe and Grandmother talking in the kitchen. Grandmother sounded tired.

'Aunt Harriet,' Uncle Jupe said, 'if there is any way that Anne and I can help you, we will do it. But you need to tell us.'

She could hear Grandmother sighing. Amelia did not know what was worrying her, but something was.

'I'm not sure about this man,' she said.

'Reinhold? He seems nice.'

'There's something ... something I don't like.'

'My cousin Lucy is a grown woman,' Uncle Jupe pointed out. 'And she loves him.'

'How did he spend the war?' Grandmother asked.

'Like any German,' Uncle Jupe said. 'He fought.'

'But after the war ... what did he do then? He's very reticent, you know. He finally ended up in Malta and then tracked down his nephew in Dresden. But we know nothing about him.'

'I'll find out,' Uncle Jupe said.

And he did.

Reinhold Kobaldt spent two years after the war in a cage in the North African sun, a prisoner of the British. This, however, did not appear to have affected his attitude towards his captors. It was as if he just took it on board as the price to pay for having lost the war. When Uncle Jupe told Grandmother – Amelia was again on her window perch and they were in the kitchen – it seemed marginally to soften Grandmother towards Lucy's fiancé.

'So there is justice somewhere,' Grandmother observed. It seemed an odd comment to Amelia, but there were so many odd comments made that she just took them on board, one by one.

'Tough justice for doing your job,' Uncle Jupe commented. He was usually very gung-ho and let's get on with it, but his comment held a modicum of compassion.

'Yes, but what did he do to deserve that?' Grandmother asked. 'I'm sure they didn't cage regular officers – at least not without good reason.'

'Does it matter?' Uncle Jupe asked. 'Whatever he did, he paid the price of the losing side. And anyway, you can't stop her marrying him,' he continued. 'And they love each other. It's not a bad start to a marriage.'

'She's loved him for a very long time,' Grandmother said. 'I don't know if she really loves him, or if it is the image of him as she remembers him that she is in love with.'

Amelia could hear the clink of glasses as drinks were poured.

Aunt Anne was there again on that occasion and she said, 'Well, I think it is lovely that Lucy has met someone and that she has the chance of happiness.'

Lucy and Rhino came back shortly afterwards from London, and she was wearing a diamond ring on her finger, and looking beautiful in a pink summer dress that was buckled on a wide belt at the waist and had a pleated skirt that spun outwards when she turned and she was smiling in happiness.

'Your father would be pleased for you,' Grandmother said, and Amelia knew then that the marriage would go ahead.

And go ahead it did.

There was a lot of discussion as to whether Amelia should go out to school in Malta, which is what Lucy appeared to want, but both Rhino and Grandmother felt that school in England would be the best place for her. This was sold to Amelia under the guise that it would give Aunt Lucymem the best chance for a start to her new life. Although she became excited about starting boarding school, Amelia did feel terribly rejected. She wanted to ask if Thomas was going to be sent away to give Rhino a clean start to his new life, but it wasn't the kind of question she could ask, and instead she stood there when she was told her fate and she said nothing.

'You'll come out to us at Christmas,' Aunt Lucymem said.

'I think Amelia and I would prefer Christmas here at home,' Mattie commented, none too politely.

But what home, Amelia wondered. There was no home. Grandmother was going to go out to Malta and was thinking of looking for a place to live, at least for the winter months. She found the English winter too cold, she said.

'But you put up with it since you moved back here with Grandfather,' Mattie objected.

'But your grandfather is gone now,' Grandmother said to her.

'You should have just left us in our home in Ireland,' Mattie pointed out. 'We were fine there.'

'You would have been put in an orphanage,'

Grandmother said, 'if your aunt had not come and taken care of you.'

Where did that leave them – Mattie and Amelia? Amelia was frightened of being forgotten and of not having a home. There was a sense of being passed over as other people's lives moved on. She listened to the constant discussion about houses and property, and wondered what would happen. Would there be beds for them in Lucymem's new home in Malta, or would Grandmother want them to stay with her? Would Grandmother even want to keep the house in Kent? And if she didn't, what would that mean? Everything other than school carried an element of uncertainty with it, and there were questions that Amelia wanted to ask, but did not know how to because she feared the answers.

Mattie had grown out of her uniform and it was passed down. Amelia got new shoes for school, and stockings and blouses. She had always envied Mattie her suspender belt and stockings, but for some reason, the suspender belt kept slipping on her, and she ended up with wrinkles on her knees.

Grandmother tried adjusting the belt, sewing in extra hooks and eyes to make it tighter.

'She has no hips,' she said to Lucy.

'She's only nine,' Lucy said. And Amelia was sure then that Aunt Lucymem did not really want her to be sent away to school. She knew that if everyone wasn't putting so much pressure on her, that Lucy would take her back to Malta, and she would see and feel the winds for herself, and explore this island of honey and bees. But it was not to be.

Mattie and Amelia – she with her multi-hooked-and-eyed suspender belts – went to school. Rhino and Lucy married quietly two weeks after the girls started back to school. Harriet came and collected them for the day and took them to the church and afterwards to a hotel for lunch, before driving them back. Amelia now experienced a sense of abandonment, as the expectations about the wedding had kept her going for those first fourteen days, and had helped her deal with the difficulties of finding herself in a large dormitory with stringent rules and a general sense of deprivation.

Homesick and isolated, she tried to get close to Mattie, but the rules were such that little or no contact was allowed between the different forms. Once Mattie asked her if she were all right, and Amelia nodded because there seemed no point in trying to express how she felt, as nothing could be changed. She was there to be educated and there was no escape from everything else. She went to bed at night, slipping between her tightly pulled sheets and lying there in the dark, unsure come morning if she had indeed slept or not. She fell into the routine of the school hours, obeyed the rules, and she worked. Study became the only outlet from the rigours of life there.

The term moved on wearily. Mattie was good at lacrosse and hockey, and Amelia discovered her sister was the school star – something she had never shared with the family at home. Amelia found she was less than adequate at sport, and was always one of the last to be picked for teams. They were not allowed to play with gloves on, and her hands were constantly frozen and they hurt. She was good at English and really enjoyed art, but she excelled at Latin and Greek, and concentrated on working hard in the vague hope that a good report and being top of her class would make her aunt see that she could do well in school, in any school, and maybe she would keep her in Malta when they went out at Christmas.

She wrote to Aunt Lucymem every week, carefully composed letters telling her how she was doing and how much she missed her. She hoped Lucy was happy.

The girls in her year admired Mattie. Many had tried to befriend her – always unsuccessfully. There was something about her spirit and her air of indifference that drew others towards her, but she was not interested. She did not seek friendship, nor did she care if anyone spoke to her. Mattie was simply putting in time. Amelia, on the other hand, was always hopeful of making a close friend, but her quietness and introspection made it difficult for her to relate to her classmates, all of whom seemed outgoing and boisterous. Her hopeful efforts invariably fell short, and she learned to stay reliant on herself.

The post was slow and only two letters arrived from Malta all that term. Lucy wrote about Rhino's house, and the start of her life with him. She spoke about the weather and Thomas, a family friend named Friedrich, and of course asked endless questions about how both girls were.

Regular letters came from Harriet. But they were brief and Amelia felt her sadness in them. Harriet had been out to Malta and had found a potential new home and was now back in England sorting things. Amelia read and reread the letters, trying to see where she fitted into them. The one hopeful thing was that she and Mattie would go back to Malta with Grandmother for Christmas and she would get to see it all for herself, and maybe, just maybe, she would be able to stay there with Lucymem.

'I'm not going to Malta,' Mattie said, on reading one of the letters. 'They need not think they will get me on a plane.'

Amelia knew that her grandmother would not let Mattie stay behind and was confident that they would go. She knew how stubborn Mattie could be, but her stubbornness was still that of a child, and Grandmother reigned supreme in their home.

But in the event they did not go to Malta for Christmas. Instead Rhino, Aunt Lucymem and Thomas came to England. And Rhino was absolutely livid.

A few days before they were due to depart for Malta, there was a festive atmosphere in school with the sense of both the running down of the end of term as well as the possibilities ahead of a great Christmas, despite the ongoing rationing. Mattie, who had used her matches, since the fire in Ithaca, only to light candles on the table or the fire in the grate, finally pulled a stunt that outdid even Ithaca.

Amelia felt that any observant adult would have noticed the fervour with which Mattie had entered into the spirit of Guy Fawkes early in November, and the way she watched the school bonfire going up. It had been a great bonfire, the biggest she had ever seen, and Mattie, standing there watching it too close to the flames, had had to be pulled back by two teachers. Amelia had got the impression she was thinking of jumping into it, whereas they simply thought she was too close to it for comfort. Had she been they, she would have commented on her sister's pale face and her too-bright eyes both that night and the following day, and she would have been worried. She was worried on one level, but they were the adults and she thought they had everything under control. That was what adults did, or so Amelia believed.

There were coal fires in the classrooms and various girls vied for the task of going to fetch the coal from the bunkers behind the school. Unlike many of her classmates, who used any opportunity to escape from schoolwork, Amelia did not aspire to this task in her classroom, and she was pretty sure that Mattie would not want to do it either. Amelia found the coal bucket too heavy, and the shovelling of the coal a filthy business, leaving her hands dirty. Not to mention the inside of her nose! She once had a cold and was sent to collect the coal. For days afterwards she blew coal dust out of her nostrils. She knew that Mattie liked to be clean and, while not particularly caring about her appearance, she would balk at the idea of shovelling coal. However, that week before Christmas saw a change in Mattie's attitude, and on a daily basis she fetched the coal for her class.

Amelia had seen her from her classroom window walking back and forward through the courtyard to the bunkers and she wondered why her sister had such a spring in her step.

Whether it was having access to all that coal that inspired her or whether it was having time to think uninterrupted by class-work and the routine of being schooled, Mattie did use that time to concoct a lethal plan. As term was drawing to a close, and the flight to Malta was rapidly approaching, the fear that Mattie felt about flying was gathering momentum.

The science laboratory was in North House on the ground floor. Above it the dormitories for an entire year stretched the length of the edifice. There too was Amelia's narrow bed and small locker.

As it was the second last day of school, and the following day was for packing and clearing out, there was an overly relaxed atmosphere in the classroom and the girls were working on various projects of their own choosing, with the science mistress reading at the desk at the top of the room.

Mattie, who had little interest in most of her school subjects, had a great interest in science. She enjoyed chemistry and had no problem in remembering formulae, to the despair of her other teachers who were frustrated at her average marks in every subject and her full marks in that one.

A new industrial-sized container of ethanol had been delivered to the laboratory cupboard earlier that morning, but Mattie was unaware of its arrival. The cupboard was situated directly behind the teacher's desk.

While the class was busy, each girl with her own or a shared project, Mattie took a small bottle of ethanol off a shelf and poured a line of it around the entire perimeter of the teacher's desk, and then, completely unnoticed by the others, took a splint and casually lit one end of the trail. Initially the teacher did not notice even as the fire whizzed around her desk, encircling her like one of the condemned in hell, but a scream from one of the girls quickly caught her attention and she leaped to her feet and through the flames.

Some of the girls were laughing so hard they could hardly stand up, but the science mistress shouted at them to get out. There were quite simply too many flammable items in the vicinity, including the large container of ethanol, and she had astutely assessed that a small circle of fire could not easily be contained.

One explosion after another rocked the classroom and, shaken and shocked, the girls stood outside in the freezing cold as flames licked upwards and slowly but very surely demolished North House.

Harriet Entwhistle was sent for and she arrived in a state of mixed fury and serious perspiration. The roads had been icy and she had not enjoyed her unexpected journey to the school with the car skidding twice on black ice.

The girls had been supposed to take the train back two days later, but as a complete dormitory was now demolished, not to mention a laboratory and the study hall, her arrival coincided with that of many other parents. The driveway to the school was jammed with the last fire engine and some fifty cars.

Harriet was immediately escorted to the headmistress's study, where she found herself in the unenviable position of having to listen to a rant about her elder granddaughter.

'The shame of it,' she hissed as Mattie put her bags in the boot of the car. 'The shame.'

Those were the only words she would utter.

Amelia wanted to dissociate herself from what had happened, but was afraid to say a word. Every single item Amelia had brought to the school was gone, and all she had left was the clothing she was wearing, her grandfather's fountain pen, which had been in her gymslip pocket, and her precious notebook, which she invariably carried with her. The long journey home was made in silence, with Mattie and she sitting in the back of the car being thrown from side to side as Grandmother was clearly trying to break the speed records. They did not even stop for tea and scones along the way, which was usually part of the trip on the occasions they had brought or collected Mattie from school in the past.

'Say you're sorry,' Amelia whispered to Mattie at one point as they took a hairpin bend on two wheels.

Mattie looked somewhat triumphant and

hissed 'no' at her. Amelia closed her eyes and prayed for a safe arrival home.

'You will not be flying to Malta,' Grandmother announced. 'And your aunt and uncle are flying home.'

Grandmother stopped the car at the village and she got out without saying a further word to either of them. They sat in silence, waiting until she reappeared carrying some bags of food.

Uncle Jupe collected the others from the airport that night, while the girls and their grandmother sat in the house in Kent in an empty cold silence. Amelia worried about Bruce. He had gone to live in Malta and she was concerned that no one would care for him while Aunt Lucymem was absent.

Uncle Jupe drove up to the house at about ten thirty. Amelia was reading in the drawing room, and Grandmother was staring at the fire in the hearth. Mattie was sitting in Grandfather's armchair and appeared to be dozing. Uncle Jupe's arrival put paid to that.

'If you were one of mine I would take a horse whip to you,' he said to Mattie.

'Don't let that stop you,' Grandmother said from her chair. She pulled herself to her feet with a degree of exhaustion in the movement, and went to greet Lucy, who had just come through the door.

'Darling,' she said.

'Oh, Mother,' Lucy said, embracing her. 'Oh, Mother. Oh, Mattie.'

Amelia felt rather ignored, but equally felt that

that might be the best way to keep it. There was so much fury around her that she did not really want to be noticed, although she wanted Lucy to hug her. She hated what Mattie had done, hated the way it made her feel, the burden of guilt, some sense of responsibility simply because Mattie was her sister.

It was Uncle Rhino who stepped into the awful despair that was apparent in the room, and he hoisted Mattie by the arm out of her chair, and hauled her out the door, virtually lifting her off her feet. He half lifted, half dragged her through the house and they heard the back door being unbolted, opened, and then shut behind them.

'Oh, no,' Aunt Lucymem said, rising to her feet from the chair in which she had just settled.

'Sit down,' Grandmother said to her. 'Just sit.'

'She's right,' Uncle Jupe said. 'This has been a long time coming. And so just let it happen.'

He introduced Thomas to Amelia. Amelia had not even been aware that there was someone else in the room, as she was so swept along by the unfolding events.

Thomas was a tall, thin boy. She took in his straight blond hair, his grey-blue eyes and tanned skin. He came forward hesitantly, and shook her hand.

'I am pleased to meet you,' he said quite formally. He looked at her carefully and she at him. His face was clean-cut and interesting, very defined, and his eyes were kindly.

'Me too,' she said, trying to take in this new half-cousin, and at the same time listening for noises from the back garden. There were none.

'Where are you going to sleep?' she asked him with interest.

'He's going to sleep in here on the sofa,' Grandmother said. 'I hope you'll be comfortable on it, Thomas.'

'It looks very comfortable,' he said politely.

Amelia was distracted between her concern for Mattie and the politeness of Thomas, and her surprise at how agreeable he seemed.

'I better get going,' Uncle Jupe said. 'I've a long drive back home. Anne said you are to come to us on Christmas Day,' he added.

'Are you sure?' Grandmother said.

'Of course I'm sure,' he said to her. Amelia was struck by his concern and sympathy. He came over and put his arms around his aunt. 'It will be all right,' he said to her. And suddenly these turns of event did not evolve just around Amelia and Mattie, but Amelia saw for a moment into Grandmother's life. Her eyes, which had always sparkled, and her energy, which Amelia had never thought about, had always been apparent. But at that moment she was suddenly an elderly lady, there were lines on her face, her neck was thin and wrinkled, and Amelia realised that there were tears on her cheeks.

She rushed over to her, and she too put her arms around her.

'She didn't mean it, Grandmother,' she said, trying to reassure her, although as she said it she knew she was lying.

'The awful thing, Amelia,' Grandmother said to her, 'is that she did mean it. And we both know that.'

234

Uncle Jupe got her back into her chair, postponing his departure, and he went to get her a brandy. Aunt Lucymem was just sitting there on the sofa and Amelia went over and sat beside her. She still hadn't been hugged and she desperately wanted Lucy's attention.

When she sat beside her aunt, Lucy responded saying, 'I'm sorry, darling. This is just so awful,' and then she held her close, and Amelia thought it would be all right.

'Come and sit beside us, Thomas,' Lucy said.

He sat down on a corner of the sofa and every so often his eyes met Amelia's and she wondered what he was thinking.

Grandmother sipped her brandy and then Uncle Rhino reappeared. Amelia could hear Mattie's footsteps on the stairs and then silence from above.

Uncle Rhino was putting his belt back into his trousers and Amelia stared at it in horror. They had never been hit. Ever. No one had ever raised a hand to either of them. Lucymem, watching what he was doing, put her hand to her mouth and swallowed hard.

'I don't think she will do that again,' Rhino said to the room.

Amelia looked at Thomas and he raised his eyebrows at her. She felt that there was an ally in the room and that was nice because until that moment she was not sure where she stood with anyone – whether the family saw her as being involved simply because she had been in school with Mattie, or whether everyone thought that by being Mattie's sister she must condone what had happened.

Rhino was so angry, and his ire seemed to include her, and she did not know how to justify herself, or if she should even try.

'Did you have to?' Aunt Lucymem murmured.

'We discussed this on the plane,' he said. 'And yes, I did.'

'It won't have done her any harm,' Uncle Jupe said. He was still hovering in the doorway. 'And with a bit of luck ... who knows ... maybe it will have saved her from something worse.'

'She could end up in prison for arson,' Grandmother said to Lucy. 'Have you thought of that? This has to be stopped, and I for one am grateful to Reinhold for teaching her a lesson.'

'But...' Lucy said gently, almost feebly. She wrung a handkerchief between her fingers. Amelia had never seen her aunt like that before. She always thought of Lucymem as being determined and confident, but she was now clearly very upset. Amelia wondered about it. Lucy had handled the fire in their home in Ireland with a great deal more strength and resolve than she was handling this. She didn't like seeing Lucy wringing the handkerchief and twisting her fingers, and the drawn look on her face.

'Have you any idea what it was like facing her headmistress, Miss Greenfield?' Grandmother almost spat out the words.

Lucy shook her head.

'I convinced her not to press charges. I don't know how I did it, but I did. They have had to close the school early. They will lose some forty girls because of the lack of space... Don't tell me that Mattie does not deserve all that she just got.'

'Oh dear,' Aunt Lucymem said. There was further twisting of the handkerchief.

Amelia was now feeling really frightened seeing her aunt like that. She simply didn't seem to know what to do or how to react.

'I'll get you and Rhino a drink too,' Uncle Jupe said. 'Then I really will have to be off.'

More brandy was poured and Grandmother suggested to Amelia to bring Thomas out to the kitchen and get something to drink.

He also seemed quite relieved to leave the room.

'Mattie is really very nice,' Amelia said to him. After all, she thought, Mattie was her sister and she did not want Thomas not to like her.

He didn't say anything.

'She didn't want to take the plane to Malta,' she explained. 'She would have done anything to stop going. Setting fire to the school was better than some of the things she might have got up to,' she continued.

'Why didn't she want to fly to Malta?' he asked, showing momentary interest in what she was saying.

'She saw a plane crash when she was just little,' Amelia explained, as she poured them some milk. 'Ever since then she has been very interested in fire. And she is afraid of flying.'

She did not know how she knew that her sister was afraid of flying, but she did. Mattie had not said as much, but that day in school, when they had got the letter confirming the dates for Christmas and Mattie had said she was not getting on a plane, Amelia instinctively knew why. She reasoned that she would have been afraid of going in a plane if she had seen what Mattie had. She tried explaining that to Thomas.

'I'd feel like her if I was her,' she said. 'Only I'm not her. I was busy being born the night of the plane crash and I really want to go on a plane.'

Whether or not this made any sense to Thomas was unclear.

'My uncle says that she is selfish,' he said, taking the glass of milk from her.

'She is really quite nice,' Amelia said defensively. 'And she can be quite good fun,' she added, even though she could not at that moment think of Mattie being much fun at all.

'My uncle says she will grow up and out of this stage. And that he is going to see that that happens quickly so that Lucy doesn't have any more trouble in her life.'

Amelia wasn't sure that she liked him calling her aunt by her first name. After all, she did not call Rhino by his. She had been told to put 'Uncle' before it, but she didn't say anything.

'My uncle says that Lucy shouldn't have to put up with any of this nonsense,' Thomas continued.

Amelia really hoped she personally was not included in that word 'nonsense'. There was something very dismissive and troublesome about it, and she did not want Aunt Lucymem to see her in that light.

'Vulcan was the God of Fire,' Thomas suddenly said to her surprise.

'I know,' Amelia replied. 'He was the Roman god. He came from Hephaestus, the Greek god.

He had a smithy on the island of Hiera – one of the Aeolian islands.'

'Vulcan was one of Jupiter's sons,' Thomas said, eyeing her with interest.

Suddenly they both laughed.

'Uncle Jupiter has a son called Mars,' she said, and they both laughed again. 'You'll meet him on Christmas Day. We're going to their house,' she said, even though she knew that Thomas had already heard that in the drawing room. But she wanted him to think she was in on all the family activities, although at that moment she felt like she knew nothing. She had the feeling she did not even have a school to go back to.

'Does your uncle have a daughter called Venus?' Thomas asked. 'She married Vulcan, the God of Fire. And Mars was one of her lovers.'

They both laughed again.

'No,' she said. 'Ophelia is his daughter.'

'What a pity,' Thomas said with a grin.

This was wonderful. She had not met anyone who knew about mythology like she did.

'Venus is the Roman version of Aphrodite,' Thomas said obligingly.

Amelia nodded knowingly. This was getting better and better.

'I was in a fire,' Thomas said to her. 'A big one. It lasted for days.'

She did not say anything. She wondered what way his mind was going. She knew that she could never really tell what was happening in people's heads unless they said, although sometimes with Mattie she knew if there was another meaning.

'In Malta?' she asked.

239

'No. In Dresden. Where I lived until the fire that destroyed it.'

He lifted up his jumper and shirt and she saw terrible marks on his body. It was as if something had eaten into him and left him with thin puckered pink skin all down one side. She put her hand to her mouth to stop herself from showing her shock. The thinness and the pinkness of it made her want to throw up.

'I know about fire,' he said, readjusting his clothing. 'They fire-bombed Dresden,' he continued. 'And then they dropped phosphorus on it so that it would keep burning.'

'I've a scar,' she said, showing him her hand and the cut from the tin of Spam. It was not in the same league at all, but it was the best she could do, so that he would know that she sympathised.

'Does Mattie have scars?' he asked.

She might have scars, Amelia thought. But they were not ones you could see. That seemed too difficult to explain, so she just shook her head.

'My sister died in the fires in Dresden,' Thomas said.

'My other sister died when the plane crashed,' she said so that he would know she had lost out too. 'Her name was Georgina.'

'My sister's name was Karla,' he said. He seemed about to add something more, but then he stopped and turned away.

When she went to bed, Mattie was buried under the bedclothes and neither said anything as Amelia undressed in the dark and slipped in between the sheets. The bed was cold and it took ages to get warm and to fall asleep. She wondered if Thomas knew about Aeolus, and she thought about the conversations they would have the following day, all about the Greek and Roman gods, and Odysseus and his journey to Ithaca. And then she fell asleep.

Moral excellence comes about as a result of habit. We become just by doing just acts, temperate by doing temperate acts, brave by doing brave acts.

Aristotle

CHAPTER TEN

The following morning Mattie woke up in surprisingly good spirits.

Amelia eyed her cautiously from the next bed.

'No school,' Mattie said gleefully. 'And no flight to Malta.'

These might have been joyous thoughts for Mattie, but they were not for Amelia. School hadn't been so bad, she thought, and she was starting to get used to it. And the thought of Malta was what had kept her going all term. Wisely she said nothing. Mattie made no reference to the previous evening, so neither did Amelia. If Mattie was in any kind of physical pain, it was not apparent. Amelia would have liked to tell her about Thomas knowing about mythology, but she knew her sister would not be impressed.

They went downstairs together, and at the kitchen door Mattie suddenly squeezed her hand. Amelia did not know why. She did not know if it was to give her reassurance or to comfort herself. But she squeezed Mattie's hand back hopefully and they went in together. They were all seated around the long table – Grandmother, Lucy,

242

Rhino and Thomas.

'Good morning,' Grandmother addressed them both.

'Good morning, Grandmother,' they replied in unison. Good start, Amelia thought, as she turned to greet the others, going over to give Aunt Lucymem a hug and a kiss.

Rhino was holding Lucy's hand, so Amelia only got half a hug, but she kept her arms wrapped around her just so that Rhino would know Aunt Lucymem was hers too.

'Will you have toast?' Lucy asked, getting up to give Mattie a hug too.

'Yes, please,' they both said. Amelia could feel that they were both being careful, not sure what was going to happen.

'They're old enough to get it themselves,' Rhino said.

'I quite like doing it for them,' Aunt Lucymem replied.

'Time to stop spoiling them,' he said.

So much for a great start to the day, Amelia thought. Lucy stood hesitantly for a moment until Rhino gestured to her chair, and she sat back down again. Mattie went over to the bread board and picked up the bread knife.

'How many slices?' she asked, wielding the knife in quite a threatening way.

'Um, two,' Amelia said, eyeing the serrated blade.

'Two it is,' she said, starting to saw at the bread. It reminded Amelia of cutting the bread when Grandfather was out sleeping in the garden, and then that reminded her that he hadn't been sleeping at all. And all of a sudden she started to cry. Mattie was cutting the bread very evenly, not like the clumps Amelia had made of it over those summer days. She stood there watching her, keeping her back to everyone so that they wouldn't know she was crying. She wished Grandfather were there. He used to cut the bread in the mornings. And he always made a fuss of them when they came down. She thought how she had taken so much for granted and the tears rolled down her cheeks. If Grandfather were there it would not matter that Rhino stopped Lucy from fussing over them.

'What's wrong?' Mattie asked without looking up from what she was doing. Amelia tried to keep her voice on an even keel when she replied that she was cold.

'You need to put more clothes on then,' Rhino said.

She did not say anything. What could she say? She had on a vest, a blouse and two jumpers.

'The house hasn't warmed up,' Grandmother said. 'I'd been staying in London since I came home from Malta, which is why it is so cold. It always takes time to heat in winter. And that,' she added, 'is one of the loveliest things about Malta – the warmth. It gets in to your bones, a bit like damp does, but it has the opposite effect.'

Thomas moved his chair up to make room for Amelia, and she wiped her eyes and nose on her sleeve and tried to pretend there was nothing wrong.

'How is Bruce?' she asked Thomas, hoping that no one had noticed her tears, but her voice was a

244

bit wobbly.

'What's wrong?' Aunt Lucymem asked her now, concern in her voice.

'I miss Bruce,' she said.

And she did. She missed Bruce and Grandfather, and she missed the way things used to be. It all seemed so different and empty.

'Bruce is well,' Thomas said comfortingly. 'He loves the weather in Malta. Just like your grandmother,' he added.

'The house will be warm by lunchtime,' Grandmother said, passing a handkerchief from her pocket.

Somehow the tears were ignored, and Rhino and Lucy chatted during breakfast about the weather and Christmas Day and plans that had to be made. Grandmother stared vacantly into the garden and Thomas whispered to Amelia that Bruce was being cared for by a Cyclops.

Amelia giggled. She wanted to ask him for more details when Rhino said, 'What did you say?'

'I was just telling Mealie that Bruce should have been christened Cerberus,' Thomas replied evenly.

Mealie? Mealie! Her mind did a somersault. It was the most endearing thing she had ever been called, or so she thought.

'Mealie?' Rhino said. 'The girl's name is Amelia.' His voice was cold. He didn't like her, she suddenly realised. She didn't care.

'I asked him to call me Mealie,' she lied. 'Cerberus was the three-headed dog which guarded Hades,' she explained in case anyone was

245

interested, and also because she wanted to show off in front of Thomas.

'He sounds a bit of a monster,' Mattie said. But she didn't say it unkindly. She winked at Amelia, who immediately knew that Mattie was referring indirectly to Rhino. She found she was smiling.

'Bruce likes music,' Thomas said. 'So did Cerberus – it was the one thing that could distract him.'

Amelia did not know that Bruce liked music. That pleased her. She imagined him lying in the sun listening to flutes and lyres while Aeolus let a soft wind loose.

She ate her toast in silence. The butter was down the table beside Rhino and she was too afraid to ask him to pass it to her. He did not seem to notice that other people, especially children, might need something.

Everything seemed to be an effort over the next few days.

'I don't think we're having a Christmas tree,' Amelia said to Mattie.

'Of course we are,' Mattie replied. 'We always do.'

But Amelia felt that the sense of crime and punishment that had been there that first evening had somehow not evaporated.

'Maybe,' Mattie said thoughtfully, 'you ought to be the one to ask about it.'

They exchanged glances, and while neither commented further, Amelia knew that Mattie was, for once, being sensible.

'Grandmother,' she said, knocking on her

grandmother's bedroom door.

'Come in, darling.'

'I was wondering when we're getting the tree,' she asked.

'I hadn't thought of it,' Grandmother said. 'I'll organise it when I come downstairs. Reinhold might take you and Thomas to buy one. I think we ought to keep Mattie out of this particular equation.'

Rhino suggested they did not get it until Christmas Eve.

'Why would we leave it until Christmas Eve?' Mattie asked him in surprise.

'That's what we usually do,' Rhino said coldly.

Mattie, who had been keeping well clear of Rhino, opened her mouth to speak again, but it was Grandmother who got in first.

'When in Rome,' she said, 'it's best to do what the Romans do.'

Amelia thought it was a great expression and she wrote it down in her notebook. The only story she had written in it was the one she had made up after Grandfather died. It was nice to get the book out again and to have something to write in it and to use Grandfather's pen. At school she had kept them close for comfort, even though she could think of nothing to write.

On Christmas Day they all piled into the car and drove to the Jupes. Their house was very grand, nearly as large as the Cholmondesley one in Ireland, but squarer, not with wings and outhouses. Amelia loved their front drive, though – it too reminded her of Ireland with its sweeping

247

driveway around a large circle of grass. But the Jupes had a fountain.

It was a cupid fountain, with the naked cherub standing staring downwards, his wings uplifted on his shoulders. Thomas kept staring at the putto when they got out of the car.

'It's beautiful,' he said when he was asked what was interesting him so much. His voice was sad. 'All our sculptures got eaten,' he said.

'Eaten?' Grandmother asked. She looked at him in amazement. 'How do you mean, *eaten?*'

'The fire ate into them,' he said.

'The bombing of Dresden destroyed most of the art,' Rhino said. He was in better and more expansive form. It had taken him a few days to get over the whole Mattie affair.

Amelia had not known that people could be like that. Until then, if there had been any arguments in their lives, they had been sorted out fairly promptly, and then they had moved on. Except, of course, problems with Mattie. But then Mattie carried everything for ever, Amelia thought. But Rhino wasn't like Mattie either. He had scowled a lot at both girls over those days, and not participated in the evening games of cards, or helped decorate the tree.

'Sculptures got eaten away by the phosphorous,' he explained.

A bit like Thomas's body, Amelia thought. How awful. She wondered what the sculptures looked like.

Uncle Jupe obligingly turned the fountain up to its full force and they stood and admired it as water poured from the cupid's mouth and

248

spouted into the stone basin.

'It's lovely,' Thomas said politely. 'Thank you for turning it up.'

Then they went in and Mars and Ophelia appeared.

What was it about human beings, Amelia wondered. Was it that they were so close to their ancestors that they still behaved like them but with a modicum of social manners attached? She had seen Bruce sniffing other dogs' bottoms with extreme interest. And in the zoo she had seen penguins all standing together just looking at nothing, and chimpanzees sitting down for a good session of flea hunting on each other's bodies. She was reminded of that when the five children went into Mars and Ophelia's playroom. They watched each other and there were long silences as if they were trying to incorporate a new member into their ranks. Mattie threw herself in a chair and stared out the window. They did not have the adeptness of adults for small talk, so there was a certain amount of shuffling and then asking each other what they had been given as Christmas presents, before Amelia went over to the bookcase for a quick browse. Neither Mars nor Ophelia seemed particularly at ease, and Thomas just stood there until Amelia suggested to him that he looked at the great selection of books that were on the shelves.

Slowly the barriers came down and Mars said to Mattie, 'That was some stunt you pulled. I believe you burned down a complete building that was dating from the eighteenth century.'

Mattie grinned. It was the first real smile Amelia had seen her give since the fire.

'I'd say the Germans tried to do that for years,' Mars said. 'And you managed in a single morning.'

Mattie stood there grinning.

Ophelia looked at Amelia. And she at her.

Mars said, 'Oh, sorry, Thomas. I didn't mean that you had been trying to burn down our historic buildings. You as a German, I mean.'

Thomas suddenly laughed. 'No, I don't have the same proficiency in that regard as our cousin Mattie.'

His vocabulary was wonderful. Amelia loved him. She couldn't take her eyes off him. His blond hair looked so soft, and his eyes were like pools of blue and grey depths in his smooth tanned face. She thought of the terrible burns under his clothing and now they did not shock her or sicken her. Instead she wondered about touching them, and maybe healing them...

'It was magical,' Mattie said. 'The fire went in circles, round and round, before it took off.'

'What did you use?' Mars asked.

'Skill,' Mattie said.

Amelia felt that they were all suddenly very close, and she also loved the fact that they were now all cousins.

'Are we cousins?' Ophelia asked Thomas when Amelia said they were now all related.

'I think we must be. After all, my uncle is married to your aunt.'

'She's not my aunt,' Ophelia said. 'Lucy is my cousin removed by a generation. Her mother is our grand-aunt.'

Oh, the precision; how the Jupes liked things to be clearly spelled out, Amelia thought.

'I'm sure that makes us some sort of cousin,' Thomas said. 'I don't have very many...'

'How many do you have?' Ophelia asked him.

'Well, not many at all,' he admitted. 'In fact just Mattie and Mealie. I rather hoped that my family circle was expanding.'

'Oh, you can be our cousin too if you like,' Ophelia obligingly said to him. 'We don't mind, do we, Mars?'

Mars agreed that he didn't mind, and they got out the Monopoly board. Amelia groaned internally. The Jupes were addicted to Monopoly. It was in their genes. They could play it for days with a fierce determination and dedication. Uncle Jupe owned property all over London, and was always on the look out for more. Her cousins were just practising by playing the game.

Regardless, it certainly broke the ice. Amelia participated in the hope that she would lose all her money immediately and be eliminated so she could go and look at Ophelia's books, but as luck would have it she got off to too good a start and the opposite happened.

Thomas, though, was very impressed with her prowess, so that was a consolation. The game was new to him, and once she realised that she was not going to be eliminated in the first hour, she didn't want him to be eradicated either. How she hated that game. She hated the tedium. And the difficulty in trying to keep someone else in it when they were determined to throw bad

251

numbers on the dice and spend their time in gaol.

They were called for Christmas dinner mid-afternoon. By this stage, Ophelia had been eliminated and was playing with her presents. Amelia was now a multimillionaire, and the rest of them were battling it out, each wanting to be the last in there with her.

Dinner was a grand affair in their dining room – a room Amelia loved, with its large mahogany table and portraits on the walls.

'We have family portraits too,' she said quietly to Thomas after they sat down. 'They're in our house in Ireland and they will be there for us when we grow up. The people who bought them – they were Germans too – they said they would keep them for us.'

'That's very nice,' Thomas said. 'When did you live there?'

'Long ago,' Amelia said.

It seemed years and years since they had been there. She wondered what Sean was doing and if he ever thought of them, and if the sea, with its shades of grey and green, still lapped up and down the sand, throwing up shells and pebbles, seaweed and driftwood. For a moment she thought she could smell the brine.

Thomas opened his mouth to speak, and then thought better of it. She was sure he was going to say that he too had once had family portraits but that they were all gone now, lost in the war. So much was lost in the war, she thought. Little people like them ended up as pawns in someone else's game, that's what Grandfather had said.

Over dinner it transpired that Uncle Jupe had pulled every string imaginable and had managed, over the previous couple of days, to get Mattie and Amelia into Ophelia's school. There went her hopes of going to live in Malta with Lucymem. And once again she found herself fighting against tears as she tried to swallow her turkey and her horrible Brussels sprouts. And the gravy didn't taste like Lucymem's or grandmother's.

Rhino seemed better with other adults around, and he was quite interesting talking about their life in Malta, his construction company and the grapes on the vines outside the farmhouse, plans he had for beehives and possibilities of a honey market. Amelia liked listening to this and she cheered up considerably because Lucymem seemed in better form too and she looked so pretty and happy when she laughed. The adults drank loads of wine and got very jolly and it was a better distraction than that awful game of Monopoly that she was afraid was going to call them back as soon as the meal was over.

Then Rhino spoke of the destruction that had taken place in Malta and of the spirit of the people in rebuilding their country. Mattie put her knife and fork down, and watched him through her eyelashes, keeping her head slightly lowered.

'They were starving,' he said, 'and yet they fought back. They held on against all probability. That kind of courage is unique.'

'I think I read somewhere,' Uncle Jupe said, 'that Malta was the single most bombed place in the war.'

'You're right,' Rhino said.

'Is that where you were bombing?' Mattie asked him. Her voice was totally polite, but the slight shift of her eyebrows put Amelia on edge. She knew that Mattie was trying to rile him.

'I don't like to talk about the war,' Rhino said. 'Like many, I did my duty.'

'But don't you have regrets?' Mattie asked. 'I'm sure I'd have regrets if I bombed somewhere and knew that people died because of me.'

'They didn't die because of any one person,' Lucy said to her. 'People did their duty as it was perceived at the time. Rhino did his.'

Her tone said that that was the end of the conversation.

Amelia thought how strange it was that these people, only six years earlier, had been fighting against each other, and here they were drinking to the rebuilding of cities and talking about the effects of the war. There was something about it that did not make sense. They were so polite and decent while sitting around the dining-room table, and yet only a few years before they were firing guns at each other, and bombing each other's cities. They killed children, obliterated them on mountainsides and in fires of phosphorous; they burned and starved and murdered. Only it wasn't murder because it was war. And now they sat and drank wine together. She wondered if that was what happened after all wars. Did it not make the war pointless if they were all friends again later? She remembered that when Odysseus finally returned to Ithaca he had killed those who had taken over his home. Was that the right thing to do? What made it right then, and yet it would not be right now? It was the kind of thing Grandfather would have explained and she wished she had thought of it to ask him while she had the opportunity.

When dinner was over they drank to a new future. Amelia was not sure, though, whether they were now referring to after the war, or to Mattie's and her new start in a different school.

'I was thinking,' Mattie said evenly, eyeing her plate but clearly addressing Rhino, and clearly unable to let the earlier observations pass, 'that if I am supposed to feel guilty about burning down the school lab, it must be really very difficult ... there must be so much guilt, I mean ... if you know that you actually destroyed people's homes and their lives...'

'If you are trying to compare what you did last week with my life during the war,' Rhino said to her, 'I think you haven't learned any lesson at all.'

'Oh, she has learned a lesson, haven't you, Mattie?' Lucy interrupted quickly. 'You see, Mattie, it is not the same thing at all.'

'And it wasn't just a lab you burned down,' Grandmother said. 'It was a whole building.'

'Yes, I know,' Mattie said. 'And of course I'm devastated about that.' Her voice said otherwise. 'And of course it was only meant as a prank – it just got out of hand. What I meant was, seeing that I am eaten up with guilt, I really wondered what it must be like to know that you actually killed people.' It was difficult to read irony, or indeed anything, into her voice, which seemed even and sincere, but Amelia knew she was pushing things very far.

'It's not a very good feeling at all,' Rhino said to her, ignoring whatever she might have been getting at. 'But the war is over. What you see as the bad side – well, we lost. And we paid a price too.'

'Let's leave it at that,' Lucy said. 'Please.'

Her voice was begging for a change of conversation and Amelia suddenly said, 'War is evil.'

'Yes, that's what my father – your grandfather – said. It's what he brought me up to believe. He said we were all the losers,' Lucy replied.

Thomas, sitting beside Amelia, suddenly touched her knee with his. It might have been accidental but she was sure it was in support and that he understood that she was afraid of what Mattie might bring up next.

But Mattie finally let the topic go.

After Christmas, there was yet another farewell for Mattie and Amelia when Lucy, Rhino and Thomas returned to Malta, and shortly afterwards so did Harriet, who had finally made the decision to buy the house in the heart of Sliema, the house she had told Amelia about in her letter the previous term.

'It is the nicest little house, terraced but I like the security of that,' Grandmother told the girls. 'On a narrow street, with a single step leading from the pavement to the front door.'

'How many bedrooms?' Amelia asked.

'Enough for all of us.'

'But we'll stay with Lucymem?' Amelia asked.

'Of course you will. But then you'll come and visit me, and there will be a bed for each of you. It's not as big as what we're used to,' Grandmother said. 'But I like it. It's Maltese and it's going to be my home. It has a wonderful courtyard in the back, interconnecting rooms that wind through the house, a stone staircase to the upper floor. It's just perfect. I find it quite exotic. Not a bit like Eden House in Kashmir, or this home here. Equally lovely, but in a different way.'

Amelia thought that Grandmother sounded happier and more hopeful. But at the same time she did not like both Lucy and her being abroad at the same time. It made her feel very alone and frightened.

It was Uncle Jupe who took them with Ophelia to their new school.

Before they left, Mattie was given a long lecture to do with matches, fire in general, the family name and what would happen to her if anything untoward – however accidental – should happen.

Amelia was not sure if it was safe to try to settle in the new school or not. She wasn't sure if Mattie had further plans, and it seemed a bit of an effort to try to make friends with girls whom she might shortly have to leave. She had to face new girls, a new dormitory, new teachers, and this time it was not even at the start of the school year, and everyone else had friends already.

Ophelia had been told to keep an eye out for her, but she ignored her completely and never so much as said hello. Instead she got on with her own life and her own long-established friends in school and left Amelia to her own devices. And it was Mattie who very occasionally asked her in a rather grown-up voice if she was settling in all right and if she was warm enough at night.

The dormitory seemed colder than the one in her previous school, and Amelia was never warm enough but she could not say it. She bore it in silence and with an acute sense of loneliness. There was no way out of the situation, and because Mattie appeared to be making an effort Amelia reassured her on all fronts, not realising that Lucymem was being told how happy she was and how at home she felt, and that this was the perfect school for her.

And so they stayed in that school where she wore two pairs of socks in bed at night and kept herself very much to herself. She sensed that Mattie had decided that if they appeared settled, there would be less chance of having to take a plane and fly to Malta. She also thought that maybe Mattie was afraid of further contact with Rhino. Mattie had never referred to that night when he had taken her out to the back garden. But as the winter months progressed Amelia hoped that they might be rescued when term ended. The post seemed even worse than before and Lucy's letters did not tell her anything, other than that there were plans for Easter. She hoped and hoped those plans included a trip to Malta.

Friendship is a single soul dwelling in two bodies…
Aristotle

CHAPTER ELEVEN

With the stress of her father's death and the journeys back and forwards to Malta, it was after Christmas before Lucy discovered she was pregnant. Her initial excitement at finally being with Rhino, and being married to him, at moving into his home, of learning to accommodate a man in her life, had carried her along. Things suddenly seemed to be happening in the right order at the right time, and settling somewhere peaceful, on the edge of a rural village on the south side of the island, offered her hope and comfort.

But despite Rhino's apparent efforts at helping her to settle, she felt an outsider. He had his friends, in particular Friedrich, but their friendship was such that she sometimes felt an outsider. She felt there was something slightly sinister about Friedrich and she had no idea what he really thought of her. He was charm itself, always solicitous, but also demanding of Rhino's time, and she often found that when she had cleared away the plates after dinner and washed the dishes, it was difficult to go and join them in the courtyard. Their relationship sometimes seemed so exclusive and she felt like an intruder coming out to join them. They always switched from German to English on her return, Friedrich always standing to pull out her chair, Rhino suggesting he would make the coffee and leaving her and Friedrich to talk. But she could never break through the barriers of politeness with Friedrich. He never suggested that she call him Fritz, as Rhino addressed him, and that in itself made her feel removed. He looked at her with his single eye and she felt as if he were looking through her, as if her existence as a human being and as Rhino's wife did not register.

Rhino had another friend, Maria Borg Cardona. It was ever unclear if her friendship was really with Rhino or with Friedrich, but either way she spent a lot of time with them. She was younger than Lucy, and had been widowed in the war. She lived in a small house in the next village with her son, Lucas. Petite and dark, Maria was a mixture of toughness and gentleness, and Lucy sometimes wondered if Maria and Rhino had been involved in some way before she appeared on the island. She was very pretty and she hung on the men's words. And while Friedrich showed dismissiveness or disdain towards Lucy, he was very solicitous of Maria. Maria spent a lot of time in the farmhouse and helped out in a rather odd way, almost as if she were married to Rhino. Like Friedrich, she had a key to the farmhouse, and dropped in most days, doing some of the household chores, or sitting in the courtyard with Friedrich while Rhino was at work.

Lucy found it very disconcerting. At first she assumed that Maria was the daily help, and she said nothing, even though she found it hard to understand what precisely Maria's role was, as the woman fluctuated between helping out and sitting drinking coffee.

'You know, Rhino,' Lucy said on one of the early days in the first week of their marriage, when Maria had stayed on late, as if waiting for Rhino to return from work, 'we really don't need Maria to come in every day, and certainly not for as long.'

'Don't we?' he said, unbuttoning his shirt as he started up the stairs and going to the bathroom to wash. 'Well, I think she enjoys coming by.'

'How many hours do you pay her for?' Lucy asked.

Rhino looked at her in surprise. 'I don't pay Maria. She's a friend.'

'But she comes and cleans,' Lucy said, puzzled.

'Oh, I know. It's one of those odd situations that evolved,' Rhino said vaguely.

'But why would she come here most days and do the housework? And what does she live on?'

'Friedrich looks after her,' he said after a moment's pause.

'What? Friedrich? Why? Why on earth would Friedrich look after her?' If Lucy was puzzled before, she was really bewildered now.

Rhino looked at her thoughtfully. 'Perhaps Friedrich should be the one to tell you,' he said slowly.

'Please, you tell me.'

But Rhino would not be drawn. 'Just leave it for now,' he said.

It bothered Lucy. Rhino mostly came home in

261

the middle of the day and stayed for a siesta, returning to work at about four in the afternoon. Maria usually left the house at about two o'clock, but Lucy had noticed that on the days that Rhino did not come home until later, Maria was inclined to stay on. Between Friedrich and Maria, Lucy was never quite sure whom, if anyone, she was going to find in the house when she came in. Both had keys, and both just let themselves in and out as they pleased. She did not dislike either of them, although she knew that Thomas did not particularly like Friedrich. It was more that she did not quite understand what was going on and what the relationships were. That she let this pattern of behaviour continue in the early days was due to her attempt to adapt to Rhino's way of life and not wanting to disturb his routine while she felt her way into married life.

She would have liked to ask Friedrich about Maria Borg Cardona but had no idea how to broach anything so personal with him.

Since their return after Christmas, Lucy was feeling more and more tired, and had taken to coming down later in the mornings, but when she did she now always found Friedrich there, drinking coffee in the kitchen as if it were his own home, with Bruce sitting beside him on the stone floor, his sad eyes gazing up hopefully.

Coming downstairs some ten days after their return, Lucy hesitated at the door to the kitchen, suddenly feeling that it was not her home at all. She had a strong sense of disorientation. She could hear Maria outside on the flagstones, presumably hanging up their laundry, and she knew that when she went around the kitchen door, she would see Friedrich there with Bruce and she found herself totally unnerved. She had been brought up with servants around the place and had no problem in dealing with them in any way at all, but this was different. Friedrich was no servant, and Maria did not fall into that category either.

A wave of nausea washed through her, and she reached out to hold on to the doorjamb. At that moment Maria opened the back door and a gust of wind moved through the house into the dining room, and the kitchen door slammed shut on Lucy's fingers. The nausea that was rising in her was suddenly replaced by sheer white pain. She thought she might have screamed but was not sure, and then she fainted. When she came around, it was Friedrich holding her, lifting her in his arms and carrying her out to his car. He helped her on to the back seat with Maria hovering gently beside him.

'Fetch Rhino,' he said to Maria. 'Tell him he will find us at the hospital.'

On the back seat of the car, Lucy tried not to think about the pain in her fingers or the terrible sickness that she felt. It made her think of Amelia and her days alone in the garden with her hand so badly cut and wrapped in a dirty tea towel. And the memory of that made her want to cry. The pain in her hand was excruciating, and she felt she might black out again. She wondered where exactly her mother was. She knew that Harriet was closing up the house in Kent and preparing for the journey to Malta, but she desperately wanted her here with her now.

In the hospital, she was quickly seen to, and it was Friedrich who went with her to have her hand X-rayed, and Friedrich who held her other hand as the bones were reset and put in plaster. And sometime later, when the nausea started again, it was Friedrich who was with her when she was told she was pregnant.

She lay on the bed looking at the doctor in complete surprise.

'About four months,' she was told.

'I had no idea,' she said.

'This will explain the various symptoms you have been experiencing,' Friedrich said to her.

She looked at him in surprise. 'What do you mean?'

'Rhino told me about your tiredness and your loss of appetite,' he said to her.

He appeared slightly agitated, pacing the room and then coming and stopping by the bed and looking at her. She could not work out if he was looking at her with concern, or with some other expression on his face.

She was completely taken aback at the fact that Rhino had discussed her. He had said nothing to her that implied he had even noticed that she was not feeling completely well.

When Rhino eventually arrived at the hospital, it was Friedrich who told him Lucy was pregnant as soon as he came into the cubicle where she was resting. Rhino looked from one to the other and then came over to her, sitting on the chair by her bed and holding her hand.

'Is this true, my little Lucymem?' he asked.

She nodded.

'Oh, this is wonderful,' he said. '*Mein Gott*, but this is great news,' he shouted in excitement.

'Gently, now,' the nurse said. 'Your wife has had an accident, you know.'

He was contrite, leaning down to kiss her forehead, and then to put his hand on her stomach.

'It's just a baby,' Friedrich said from behind him. His voice was slightly teasing, but Lucy was not sure what was behind it.

She came home from hospital and found that she was really dependent on both Maria and Friedrich. Everything was an effort with her hand in plaster, and now that she knew why she was so tired, she did not know if that made it better or worse.

When Maria was not there, Friedrich was. No matter how Lucy tried to make herself appear in control, it made no difference; both were so firmly wedged into their house, and Lucy, who had always been confident in her own abilities, found more and more that she could not handle the situation.

'Can I make you coffee?' Friedrich asked her. They had been waiting for Rhino to appear for lunch, but had eventually given up, and had sat down for their meal. Lucy kept wondering at what point it had happened that Friedrich had just become part of the family. He had his meals with them. No invitation was ever proffered. He simply appeared as if expected, and he was just accepted. They had had lunch together and there was still no sign of Rhino.

Thomas was in school, and was not due back until later in the afternoon.

'Coffee?' asked Friedrich again.

'I'll get it,' Lucy said, trying to assert herself as mistress of her own home.

'Nonsense,' Friedrich replied. 'We are a great pair. Me with my one eye and you with only one useful hand at the moment, and I think I'm as comfortable in your kitchen as I am in my own. If not more so.'

And that said it all, she thought. He was just very comfortable in her and Rhino's house. There was no real affection between him and her, and yet he was always there. He knew her every move, he talked to Rhino and, as she now knew, they talked about her. He was solicitous of her, her hand and her pregnancy, and yet she did not feel he liked her. It made no sense for him to be there all day. There was the added frustration that Rhino talked to Friedrich about her, and yet would not tell her whatever it was about Friedrich that she wanted to know. She thought repeatedly of broaching the subject with him, but he was so distant and formal with her that she had no idea how to break through the barrier. Sometimes she felt he was simply watching her and waiting, silently. Once when she had gone upstairs for an afternoon sleep and Rhino, who had been home, had gone back to work, leaving her asleep in their bedroom, she woke to find Friedrich standing in the doorway watching her.

'What is it?' she asked in consternation.

'I was just checking you are all right,' he replied.

But she had the feeling he had been there for a while, just standing staring. And it unnerved her.

Lucy found pregnancy much as Hilary, her sister, had done – a tiresome procedure that exhausted her both mentally and physically. With this tedium, came a slight irritability.

'I can understand Maria having had a key before we were married ... at least I think I can. I think she came in to help you, but there is no need now,' Lucy said one evening over dinner to Rhino. It was one of those rare evenings when Friedrich was absent. 'And also I really don't see why Friedrich needs a key to our home.'

'It's useful that they can get in and out while we are away,' he said.

'But we're here now,' Lucy said to him. 'Shouldn't they give their keys back now that we are at home?'

'Oh, I don't have a problem with them having keys,' Rhino said. 'They've always had them. Think of the day you caught your hand in the door – it was as well Fritz was here. Maria too. She was able to come and fetch me. Also, if we go away, like we did before, it will be reassuring knowing that Bruce will be properly looked after.'

Thomas, listening to this, said nothing, but Lucy felt that he had cast a sort of comforting glance at her. She knew that he did not like Friedrich any more than she did. She felt him withdrawing whenever the other man was around

267

– preferring his own company or taking Bruce for a walk.

The days went slowly, reassurance over the girls coming through their letters – they were happy and safe and seemed to be well settled in school, but Lucy worried about them, each in a different way. She had a lot of time on her hands, too much in fact, because between Maria and Friedrich there was nothing she was doing for herself. She passed much of this time in thought. She missed the girls, especially Amelia. She missed her proximity, her affection, her attention, her neediness, always so politely hidden, but always there. She worried about her, and in her heart she feared that boarding school had not been the right place to send her. It was different with Mattie. There had been almost a sense of relief when Mattie had settled in her first school. Granted, that relief had eventually blown up – quite literally – but there had been a period when Mattie out of sight made things a lot easier, and gave Amelia a chance to grow in her own right. Lucy knew, though, that to have brought Amelia to Malta with them might have alienated Mattie even more, and she hoped that the two girls being in school together would offer them both comfort.

Lucy did not quite understand Rhino's feelings towards the girls. He was entitled to be furious with Mattie – indeed it was a normal reaction, and he was supportive of Lucy during that period. But when Mattie had been punished, Lucy felt that he should have taken her back into the fold in some way. Quite what she meant by that, she was unsure, but she felt that his coldness afterwards did nothing to alleviate the tension in the house. Also he was unfairly cold towards Amelia who had, after all, done absolutely nothing.

It made her query his love for her. It was not that she doubted it, but it was not quite the way she expected. She had embraced Thomas because he was Rhino's adopted son. She would have liked him anyway, because Thomas was an endearing boy, but the feelings she had for him were to do with his belonging to Rhino. And yet Rhino could not do that for her girls.

Added to that, he had no understanding of her feelings about Friedrich's almost permanent presence, as well as Maria hanging around the place, hoping just to see him. It made her uneasy but she was unable to confront him again.

She was also very isolated. She had had few friends in England, but the family life had totally preoccupied her. Now there was no one other than Rhino, Thomas and her mother. And at that point she hardly included her mother in the equation because Harriet's visit to the island had been short, and she had not as yet returned.

Briefly she thought of Hilarymem and wondered how she had settled into her country home in Ireland. She recalled asking Hilary if she were afraid of her new life after she got married, but Hilary's confidence, learned from their mother, had been supreme. Hilary would survive wherever she was, of that she was sure, and her reaction to Lucy's question had reassured Lucy.

But now she was feeling lost.

It was not that she thought that she and Rhino were putting up a front, it was more that their marriage didn't cohere the way she would have liked, the way she assumed marriage was. Her mother had once been in the same situation, she supposed. Harriet had gone as a young woman to India with a husband she hardly knew and yet their marriage had been solid – a solidity that had led Lucy to believe that that was the meaning of marriage. And even in those later days, after the war, when her father had been withdrawn and more aloof than when they were children, her mother had appeared to take his behaviour on board. She had accommodated him all the way.

But now it seemed to Lucy that her father had accommodated her mother too. There were things that he had done to make her mother's life easier. He had encouraged her in his own way. He had never appeared embarrassed at some of her mother's more extreme announcements, even when she, Lucy, was wilting with mortification. He had always encouraged her mother's activities, embraced her friends, relied on her support and given support back. Presumably her mother too had once felt friendless in a foreign place. And yet she appeared to have the ability to rise above a situation.

Harriet Entwhistle finally arrived in Malta, Friedrich having come with Lucy to the airport to collect her at Rhino's request.

'Well, you can't drive with that hand,' Rhino said when Lucy objected. 'And quite honestly, I can't afford to take the time off.'

Lucy knew she was being unreasonable but she did not want to have Friedrich driving her. When they arrived at the airport, he got out and came round the car to open her door. Very politely she suggested that he stay in the car while she went inside.

'Lucy,' he said very evenly in his clipped tones, taking her by her arm and helping her out, 'Rhino would not forgive me if I was not there to greet your mother and to help her with her bags.' He looked at her with his one eye and she knew that he was weighing up the situation.

She felt he could see through her small effort at rebelliousness, and knew that he had outwitted her. They walked in silence into the airport.

'You are pale for a girl in the sun,' Harriet said, when she came through customs, hugged Lucy and then stepped back from her to look at her carefully.

'Oh, Mother, I have such news for you,' Lucy said, trying to steer Harriet away from Friedrich. She wanted to be the one to tell her mother of the expected baby, and she did not trust Friedrich not to say it as he had to Rhino in the hospital. 'Excuse us, please,' she said to him.

He hesitated.

Lucy was aware of Harriet carefully watching and listening, and she tried saying firmly, 'Do go ahead to the car, Friedrich. My mother and I will join you in a moment.'

'Of course,' Friedrich said. He smiled politely at them both and took Harriet's cases. The rest of her possessions that she was bringing out from England had been packed and shipped, and were

271

somewhere in the Mediterranean on their way to join her.

'Now, darling,' Harriet said to her, as they watched Friedrich's upright gait disappearing towards the doors, 'tell me your news first and then tell me what that was about.'

Harriet rejoiced at Lucy's pregnancy. She hugged her daughter and there were tears in her eyes as she said, 'How perfect. How absolutely perfect.'

Instead of staying with Rhino and Lucy, she insisted on staying in the Phoenicia Hotel to which she had become particularly partial, while she waited for the paperwork on her house in Sliema to be sorted.

It had surprised Lucy that her mother wanted to move to Malta. But now she was pleased. One of life's little ironies, she thought. There had been a time when the last thing she would have wanted was her mother on the same continent as her, let alone the same island. Now, her mother's presence, even though it was some five miles away, was something she could look forward to in this period of loneliness. With her customary zeal and organisation, Harriet had the deeds signed and transferred in a matter of days, and by the end of the week was ensconced in her new home.

To escape the daily invasion of Maria and Friedrich, Lucy took to driving Thomas to school and then going to visit her mother. She was tentative at first on these visits, unsure in some sense of how to proceed. Her mother was busy – busy in a way that she, Lucy, was not. Her mother had already made friends with other people on her street. She had started both a mah jong morning and a bridge afternoon. She had already been invited to dinner both in another English woman's home, and by a Maltese man who appeared devoted to her. Lucy watched in amazement as this progressed, and in return her mother watched her with concern.

'I think you should tell me what is wrong,' her mother said to her one morning after Thomas had been dropped to school and Lucy had arrived looking pale and tired.

'I don't know,' Lucy said. 'I don't know.'

She didn't know where to begin, or how to explain the incredible feeling of not belonging. It was made the more difficult because she had never had a close relationship with her mother. They had always seemed somehow remote from each other, Lucy growing up apart and being independent from an early age. And even though their lives had been so closely interlinked since her parents' return from India, she had still retained her independence, partially to do with the house in London, and partly because of her role as parent to Mattie and Amelia. But since leaving England she had become more and more unsure of her own place and her own abilities, and after the return to Malta in January, these feelings were reinforced to an extent that was beyond endurance.

'There is nothing I am unable to listen to,' Harriet said. 'Just tell me. Is Rhino kind to you?'

'Yes,' Lucy said. 'He is. I think he is a kind man.'

'Does he love you?'

'Yes.'

'Are you worried about the size of his head?'

Lucy shook her head.

'Do you feel that you are important to him?'

Now Lucy was silent, thoughtful as she mulled over these words. She felt that she was important to him, but she wondered if she were important enough.

'He talks to me when he comes in from work,' she said. 'There is nothing I don't know about the water situation, difficulties within the construction company, problems with employees ... you know ... all the usual business things.'

'Is it not enough that he talks to you? That you are the important person in his life? The one he shares things with? Is there something else, something you are not telling me?'

'I feel foolish telling you this,' Lucy said. 'I thought marriage would be more. I thought... I don't know what I thought. I just didn't think it would be like this ... you know, if I go home now, Maria ... our friend, I suppose, although she is more like a family attachment, will be in the kitchen making coffee, rearranging the crockery, hanging my dishcloths out to dry...'

'I beg your pardon?' Her mother seemed really surprised. 'The woman is like a family attachment? A maid? Or a friend?'

'Yes,' Lucy said. 'Yes. It's odd, I know, but actually she's not really the problem ... at least I don't think she is the problem. She's there too much, but that isn't it...'

'Go on,' Harriet said.

274

'It's really that I have no space ... no time alone with Rhino, or not enough time.'

'The evenings?'

'Friedrich is always there. He's there all the time.'

'You don't have to let him in,' Harriet said. 'You can just say you are busy.'

'He still has a key,' Lucy said, and then went on to explain why he still had the key and how Rhino saw no reason to change things from the way they had been before he married her. 'Maria has a key too,' she added. 'It suits Rhino,' she explained.

She put her hand on her stomach. She could feel the familiar tightening of the muscles and the accompanying pain. She winced slightly.

'Are you all right?' Harriet asked.

'I keep getting these contractions,' Lucy said. 'They're not real. The doctor said they are normal.'

Her mother, watching her, said nothing for a moment. 'You're not forceful enough,' she then said to Lucy. 'Do you think I would ever have let someone else have the key to my house?'

'I don't know how to get them back,' Lucy said. 'Now that I've asked Rhino and he said to leave things as they are, I feel in a really difficult position. If I ask either of them, I'm going against his wishes.' The muscles contracted again and she clenched her hands in pain.

'When are you seeing the doctor next?' her mother asked.

'In a month's time,' Lucy answered.

'Well, we're going to remedy that. I want to

275

know what is going on and why you are so physically uncomfortable. I'll make an appointment. Now, at what time does Friedrich arrive in the mornings?'

'About ten o'clock. I used to lie in bed in the morning and Rhino brought me up tea before he drove Thomas to school, and Friedrich would be there when I came down. Now, in the last few weeks, I make myself get up and drive Thomas. If I don't come and visit you, I just drive around a bit, or go to the shops...'

'I see,' Harriet said thoughtfully. 'Tomorrow morning you are to lie in again. Tell Reinhold tonight that you are too tired in the mornings.' Looking into her daughter's face, she thought that was no lie. Lucy looked drained. 'No. Just leave it to me. Now, which do you want to learn, bridge or mah jong?'

'Oh, Mother, do I have to?'

'Yes. Bridge I think is the better option – you'll meet more people that way.'

And Lucy succumbed as the cards were taken out, and her mother brought her back to her childhood when as a family they had played – basic bridge, her mother called it.

'Basic will get you anywhere,' she said firmly, just as she had said when Hilary and she were children. 'It's like tennis. Learn it early, and you have it all your life. It's a great way to meet people. I'm asking some friends over on Thursday – you'll partner me.'

For the next hour they bid hands together and Lucy remembered that pleasure as a child, playing with her father, Hilarymem with her

276

mother, on Sunday evenings when the Indian night had fallen, and there was silence outside bar the occasional barking of the dogs.

'How come you feel so at home here?' she asked her mother afterwards.

'Home is where you make it.'

'Why did you decide to move to Malta?' she asked.

'Why do you think? To be with you, of course,' her mother said.

For some reason that had not occurred to Lucy. She thought her mother would go on about the weather, which was what she usually said when people asked her. That she was there because of her daughter was a very comforting idea. The more she thought about it, the more it came to her that Harriet's sense of love and duty to her family was overriding. She had been a very good wife in every sense, and had come to help with her grandchildren as soon as she could. She had done her best, fulfilled her role as wife, parent and grandparent. This was reflected in the way she had wanted to relieve Lucy of the responsibility of raising Mattie and Amelia, and that she had in fact been there for Lucy all the time, even though Lucy had not seen it like that way back then.

The following morning, Harriet was waiting outside Lucy's house from a quarter to ten. In due course, Friedrich Arnheim drove up and parked behind her.

'You've taken my place,' Friedrich said to her by way of greeting. 'But you are very welcome.'

His courtesy and charm were to the fore, but Harriet had felt him bridle at her presence.

Harriet looked around with interest. 'I didn't realise there were places,' she said smoothly, as Friedrich deftly moved the keys in his hand, finding the one to open the outside door.

'Now, I want you to give me the keys,' Harriet said.

'I beg your pardon.'

Harriet removed the keys from Friedrich's hand. 'I'll just take the ones for the outer and inner doors – don't worry,' she said.

'But they're my keys,' Friedrich said in surprise.

'I think not,' Harriet replied. 'I think they are the keys to my daughter's house.'

'But I need them,' Friedrich said.

'Not as much as I do,' Harriet replied. 'My daughter and son-in-law would like me to be able to get in and out, especially now, with Lucy pregnant. AND she doesn't need the disturbance of someone who is not family around here all the time. Are you married?' she asked pleasantly.

'No, no, I'm not,' he replied.

'Do you have a home of your own?' Harriet asked.

'Indeed,' he said shortly.

'Then I'd be inclined to tend to your own home.' Harriet's voice never lost its pleasant edge, nor did she let slip the agreeable smile on her lips but her eyes were not laughing. 'It's an unusual friendship you have with Rhino, is it not?'

'It's a long-lasting friendship,' Friedrich replied. 'Please do take the key,' he added evenly.

'Would you like to come in for coffee?' Harriet asked.

'I have changed my mind,' he said. 'I have other things to do today. We will meet again,' he added. He clicked his heels together before turning and walking back to his car.

Inside, Harriet found Lucy still lying in bed, and she made them both tea, bringing it upstairs on a tray.

Harriet sat on a chair beside the bed with the fan turning slowly in the ceiling. She poured the tea, and Lucy pulled herself up on the pillows and looked at her.

'You really got the key from him?' Lucy said in amazement.

Harriet smiled. 'You doubted me?'

They both laughed.

'It's going to be just fine now,' Harriet said to her.

Lucy reached out her hand and took her mother's. 'Thank you,' she whispered.

'For what?' Harriet asked. 'For not taking any nonsense? Don't thank me for that. I've never taken any nonsense. I wouldn't know how to.'

Back downstairs she found Maria had arrived and was brushing the flagstones out in the courtyard.

She introduced herself and watched the younger woman for a few moments. Maria was pretty, with black hair and tanned skin. She had huge brown eyes with thick lashes and a gentle smile in her open and dramatic face.

279

'You know, Maria,' Harriet said, 'you are invaluable to my daughter. I don't know what she would do without you.'

'Thank you, Mrs Entwhistle.'

'Do you have a family of your own?'

'There is just my son, Lucas, and me. My husband died in the war.'

'I'm sorry to hear it,' Harriet said. 'But *c'est la guerre*, as they say in Paris. You know, I don't think you should be coming here every day. I think Lucy and Rhino need time to themselves.'

'But I'm quite happy to come in and to help out. Poor Lucy and her hand...'

'No, I won't hear of it,' Harriet said firmly. 'You need time with your son. And my daughter and her husband need quiet time together.'

'But–'

'How did your husband die?' Harriet interrupted. Her voice sounded sympathetic.

'He died in the bombings.'

'It's a terrible shame, losing anyone like that, especially a husband,' Harriet said.

'I picked up the pieces.'

'I'm sure you did,' Harriet said. 'And you need to keep the pieces together, of course. Lucas will be glad of the extra time with you.'

'He doesn't come home from school until later,' Maria said.

'Well then, it will give you time to keep your house as clean as you keep here, and you will then have more time for Lucas.'

'I should really confirm this with Rhino,' Maria said. 'He and I are old friends. He's going to find it very odd if I stop coming around.'

'I don't think he will. Anyway, I will talk to Rhino,' Harriet replied. 'Don't you be worrying your head over this. It is for the best. Now, I'll take your keys, as I want to be able to get in and out whenever Lucy needs me.'

Maria handed over the keys almost disbelievingly, and Harriet ushered her out.

With Maria gone, she went back upstairs to Lucy, who was sitting up in bed with her teacup in her hand.

'Now, first of all is there anyone else you want me to sort out?' Harriet asked her.

Lucy shook her head.

'How about Thomas? Is he behaving?'

'He is just the greatest boy,' Lucy said. 'He's such a pleasure to have around. Sometimes I think we are skulking together in the house after dinner. He's in his room studying and I'm putting in time until Friedrich leaves.'

'Speaking of whom, do you want me to keep the keys?' Harriet asked Lucy. 'We can simply say to Reinhold that Friedrich and Maria gave them to me as it was important I could get in and out to you, and that neither realised that the other had handed them over. Now, shall I do dinner for you this evening? I've brought meat and vegetables with me?'

Lucy concurred willingly and spent the day resting.

Rhino said that they could have had extra keys cut, but if Friedrich and Maria were happy about it, then of course there was no problem.

'Oh, I think they were both delighted,' Harriet reassured him. 'They have their own lives to lead.

They must not be too dependent on you two – nor indeed must you two be too dependent on them.'

Both she and Lucy noticed Thomas was smiling as he started eating, and Rhino turned and asked him how school had been.

'It was fine, thank you,' Thomas replied. He looked up at Lucy and said that she looked better.

'Better?' Rhino said, looking over at Lucy across the table.

'I've been feeling a bit tired,' she said. 'It's so nice of Mother to help me like this.'

'I will get you someone to clean for you,' Harriet said to Lucy.

'But Maria–' Rhino objected.

'Much more dignity for Lucy to have a maid, rather than a family friend helping out,' Harriet said. 'Don't worry about it, Reinhold. These are female matters.'

The slight crispness of the days was already easing. Spring in Malta was like nothing Lucy had encountered before and her energy levels increased dramatically, just as the pains in her stomach eased. A trip to the doctor with her mother confirmed that everything was all right, and for a while Lucy was more relaxed.

'I really do feel better already,' she admitted to her mother when she arrived for bridge a few days later.

Her mother smiled. 'There are some things we don't need in life,' she said obtusely. 'And once we identify them, we have to get rid of them.'

'Thank you, Mother,' Lucy said.

'Cankers, sores, gangrene, Maria Borg Cardona and Friedrich Arnheim,' her mother said, and they both laughed.

Harriet's guests arrived on time. Lucy was amused by the varied ages of the group. Harriet was probably the oldest but she wore her age with dignity and it was difficult to tell how much older than the rest she was. She, Lucy, was clearly the youngest. There were two women, Marianne and Jacinta, who were good friends and had been playing bridge for some time. Then there was a neighbour of Harriet's named Lou, a dark-haired, swarthy woman whom Lucy found slightly difficult to understand, as her Maltese accent was stronger than the others. There was a man called Henry and his half-brother, Jock, whose father had been Scottish and who had been educated in Glasgow. And finally there was Geoffrey Lord, a tall suave man with grey hair, who took Lucy's hand and kissed it.

'I have been looking forward to meeting you,' he said. 'Your mother spoke so often of you.'

Lucy wondered at how her mother had managed to find so many new friends so quickly.

'Your mother has spoken so highly of you and Reinhold, whom I have not yet met,' Geoffrey continued. 'I would like you to join Harriet and me for dinner. Does Saturday suit?'

The accents fascinated Lucy and she found herself listening to the sounds rather than to the content, and had to force herself to stop when twice a question had to be repeated for her. She realised that these were the first real conversations she was having with any Maltese, other than quick exchanges in the shops or with Maria. In some ways it made her feel inadequate because she knew the people were friendly and that the reserve was coming from her.

'I insist on playing with Lucy,' Geoffrey said when they were pairing off.

'Oh, you should be flattered,' Marianne said to her.

'He's by far and away the best,' Jacinta added.

'He learned in the army,' Marianne continued.

'Who didn't?' asked Henry.

'Well, you didn't for one,' Marianne retorted. 'In fact, no one else here did.'

They were comfortable with one another and there was a lot of banter, and Lucy found herself quickly eased in to the group. She ended up playing with Geoffrey and had no real trouble as he adapted to her simple system and occasionally just took control and bid to game when she was in a quandary as to what to do.

By the time evening came, she had been invited to tea in Jacinta's, and for a walk with Marianne as well as to dinner at Geoffrey Lord's house.

'That went well,' her mother said when they had left and she was clearing the teacups away.

'And we're playing at Henry's next week,' Lucy said. 'I didn't think they'd want me back after seeing my play.'

'You did very well,' Harriet said. 'I was proud of you. And I think you quite surprised them – for someone who hadn't played since she was ten! You should be pleased with yourself.'

Lucy was pleased.

Apart from anything else, Lucy now had something interesting to write to the girls about. They were not coming out for Easter because both Rhino and her mother felt that it would be too much for her, and that holiday was such a short one.

'They can come in the summer and they'll have weeks and weeks. It will be much better for everyone, and the baby will be born by then, so you'll be recovered,' her mother said.

'I think this will be very hard on the girls,' Lucy said. 'Especially Amelia. I know how much she wants to come out here – *needs* to come out here, in fact.'

'The girls will be fine,' Harriet said. 'A few months more will make no difference.'

'Mother,' Lucy continued thoughtfully, 'would you think of going home for the Easter holidays? I don't want to burden you with yet another trip, but I can't help thinking that the girls need you or me for that period.'

'Well, funnily enough,' Harriet replied, 'I was thinking of going home. I'm considering selling the house in Kent. It's lying there unoccupied and quite honestly I don't see us returning to it again. So, I could spend a week there with the girls while we tidy up and sort things, and then a week in London before they go back to school.'

'Have you had any thoughts on the London house?' Lucy asked her.

'I don't think we should let it go. It is a base for all of us in England, nicely situated, and, anyway, at this point I don't even see it as my property any more. I see it as yours. So if we come to make any decision on it, we will do it together.'

Two days before Harriet was due to leave Lucy woke in the night. There was perspiration dripping down her body and she lay for a moment wondering if she were hot or cold. She was shivering but had the feeling that she might be running a temperature.

Rhino, sensing her stir, rolled over to face her.

Recently they had seemed withdrawn from each other. He was late coming home from work, and was often very silent. He was always solicitous of her, always chivalrous and attentive, but in a remote way.

She had tried asking him if something were the matter, but if there was a problem he was not prepared to discuss it.

There had been the smallest of arguments over Harriet removing the keys from his friends.

'I don't think your mother should have interfered like that,' he had said to Lucy some time afterwards. Lucy instinctively knew that he had been talking to Friedrich.

'I think she meant well,' Lucy replied.

'Fritz has had a key for here since I moved in,' he continued. 'He's my friend. He and I have been through more together than most people… I do not want him to feel rejected by me.'

But maybe I feel rejected in his presence, Lucy thought, but she did not say that aloud. It seemed harsh and accusatory, and she did not know how to speak about it with him. She also began to feel that maybe she had been foolish in having a problem with Friedrich always being there because, in his absence now, she felt on no sounder ground with Rhino. Friedrich still came over, but only in the evenings, and now only a couple of times a week. And Lucy sensed that Rhino's late return on the other evenings of the week meant that Rhino was going to him instead – to Friedrich or to Maria, or maybe to both.

She had felt jealous once before in her life, and that was when Matthew courted and married Hilary. But this did not feel like jealousy – it was more like fear. Somehow things between her and Rhino were no better since Harriet had intruded.

The second argument that arose between them was to do with Maria. At first Rhino did not realise that she had stopped dropping in, and then he assumed it was because Friedrich was not around, but then one day he mentioned he had dropped into Maria's to see how she was.

'I think we might ask her to dinner,' he suggested.

Lucy was startled. 'Maria?'

'Yes. I don't see her any more and I like her. What's wrong with that?' His voice was a little cold. He had never spoken to her like that before. It felt wrong to her but she did not know what to say. Anything she said would sound like jealousy. There was something about this that made her feel threatened, and she felt him withdraw further from her. Since she had broken her fingers and her pregnancy had been ascertained, Rhino and she had not made love. He held her tenderly in bed, sometimes until she went to sleep, but the few shy overtures she had made had been politely rejected with the pretence of not realising what she was doing.

So she had stopped. It was shameful being rebuffed and easier just to take what was on offer from him.

When she woke dripping with perspiration and shivering, and Rhino turned to her, she wondered for a fleeting moment if he wanted to make love to her, but instead he turned on the light and felt her forehead.

'You don't feel hot,' he said. 'But you're soaking wet.'

He ran her a bath and changed the bed linen while she lay in the warm water, and then he dried her and helped her back to bed.

'Pain?' he asked.

She shook her head.

There was no pain. It was something else. Something that was rising in her and seemed to be enveloping her. It was like a wave coming over. Memories of Hilary – Hilary giving birth to Mattie that long night and the following day, walking on the beach to rid herself of Hilary's screams. And then Amelia – Amelia's arrival followed by Hilary's death. All the fear in the world seemed to be inside her head. Rhino and his combination of being solicitous and yet remote; her feelings of isolation ... it all seemed too much.

She lay in the bed and she cried. He was concerned, asking her over and over what was wrong, but she could not put it into words.

Everything was wrong.

In all things of nature there is something of the marvellous.

Aristotle

CHAPTER TWELVE

Harriet cancelled her trip to London. She phoned her nephew Jupe, and the school and the girls were informed of the change of plans. Sitting by Lucy's bed, holding her hand, she tried to identify what was wrong. The doctors were adamant that physically Lucy was fine, and yet looking at her, Harriet knew something was greatly amiss. Her eyes were surrounded by dark shadows and she could hardly eat.

'You can tell me anything,' Harriet said to her, an echo of a conversation earlier that year.

Lucy shook her head. She had confided in her mother before and somehow the problem had escalated. The previous arrangements seemed preferable to where she now found herself. She lay there with hazy memories of what it had been like before Harriet took the keys off Friedrich and Maria. Friedrich sitting in the garden with Rhino, Friedrich sitting back with his legs crossed, Rhino laughing, a glass of brandy in front of each of them, the sound of German wafting through the kitchen window as she tidied up after dinner, and Thomas coming in and taking a piece of fruit, sharing a few words with her before heading up to his room. Suddenly that all seemed companionable. It was preferable. It had not been so bad.

And even Maria hovering in the late morning, waiting for Rhino to come home just so that he would exchange a few words with her...

All of that was definitely a better option.

'She's not eating, Reinhold,' Harriet said to her son-in-law. 'Have you any idea what is wrong?'

He shook his head.

Harriet wondered as she watched him what he was thinking. All the charm that had been so apparent on her first meeting him was still there, but it was difficult to get beneath it.

'It's unbearable as a parent to see her in this state and not able to help her,' she said as gently as she could, in an effort to get him to talk, although she wanted to shout at him.

'Yes,' he agreed. 'She is so fragile.'

Fragile? This was not a word Harriet would have used about Lucy. She thought of Lucy as being determined and independent, and yet she now realised that those aspects of Lucy had changed. Her daughter *was* fragile and she wondered how that had happened.

'My girls, Hilary and Lucy,' she said slowly, 'were so similar in so many ways and yet so different. But the one thing they had in common was a fierce determination and a sense of self. I'm not seeing either of those things in Lucy now. And I don't know when it changed.'

'Friedrich was wondering,' Rhino said thoughtfully, 'if Lucy could be afraid of childbirth. She

290

has told me of the awfulness of Hilarymem's death and Friedrich suggested that maybe she is panicking.'

Harriet listened to this with a mixture of distress and interest. She could not work out where Friedrich fitted in. Clearly Rhino told him everything, and it was Friedrich who pieced things together. She found it baffling.

She tried again, but there was little more she could get Rhino to tell her. She wondered about other things within the house, how marriage had affected Rhino, how having a wife had curtailed him, and if the idealistic notion both he and Lucy had carried for all those years had not held up. But they were thoughts she could not broach with him, because she knew he would not answer.

A man's man, she thought. Farmer, builder and soldier first. And perhaps on top of that, he put male friendship above his spouse.

She wanted Lucy to talk to her, but she was too concerned for her to push these questions on her and, in the event, Lucy's doctor, who came the following day again, suggested moving Lucy to hospital. Now they were concerned about her inability to eat and he felt that round-the-clock medical attention was needed.

In hospital, Lucy started to sleep and the shadows around her eyes faded. Less than a month later she went into labour suddenly, five weeks early, and as morning light broke through the hospital windows, she gave birth after long and painful hours, to Charlotte Hilary Kobaldt.

In the corridor outside, Harriet sat upright on a

hard chair, ankles crossed with her customary elegance, and Rhino, unshaven and grey, paced up and down, occasionally stopping in front of her as though looking for words of comfort, before continuing his endless trekking.

Friedrich Arnheim arrived shortly before Charlotte was born. He appeared suddenly in the corridor and Harriet watched as he put his arm around Rhino's shoulder.

'It will be all right,' he said to his friend.

Rhino nodded.

Harriet wondered how Friedrich knew that Rhino was in the hospital, and when he came over to speak to her she asked him.

He hesitated for a moment and then said, 'I called at the house and when I saw the car had gone, I guessed where Rhino was.'

'At three o'clock in the morning?' Harriet asked.

'I was on my way home from a friend's house,' he replied. 'I've been keeping an eye on Rhino since Lucy was brought in here.'

'You're very kind,' Harriet said, but she was puzzled.

'That's what friends do,' he replied. 'Rhino was there for me...' he touched his eye patch, 'I am here for him.'

But all of that was put aside, forgotten, when they each held Charlotte in their arms. Friedrich brought Thomas in to see the baby and Lucy was grateful to him. Thomas's pleasure was blatant, both at seeing Lucy and at the baby. She chided herself for her inability to warm to Friedrich, none of which mattered now as she cuddled Charlotte in her arms, nursing her, holding her – the worries and fears of the previous months obliterated by the love and joy she felt.

'She looks so like Amelia did when she was born,' Lucy said to Thomas.

That was what Thomas wrote in a letter to Amelia. The girls already knew from Harriet that Charlotte was born, but it was the letter from Thomas that Amelia read over and over. It was the first letter she had ever received from him and she read it with mixed emotions.

Charlotte Hilary is so tiny, like a baby in Greek mythology. I thought they might name her Hebe or Hera. But no, she is Charlotte after Rhino's mother and Hilary after yours. So now I have another sister – of sorts, and you another cousin... Lucy says she is the image of you when you were born.

Amelia felt very emotional. There was relief about Charlotte's birth and Lucy being well. She did not know until after the birth how ill Lucy had been and it frightened her now to think that Lucy might have died like her own mother had. She felt pangs of fear about how Charlotte was now Lucy's baby, and this added to her uncertainty of who she really was and where she belonged, and whether she would have any importance in Lucy's life any more.

Everything seemed so unclear. Thomas's letter added to those fears on one level, but on another she felt happy – happy that he had written to her, happy that he spoke of Greek mythology, which was their shared link, happy that he was connecting with her. Amelia had felt desperate disappointment about there being no trip to Malta for Easter, followed by Harriet's sudden cancellation of her visit to England. Instead there was the realisation of endless days of Monopoly in the Jupes, with the only relief being that she would have complete access to Ophelia's books, all of which she had now read at least once. There she was warm and was cared for, but in many ways that made her more aware that she was a visitor in other people's lives with no real place of her own.

Mattie did not appear especially interested in the new baby's arrival, passing Amelia the letters from their grandmother and shrugging off any questions that Amelia might ask. But Amelia knew that Mattie had rejoiced in the postponed trip to Malta.

In the days coming up to the end of summer term and their departure for Malta, Mattie became more and more morose.

Despite Amelia's fears of what she might do in order to avoid flying, nothing happened.

Amelia had no doubt that she was very worried about the flight but was unsure if the threats that had been made would be adequate in tempering her actions. Amelia had seen her looking up at the occasional plane that flew over the school. It was a look that made her seem far away, a look of both fear and expectation, and Amelia could not imagine what it was going to be like, being in an airport and then getting on board an aeroplane – if indeed they ever got that far.

Uncle Jupe collected the three of them from school and took them back to the Jupes for two days before they left. They had all grown and Aunt Anne took them to town and bought summer clothes and swimming costumes, Ophelia sulking as she was unused to sharing her mother with anyone other than Mars. Mattie convinced her aunt they should go to the country house to collect some of their old summer things, and they drove there on the way back.

The house was cold and empty, despite the warm summer day, and the dustsheets on the furniture made the place seem ghostly. There was a hollow oldness about the place, and the kitchen cupboards were bare.

From their bedroom window Amelia looked down into the back garden, overgrown now with an air of abandonment. The grass on Grandfather's once-carefully maintained lawn was clumpy and full of heaps. She wondered what they were. She went downstairs for a closer inspection.

There were holes in the grass with heaps of earth beside them. She looked at them in puzzlement.

'What are they?' she asked Mattie, whom she had called out to join her.

'Don't know,' Mattie said, looking at them with interest.

'They're mole holes,' Aunt Anne said. 'How strange.'

They must have burrowed their way in under the garden walls, their aunt told them. There was something lovely about it, Amelia thought. She was taken with the idea that even though they had deserted this house, there were still tenants in the garden. Somehow she knew Grandfather would be pleased. She would have loved to spend a night there, but there was no time.

They collected their things, even though there was nothing that fitted Mattie. She gave Amelia some of her old shorts and tops, and their aunt helped them throw out everything that was too small.

The following day in the airport, Mattie was silent. She still had the ability to withdraw completely into herself and to appear unaware of outside events.

'It will all be fine,' Uncle Jupe said to them as he checked in their bags.

Amelia could see him taking in Mattie's pale face.

'You're going to have a wonderful time, girls. I wish I were going with you,' he said cheerily.

'You could go instead of me,' Mattie said.

Uncle Jupe laughed and said he wished he could. He brought them as far as he was allowed before giving them each a hug, and out they went to board the plane. Amelia could see Mattie's hand clinging tightly to the rail on the steps. She didn't think her sister was going to climb up, but the surge of people behind her pushed Mattie along in a way she clearly had not expected. She found herself, against her will, seated on the plane clutching her bag on her lap.

Her face was closed. It had blanked and Amelia

could get no response from her. She was concerned Mattie might do something on the flight, but instead she kept her eyes closed all the way to Rome.

Amelia wanted to ask her about the mountains over which they were flying. She looked down on high, jagged, snow-covered peaks that seemed to stretch endlessly until they dropped into the sea. She was fascinated by the purity of the snow and the levelling off of the whiteness as fertile ground appeared below in valleys with rivers meandering through. She wondered if they were the Alps, but Mattie's silence was impenetrable and there was no one she could ask.

In Rome they changed planes before flying onwards. The temperature in Rome had hit them with disbelief. Neither had any idea that heat could feel like that. Beads of perspiration trickled down their backs. Mattie looked pale and drained, which Amelia knew was not just from the heat. The second journey by plane was not as long, but once again Mattie sat with her eyes closed, and her arms clasped tightly around her, hanging on to her bag as though it might give her comfort or protection.

Amelia watched out the window as a different scene unfolded – blue sea seemed to stretch endlessly as they flew southwards. Then the island of Sicily, with its rugged mountains and its towns dotted all along the coasts and in between the hills. Again, blue sea with the occasional ship visible as a small dot way below them. At last the start of the Maltese archipelago appeared.

The plane flew in over Gozo and immediately

afterwards over Comino and Cominetto and then there was a view of cliffs as though the island of Malta had been tilted upwards at some point in the past. Within no time they had circled round and buildings appeared in pale yellow all along the north coast.

Amelia saw with shock that there were tears streaming down Mattie's face. She reached out and took her hand. They squeezed each other's fingers tightly as the plane descended.

'It's OK, Mattie,' Amelia whispered. 'We've landed. It's all right now.'

Mattie seemed to pull herself from somewhere far away and opened her eyes with a puzzled look.

'Landed? Oh. I didn't realise.' She pulled her hand away and wiped her eyes vaguely, as if she did not know that she was crying or what she was doing. Then suddenly she reached out a hand again and they sat there for a moment holding each other. 'Are you afraid?' Mattie asked her.

Amelia didn't know what to answer. She was afraid on some level – afraid of what was ahead as well as wanting it. As well as needing it. She nodded.

'Are you afraid of Rhino?' Mattie asked.

Amelia wondered how this had turned around from Mattie crying, Mattie who clearly had been afraid or upset during the flight, and now it was she, Amelia, who was having to expose herself to her sister's questions.

'I want it to be like it was,' she said. 'Like it used to be.'

'So do I,' Mattie replied.

But they spoke at cross-purposes. Amelia wanted back her family as she knew it – both as it was in the beginning with Lucymem and Mattie in Ithaca, or in Grandfather and Grandmother's house, with Grandfather and Grandmother watching out for them. Mattie wanted it back as she had known it when she was just a tiny child.

'Grandfather once said to me,' Mattie confided, 'that things move on in life, and we have to accept them.'

It was the first time that Amelia had realised that Grandfather had shared his wisdom with Mattie too, and it pleased her. All the words of his knowledge were stored in her head, and Mattie mentioning him made her feel they were on the same side.

'Uncle Jupe said to me that Rhino is not such a bad person and that we should both give him a chance. It might be easier here, on his territory,' Mattie continued.

This was by far the most serious conversation they had ever had. Amelia was amazed by it, and it took her a while to work out that Mattie had assumed a role she had hitherto had no interest in. She was playing big sister.

There was something intensely reassuring about this.

'Are you looking forward to seeing Charlotte?' Amelia asked in a small voice.

Mattie shrugged, withdrawing again. 'I'm not that keen on babies,' she said.

'I liked being the baby,' Amelia now confided to her.

'You'll always be a baby,' Mattie said to her as

they opened their seat belts and started to get up. Amelia wasn't sure if that was kindly meant or not.

'Aunt Anne said Lucymem has the right to happiness,' Amelia said suddenly, remembering the conversation she had heard the previous year.

'Yes,' Mattie replied.

But both were thinking, was Lucymem not happy before? Were they not enough for her? Were they rejected, as they feared?

Neither knew. Neither was old enough to follow the sequence of their personal history and how it had affected their beloved aunt, and they both knew that.

Their grandmother had come to meet them at the airport, with Thomas lingering in the background but looking out hopefully for them. Grandmother was dressed in bright yellow silk and stood out in the crowd. Any fears that Amelia had had about her finding them, or they her, dissipated on arrival. Harriet was like a glowing sun in the bustle of waiting people, and her voice was loud and clear as she hailed them coming through the doorway. Amelia had hoped, indeed had assumed, that Lucymem would be there to meet them, and she looked around for her. Their grandmother embraced them both and Amelia found herself trying to linger in the embrace – she did not want the contact to cease.

'Goodness, you've grown,' Harriet said to them, standing back and taking them both in. 'I would hardly have recognised you. And you look so alike – I'd never seen that before.' She seemed really surprised.

Amelia looked at Mattie.

Mattie was tall now; her dark hair curling down beneath her shoulders, her body had lengthened so that she looked like a healthy young animal with a long slim neck and tiny breasts. Amelia felt like a shadow of her, and had no idea that they looked alike, although she too had hair nearly Mattie's length when she let it out of her plaits. Her hair had grown back well since it had been cut the previous year. Mattie looked beautiful, she thought. She wouldn't mind looking like her when she grew up, and it was comforting that Grandmother could see a resemblance.

Thomas came over. He too had grown, his shoulders were broader and he was very brown. Although he greeted Amelia with an endearing 'Hello, Mealie,' it was Mattie he couldn't take his eyes off.

They came out of the terminal into the car park and Amelia looked around in excitement and expectation.

They had arrived, at last, in her island of honey and bees. The sun baking down on the car had heated it to a temperature Amelia couldn't believe.

'We'll cook in here,' she gasped as they got into the car.

'Don't be a baby,' Mattie replied. She suddenly appeared older and she turned several times towards Thomas with a slightly complicit look in her eyes that Amelia could not understand. She turned away from them and wound down the window on Grandmother's advice.

'I meant to leave the windows open,' Harriet

said. 'But we were rushing to get in to meet you and we closed them without thinking. It's what we always do. Because of the dust, you know.'

'Where's Lucymem?' Amelia finally asked.

'She's feeding Charlie at this time,' Thomas said.

Amelia wondered if he shortened everybody's name and was about to ask him when Mattie got the question in first.

'I notice you've shortened Charlotte's name,' she said, adding coquettishly, 'You haven't shortened mine.'

'Someone got there first,' he replied. 'I suppose I could lengthen yours. Would you like that, Mathilda?'

'No. Although my name is Mathilde, with an "e" not with an "a" at the end, but I like being Mattie,' she laughed.

'It suits you,' he replied, and Amelia saw their eyes meeting and staring at each other for a moment, before Mattie turned round and settled herself beside their Grandmother.

'What's the baby like?' Amelia asked. She didn't know whether she wanted to hear that Charlotte was really beautiful or truly ghastly. Any answer would probably have been the wrong one.

'She's just like a baby,' Thomas said. 'She cries a lot.'

That pleased Amelia. She hoped she would be the one to stop Charlotte crying. She had a sudden vision of holding Charlotte and everyone saying how wonderful she was with her.

'I don't have much time for babies myself,' Mattie said in her new grown-up voice that

302

implied a person who knew her likes and dislikes and certainly was not going to be involved with a howling cousin.

'She's quite sweet really,' Thomas said.

'And I am now a grandmother blessed with three darling granddaughters,' Harriet contributed.

Amelia wondered if that made Thomas feel excluded.

'Not forgetting a Thomas in my life,' Harriet continued, looking over her shoulder at Thomas, as though reading Amelia's thoughts.

'Rhino has adopted me,' Thomas informed them. He sounded really pleased. 'He did it in Germany and I've changed my name to Kobaldt,' he added. 'That makes me really your cousin now.'

Amelia wondered why Lucymem had never adopted her and Mattie, and as if reading her thoughts again, Grandmother said, 'Lucy was made Mattie and Amelia's guardian so she had no need to adopt them.'

But Rhino had been Thomas's guardian, and Amelia really wished that Lucy had adopted her too. Adoption sounded reassuring. It gave you a connection. It made you belong to someone.

But there wasn't time to think about that as they drove down bumpy roads and headed towards the coast.

Amelia was aware of dry-stone walls and rough terrain, cacti in fields and on the walls, the shocking pinks of exotic flowers and the brightness of the light. The feeling of excitement she had about coming to Malta returned as the sea appeared and the blue she had been observing on the plane was now so much closer.

'It's so very blue,' she said.

'What colour did you think it would be?' Mattie asked her.

But Amelia did not hear the question as her mind was already down at the sea.

Silver-white rocks edged their way into the sea, forming a promontory of sorts, lined with white froth, although the water seemed not to move at all.

'That's where I swim,' Thomas said. 'Down there, off those rocks. We'll go later or else tomorrow. We'll go every day.'

All Amelia could think of was the joy of slipping into the water and escaping from the heat. She looked at Mattie but could only see the back of her head as Mattie's face was turned to the window.

Amelia was in bed that night before she had the chance to think about the day, about the excitement of coming in through the outside door and the arcade of grapevines, about her joy at seeing Bruce again. He had come pottering in from the back and on seeing them, bounded over, slobbering on them, tail wagging in delight. She had buried her face in his fur, arms around his neck, breathing him in, feeling the heat of his body, loving him as she always had.

Lucymem had hugged them both, her delight in seeing them apparent. Then she introduced their baby cousin. Charlotte had gurgled when lying in Amelia's arms, and Lucymem showed her how to hold the baby's head so that it was well supported. Charlotte was tiny, with a fuzz of blonde hair and minute limbs. Amelia touched her little fingers and toes, and when she had got enough confidence to both hold her and to touch her, she stroked Charlotte's round baby cheeks and kissed her on her smooth forehead.

Their bedrooms were small, with little room for anything more than a bed and a cupboard, but the view from their windows was down over a pathway that wound its way towards the sea. The tip of the rocks was visible on the shoreline, and as Amelia unpacked her bag she was drawn over and over back to the window and the enticing vision in the distance. She wanted to get down there – down to the rocks, to climb across them, to imagine Poseidon down at the water's edge with a staff in his hand, and the sea at his command.

By the time they had unpacked and had a cold drink, Rhino had appeared. He arrived hot and tired but he seemed pleased enough to see the girls. After washing he came and held Charlotte in his arms and spoke to the girls about their journey.

'Those mountains are the Alps,' he told Amelia when she asked him. 'Once when I was very young we came up from the farm in Kenya and stayed with cousins. We skied in the Alps. I remember the cold but also the excitement.'

Because she was now so hot, Amelia could hardly remember what it was like to be cold. She liked the way Rhino had answered her. He seemed nicer than she remembered and that was a relief.

They ate dinner outside in the courtyard behind the house. Mattie, who was not prone to helping in the kitchen, had cut the tomatoes and cucumber, while Rhino and Thomas grilled fish outside near the table. Harriet had departed as she had been invited out to dinner.

'I'll be back tomorrow,' she told the girls. 'A friend of mine is going to take us out on his boat.'

'You can't do that tomorrow,' Rhino objected. 'Fritz is going to come over to take us out on the boat. Make it another day.'

'Reinhold,' Harriet said, 'I absolutely insist on spending the first day with my granddaughters. I haven't seen them in so long. Friedrich Arnheim will have to take them out another day. I'll be over at ten in the morning – give you girls time for a lie-in, which I'm sure you both need. School and travelling and everything – get extra sleep and lots of sunshine and you'll both be as happy as clams on a rock.'

Rhino was overruled by sheer strength. Amelia was aware of something beneath the surface but she could not work out what it was.

During this interchange Lucy said nothing. She smiled at them all and let events around her unfold. She had Charlotte in her arms and every so often she nuzzled the baby as if taking in her smell and her touch. Harriet kissed her before leaving and told Thomas to watch out for the girls.

'Show them around, won't you?' she said to him.

He assured her that he would, but Amelia

wondered where she would fit into the equation, because he couldn't keep his eyes from wandering to Mattie, who was sitting on a wooden chair tugging gently at the curls on her left shoulder.

'This is the life,' Mattie said. Her voice sounded really happy and her face had a smile on it.

'Mama came here once, didn't she?' Amelia said. She liked to think of her mother once upon a time on this island.

'I don't know that your mother did disembark that day,' Rhino said, lighting a cigarette.

'Oh, she did,' Lucy said quickly with a smile. 'She and Matthew went for a walk. She told me how much she liked it here.'

Amelia felt pleased, and she smiled at her aunt. She imagined her mother, as she knew her from photographs – always in black and white – walking, holding her father's arm down winding pathways like the one she could see from her bedroom window. In this fantasy, her mother was dressed as Lucymem was now, in a cotton frock with bare legs, smiling gently at her father as Lucy smiled at Rhino. And in this dream she emerged as a baby in her mother's arms, held with the love she could see when Lucy held Charlotte. She started to feel petulant and hot, and was sorry that her grandmother had left.

Grandmother came by boat the following morning. Her friend Geoffrey Lord moored off the rocks and came in on a tiny dinghy to collect them.

Amelia had skipped down the path from the

house with a feeling of freedom and joy. Her bones felt as if they were warming for the first time in a long while. The heat from the previous day now soaked through her and, in shorts and a cotton blouse, she ran ahead of Mattie and Thomas, who were walking slowly side by side.

Amelia was excited at being down on the rocks and waving to her grandmother, who was standing like a goddess or figurehead at the prow offshore, and she wanted to swim out to the boat. They had their swimming costumes on under their clothing and they were going to leave their shorts and shirts on the rocks, but Geoffrey said to put them in the dinghy, as they would need them for protection from the sun.

Geoffrey then found that he was the only one in the dingy going back out, as the three of them swam across together.

They sailed along the coast, the boat dancing on the sparkling water, and even Mattie still looked happy.

That evening Friedrich was coming to dinner and Thomas said in an aside to Amelia, 'You're going to meet Cyclops.'

'Cyclops?' Mattie asked, overhearing.

'They were a race of one-eyed monsters,' Thomas said.

'And the most famous,' Amelia explained happily, 'was Polyphemus, son of Poseidon, God of the Sea. And Odysseus blinded him,' she added.

'Well, wait until you meet this Cyclops,' Thomas said.

She and Mattie waited with expectation to meet Cyclops, and when he arrived it was all she could do not to giggle. He was very handsome, as tall as Rhino, smooth and blond and he had one startlingly pale blue eye, and a black patch over the other.

Mattie, with her customary directness, asked him what had happened to his eye.

'This one?' he asked pointing at his good eye, in momentary wit.

'No,' Mattie said. 'I meant the one behind the patch.'

'There isn't one there,' he replied, and said no more.

Twice during this conversation Amelia tried to get Thomas's attention, but he ignored her and just watched Mattie with a funny smile on his lips.

It was a long summer.

Amelia read most of the time. While she went swimming with Thomas and Mattie and they kept an eye on her, she felt excluded. She tried her best to connect with Thomas, but he was different from the way he had been at Christmas and there were no further joyous references to any of the gods of wind, earth or sea, and it was Bruce who usually kept her company. She was not allowed to go bathing by herself, and yet she did, with Bruce beside her paddling in the water and trying to nudge her towards the rocks, as if he knew she should not be there alone. Where they swam was completely deserted and they never saw anyone else.

'Our private cove,' she whispered to Bruce as they both sat on the rocks, Amelia drying the telltale traces of her illicit swim from her hair, before digging her comb from her shorts pocket.

Everything dried so quickly in the heat that she had little problem in keeping her activities from the others.

It was a Wednesday evening and Lucy and Rhino were taking Charlotte to the doctor. Despite the old-fashioned ceiling fan in the master bedroom, Charlotte slept fitfully at night and cried inter-mittently. Amelia was going to go with them into town, while Thomas and Mattie were going for a swim. Mattie and Thomas had already left for the rocks, and Amelia was about to get into the car with Rhino, Lucy and the baby, when she changed her mind.

'It's still so hot,' she said. 'May I stay, Lucy-mem?'

Lucy willingly agreed. 'Go and join the others and have a swim,' she said to her niece. 'You'll have more fun than sitting in a hot car and then in the doctor's. We'll be gone a good hour and a half, I think. Maybe longer.'

Amelia waved them off and then went back inside. She went up to her room to change into her swimsuit, before trailing down the pathway to the water. At one point the sea was completely blocked from view by the stone walls, and then she emerged just above it, looking down on the rocks. The light coruscated on the water as it dappled against the edge. Shades of blue stretched to the azure horizon. She was looking at the sky when movement beneath her caught her attention. She stopped in astonishment as she tried to take in what she was seeing.

Mattie was standing still on the rocks, and Thomas was slowly peeling her swimsuit off.

Amelia stood frozen in disbelief before crouching down so that she would not be seen. Thomas touched her sister's shoulders and then put his hands on her breasts. Amelia gulped and discovered she could not swallow. It was as if there was an enormous lump in her throat. She could not identify what was happening, did not know if it was jealousy or some other emotion. She did feel a thrill of excitement, but with it was a pain through her heart because she loved Thomas passionately and she felt as though she was being torn apart.

Her sister by now had completely removed her costume and was standing naked on the rocks.

Amelia was reminded of a scene from one of her myths of a woodland nymph, only this time it was a sea-nymph. Mattie, standing still, reached out and ran her fingers over Thomas's chest. Amelia was too far away to see clearly what she was touching, but she knew it was his livid scars. She could not breathe as she watched.

Then suddenly, Mattie turned and dived into the sea.

Thomas stood with his hands now by his sides looking out towards the water where she had disappeared. Then he too ran across the rocks right to the edge, before poising himself as he looked into the water. Then he dived in after her.

Amelia wanted to join them, to stop what was

happening, but she did not have the courage to go down further. She watched them bobbing about and chasing each other in the blueness below her and with tears in her eyes she walked dejectedly back to the house.

She had brought Grandfather's paints with her from England, and she got them out and settled herself at the garden table, but all she could paint was the sea and the silver rocks glistening within. She wanted to draw her sister naked on the rocks and Thomas as Adonis before her, but she could not. She did not dare. She knew that someone would come across the painting unless she tore it up, and Mattie would identify herself. She could not expose herself spying on them because Mattie would make her pay.

Instead she painted a mermaid sitting on the rock with long dark hair curling over her shoulders, and an enormous toad sitting watching the mermaid with a look of contentment on his fat face.

She felt cross, rejected and hurt.

There was no immediate sign of any change when Thomas and Mattie returned from their swim. But later in the evening, when Rhino was grilling fish for dinner, Amelia saw Mattie looking at Thomas with a sleepy look in her sparkling eyes and she began to wonder if that afternoon had been the first time there had been that kind of contact between them. It was impossible to tell. She thought back over the previous few days and could not remember whether or not she had seen that intimate look before.

Her exclusion was complete.

Lucy was engrossed in Charlotte and running the home. Rhino never noticed her. Mattie and Thomas were so absorbed in each other and yet busy pretending there was nothing going on. All Amelia's hopes of closeness and reconciliation with Mattie had fallen away; even the joy of holding hands on the plane paled now – now she was alone. Everyone else had bonded in different ways and she was left out. It was a miserable feeling and she tried telling herself to snap out of it, as her grandmother would have said, had she known.

But snapping out of it was not that simple. It was easier to indulge in feeling miserable, knowing that she was in some way being wronged by everyone.

The days slipped into each other, one into one, and while there was plenty of laughter and fun, swimming and sailing, Amelia became more and more aware of Thomas and Mattie's involvement with each other, and wondered that the adults did not observe it.

Grandmother commented on how lovely it was that the three children got on so well, but Amelia felt left out, trailing along as the little sister when Thomas and Mattie went swimming, feeling that they did not want her with them, although they were careful to hide it.

Later in the second week, Friedrich took them out on his boat. Rhino was with them, while Lucy stayed at home with Charlotte.

313

In the Blue Lagoon off Comino, bobbing in the water by the side of the boat, Amelia could hear Friedrich's clear clipped voice travelling down the side. He and Rhino were intermittently varying between German and English.

Thomas and Mattie had disappeared, and Amelia could smell Rhino's cigarette in the stillness of the morning. Lucas was with them on this boat trip – Lucas, who had appeared seemingly from nowhere. He was the son of a friend of Rhino's, a woman called Maria Borg Cardona, whom they had briefly met in the shops. She was very kind and friendly, delighted to meet them and mentioned that she had a son a little older than Amelia.

Thomas said afterwards that Lucas was in his school, a class or two behind him and that he did not know him very well, but that he seemed nice. He suggested that the next time they were doing something Lucas would be invited along.

But Amelia disliked Lucas intensely when they met because she instinctively felt he had been brought in to befriend her and to keep her away from Thomas and Mattie. They were close enough in age – a little more than a year and a half between them. But she wanted him to go away and leave her alone.

He was a skinny, dark-haired boy with huge black eyes under thick dark eyelashes. Friedrich, who appeared to know him well, brought him along that day.

Lucas swam in small circles around her in the water and she ducked down and swam under the boat, coming up on the other side, to escape him.

She put one foot on the ladder to pull herself up, and then paused as voices drifted down the side of the boat.

'I don't see enough of you,' Friedrich was saying to Rhino. Amelia shook her head to clear the water from her ears.

'It isn't possible, Fritz,' she heard Rhino saying. 'Those days are over.'

What days? Amelia wondered.

'I miss you,' Friedrich said. His voice was odd: a mixture of petulance and greed. Amelia could imagine the look on his face even though she couldn't see it. She headed up the ladder smoothly and quickly in time to see Friedrich's hand on Rhino's bare leg. They were both wearing black bathing trunks and one of Friedrich's fingers was inching its way up Rhino's leg and under the tight material. Rhino was lying back on the deck, his head on a pile of towels. Amelia stood for a moment and watched as Friedrich's long elegant fingers, little finger complete with signet ring, stroking the blond hairs on Rhino's thigh, one finger out of sight. And then Amelia coughed, and shook her head and spluttered like a dying fish.

Their reaction was instantaneous. Rhino jumped to his feet and stood looking at her with a shocked expression on his face. Friedrich came rushing over with a towel, asking if she were all right.

'How long have you been there?' Rhino asked.

Amelia said she had only just got out of the water and that her eyes stung and there was water in her ears and that she couldn't see or hear anything. She was trying to be reassuring so that they wouldn't know what she had seen, but as she said that she couldn't hear anything, she knew that Rhino would know she was lying, because how could she have heard his question if she couldn't hear a thing?

'I think I went down too deep,' she said, coughing a bit more and trying to appear as if there was nothing on her mind other than recovering from drowning.

Lucas appeared and said that she had given him a fright, the way she had disappeared, and that seemed to confirm her story, or so she hoped.

However, she was shaken by what she had seen – shaken to the core – and she felt that Rhino was overly solicitous over their picnic lunch, and he referred continually to Lucy and Charlotte, and seemed to fret that they weren't there. But Amelia suspected this was for her sake.

She felt afraid.

Back at the house Amelia wanted to tell Lucy-mem what she had seen. But she had no idea how to explain it and feared her aunt would think she had imagined it, because how could such a thing happen? Amelia felt she should warn her aunt but she did not know how to do it, did not know what to say or how to explain what she had seen or if indeed she could have seen such a thing. Could it have been her imagination?

Lucy was again uncomfortable with Friedrich being around, nor did she like him using the girls' arrival to ensconce himself back with the family, and while she was pragmatic enough to know that Rhino had married her and it was she he had chosen to spend the rest of his life with, none the less she was not at ease.

She sometimes thought that maybe it was because she did not have a close friend, she was jealous of their friendship and she disliked herself for that. She knew their friendship was closer than hers and Rhino's, and that was what was so disconcerting. They talked endlessly when they were together, which showed Rhino's ability to be able to converse, and yet when Friedrich was not around, Rhino did not talk closely with her. It irked and puzzled her endlessly.

'We should have Friedrich and the Borg Cardonas over to dinner,' Rhino suggested again.

It had been a long time since he had brought up the subject. Grandmother was there for dinner. She lifted her wine glass and drank.

'It would be good for Amelia to see someone her own age,' Rhino continued. 'Young Lucas is a nice boy, and it was lovely having him out with us on the boat.'

'Oh, no, thank you,' Amelia interjected quickly. 'I really don't need someone my own age to play with.'

'Fine,' Rhino replied. 'We'll ask Maria to dinner without Lucas. And we'll have Friedrich too.'

Lucymem looked at Grandmother. One of those adult looks took place that Amelia invariably observed and made her wonder what they were thinking.

Grandmother said, 'Oh, do, please do, invite me too.'

'I've asked my mother and her bridge friend Geoffrey Lord,' Lucy said to Rhino. 'Six will be about the same amount of work, and it's a better combination.'

If Rhino felt any reluctance he did not show it.

'Can't we have dinner with you?' Mattie asked.

'Only if Lucas is invited,' Rhino said. 'He can't be excluded.'

Neither Mattie nor Amelia saw why he could not be excluded, but they didn't say anything to that effect. Thomas as usual said nothing, just observed and listened to the interchange.

'Then invite the little twerp,' Mattie said.

So Lucas came too. Amelia felt sorry for him. Maybe he was like her, out on a limb. Everyone else, she thought, was a nymphomaniac. She had recently come across this word while looking up 'nymph' in a dictionary, and while she was afraid to use it out loud, it certainly featured in her thoughts.

Rhino and Friedrich were nymphomaniacs. So were Thomas and Mattie too. They were always going off together and doing things – things like Grandfather's rabbits used to do, except it took them a bit longer and it involved a certain amount of petting and touching each other both before, during and after. She had no recollection of the rabbits behaving like that.

Rhino touched Lucymem sometimes. He put his hand on her shoulder, and she invariably looked up at him with love in her face. And although Amelia wanted all her love for herself, she did want Lucy to be happy and she knew that Lucy loved him.

She sat through the dinner party, watching Friedrich flirting with Rhino. It was discreetly done, and no one else appeared to notice. But Amelia knew. She knew what she had seen, and she could feel something happening that was so disturbing she did not know how to put it into words or to explain it in her mind.

Grandmother's friend Geoffrey was sitting beside Maria and he endeavoured to talk to her. But he was only partially successfully, because every time that he paused Maria turned to Rhino on the other side to draw him into their conversation. A lot of the talk was to do with the rebuilding of Malta, which had, Geoffrey confirmed, been the most bombed place in the whole world.

Rhino appeared uncomfortable and made a few comments about the horrors and the inevitability of war. While Amelia had been born during the war and had lost her parents because of it, she didn't have any recollections in her childhood of its effects. She sat there listening, but her mind was on Friedrich and she wondered where his hands were when they were not on the table.

'I thought Dresden was the most bombed place,' Thomas ventured.

'What was done to Dresden was inexcusable,' Geoffrey said. Amelia was glad he said that, because she wanted someone to offer some sympathy to Thomas.

'Everything was inexcusable,' Grandmother

said. She sounded momentarily like Grandfather. That was what Grandfather had said – war was inexcusable, and the innocent suffer. 'But don't forget,' she continued, 'as Churchill said, "They have sown the wind, they shall reap the whirlwind." He said that after the bombing of Coventry.'

'What is right, what is wrong in war?' Rhino asked. 'Who judges? How can we judge?'

'Every innocent who suffers – that is wrong,' Geoffrey said.

'But who is innocent?' Rhino asked. 'If you are on the wrong side, then you are not innocent. And who judges what is the wrong side? Is it history? Or is it the victors?'

'Thomas suffered,' Mattie said suddenly.

'We all suffered,' Maria Borg Cardona, who was always so gentle and friendly, said in a cold voice to Mattie.

'Did Lucas?' Mattie asked innocently.

It transpired that Lucas had suffered too. Geoffrey Lord described the air raids in Malta, the evacuation, and the rush for the shelters, the bombing of land and sea.

'That's when Lucas lost his father,' Rhino said. 'Lucas had not even been born.'

Geoffrey went on to describe queues for food, and the endless hunger, the drone of planes in the distance and the fear of the inevitability of it all. When he mentioned the drone of planes, Mattie's face went blank as though she could not hear him.

'You girls were safe in your little green island,' Friedrich said to them.

'I beg your pardon?' Mattie said, snapping out of her reverie, her eyes narrowing and turning to look at him. 'What do you know anyway?'

'Ireland – neutral country. Cowardly, in fact.'

'That's what you might think,' Grandmother said sharply. 'You know they lost their parents and their sister during the war.'

Neither Friedrich nor Maria had not known that. They both looked mildly surprised.

'Did they?' Friedrich said. 'The accident was war-related? This I did not know. I am sorry.' His voice was as clipped and as icy as ever, but Amelia felt that he looked at both girls with a mixture of curiosity and sympathy.

'It's God's blessing that these two girls are here this evening,' Grandmother said to him.

Neither Mattie nor Amelia was used to having their past talked about, and they glanced at each other. Mattie's face was slightly twisted. And Amelia wondered again what Mattie had seen that night and what she remembered.

She asked her later.

Mattie, Thomas, Lucas and Amelia went for a walk in the moonlight down to the rocks, while the adults sat out on the terrace drinking coffee and smoking. Amelia felt safe asking her, because of Thomas being there and she knew she would not be attacked in front of him.

Thomas picked up on her question with interest. 'Yes, Mattie. What do you remember?' he asked.

He linked his arm through hers, and maybe it was because of that supportive contact that

Mattie actually told what she recalled.

'I couldn't keep up with Father,' she said. 'He used to bring us up the mountains and sometimes we could see lights far away in the distance. There was a storm that night. It came up suddenly from the south. I think that at first he had been carrying both my sister, Georgina, and me, but it was uphill and when the first drops of rain started falling he put me down and I was running to keep up with him. And then he put Georgina down too. I remember holding her hand. He was ahead of us when we heard the plane. At first there was nothing, only the rumbling of thunder, and then the sound of the thunder got louder and louder and there were lights...'

They walked on down the pathway. The moon, although full, was slightly diaphanous and it lit a long silver light across the sea that seemed unimaginably still.

'What happened then?' Thomas asked.

'I thought it was lightning. I was afraid. I let go Georgina's hand. I think I must have run. There was the most almighty ball of fire and a sound like the mountain was breaking up. I don't remember anything else,' she said. 'But I let go her hand.'

'I was born that night,' Amelia contributed so that Thomas would see her in the picture.

'She was born in a car not that far from where the crash occurred,' Mattie said. They walked the rest of the way in silence, and when they got to the rocks Mattie suggested that they went for a swim.

'We've no costumes,' Amelia pointed out.

That didn't deter the others. They stripped off their clothes, shouting at her to join them. And with a great deal of trepidation she did. She didn't want to be excluded and she didn't want to sit there and watch them naked, so she did the same thing.

There was a wonderful feeling of freedom when she dived in off the end of the point into the sea. She emerged in the stream of moonlight and felt like she had been reborn. They swam around each other in circles, diving like dolphins and coming up to breathe. Until eventually they climbed back out. Although the night air was hot, the sea was warmer, and they sat shivering while they tried to dry off. They had had on their good clothes because of the dinner party, and Amelia's cotton dress stuck to her when she tried to button herself into it.

'Let me help you,' Lucas said while her arms were twisted behind her back, trying to slip the tiny buttons into their holes. He had pulled on his shorts and she did not know whether it was the moonlight, or the fact that they had talked about their past and it was now shared, or what it was, but she suddenly liked him. Her hair was dripping and he scooped it up in his hands and squeezed it.

'That should help a bit,' he said.

She thanked him shyly. Just as she had tried not to look at them naked, she assumed they had tried not to look at her. But of course she had seen, how could she not have?' And knowing that he had seen her stirred something in her. She wished she was older and beautiful and like Mattie with her grown-up body, and suddenly and unexpectedly she wanted Lucas to like her.

'Where were you born?' she asked him.

'In an air-raid shelter.'

Well, it was probably better than in a car, she thought, from his mother's point of view, anyway, as it didn't make much difference to him where he was born, as long as he had been.

'I'm probably the only one not scarred by the war,' he said. And she thought of Thomas's terrible scars and of the torment that went on in Mattie's head, and she wondered what he meant, because she wasn't scarred, but she didn't ask him. She didn't want to know the answer.

'Do you want to come swimming with us tomorrow?' she said instead.

He seemed pleased and said yes, he would. He would cycle over the following day. And that night, all the feelings of exclusion that Amelia had felt over Mattie and Thomas evaporated. They were gone as if they had never been there.

She had a friend.

Their games were not quite as grown up as Mattie and Thomas's, but they were fun. The following day Lucas took them to Hagar Qim on their bikes. It looked to Amelia like piles of strange enormous stones and nothing much else, but they clambered up on them and Lucas told them that it was an ancient place, thousands of years old, where people once came to worship, and Amelia suddenly was aware of the movement of time outside of it, because in there among the stones it felt completely ageless and unchanging. They climbed up, scrambling from one stone to the next. The boys had their T-shirts tied around their waists.

'I worship the God of the Sun,' Thomas said, reaching the top of a stone and raising his arms to the sky. The puckering of his burned skin was even more apparent than when they went swimming. As he grew and his shoulders broadened, the skin on his left shoulder and down that side of his body had stretched even more and looked thinner than when Amelia had first seen it the previous year.

'I worship the God of the Sea,' Lucas responded, looking down to the south where the sea lay motionless like a silent blue blanket before them.

'I worship the God of Winds,' Amelia contributed.

'I bask in the heat of the day,' Mattie said.

'You have to worship something,' Amelia said, wanting Mattie to enter into the spirit of the moment.

'I don't see why I have to do anything, but if you insist then I worship the God of War,' Mattie said.

'That's not very nice,' Lucas said. He reached out and touched Thomas's scarred body. Amelia felt a shiver going down her spine. She thought of Friedrich's hand on Rhino's thigh, his fingers sliding upwards, inching their way... For a moment she imagined Lucas touching her as she had seen Friedrich doing, and she shivered.

'What's wrong with it?' Mattie asked.

'War scars,' Lucas said.

'War displaces,' Thomas said.

'War destroys,' Amelia said.

'Yes, but our lives are the result of war so if we worship the God of War then maybe he will be kinder to us,' Mattie said, closing her eyes and stretching out like a lizard on the rock.

'Who did you say you worship, Amelia?' Thomas asked.

'I don't know,' she replied, unsure if her contribution had any meaning at all. 'Maybe the God of the Wind,' she repeated tentatively.

'Zephos?' Thomas asked.

'Maybe. Or maybe Aeolus.'

'I think he was just the custodian of winds,' Thomas said.

'I know. The four winds. But I always like him. I like his name.'

'Wind brings storms,' Mattie said. 'And storms bring disaster.'

'Better than war,' Amelia retorted.

'I don't agree.'

'There are more than four winds,' Lucas said. 'We have eight here – there are the ones from the in-between directions, but I don't know their names.'

'I know all their names,' Thomas said. 'Tramuntana and Nofsinhar, Punent and Lvant – and then the winds between north, south, east and west are Grigal, Xlokk, Lbic and Majjistral,' Thomas said. 'Northeast, southeast, southwest and northwest.'

'Doesn't matter what they're called,' Mattie argued. 'Winds bring trouble.'

'Come on,' Lucas said to Amelia, 'let's go down to the sea.'

Amelia knew he was trying to divert the argument that would so easily blow up between her and Mattie. She wanted to hover longer in case Thomas had more information to share, but Lucas was moving off, so she scrambled to her feet and followed him down across the rough grass, leaving the other two up on the stones.

'Mattie always blames someone,' she said when she caught up with Lucas.

'Yes, but she doesn't argue as much as she did when I first met her a week ago,' he replied.

Amelia shrugged. He could have been right, but she was unsure, as she was the one who was invariably in Mattie's line of fire.

There were cages among the tufted grass, and kneeling down Amelia saw a tiny songbird trapped in one. She stood in horror, gazing at it.

Lucas came over to look, and he opened the catch, releasing the bird, which promptly flew away.

'So cruel,' Amelia said.

Lucas said nothing. And she felt that by criticising something in Malta she was criticising him, which she certainly had not intended to do.

'I didn't mean that you are cruel,' she said, getting back to her feet.

'I know you didn't. You're right, though. It is cruel. And if people are cruel to animals who can't do anything to defend themselves...'

'It doesn't say much for people, does it?' Amelia said. She felt sad. Sad for the tiny creature they had just released, and which probably would get caught again.

They moved on down the slope, releasing the birds that were trapped, and Amelia tried to break the traps so they could not be reset.

'Stop what you're doing,' a voice shouted.

Both Lucas and Amelia jumped in surprise. A man with a gun half cocked stood above them on the incline.

'What do you think you're up to?' he shouted at them. Dark-haired, heavy-set, scowling, he put his gun down on the ground and started running downhill towards them. Reaching them, he gave Lucas a violent shove, which sent him rolling down on his back. Amelia put her hands up to defend herself, but he grabbed one of her wrists and spun her round.

'Stop that at once,' another voice yelled, and the sound of a shot split the air. Mattie was standing further up the hill where she had picked up the hunter's gun. 'Let my sister alone,' she called, approaching them carefully, holding the gun in front of her.

'Don't be silly,' the man said, releasing Amelia and stepping towards Mattie.

'I wouldn't do that if I were you,' Mattie said.

'I want my gun back,' he said.

'We'll take it to the police and you can get it from there,' Thomas said, coming down the hill behind Mattie.

'Now back off,' Mattie shouted.

Lucas had got back to his feet and he came and stood beside Amelia and put his arm around her.

'It's all right,' he whispered.

Amelia already knew it was all right. It had

328

been all right from the moment Mattie had appeared with the gun and had protected her. Everything was all right then.

Mattie took the gun back to the house and stowed it in her bedroom, apparently with the intention of keeping it. But over dinner that evening, Thomas told the story of what had happened and how courageous Mattie had been.

'Where's the gun now?' Lucy asked after a bit.

This forced Mattie to admit that it was upstairs under her bed.

'We're going to take it to the police station tomorrow,' Thomas reassured the adults.

Lucy was aghast that the gun was in the house. Rhino had one, but she knew that he knew how to look after it. The idea of Mattie with a gun was quite disturbing.

Friedrich, who was there again for dinner, as he was most evenings now, said that he would take the gun in.

'But I want to do it,' Mattie said.

'I'll drive you over,' he said agreeably, 'but I think it might be better if I hand it in. We don't want you getting into any more trouble, now, do we?'

'What do you mean?' Mattie asked.

'I've heard of some of your escapades from Rhino,' he replied with a smile, his icy eye fixed on her.

'Rhino has a big mouth,' Mattie muttered under her breath.

Change in all things is sweet.

Aristotle

CHAPTER THIRTEEN

The summer days slipped away. That first holiday in Malta set the pattern for many following. That first summer, in the early mornings, Amelia got up to have time with Lucy. She shared in bathing Charlotte and feeding her, using this time to be close to her aunt and to talk to her. She asked her things about her mother, little things that she wondered about now, but had not in the past.

'Lucymem, are you like Mama was?'

'I always saw myself as an echo of Hilarymem,' Lucy replied. 'I always wanted to be noticed by her. I was always seeking her esteem. I imitated her, copied how she sat, learned from her, I suppose.'

This reminded Amelia of herself and Mattie, and she thought how like her aunt she really was. She also knew that in many ways she had learned from Mattie how not to behave.

'I love when Mattie smiles at me,' she said. She was sitting on a chair in the kitchen with Charlotte in her arms as Lucy prepared the dinner. Amelia put her face close to Charlotte's head and nuzzled her downy hair and breathed in her fresh warm baby smell.

Lucy, crossing the kitchen, stroked Amelia's

hair. 'We all love when Mattie smiles at us,' she said.

'I love when Charlotte is smiling at me too,' Amelia said. 'It's a really good feeling when she's looking at me and then her lips go into a smile.'

'You're such a nice child,' Lucy said to her.

'So is Mattie,' Amelia said quickly.

'In her own way, so is Mattie,' Lucy said slowly. 'In her own way,' she repeated.

It was difficult to know if Lucy was aware of what Mattie and Thomas were up to. It seemed unlikely that she could not have picked up on something, and yet she gave no sign if she did, but then, Amelia reasoned, Lucy was so absorbed by the baby, and was so busy now that there were six of them in the house.

Lucas now appeared every day, cycling over shortly after breakfast. Amelia found herself looking forward to the clatter of his bike coming across the flagstones, and the sight of his face appearing at the window, with his big black eyes and his spiky hair. He always looked hopeful and cheery, carrying a paper bag with his sandwiches.

When the four of them set out each day, they now started to separate, Thomas and Mattie going off in one direction and Amelia and Lucas in another, promising that they would meet to eat their packed lunches, but mostly not doing so. The first time Amelia and Lucas set off by themselves, they circled back to the rocks below the house to swim, because Amelia said it was her favourite place.

'Remember that night we swam here after the

dinner?' Lucas asked her.

'That was fun,' she said shyly, as the memory carried with it the image of the four of them naked.

'We could swim like that again,' he suggested.

She pretended she did not know what he meant. 'Come back at night to swim?' she asked.

'No. I meant, just taking our things off and swimming in the sea.'

She felt herself blush. Nighttime had been one thing, but this was broad daylight.

There would be no pretending not to see. She didn't say anything.

'Come on,' he said. 'I will if you will,' and he started to pull off his T-shirt. She watched him for a moment and then slowly she followed suit, keeping her back half turned to him.

'Let me see,' he said, standing in front of her.

She hesitated, then slowly she turned round, and unhurriedly pulled off her clothing, stepping out of her shorts and leaving them lying where they were. She stood there, motionless and shy, watching him and not knowing what to do.

Suddenly he kneeled down in front of her, his knees protected from the rocks by her discarded shorts, and he kissed her between her legs. She shivered and then she touched his hair, before turning and running across the rocks and diving into the sea. He caught up with her in the water and neither said anything. They bobbed there looking at each other.

'I like you,' he said.

I like you too, she thought.

They developed their games, teasing each other, always going one step further, the sun baking down on them while they explored each other. At night the moon coyly watched, while they touched and stroked and petted. Summers they spent in Malta, and Lucas and Amelia used those long hot days and nights of freedom in which to craft this art.

Over those next few years Mattie and Amelia travelled back and forth to Malta, flights out that they both learned to love, always holding hands as the plane landed, both gradually relaxing in each other's company. Then there were the flights home that they both dreaded, bringing with them the return to school, and long days and nights of incarceration. Mattie was a different person in Malta. Amelia did not know if it was because of the sun and the sea, the heat and the freedom, or whether the distance they travelled actually removed her from the past.

Back in England, in school or with the Jupes, she reverted to being the same closed person she had been before. In Malta she and Thomas raced along the narrow roads on their bicycles, with Lucas and Amelia purposely losing them at some stony crossroads, pairing off as though in silent agreement.

Amelia still painted and drew, but less so in Malta. These were pursuits that she kept for the Easter holidays when they stayed with the Jupes. They found the three terms between summers long and cold; neither mixed particularly well at school and Amelia knew loneliness then in a different way from before. Finding friendship in Malta had reinforced it. She longed for June and knew that Mattie felt the same. This became something they shared and it forged a bond between them. As summer term drew to a close they sometimes counted the days between them, passing each other on bare corridors, and whispering 'ten days to go', 'nine days to go', and on and on, until they reached the end.

Each trip saw new changes in their cousin, as Charlotte was a mere baby in arms on their first visit, and a year later she was standing, and a further year she was talking. Friendly and sweet, she endeared herself to them both, remembering them from one year to the next and running to meet them with excitement when they returned, holding their hands, wanting to be swung off the ground between them, sitting on their knees and playing with their hair. She adored them both, wanting to be with them when they were going out, begging to be carried on Mattie's back, asking Amelia to read to her, needing one of them to tuck her up in bed at night.

As time passed it became clear to the girls that there was a rift developing between Lucy and Rhino. He was a difficult man to understand. He appeared to love her but did not seem aware of her needs. He liked to know where she was and what she was doing and he ruled her life in a way that was not healthy.

Somehow Friedrich had been given back a key for their house, although Lucy never found out how that came about, but before she knew it,

Friedrich was once again ensconced in her kitchen or sitting out in the garden. It did not much matter to Mattie and Amelia because when they were there they were always out on their bicycles with Thomas and Lucas, exploring and enjoying themselves, and when they were at home Lucy had more time for them because Friedrich and Rhino would sit together in the evening in the garden while Lucy busied herself with dinner for them all.

One evening after dinner, as Rhino and Friedrich took themselves out to the garden to smoke, Mattie said to Lucy, 'Why don't you join them? Thomas, Amelia and I can clear up by ourselves.'

'You usually do anyway,' Lucy said.

'Yes, but you don't usually go out and relax – you're always busy doing something,' Mattie was seventeen now. 'Go and we'll bring out the coffee.'

'I'll just tidy up a bit first,' Lucy said.

Later, when Lucas came by for their nighttime walk or swim, and they were ambling down to the rocks, Mattie said, 'I think there is something wrong between Lucymem and Rhino.'

Amelia, who for a long time had tried to dim the memory of Friedrich's hand on Rhino's thigh, said nothing.

'I think there has been something wrong for a long time,' Thomas said, breaking the silence.

'Boys will be boys,' Lucas said, and Amelia looked at him startled. She wondered what he meant. Thomas laughed.

'Why are you laughing?' Mattie asked.

335

'Silly joke,' Thomas said quickly. 'But you're right, Mattie. I don't think Lucy is very happy.'

'She never seems to want to sit with Rhino in the evenings any more,' Mattie continued her train of thought.

'Maybe it's because she's so busy with Charlotte,' Amelia suggested hopefully. 'And she's got more work to do because we're here on holiday. Maybe when we're not here she spends more time with Uncle Rhino.'

Thomas didn't reply. Mattie let the observation go. But Amelia knew she knew that what she thought she had seen those years ago had not been some figment of her imagination. It had been for real. And she suspected that was what Lucas had meant.

Grandmother's life was one long social whirl but she always made time for the girls.

'Why does Friedrich Arnheim have a key to our house?' Mattie asked that summer.

Amelia was busy thinking about how Mattie had called the house 'ours', and she was pleased that Mattie felt they had a home in Malta because they spent so much time drifting through other people's homes when they were not locked up in school. For a moment she did not take in the question, and then she heard it, and she wondered what Mattie was implying.

'Does he?' Grandmother asked in surprise. 'Are you sure?'

Oh yes, the girls were sure. Grandmother looked bothered.

The girls went back at the end of that fourth summer, with the usual sadness and sense of something ending as they said their goodbyes.

'I'll write to you,' Lucas said to Amelia.

'Not to school,' Amelia said. 'We're not allowed letters from boys.'

'I'll get your grandmother to enclose it with hers. She does write to you, doesn't she?'

Amelia nodded. She wondered if Mattie and Thomas were having a similar farewell on some other group of rocks. She and Lucas were sitting on the last rock right out as far as they could be, side by side, arms and shoulders touching.

'I hate going back,' Amelia said.

'I hate you going,' Lucas replied.

He put his arm around her shoulders and they sat as the moon rose high in the sky and the water lapped and lapped just beneath their feet. And for a fleeting moment Amelia thought of another beach and tides and wind and then she leaned against Lucas and she sighed.

Their games had changed as reticence on both parts emerged and a safe friendship had formed between them. They seldom played their games any more, just being happy in each other's company.

It was some time later that Lucy came to her mother for morning coffee. The girls were gone and Charlotte had started nursery school. She was skirting around various things when Harriet said, 'Lucy, will you please tell me what is going on?'

Lucy did not answer at first.

'I know you're not happy,' her mother said. 'I think you really ought to tell me.'

'I don't want to bother you,' Lucy said. 'There isn't anything you can do anyway.'

'Tell me, and let me be the judge of that. I love you,' her mother said. 'I will move mountains for you.'

And so the story unfolded of Friedrich's returned and permanent presence, and Lucy's increased feelings of lack of self-worth.

'I used to feel threatened by his presence, but also by Maria Borg Cardona's. In the meantime, I realise ... I've learned that really Rhino feels nothing for her but a friendly affection. Possibly based on the war experience ... you know. But it's Friedrich I can't bear. He's just always there.'

'First of all, what do you mean about Maria and the war?'

'Oh, you know,' Lucy said. 'You must know – Rhino bombed Malta – you must have realised that?'

Harriet said nothing.

'I think that although he sees it in context,' Lucy continued, 'he cannot forgive himself for certain aspects of suffering. Hence his affection for Maria and Lucas. He is very generous to them. It used to bother me. But not any more.'

'Have you spoken to Reinhold about Friedrich?'

'Yes.' Lucy had.

She had tried to tell Rhino that she couldn't handle this man always being there, making inroads into their marriage, marginalising her by degrees until she felt that all she was, all she had become, was a mother and a housekeeper.

'Not that there is anything wrong with being those things,' she sighed, having explained the conversation to her mother. 'I like it. It's what I wanted. But I thought there would be more. I wanted more.'

'There is more,' her mother said. 'There most definitely is more. That is not what marriage is about. Marriage is about joy and fulfilment, about mutual compromise and respect, about putting the other person high up – very high up on one's agenda.'

'I feel a failure,' Lucy said.

'Do you love him?' her mother asked.

Yes, Lucy loved him. She loved him desperately.

'Do you respect him?' Harriet enquired, but Lucy was no longer sure of the answer to that question.

'I suppose so,' she said. 'Yes, of course I do.'

'Do you love yourself?'

Lucy shook her head. 'What is there to love?' she asked by way of reply, and Harriet pursed her lips.

'This won't do,' she said to her daughter. Her voice expressed both shock and dismay. 'This won't do at all. This is not the Lucy Entwhistle I once knew. It was Hilary I worried about – Hilary who wanted to marry and be a wife.'

'But that's what we were brought up to do,' Lucy objected.

'Yes, I know. It's what we're meant to do,' Harriet said. 'But... I said that it was Hilary I worried about, and in fact that isn't true. I was worried about Hilary's choice of husband. That is all. I worried about you because you were so strong and determined and full of inquisitiveness about life. I worried because I couldn't imagine you settling down, and how can one be happy if one has not settled down? After you took over the rearing of Hilary's children, I then worried about you not meeting someone, not finding someone to fulfil you.'

Lucy said nothing at first. Then, 'I always loved Rhino. Since I first met him.'

'Is it possible he is not how you remembered him?' Harriet asked.

'That would not be fair on him,' Lucy replied. 'He probably is just as I remembered him. I suppose I did not know him.'

'But how could you have known him?' Harriet asked. And after a moment's pause, 'Are you prepared to lose him?'

'I've already lost him,' Lucy said.

'Then leave him.'

Easy words to say, but a difficult action to see through to its bitter end.

Lucy returned home, went about her usual chores with Charlotte playing with her dolls on the floor beside her, and Thomas, coming home from school, lifted Charlotte up and hugged her.

'I miss Mattie and Amelia,' he said. 'Thank goodness I have you, Charlie.'

Charlotte put her little arms around him and kissed him. Later that night, when Friedrich had finally left and she had cleared away the brandy glasses and the coffee cups, Lucy went upstairs to where Rhino was getting ready for bed.

'Rhino, I need to talk,' she said.

He glanced up from the chest of drawers where he was looking for something. 'Yes, Lucymem,' he said, picking up a comb and drawing it through his hair. He was watching her now through the mirror on top of the cupboard.

'Rhino, this is not a marriage. I can't stay with it any more.'

He put the comb down, and turned round. Coming over to her, he led her to the bed. 'Don't be silly,' he said. 'You've got a lovely home, little Charlotte and me. What more do you want?'

'I want you, and I don't want to share you with someone else.'

There was a moment's silence and he looked at her. Shock crossed his face. And in that moment Lucy knew with the most amazing clarity that Rhino was having a relationship with Friedrich – a physical affair, not just an intellectual one – and she saw him clearly for the first time ever. It came in on her almost with disbelief. How could she not have seen it before? How could she not have known what was going on? He was weak. She had not realised this ever before. She had seen him as a solid entity, and had not looked through to the flaws, to the selfishness, to his continual need to satisfy himself. She did not like what she saw.

He soothed her with comforting words. 'You mean Friedrich,' he said smoothly. But she could hear the slightest tremor in his voice.

'Yes,' she said simply.

'Friedrich and I go back a long way – you know that. From before the war. Training in North

Africa. He stuck by me. And I by him. Like me, when the war was over he had little left. I at least found Thomas. Fritz found ... well, he found no one. His whole family was wiped out. He is like a brother to me.'

Again she could hear something in his voice. It was unclear if he was trying to convince her or himself.

'I love you, Lucymem,' he went on. 'Don't say such things – don't talk of leaving me. If Friedrich is around too much, I'll ask him not to come over so often. But I can't exclude him from my life. He is my closest friend. You must see that.'

'I asked you once about him and you wouldn't tell me.'

'I told you to ask him yourself. It's his story to tell. Not mine. Now come here.'

He talked her into getting into bed with him. He held her close while she tried to bite back tears, and when he made advances to her in the bed, she could smell Friedrich on his skin, and she could imagine his large and hard body heaving against Rhino, and she shuddered in revulsion, and she could feel her respect for him evaporating. She felt that she could never love him again. And when he entered her, she wanted to pull away. She wanted to scream out Friedrich's name and tell him that she knew. But she did not.

She did nothing.

'I don't know what to do, Mother,' she said. 'He even said it himself. Friedrich is his best friend. Please don't misunderstand – I don't have a best friend. I wouldn't want Rhino not to, just because I don't. But I thought – I hoped – that he and I would be best friends. I thought... I thought there would be more between us than there is. I can't bear it.'

'You must leave him. You must find yourself,' Harriet replied, as she had done before.

Lucy had not thought that Harriet really could see it so clearly. She thought the first time her mother had said it that she had not meant it. But here was Harriet repeating it. Lucy thought that her mother, being of a different generation, of a different ilk, of the old school, would not see that as an option. She hardly saw it as an option herself.

'I don't know how to,' she said, chewing her lip.

'Oh, yes you do,' Harriet replied. 'You will do it with the strength and determination you have always shown. You will pick up the pieces of your life as you picked up the pieces of Hilary's. No one could stop you from taking on Mattie and Amelia.'

'But I knew that was the right thing to do,' Lucy said.

'And what do you think is the right thing to do here? Sometimes we have clarity when we look at other people's lives. Like I have clarity when I look at yours. I don't know when I last saw you laughing.'

Lucy was torn. She was caught between her upbringing and her approach to marriage and the slow-dawning realisation that the position she was in was untenable.

'Where did I go wrong?' she asked.

'I don't think that you did go wrong or do wrong. In my opinion the compromise that has to be reached in a marriage was not reached in yours.'

They left the matter there, and Lucy did nothing. She waited, hoping that things would improve.

They did not.

The strength she had had in the past was not there. She did not seem to have the resources to tackle the problem, and Friedrich seemed more and more entrenched in their home.

It was months later and Rhino and Lucy were having dinner in Harriet's house, with Charlotte asleep in a bed upstairs.

'I was thinking how nice it would be to take a trip to Europe,' Harriet said.

'What a good idea,' Rhino replied. 'It would be lovely for you.'

'Not just for me, Reinhold. I was thinking of inviting you and Lucy to come too. And Charlotte, of course.'

'I couldn't take time off,' Rhino responded, just as Harriet had known he would. She looked at him and said nothing. 'We're very busy, and I'm expanding all the time,' he continued.

'What a pity. But, Lucy, you could come. It would do you good. I'm getting old, and I'd love to have some time with you and Charlotte.'

And with her customary force of argument, Harriet convinced them both that Lucy and she would go abroad, Charlotte going with them, while Rhino stayed and worked.

Thomas looked at Lucy when she told him, and for a moment she thought she saw a look of consternation in his eyes but then his usual impassivity took over.

'Will you go to England?' he asked.

'I don't know, because it is a surprise trip,' Lucy told him. 'Mother won't say. All I know is that we are going to fly to Rome.'

'For how long?'

'In Rome? Again, I don't know. Altogether my mother says six weeks. I imagine only a week in Rome. But I'm not sure.'

'I'll miss you,' Thomas said. 'And Charlotte.'

Charlotte, now four years old, had Lucy's fair hair, and her father's blue eyes, and her personality was like Amelia's. She was a calm child and she adored Thomas. She called him her brother.

'I will miss Charlotte a lot,' he repeated.

'She will miss you too,' Lucy said to him. 'And so will I.'

He did not ask if they were coming back. And Lucy, who had no definite plans, could not imagine not coming back, but when she said goodbye, she felt that it was all changing.

She also knew that by leaving for six weeks, she was making things easier for Friedrich. She did not like that feeling, but as Harriet said to her, she wouldn't be there to see what happened, and she should use the time to heal herself and to find out what it was she really wanted.

Her daily routine fell away quicker than she

thought it would, each day now bringing with it an element of surprise and excitement.

They got up in the morning, sometimes not even sure which city they were in and having to remind themselves by looking out the window to see what view was in front of them. Each opened like a new page in front of Lucy and once again she was astounded by the magnificence of Rome, only this time she was focused on it, not like she had been five years earlier when all she could think about was getting to Malta. Florence surprised her all over again with its narrow streets and its more recent sense of history, and Venice captured her.

They were in Paris when Harriet asked her how she felt about going back to Malta.

'I don't think I want to go back,' Lucy admitted.

'I thought as much.'

'How about you?'

'Oh. I want to. I love it there. It answered many of the questions I've looked for since we left India. I love the climate,' Harriet replied. 'I love the people.'

'I like those things too,' Lucy said, but, of course, for her, they were not the prime issue. The problem was Rhino, it was the erosion of her marriage, it was the isolation in their home, and it was the loneliness that enveloped her. She could not tell her mother all of this because it added to her feelings of failure.

'When were you happiest?' her mother asked.

It was a thought-provoking question that brought up memories of when she had met Rhino

346

for the second time, almost accidentally in the Co-Cathedral in Valletta. That was happiness. That had been joy. That meeting had been full of promise. The light coming through the windows had caught them in an instant like the insects in the amber, and they were trapped as they had seen each other – an image of perfection in the aeons of time.

She asked herself over and over what she really wanted. And despite the feelings of rejection and the loss of love, she finally found she still wanted their marriage to work. The idea of destroying Charlotte's happiness was anathema to her. There was the added problem, as she saw it, that Harriet had moved to Malta because of her. That her mother had clearly settled and was happy there did not negate her sense of obligation to Harriet. For Lucy to leave Malta would also mean abandoning her mother. Her obligations appeared to her to outweigh her marital problems, and distance from Malta made her feel that she had the strength to try again.

They were in Amsterdam when she said to her mother that she needed to give the marriage another attempt.

'Are you sure?' Harriet asked her.

Lucy nodded. She was sure. She explained that she needed to give it another go, if not for her own beliefs in the sanctity of marriage and for the sake of the hopes she had held when she entered into it, then for her daughter. She did not mention the need not to disrupt her mother's life.

When Charlotte looked up at her with her big

blue eyes, she saw Rhino in them. It was like looking into a genetic pool, and leaving him at that moment seemed a rejection of her own daughter. She thought of the girls in their boarding school in England and how the war had taken their parents. She knew that life threw enough bad things at children without her deliberately adding to it by taking Charlotte from Rhino. She was not sure if she was doing the right thing in going back. Nor was she sure that she would be better able to handle the situation, but separation from it had given her a new lease of energy and she felt determination by returning to Malta.

Harriet accepted her decision without trying to talk her out of it.

'You must do what you think is right,' she said. 'But you must never feel trapped. Just promise me, if it doesn't work that you will leave.'

Harriet took the boat on to England while Lucy and Charlotte flew back to Malta to try once again to make the marriage work.

Friedrich met them at the airport – suave and smooth he greeted them. He kissed Charlotte, who had always loved him. And Lucy, standing stock-still in disbelief that Rhino could not have made the effort to come to collect them, tried so hard to bring a friendly smile to her face.

'Thomas wanted to come and collect you,' Friedrich said. 'But Rhino and I felt he should not be taking the afternoon off school. So I came instead.'

Back at the farmhouse, Friedrich brought their

bags upstairs and Charlotte lay down for a nap. He joined Lucy in the garden and, offering her a cigarette, which she declined, he lit one for himself.

'You know, Lucy, you and I have never talked that much. I don't know why. It just is so. I do not talk much, as you know.'

Lucy watched him. She knew he talked to Rhino. She'd seen and heard him talk with Maria Borg Cardona.

'But I thought that perhaps I might tell you my story.'

She listened. She knew she was curious, but she was also angry. Angry that he had come to the airport and not Rhino, angry that he was sitting with her in the garden six weeks after she had left home, and there was no sign of Rhino to greet her.

'Once,' he said, 'I did a favour for Rhino. And as a result of that momentary act of kindness, I lost my eye.' His long fingers touched his eye patch and he looked at her with his other one. 'I therefore could not fly. We had been trained as fighter pilots and I found myself in a different role in the war. I served my country and, like Rhino, I was captured at the end and, like Rhino, I served my sentence in quite brutal circumstances. I am only alive because Rhino stuck by me during those few years. His humanity to me, our friendship – it is what I live for. I have nothing else. I am not interested in anything else. I do not wish to come between Rhino and his happiness, and if that happiness is you, I will not do anything to destroy it. I ask you the same.'

Lucy sat there speechless. She had no idea what he was really saying. Was it that they would fight it out for Rhino? She could not imagine that he was being serious.

'I don't understand,' she said slowly.

'I am asking you to permit me to remain Rhino's friend.'

'But that's not my choice,' she said. 'That's Rhino's.'

She wondered now who had decided Friedrich should come to the airport and if they had concocted this conversation between them. She was angry and felt manipulated but did not want to tell Friedrich what she thought of him, as she knew anything she said would go back to Rhino. She did not want this conversation, and she withdrew from it by going inside to unpack.

'Let yourself out when you are ready,' she said over her shoulder. She left him sitting there in the shade, cigarette in hand, legs crossed, looking ahead.

Probable impossibilities are to be preferred to improbable possibilities.

Aristotle

CHAPTER FOURTEEN

The school years, like the summer holidays, slipped past. The routine of class and study kept the Cholmondesley girls grounded, each in her own way. Mattie's aspirations and Amelia's differed greatly, as did their approach to things. For Amelia, the time passed when she was working, so she worked hard. For Mattie, time had always hung on her hands but after that first summer in Malta, her attitude changed. She brightened up, as if the sunshine there had lit her up inside. Amelia still saw her in school with a sulky introverted look on her beautiful face, but the glow she took back from their trip remained in some aspect of her personality.

Fears that Amelia once had of Mattie burning down another building had faded. She knew that Malta had helped Mattie to move forward, perhaps even healed her a little.

They came back to England each time with their skin tanned and in some way their blood seemed warmer, richer, fuller and augmented them, so that they could handle the coldness of the cold climate.

Efforts they had made each summer to remain

in Malta had fallen on deaf ears, which Amelia now saw as a good thing. Apart from anything else, it gave Mattie something to look forward to, and it meant that they were not exposed on a daily basis to the slow but seemingly inevitable breakdown of the relationship between Lucymem and Rhino. Amelia was haunted by her memory of Friedrich's hand. She had tried so hard to tell herself that she had imagined it, that there must have been something else behind it, some other adult meaning that she could not understand. She sometimes thought of trying to discuss it with Mattie, but she was afraid of Mattie sneering and not believing her. She worried about Lucy, what would happen to her, how she would cope if she ever found out that Friedrich loved Rhino – and worse, that Rhino harboured something for his friend.

One night back in school, she woke up suddenly, having had a dream, and she could see Rhino and Friedrich that afternoon on the boat up at the Blue Lagoon, in their black swimsuits, and their strong bodies and blond hair, and she thought of the Greek gods. She lay there for a long time, thinking of all the different things the gods had done – and some of them were very strange. Zeus had put the baby Dionysus into his thigh until he was born. Hermaphroditos was the son of Hermes and Aphrodite. He had been loved by the nymph Salmakis, who prayed she could be with him for ever, and the gods, on hearing her prayer, merged their two forms into one to form a being that was both male and female. She thought how Rhino and Friedrich looked like gods that day on the boat and she knew that strange things could happen between people. She wished that Lucy would never know and would never be affected by these events.

Mattie, being that much older, finished school ahead of Amelia and applied for university in London. She had also applied to the Royal Air Force for reasons that she never explained to anyone, but when finding that she would not be allowed to go to war as a fighter pilot because she was female, she abandoned that course of action and she turned them down instead.

Mattie's interests were not very widespread and included little more than fire and aeroplanes. Her fear of flying had been diluted over the years until it finally disappeared and was replaced with the same enthusiasm she had always shown in fire and conflagration.

Since the day they had gone to Hagar Qim, Amelia had become increasingly intrigued by antiquity and archaeology, and she encouraged Mattie to look at it as a possibility.

'Archaeology,' Mattie mused. It did not seem such a bad idea to Amelia, because if Mattie studied it, Amelia could pick up bits of information from her. Mattie gave it more consideration than Amelia imagined she would. Going back to something further than her own history and looking at its effects on life and the progress or otherwise of mankind began to interest her. However, after reading the literature outlining the extent of the course, Mattie finally decided that it was not for her.

She had been forbidden from studying chemistry in school following the fire, but there was nothing to stop her taking it up at university level provided she did a course in it beforehand to bring her up to the right level.

'Mattie,' Amelia said as Mattie's last term in school was coming to a close. 'You're going to be in the London house next year. Do you think I could come to?'

Mattie grinned.

'Why the smile?'

'Well, I'd prefer you as my housemate, and Grandmother and Lucy have said in letters that I have to have someone there with me.'

Amelia's heart soared. 'Do you think we can talk them into it?'

'We can talk them into anything if we put our minds to it,' Mattie said. 'You're so bloody diligent – they'll see you as a positive influence on me. Yes, this will work. You're such a Goody Two-Shoes.'

Amelia might have taken offence, but instead she saw compliance and agreement as the best way forward. 'Which of us suggests it?' she asked.

'I hate saying this, but I think it ought to come from you. And then I'll show a little reluctance and let them coerce me into it.'

'Well, don't show too much reluctance in case they think it might cause friction.'

They hatched their plan and Amelia first approached Uncle Jupe, who surprisingly thought it was a great idea, and said he would broach Harriet and Lucy.

The London house was cleaned once a month by the cleaning lady of the Farringtons next door, and was less musty than Mattie and Amelia expected.

They did not go to Malta that summer; instead they started living in North London, opening the windows to air the place, throwing out old things from their childhood and cleaning out the presses in the kitchen. Harriet expressed interest in coming over to help them, but was convinced by both Uncle Jupe and Mattie that there was no need. Uncle Jupe said that he and Anne would drop in regularly, that it was giving Mattie a new sense of responsibility and how wonderful it was watching her respond to this. Roger Farrington and his wife, both still living next door, gave what assistance was required, but the girls were very self-sufficient and had little interest in outside influences.

Mattie painted her bedroom red and would have started on other rooms in the house had Amelia not convinced her that it might not be the best idea.

'Grandmother might get to hear of it, and I don't think she'd like it,' she said, when Mattie said what she was planning on doing to the rest of the house.

'Are you going to tell her?' Mattie asked crossly.

'No, I'm not, but the Farringtons will find out. They'll see through the windows. And Uncle Jupe is going to be checking up on us. Don't do it, Mattie. It's not worth it. Your own room is fine. No one will find out. But I wouldn't paint anywhere else red.'

So with the Air Force abandoned, Mattie started at her college in London where she studied a foundation course in chemistry, and discovered that she had no problem whatsoever in catching up on those who had done it in their A levels. Formulae, equations and compounds came easily to her, especially if she could see the potential in creating explosives.

Once again the Farringtons helped in the finding of a school for Amelia, which Uncle Jupe and Aunt Anne inspected and found acceptable.

Thomas was the first to join them. He came to London at the end of that summer to study business with a view to going into Rhino's now well-established construction company and eventually running the financial side of it. Thomas's relationship with Mattie had changed. The passion was gone, and the two of them were like old friends. Occasionally a spark from the past would ignite between them, but the rest of the time they let each other be.

Mattie's money had come through and at nineteen years old she bought a motorbike and red leather clothing. The girls discovered a world they did not know existed, so hermetic had been their existence, between the Jupes and Malta.

These were the dying days of teddy boys and the rise of mods and rockers, cults replacing cults without the Cholmondesley sisters having been fully aware of either.

Amelia and Mattie headed for Carnaby Street, Regent Street and Knightsbridge. They heard music that had been prohibited in school and had not been part of their summers in Malta. They bought clothes for themselves for the first time. They shared in a way they had not shared before. Amelia no longer boarded at school so they were together every day. Mattie's hours were more flexible and she did the shopping, and then, because Amelia's school work was so time-consuming and Mattie was totally disinterested in cooking, Thomas took over the kitchen chores.

Then, when Amelia was in her last year in school and had been accepted into the best art college, Lucas joined them. Their *ménage à quatre* had the elements of a commune about it, but with four very distinctive personalities.

Mattie's red phase had expanded, and her wardrobe consisted only of scarlet garments. Even her underwear had all been dyed. She had no interest in being allied with any cult. She avoided the motorbike gangs with disdain.

Thomas, now exceptionally tall and lean with his broad shoulders, and still with traces of different accents in his voice, was very comfortable in himself and Amelia had long forgiven him for transferring his affections to her older sister. She no longer remembered that she had moved from hero-worshipping her grandfather, to worshipping him. She loved him as a cousin and trusted him as a friend. Sometimes she thought of him as a big brother, someone who was there for her, who kept the structure of the house in place, a positive influence on Mattie and a stalwart prop in their odd home.

The surprise element was Lucas. When he

joined them the year he had turned eighteen, his behaviour and appearance had changed dramatically. At first Amelia was not understanding of it, but when her attention was drawn to it, she had to acknowledge that there was something different in him. She and he had played their games together for several years, but she had withdrawn from them when she was in her mid-teens when the intensity of what they were doing became too much for her. He had seemed quite content with the change of tempo. She still liked him and they still teased each other, but neither seemed to want more than that. She had not realised that Lucas had pulled back from their activities just as she had done. She thought that she had been the one to redirect their friendship. It only began to occur to her now that it had been mutual.

She did not know words like 'camp' and 'effete', not until Mattie used them and she asked what they meant.

'He's a bugger,' Mattie replied. It had always been Mattie's favourite word.

Amelia looked at her startled. 'Lucas?'

'Yes,' Mattie grinned. 'With all your classical knowledge, even you must know what that means.'

Amelia thought of Friedrich and Rhino on board the boat, and realised she had known what it meant for a very long time.

Lucas was now a little taller than Mattie and Amelia, and he enjoyed wearing their pyjamas – much softer fabric, he assured them. His hair was slightly too long, and hung in a limp point down the side of his face. He was exceptionally fussy about moisturising cream and insisted that Mattie and Amelia took his advice. Amelia watched this at first with some bewilderment, unsure if it were all some kind of joke although it would have been out of character for Lucas to joke at their expense. Rhino had taken over his education and had sent him to London to commence a degree in medicine. However, he had transferred to the art school where Amelia was planning on going.

'But what about fees?' Thomas asked him. 'Isn't Rhino paying the wrong place?'

Lucas reassured him that that was all under control, his allowance covered his fees and joyfully the art college was less expensive than the medical school.

'AND – an added bonus – the medical course takes two years longer than the art one, so I'll be able to stay on and on,' Lucas said.

'Isn't Rhino going to notice in six years' time that you are not qualified as a doctor?' Amelia asked tentatively. Such deception was beyond her imagination.

'I doubt it,' Lucas said. 'First of all he is too busy juggling your aunt Lucy and dear old Cyclops. And secondly, he isn't paying. Cyclops is.'

Amelia was not sure that she liked Lucymem being spoken of like that. She would never have said anything that in any way belittled her aunt, but the others were all so grown up and they all laughed, so she did too.

'Poor old Rhino,' Mattie said. 'Being devoured

by a one-eyed monster.'

'Maybe it is the other way around,' Lucas said with a laugh. 'Who knows what Rhino does to the eye socket in the Cyclops' head!'

'Lucas,' Thomas said, 'keep the vulgar comments to yourself when the girls are around.'

Mattie was laughing. 'Anyway, why is Cyclops paying?' she asked.

'Why not? He's fond of me,' Lucas said with a laugh.

'What? What are you saying?'

'No, not like that. He just likes me. I suppose.'

Lucas was taken with Mattie's red motorbike and matching leather gear, and he wanted to buy the same so he could sit on the back of it and look like her sister.

'Well, you can't,' Mattie said. 'Red is my colour. Go get your own. And anyway, I have one sister and that's more than enough for me.'

'Leather,' said Lucas, ignoring her comment. 'I just love it, darling.'

He sat in quite a prim way, with his legs tightly crossed, and he drank with a little finger upwards. He bought a red silk cravat, so that 'we'll connect', as he put it to Mattie, but he abandoned the notion of the red leather clothing.

Thomas bought a motorbike too. Amelia envied them their freedom, but knew to be happy with the fact that at least she was no longer in boarding school and that in itself was liberation. She went in and out to school by bus, using the time for thinking, for going over her work, for learning things off by heart. She looked forward to the evenings at home. Occasionally there was no one there, but usually there was at least one of the others, if not more. Lucas now did the cooking.

'I trust no one to be sufficiently hygienic,' he said. He had become as fastidious in his cooking as he was in his appearance. Never had onions been so neatly chopped, nor beef so well pounded, and although the rest of them took it in turns to clear up afterwards, even this was an operation that he oversaw with extreme care, wiping down surfaces after they had finished.

To Amelia's dismay they all loved Monopoly and there was a permanent game on the go on a table in their drawing room. But she was older now, and capable of saying that it wasn't for her. She was studying anyway in the evenings, and the last thing she wanted was to be buying some station or sitting in gaol, so they left her out of it and she got on with her work.

Sometimes at night Lucas got into bed beside her and they slept curled up together. He was no longer interested in her body like he had been when they were children, but she did not want anything else either. She liked the companionable state of affairs, and there was something lovely about being held in bed and just sleeping in someone's arms.

The first time he came into her room late one night, she had been half-asleep.

'Do you mind?' he asked, as he lifted the bedclothes and slipped in beside her.

At first she was unsure what he was planning, but it transpired that all he wanted was to put his arm around her, and sleep against her.

It was all she wanted too.

There were times during those years living in North London, attending school as a day girl, when she could not imagine life being better. As their house filled up, first with Thomas and then with Lucas, Amelia began to feel that she had found a niche. Mattie occasionally played parent and wrote a note to school when Amelia was ill with the flu or when they had to go to a funeral when Roger Farrington's wife next door died. The Farringtons had been kind to them when they moved in, although Mattie was inclined to see them as being interfering but in fact they were not. They were decent people who expressed an interest in the girls. Amelia always remembered them with kindness from when she and Lucy-mem lived in the London house years earlier. The Farrington boys, with whom she had once played, were both away boarding in a Scottish public school, and spent a lot of their holidays with their grandparents in Ayr, so there was very little contact with them. She admired the Farringtons for never showing surprise or shock in the activities that were going on in the house next door to them, between Mattie in red on her motorbike, Lucas taking in the milk dressed in the girls' pyjamas, Thomas with his unusual mixture of accents and his occasional flights of speech into German when shouting at his housemates to hurry up, and Amelia traipsing off to school every day in her uniform.

She was taking the bus home one day from

school, and as it pulled in to the kerb about four stops from home, she looked out the window and there below her was Mattie dressed in a smart dark suit, her hair tied back. She turned slightly away from the bus and Amelia could see her hair, dark and curly, lying down her spine. She was wearing stockings and flat shoes.

Amelia was stunned. She had never seen Mattie dressed like that, and in fact did not know she owned such clothes, and she wondered what her sister was up to. She was about to knock on the window to try to get her attention when the bus pulled away. When Amelia got home Mattie was already there, sitting in the kitchen at the table, reading a paper.

'Did you get a taxi?' Amelia asked.

'How do you mean?' Mattie looked up at her.

'I saw you at the bus stop,' she said.

'I don't know what you're talking about,' Mattie replied, returning to the newspaper. 'I've been home all afternoon.' She was dressed in red as usual.

There was a teapot on the table and Amelia reached out and touched it. The heat was gone out of it. For the life of her, Amelia could not see what her sister was playing at. She had definitely seen her at the bus stop, and yet here she was, sitting at the table with all the appearance of having been there for some time. She went upstairs to change out of her gymslip.

Listening carefully on the landing to be sure that she had not been followed, she slipped into Mattie's room and looked around for the dark skirt and jacket she had seen her in. Her place was a bit of a mess, with underwear and damp towels scattered on the floor amidst red jumpers and other bits of clothing. She looked quickly in the wardrobe but there was no sign of the suit there either.

Puzzled, she went to her own room and changed.

It was two days later when she saw her again in the same clothes at the same stop. She leaped to her feet and jumped from the bus just as it pulled off. Mattie was now walking down the road.

'Mattie,' Amelia yelled. 'Mattie, stop.'

Mattie hesitated for a moment as if listening, and then she stepped out into the road and was hit by a car. It happened so fast that Amelia could do nothing. She saw it as if in slow motion. Her sister bounced on the bonnet of the car and was tossed back onto the road where she lay in a crumpled heap.

Amelia raced forwards, as did many other people.

'Please, please let me through. She's my sister,' she begged, pushing herself through the crowd. The driver of the car had got out and was standing there on the road, shaking. He was saying something like 'I didn't see her' over and over.

Someone yelled to get an ambulance. People were crouching beside the fallen girl. One man said he was a doctor and asked everyone to move back.

'She's my sister,' Amelia pleaded. 'Please let me through.'

She was let through and she kneeled down and

held her hand. Mattie's face was white and badly cut, with blood running from her forehead and down over her eyes. Amelia tried wiping it off with her scarf. She held her hand and she prayed for a god, if there was one, to come and save Mattie.

She was unconscious and the doctor opened the buttons at the top of her blouse. One of Mattie's arms was twisted behind her. The ambulance came surprisingly quickly and the ambulance men placed her carefully on a stretcher.

Amelia looked around and, finding Mattie's shoes, she picked them up and climbed into the vehicle with her.

That journey to the hospital was the longest trip she could imagine. She was not allowed to be beside the stretcher. They made her sit at the back while they busied themselves with Mattie's prone body. She held her sister's shoes on her knees, touching them over and over with her fingertips, wondering why she had never noticed them before, horrified at the scrapes across the leather, which she knew were reflected on her sister's torn and battered body.

'What happened?' one of the crew asked her.

'I called her. I called her name and she stepped out into the road. I don't know if she heard me. I don't know what happened. Or why. I don't know anything...' Amelia was incoherent in her distress.

At the hospital Mattie was rushed away on a trolley and a nurse helped Amelia to a chair.

'It's all right,' the nurse said. She sent for tea, sweet tea with far too much sugar in it, but Amelia did what she was told and drank it.

Time appeared stationary and she sat there in a daze while people came and went and somehow the dragging minutes passed while she was not aware of it.

'Your sister is in theatre,' she was told. 'Head injury, broken arm, broken ribs. Just stay here and we'll be back to you.'

When she saw Mattie later she was asleep, with bandages around her head and her arm in plaster. Amelia could only see a little of her face. Her nails were longer and more polished than she recalled ever seeing them and there were bruises and cuts on her hands. She stroked her arm gently and whispered to her that it was going to be all right.

There was a handbag on the bedside locker. Amelia picked it up and stroked it as she had Mattie's arm, before replacing it on the metal surface. This was a side of Mattie she had never seen before – there was something about the handbag, something about its shiny imitation leather that upset her. She puzzled over what Mattie had been up to, and for how long she had been at it, whatever it was. She sat there until the nurse told her to go home for the night. The nurse said they would make contact if there were any changes but that they expected Mattie to sleep through and that she appeared stable.

Amelia caught a taxi home and let herself in as quietly as she could. As she crept through the hall Mattie ran in from the kitchen.

'Where have you been?' she shouted, almost in tears.

Amelia couldn't reply.

She stared at Mattie, at her unmarked face, her long red dress, her loose black curls, and her knees weakened. She felt them give and she would have fallen had Thomas not grabbed her and carried her inside, easing her on to the sofa. They made her lie down. Mattie kneeled beside her on the floor, holding her hand.

'Darling Mealie,' Thomas said. 'We're not angry with you. We were just worried.'

Amelia stared at Mattie. She lay and stared at her. Lucas got her a glass of water. There were too many shocks going on. She could not take anything in. She felt a sense of the densest bewilderment.

'Mattie,' she finally said, struggling to a sitting position.

'That's me,' Mattie said, kneeling beside her. 'You're as white as a sheet. What's wrong, baby?'

'Mattie,' Amelia said again. She said it over and over. Mattie. Mattie. Mattie.

'She's going to faint,' Thomas said, and they made her lie down again on the sofa.

'Mattie,' Amelia whispered again. 'How can you be here?'

They all looked puzzled and glanced at each other.

'I left you in hospital,' Amelia said. 'I saw you. I left you there.'

'I'm here,' she said. 'Where have you been? What's going on?'

A good question, and one Amelia wanted answers to as well.

She told them about seeing Mattie at the bus

stop, and getting off and calling to her, and how Mattie had walked straight out into the road under a car.

'Mattie's been here all afternoon,' Thomas said to her. His voice was very calm and, kneeling on the floor beside the sofa, he took her hand from Mattie's. 'I've been with her, Amelia. And Lucas got in at about six. Amelia,' Amelia's eyes were going wildly from one of them to the other. 'Amelia,' he repeated. He was talking very slowly. 'Focus on me. I'm telling you the truth. Mattie was here all afternoon. We've been looking for you since eight o'clock. We even phoned the school. I went down to the library on the bike. We've looked everywhere. And Mattie has been looking for you too.'

'But I saw her,' Amelia said, desperation in her voice. 'And it's not the first time. There was that day – oh, I don't know when. A couple of days ago, I saw you then.' She turned to Mattie. 'I saw you at the bus stop and when I got home you were here.'

'Have you been drinking?' Lucas asked her gently.

For a moment Amelia wondered if she had been drinking, because she was desperate for an explanation.

'I don't understand,' she said.

'Let me get this straight,' Thomas said. 'A few days ago you saw Mattie at a bus stop...'

'Dressed in a black suit,' she affirmed. 'And when I got home, Mattie was here. And I thought she must have got a taxi. I thought maybe she'd got a job or something and didn't want any of us to know. I checked her room for the suit. I was that sure.'

'And you saw her again today?'

'Yes. And when I tried to speak to her, she just walked off the pavement and a car hit her. I've been in the hospital with her.'

'And what did she say?'

'She didn't say anything. She's unconscious.'

'I'm here,' Mattie said. 'And you didn't see me. Whoever it was, it wasn't me.'

That was beginning to dawn on Amelia too.

'Everyone has a double somewhere in the world,' Lucas said. 'Except me, of course.'

Well, that last bit did not surprise anyone. There couldn't have been a double of Lucas because he was unique. But then were they all unique, Amelia thought. Mattie couldn't have a double. Even Amelia, who looked so like her, could not be mistaken for her. And then she thought of the girl's hands and the long polished nails, and she reached out and took one of Mattie's hands in hers. They were very similar in shape to the girl's in the hospital, but Mattie's nails were not that long, nor were they polished in a shiny pink colour.

'It's not you,' Amelia said slowly. 'The nails are wrong. But she looked so like you. I was absolutely sure. Please tell me you believe me,' she said to the others.

'We believe you, all right,' Thomas said. 'No one could make up such an odd story. But I can see an awful problem...'

'What is it?' Lucas asked.

'Well, there's a girl down in the hospital who

has been misidentified and maybe there is someone out there waiting for her to come home tonight.'

They got their coats and went to the hospital on the motorbikes, Amelia clutching on to Thomas, and Lucas sitting back as he always did behind Mattie. It was very difficult getting the night nurse to believe them. Eventually they let Mattie and Amelia in to look at the girl, but she was so bandaged, and the bit of her face that was exposed was swollen so it was impossible to convince Mattie that she looked like her.

'For heaven's sake,' Mattie said. 'I hope I don't look like that.'

The nurse took the girl's handbag out and in it was a purse with some money, a comb and a compact. And a letter addressed to Miss Breda Mangan.

'I think we can assume that this is Breda Mangan,' the nurse said.

The letter was from someone who appeared to be an old school friend of Breda's and was full of memories and gossip about other girls.

'I'll phone the police and report this,' the nurse said. 'They'll check out the address on the envelope.'

Amelia thought she meant that she was now in trouble for having given the wrong name to the girl, but it was not that at all. Mattie pointed out on the way out of the hospital that someone might have reported Breda Mangan missing.

'Some poor parents or husband sitting at home waiting for old Breda to return,' Lucas said to Amelia.

'I'm surprised that you would think I might ever buy a handbag like that one,' Mattie said crossly. 'You must think I have no taste.'

There didn't seem much point in trying to explain to Mattie that the handbag *had* surprised her too, so Amelia didn't say anything. She felt absolutely exhausted and could hardly stand up.

When they got home they went to bed, but an hour later Amelia was still awake and she felt terribly cold, so she went in to Lucas, who obligingly moved over and wrapped his arms around her. She usually slept well like that.

'God, but I wish you were a boy,' he whispered. He always said things like that to make her giggle. She gave him a perfunctory chuckle, but her mind was elsewhere. It was in fact in the hospital in that bed at the end of the ward, where a girl was lying wrapped in bandages and totally unidentified because of her. Well, she corrected herself, not so much unidentified as alone.

Alone, because she, Amelia, had claimed her as hers and she was nothing to do with the Cholmondesleys.

The following morning Mattie rang the school and excused Amelia for the day, and then Amelia rang the hospital and was told that Breda Mangan had had a good night. She asked if anyone had come to see her yet, but the nurse on the ward didn't know. What Amelia wanted to know was had her family been informed, but again the nurse didn't know. She said to call back, that they were in the middle of changing shifts.

Amelia waited until the afternoon and then

Lucas and she went to the hospital together.

'Of course it isn't your fault, silly,' he said to her, when she explained how guilty she felt and how she feared that in some way her calling had made the girl step off the pavement. 'How could the fact that you called out Mattie's name make this Breda step off a footpath?' Now if it were Mattie, and she was up to something illicit and you had come across her, then I could understand her being agitated. No, this was just bad luck. Even if you had not been there she would still have stepped into the road.'

'That's a bit fatalistic, isn't it?' Amelia said.

'Well, we'll never know, will we?' Lucas squeezed her arm.

'Shouldn't you be at college?' she asked.

'And let you brave the hospital alone? No way. I want a nice calm bedmate who isn't tossing and turning all night.'

She had not realised that she had been tossing and turning, although she was prepared to acknowledge that she had been a bit restless and disturbed. 'Sorry,' she said.

'Don't be silly,' he replied. 'There's nothing to be sorry about. I like when you come into my bed.'

At the hospital they were told that Breda's mother was with her. Lucas asked if they might visit too when they heard that Breda was awake.

'No,' said the nurse. 'Not today. She's still heavily drugged for the pain, but she's doing fine.'

'Would you be good enough to tell her mother that we are here and we'd dearly like to say hello?' Lucas said.

'Why did you say that?' Amelia hissed as the nurse went off to tell Mrs Mangan.

'Well, I for one am very curious.'

'Mattie doesn't believe me that Breda looks like her.'

'I believe you,' Lucas said.

Mrs Mangan, coming down the corridor towards them, accompanied by the nurse, stopped in her tracks as she looked at Amelia. Her face was pale. She was thin, with short straight hair, thin-lipped and rather worn. She looked both tired and strained.

Lucas introduced them. 'I'm Lucas Borg Cardona,' he said. 'And this is Amelia Cholmondesley. Amelia was there when it happened,' he continued. 'We were concerned and wanted to know that Breda was all right.'

Mrs Mangan kept staring at Amelia as though she recognised her, though Amelia was certain she had never seen her before in her life.

'I mistook your daughter for my sister,' she said. 'Even after the accident I was sure she was my sister, Mattie. I'm so sorry that you were delayed in being told about what had happened. It's completely my fault.'

'Did you come in during the night?' Lucas asked her.

'I did,' she replied briefly. She was exceptionally abrupt with them, and appeared not to want to speak to them.

Amelia decided she didn't like her. She was sorry for her and concerned about the grief she had put her through by claiming Breda as her sister, but there was something about her that she found off-putting. There was no reason why she should have been concerned about Amelia, but Amelia felt that, after all, she had gone to the hospital with her daughter, she had been there through the whole ordeal, even if she was totally mistaken in her identification of her daughter. Breda's mother never once asked what had happened, or if Amelia was all right. Nor did she thank her. Nothing.

Lucas said afterwards that he thought that was odd too.

'But then, of course, she must be very shocked, not to mention tired. We'll forgive her this time,' he said to Amelia. 'I'm sure she had a terrible night, with worry about her daughter. And then she was forced to come and be polite to us. Let's be sorry for her instead of cross.'

'But I did think she was rude,' Amelia said.

'She may not have meant to be,' he replied.

But when they told Mattie, she asked why anyone thought this woman would be concerned about Amelia and that obviously she was completely caught up in what had happened to her daughter.

But it had seemed different in the hospital, not quite like that, which Amelia felt she would have understood. But she couldn't explain it.

Lucas made tea and commented that he couldn't wait for Breda to get the bandages off because he wanted to see what she looked like.

'She looks like Mattie,' Amelia said.

'Then she looks like you too,' he observed. 'After all, you are remarkably alike.'

374

Amelia still loved when people said that. It made her feel connected, apart from the fact that she just liked the idea of looking like Mattie.

However, when she tried to visit Breda the following day – she was now up and about, and bruised and sore, with her broken bones in plaster – she was told that she could not see her.

Lucas, who was with her, asked the nurse why not.

'Breda's mother doesn't want her having visitors,' the nurse said.

'All that my friend wants to do is to talk to her and to reassure herself that Breda really is all right,' Lucas said.

'She's fine,' the nurse replied. She had the face of the Duchess in *Alice in Wonderland* and she glowered at them both.

'We'll come back when she's not on duty,' Lucas announced to Amelia as they walked back down the corridor.

'They'll never let me in,' she said. 'They must think I'm to blame.'

'Of course they don't. Why would they think that? She's just an old battleaxe and is doing what the mother has asked. We'll get in some time later and cheer old Breda up.'

Lucas was good at cheering people up. He always made them feel better at home.

Amelia went back to school and Lucas asked Thomas if he could ride his motorbike. Thomas said categorically no, that he wouldn't trust Lucas on a motorbike and that it was bad enough watching him sitting behind Mattie on hers.

'Spoilsport,' Lucas said.

'Why did you want the motorbike anyway?' Amelia asked.

'To collect you this evening and to bring you to the hospital, of course,' he said. It transpired that he had seen the nurses' roster and that they were going to go in at eight that night when Amelia finished in the library.

'But her mother might be there,' Amelia objected.

'Don't worry,' Lucas replied. 'We're not going to meet her again.'

'How can you be so sure?'

'Well, she hasn't met Thomas or Mattie, so we'll get them to go in and check if the road is clear.'

There was something about that plan that did not seem to be a very good idea, but Amelia couldn't think what it was, so she agreed. Thomas and Mattie, with Lucas behind her, collected Amelia from the library at eight and once again they set off on the motorbikes and Lucas and she hovered outside the hospital while the other two went in.

In the event Mrs Mangan was there, and, as it happened, she had been having a cup of tea in a small and rather dismal place near reception, and coming out of the little teashop, she saw Mattie.

'What are you doing out of bed?' she snapped at her. 'And why are you dressed like that?'

Thomas later said that there was a moment of stunned silence and then Mattie, being Mattie, said, 'I don't know who you think I am, but you may not, categorically not, speak to me like that.'

A further stunned silence and then Mrs Mangan suddenly put her head down and murmured that she was sorry. 'I thought you were someone else,' she said, turning away.

'You thought I was Breda Mangan?' Mattie said, hurrying after her, as she started to believe bits of Amelia's story.

'You're not like her at all,' the other woman said. 'For a moment I thought you were my daughter, but I got it wrong.'

She walked away. Mattie was about to go after her, but Thomas pulled her back.

'Leave it,' he said to her.

'Why?'

'Believe me. Just leave it.'

Now Mattie was really curious to see Breda Mangan and she and Thomas came out of the hospital and joined Amelia and Lucas where the bikes were parked, and Thomas said they were going to have to bide their time until Mrs Mangan went home for the night.

They had to wait until quite late before they saw Mrs Mangan leaving the hospital, and then Lucas and Thomas chatted up the ward nurse, while Mattie and Amelia slipped in to see Breda.

She looked quite different now from the last time Amelia had seen her. Although her face was still bruised and she had stitches on her forehead, the bandages were off her head, and she now clearly resembled Mattie again.

She looked at them in surprise, as Mattie stared at her.

'We came to see how you were,' Amelia said tentatively. 'I was there when you were hit by the car. I came in the ambulance with you.'

'Thank you,' Breda said.

Mattie introduced them.

'You look very alike,' Breda said.

'And *you* look very like us both,' Mattie said.

Breda was from London but she didn't talk like the sisters. Amelia thought that their upbringing must have been totally different – Mattie and she talked like Lucymem and Grandmother. Breda's vowel-sounds were different. She had gone to a local school and now she worked in an office.

'Are you Irish?' Mattie asked. 'With a name like Breda, I mean – that's Irish, isn't it?'

'I was born in Ireland,' Breda said. 'I don't know where. Some village. We came to live in London when I was very little. I don't remember it at all.'

'We're from Ireland too,' Mattie said. 'We lived in Wicklow, on the east coast.'

'I see,' Breda said. 'It's nice of you to come and visit.'

The polite conversation went nowhere. There was nowhere for it to go. Breda was clearly very tired and while she kept looking at them and smiling she didn't have much to say. Mattie retreated into silence and Amelia tried to keep a monologue going about how she had first seen Breda from the bus and then saw her again.

'Were you adopted?' Mattie suddenly asked Breda.

'No,' she said.

'Are you sure?'

'Well, I've got my birth certificate. I've seen it,' Breda said.

'Why did you ask her that?' Amelia asked Mattie outside.

'Ask her what?' Thomas enquired.

Amelia reiterated Mattie's question.

'What did she say?' Lucas asked.

'Breda? She said she had seen her birth certificate.'

'Where was she born?'

'I don't know. We did ask her, and she seemed to think somewhere in Ireland, but she didn't really know. What are you thinking?'

'I have no idea what I'm thinking. I suppose I'm just intrigued by the fact that you both think she looks so like you. It's interesting,' Thomas said.

'I think we ought to go in and see for ourselves,' Lucas said.

Mattie and Amelia stayed outside.

Lucas picked up a white coat that he saw on a hook near the ward and he made Thomas put it on.

'You look older than me,' he said. 'You're the doctor and I'm the student.'

They went into the ward and Thomas introduced himself to Breda as Dr Kobaldt and Lucas nodded at Breda in the bed.

Lucas picked up her chart from the end of the bed and perused it with interest while Thomas chatted briefly to Breda, asking her how she was. Lucas was enthusiastic about visiting some of the other patients when they had finished with Breda, but Thomas said they had to go and write up reports, and he herded Lucas out of the ward.

'Enough is enough,' he said to him.

'I quite enjoyed that,' Lucas said.

'Well, you had your chance to be a doctor,' Thomas said. 'You chose art college instead.'

Back outside at the motorbikes, Thomas and Lucas joined Mattie and Amelia.

'Despite her cuts and bruises, Breda does look very like you both,' Thomas said to them.

'Especially Mattie,' Lucas contributed.

'It proves my theory that we all – and I am the sole exception – have a double or a near-double in the world,' Lucas said.

Mattie didn't say anything until they got home and Thomas asked her what was wrong.

'She made me think about Georgina,' Mattie said. 'Georgina was my sister.'

'She was my sister too,' Amelia tried.

'Not really,' Mattie said. 'You never knew her.'

'No, but I visited her grave with you. Remember?'

'She might be some distant cousin, I suppose,' Lucas said. 'Breda, I mean. That's always possible.'

'She said there was just her mother and herself,' Amelia said.

'Well, there could always be some estranged uncle, you know. I have all kinds of relatives in Malta,' Lucas said.

'What does that mean?'

'I meant that Malta is small and we all know who is related to whom. But here you could have relatives all over the place and not know who they are.'

'I miss Malta,' Mattie suddenly announced. 'I

like it there.'

'More than here?' Lucas asked.

'Yes. I'd like to live there eventually. When I've finished studying and know what I'm going to do with myself.'

It was interesting to think of Mattie with some kind of plans in her mind – Mattie who had always lived in the past and had never really shown much connection with the present until she had first gone to Malta. Perhaps because Lucymem was settled in Malta that was why Mattie looked on the place as her home.

'Is it Lucymem you miss?' Amelia asked Mattie.

'No,' Mattie replied. 'No.' Her voice was cross and frustrated. 'It's nothing to do with Lucy-mem.'

Thomas said to Amelia later that night that he thought that Mattie found peace in Malta because she was so far away from all the sadness of her childhood.

Amelia was not sure if he was right, or if maybe it was just some wandering gene in them that made them feel they had no roots and that some other place might always be the answer to their quest.

I count him braver who overcomes his desires than him who conquers his enemies; for the hardest victory is over self.

Aristotle

CHAPTER FIFTEEN

Those days left them uneasy, and in Mattie's case with a renewed awareness of the sense of loss. Mattie who had found some equilibrium of spirit was now troubled and morose again. And Amelia, who had moved always forwards with life, harped back in her mind to her incorrect identification of her older sister.

It bothered her greatly and she had a problem letting it go. She had been so sure that the girl in the road was Mattie and yet it had proven not to be. All the similarities that were so blatantly there between Mattie and Breda were dispelled when Breda spoke.

Amelia was left with a sense of bewilderment.

'Put it behind you,' Thomas said to them both as they sat silently at the kitchen table.

But it was not so easy. Mattie was churned up in some way that the others could not relate to and she hardly spoke to them at all.

'Please talk to me,' Thomas said to her. He and Mattie were sitting in the back garden in the late autumn sun, out of the breeze just beside the kitchen door.

Amelia, who had spent so much of her life listening behind doors and curtains, was now in her bedroom with the window open. Their voices drifted upwards. Lucas was lying on her bed, reading a magazine.

'I spent so much of my life,' Mattie said slowly, 'so much of it, just entangled like a fly in a spider's web...'

'In what way?' Thomas asked.

'It was as if I couldn't let go of that night – the night of the plane crash. And while I couldn't remember anything that happened after the crash I could remember everything so clearly about that day. I can recall the colour of the sea and my mother's tiredness, and the drive up the mountains, and walking in the dark – it is as if my whole life began and ended on that mountain. I spent years just going over those moments and I couldn't let them go.'

'But you did let them go,' Thomas pointed out.

'Yes I did. When I came to Malta and it was all new and different and so far away from that night, I let it go then. In fact, after that first trip I really moved away from it. But for some reason I've gone back to it. I'm back on the mountain-side. I'm back at that point of no return.' There was a slight desperation in her voice.

'There is a time like that for me too.' Thomas's voice drifted up to the listening pair in Amelia's bedroom.

He sounded so much older, Amelia thought.

'We are all caught by events that change our lives – irrevocably change them, I mean. I think

383

those moments happen all the time but we often are not aware of them, but in your case and mine, and presumably thousands if not millions of other people, there are those defining moments and there is no going back beyond them, because they cannot be undone. I remember a night ... no ... there is no point ... I cannot find words to describe what I recall ... my little sister, Klara, with her beautiful eyes... But, Mattie, believe me, what you went through, what happened – it happened. There is nothing you can do about it.'

'It doesn't seem right,' Mattie said. 'We had done nothing, Georgina and me – we had done nothing to deserve what happened.'

'Nor had I,' Thomas said gently. 'Nor Amelia. Nor Lucy. Nor your parents. Nor mine. Nor my little Klara. None of you had done anything to deserve what happened.'

'But no one is held to account for it. That's what is not fair.'

'Who would you hold accountable?' Thomas asked.

Silence met his question.

'I lost my sister,' Mattie said after a while, as if that was the point that hurt the most.

'So did I,' Thomas said. 'So whom do you want to hold accountable?' he asked again.

'Life is accountable,' Lucas said to Amelia, putting down the magazine. 'That's my philosophy, anyway. Events take place and there is nothing we can do about them. Poor Mattie.'

Amelia wondered why poor Mattie, why poor her more than anyone else?

Amelia wrote and told Grandmother and Lucymem how Mattie had become introverted again. She did not tell them about the encounter with Breda Mangan because it was too complicated to put in a letter and she knew that they would not believe that someone could look so like Mattie that Amelia would mistake her.

'Mattie never learned to count her blessings,' Grandmother wrote to Amelia in her reply. 'She'll come out of this phase again.'

But then, as Amelia knew, Grandmother always had a very gung-ho attitude to life, her blessings were invariably counted, wrongs were righted, the past was put behind her and she marched as a soldier ever onwards.

Lucy wrote too, asking what had happened, if anything, to undermine the slight optimism she had seen develop in Mattie over the previous few years.

'Should I come home to see you girls?' she asked in her letter to Amelia. 'Or should I suggest to Mattie you both come out here for a week or so? You cannot really afford to take time off school, I know. What about at the next holidays? I miss you both and Thomas too, so dreadfully. Charlotte and I talk about you all the time. Despite the glorious weather, the house seems cold and empty without you...'

Not a word about Rhino, only the implication of a silent home with just Lucy and Charlotte chatting together and nothing much else happening. Amelia could not say any of this to Mattie in case Mattie asked to see the letter, and she bottled it up until Thomas asked her if something were wrong.

She told him and Lucas. Showing them the letter, they agreed that there was something missing from it.

'There's nothing you can do,' Thomas said to her. 'They will work through their own problems there. It is not your responsibility.'

'It is worrying,' Amelia said. 'I hate the idea of Lucymem unhappy.'

'Lucymem is an adult,' Lucas said. 'She'll find the right thing to do when she is ready.'

They both sounded so grown up and so capable of dealing with the problems adults faced, that Amelia wondered how that had happened, when all she could do was worry about Lucymem and also about Mattie.

'It's easier on the outside,' Lucas said, when she voiced this aloud.

It was a while later when Mattie said that she had been to visit Breda at her home. She had gone with flowers and, despite a frosty reception from Breda's mother, who happened to be at home at the time, got invited in and was given tea by Breda.

'Tell all,' said Lucas with interest.

Amelia sat forward and looked in amazement at Mattie. She couldn't believe that Mattie had actually gone there.

'How did you know where she lived?' Amelia asked.

'Remember that night we saw her address on the envelope – well, I remembered it.' Mattie said. 'There's not much to tell,' she continued. 'I drank their tea and we chatted. And then I left.'

'And that's it?'

'I invited Breda to visit us – I gave her our address. Maybe she'll come.'

'Why did you invite her?' Lucas asked.

'Why not?' Mattie shrugged.

Breda came to visit. She dropped by one evening after work. Amelia was sitting in the window in the front room reading, and Mattie and Lucas were preparing their evening meal. Thomas was not yet home.

Amelia looked up from her schoolbook and saw Breda, dressed in a neat dark suit, looking tentative as she walked up the garden path. In her surprise Amelia dropped her book.

'Mattie,' she yelled. But Mattie, in the kitchen with something sizzling in the frying pan, did not hear her.

She rushed to the hall door and opened it as Breda stood on the step looking as if she were not quite sure whether to knock on the door or not.

'Come in,' Amelia said. 'You look so much better. I am glad.'

Breda stepped into the hall and touched her forehead. 'Hardly a scar,' she said.

'And your arms and ribs?'

'Nearly all fine again, thank you. Only the odd twinge of pain. And only one arm still in plaster. The bandages are off my ribs.'

'Come on in,' Amelia said again, and ushered Breda down the hallway to the kitchen. 'Look who has come to visit,' she announced as she opened the kitchen door.

Mattie and Lucas looked up in unison.

'Well, hello,' Mattie said.

'Hello, ducks,' Lucas echoed.

'Will you stay and eat with us?' Mattie asked.

Breda shook her head. 'I can't,' she said. She hummed and hawed a bit and then she said it might be better if Mattie did not call at her home again. 'It upset my mother,' she explained.

They were all looking at her. She appeared very uncomfortable.

'But I would like to see you again,' she added lamely.

'What upset your mother?' Mattie demanded. 'My calling over to see if you were all right? Bringing you flowers? Amelia going with you to the hospital?'

Again Breda shook her head. 'No. It's the fact that we look so alike.'

'And that upset her?' Mattie said crossly. 'Think how it upsets us.'

'Does it upset you?' Breda said. 'I didn't know that. I didn't think of that.'

'It puzzles us,' Amelia said, hoping to calm Mattie down. 'We look so alike that we even wondered if you could be related to us.'

'I don't think I am related to you.'

'Who is your father?' Mattie asked.

'He's dead,' Breda said. 'I never knew him.'

'Maybe your father,' Lucas said, 'was also Breda's. Maybe that's what is upsetting Breda's mother.'

'I don't think so,' Breda said. 'You see, I've seen their marriage certificate. And he died after I was born, but he was there when I was little. My mother has told me stories and I've seen photographs. There is one of me in his arms, when I was a baby. And others of me when I was two, before he died. I think it really is just a coincidence that we look alike. You and me, I mean.'

'It's a very strange coincidence,' Mattie said. 'Everything about us is similar.'

'Except your voices,' Lucas interjected.

'I didn't grow up in the same area as you did,' Breda said. 'And I went to a local school. I don't suppose you did.'

She did not sound bitter. There was more a sense of resignation in her voice. And she sounded sad, Amelia thought.

'The only reason we didn't go to a local school in England,' Amelia said, 'is because of family tradition. At least that is what we were told. In Ireland we went to our local parish school. Accents don't matter anyway,' she added, hoping to make Breda feel better.

'I know that,' Breda replied.

'You sound cross,' Mattie said, which Amelia did not think was fair. Breda had not sounded cross.

'It's not that I'm cross,' Breda said, trying to explain herself.

The others waited but she was not more forthcoming.

'Don't worry,' Mattie said. 'I won't come visiting again. I'd hate to upset your mother.' Her voice said that there was nothing more she would like than to upset Mrs Mangan.

Amelia and Lucas exchanged glances.

'You're very welcome to visit us,' Amelia tried.

Breda tried to smile at her, but there was a look of pain on her face. 'Please don't be angry with me,' she said to Mattie. 'You can't imagine what it's like. There is just my mother and me and–'

'You're dead right, I can't imagine,' Mattie said. 'I don't have a mother.'

'I didn't mean that.' Everything she said seemed to be making it worse.

Amelia felt really sorry for her.

'I'd better go,' Breda stood up. 'I'm sorry. I shouldn't have come here. I just thought it would be easier. She's forbidden me to see you again. I wanted to spare you coming back to our place,' she said to Mattie. 'I just thought it would be easier...' she repeated.

Easier than what? Amelia wondered.

After Breda had left, walking dejectedly down the path, and Amelia came back to the kitchen from showing her out, Mattie said, 'Bugger her, and bugger her bloody mother.'

'I don't think she meant any harm,' Amelia said.

'Well, what did she mean, "it would be easier"?' Mattie asked.

'I think she meant that by coming here it would be easier for us all, rather than you going to her house again and maybe her mother being rude to you.'

'You don't know what kind of an argument she and her mother may have had,' Lucas said.

'I don't care what kind of a row she and her mother had. She should stand up to her. She's old enough to see whom she wants, when she wants. It's none of her mother's bloody business.'

'I think you're being a bit tough on her,' Lucas said.

Thomas arrived home, walking into the kitchen and removing his helmet at the same time.

'What's going on in here?' he asked. 'I've never seen you lot so quiet.'

'Bloody Breda came to visit,' Mattie said.

Amelia and Lucas explained what had happened and what had been said, while Mattie broke a cauliflower into florets, snapping each flower apart with her fingers and throwing them one by one into boiling water.

'Put them all in at the same time,' Lucas said to her. 'Otherwise some are cooked more than others.'

'I don't care,' Mattie answered. 'Does anyone else care?' she asked around, and before anyone could answer, even if they had dared, she continued, 'See, Lucas. No one cares about the cauliflower or how it is cooked.'

Now all three of the others exchanged looks.

'She was going on about her accent,' Mattie continued, clearly going through every aspect of the conversation. 'Who cares about her accent? It's not our fault that she looks like us but talks like someone who isn't us.'

'I don't think that's what she meant,' Lucas said.

'It sounds to me more like she was regretting the fact that you and Amelia were given opportunities she was never given,' Thomas said to Mattie.

'Well, that's not our fault, is it?' Mattie said.

'I don't think she's like that. I really don't think

she saw it as our fault,' Amelia said uncertainly.

'And so she shouldn't,' Mattie snapped.

'I don't think we'll be seeing her again,' Lucas said.

'Why not?' Mattie said, now surprised. 'She said she'd visit us. Just that we couldn't visit her.'

'I don't somehow think she'll be back,' Lucas said, putting plates on the table.

'Not after that reception anyway,' he said to Amelia and Thomas later.

Amelia went out of the room and back to her book in the drawing room, as she needed both to work and to think.

She felt sorry for Breda but she also envied her. She thought about Breda saying that there was a photograph of her in her father's arms, and she thought how she would have liked a picture of her with her father. Or just to have a mother like Breda had – one who watched out for her and had been there for her all her life. Amelia would have settled for that.

Breda might regret the missed opportunities in her life, but she had the precious commodity of a mother and that was something she, Amelia, had never known, and Mattie had only had for a few short years.

She returned to Homer's *Odyssey* with a sigh, thinking that no one was satisfied with his or her lot in life. But then, why would Odysseus have been happy on his quest? He had every reason to keep trying to find a way home. He, at least, knew where home was.

As she read, her mind wandered. Alcinous said

to Odysseus, she translated, 'You have suffered a great deal. Now, at last, you have stepped on the bronze floor of my large house, I am sure you will arrive home without any further wanderings...' It suddenly occurred to her that she would like to go back to Ireland, to Ithaca and visit her past.

Wishing to be friends is quick work, but friendship is a slow-ripening fruit.

Aristotle

CHAPTER SIXTEEN

Leaving the Cholmondesleys' house, Breda closed the black-painted gate behind her, unable to remember if it had been open or shut when she had arrived at the house, wanting to leave it the way she had found it, but not knowing how. A man about to go in the gate next door said, 'Hello, Mattie.'

She looked at him in distress, shaking her head in confusion. She hurried on up the road, back to the bus stop, her mind in turmoil. Nothing made sense and that man who was probably a neighbour, saying 'hello, Mattie' to her, was the last straw.

Breda did not recall much from her early childhood, nor indeed anything of those heady days of babyhood that her mother had told her about. Nor did she remember her father, a gentle workman who held her in his arms and brought her mother tea in bed and doted on her, as her mother so often told her.

Her first memories were of their flat in London with its tiny kitchen. She remembered clambering on to the sofa, clutching a book for her mother to read to her. Her nights were disturbed. She often woke crying about something that haunted her, but to which she had no access. If she disrupted her mother's nights she was never blamed nor ever scolded. Her mother held her in her arms and told her she was the most precious human being in the world, and a gift from God.

She was cared for by a woman down the road while her mother went out to work.

'Where is my father?' she remembered asking her mother one evening when she came in tired from work. She had taken off her shoes and Breda fetched her slippers from the bedroom. Her mother was heating something in a saucepan and making toast on the grill.

'He died of diphtheria,' she sighed. When she said it, Breda knew she had told her before, but sometimes she did not remember things. That was one of them. 'It would have been so much easier if he hadn't died,' her mother said. 'But he did. And that is that.'

And that was that. Her mother sometimes mentioned him, but always with a sigh. She was a sensible and organised woman, but often given to bouts of sadness that would leave her encased in herself and Breda, as a child, sitting hopefully on the floor looking at her, waiting for her to come back to normality.

Apparently they had spent a year as evacuees in some village up north, but Breda had little recollection of it, nor any interest in it. She had only the vaguest memories of early days. She was not sure if she could remember the sound of the air raids or of the bombings. She did not recall the sirens calling them to the shelters. She only remembered her mother's arms around her, and her singing to her as she went to sleep, and the little table beside her bed on which she had two photographs, one of her father and her, and one of her mother sitting by the sea. She liked both photographs. The sea looked choppy, with white caps on the waves. Her mother's face was happy. She was smiling at whoever took the photograph. Her hair was blowing in the wind. She didn't smile much when Breda was little except when she was cuddling her. Then she smiled. She sang to her.

'Rock-a-bye, Baby', she sang. She had a deep voice, with melodic Irish overtones, but she only sang in Breda's childhood, not later. Later things were difficult. 'When the wind blows...' she sang, and Breda thought of the wind blowing her hair and the waves in the photograph and she was safe in her bed.

'Mummy,' she said, 'will I ever have a brother or a sister?'

'No,' she replied. 'There is only just you. You are my special and only baby.'

Mrs Boole cared for Breda when her mother was at work. Mrs Boole had a daughter called Jane, and Breda and Jane became best friends. When she started school, Jane and she held hands and they went in together. They were not afraid because they had each other. Her mother walked them both to school, and Mrs Boole collected them when school was over. Breda was good at reading but Jane was not. She tried to help her, but it was too difficult to teach someone how to read. They drank their milk together and they looked after each other. They knew their friendship would last all their lives. Once the Booles took Jane and herself to the seaside for two days. That was the only holiday she had ever had.

Jane left school before Breda, but they still saw each other. Breda thought she was as close to a sister as she could have. The School said she should go to university but her mother did not have the money, even with a scholarship, which she was offered, and so when school finished for her, she did a secretarial course and her mother said how proud of her she was, that she was doing so much better than she had, and that life would give her better opportunities.

She worked in a solicitor's office, typing up documents, one just a variation on the previous one. She found it dull and repetitive, but there were no other opportunities. Her mother said it was a good job, safe work and it paid well enough. She had no ambitions, no idea if there might be better options. Her mother did not want her looking for other work, and she did what she was told.

That was her world until the day that the car hit her and she ended up in hospital, and Mattie and Amelia suddenly appeared in her life.

Mattie and Amelia...

Since they had come to the hospital, she thought about them all the time. Their similarity to each other was probably not surprising. After all, they were sisters. It was her similarity to them that held her spellbound. In the hospital the nurses commented on it. She knew her mother was disturbed by it. Her mother said that people often look alike, that, after all, there are only so many features and combinations of them to go around.

But Breda was enthralled. They appeared so confident, so comfortable, so in control of their own lives.

By the time she got to the bus stop after leaving their house, Breda was still in turmoil. Mattie had really disturbed her.

When Mattie came to visit at their flat, she did what Breda's mother called 'Lady Bountiful'. She came with flowers and chocolates, and was very solicitous and chatty. Mattie kept the conversation going every time her mother tried to dampen it. Breda could feel hostility coming from her mother and in due course Mattie left, having given Breda their address, but saying that she would come again.

After she left, her mother made it clear that she didn't want the likes of them, as she put it, dropping in on them.

'I think it was kindly meant,' Breda said.

'No it wasn't,' she snapped. 'She came to spy.'

Spy? It wasn't a word Breda would have used. 'I don't think she did,' she tried. 'I think she is just puzzled at how alike we look.'

'It's just one of those things,' my mother said. 'Leave it be. She was lording it over us.'

Breda didn't understand. She couldn't think of any reason why Mattie Cholmondesley would come around to lord it over them. She had said that she was just reassuring herself that Breda was all right and that she wanted to set her sister's mind at rest.

'Why didn't her sister come then?' her mother

asked, when Breda suggested this explanation.

Breda did not say anything. There was no point in arguing with her. The truth was that if Amelia had come instead of her or with her, the same irritation would have arisen, and Breda's mother would have been equally annoyed. And she, Breda, would still be sitting there in their tiny living room, trying to pour oil on troubled waters. She wanted her mother to cheer up. She wanted her to be happy that a person as exotic as Mattie Cholmondesley would come to call and see if she were all right. And she was doing it because she wanted her sister, Amelia, to feel better about the whole accident. Though why Amelia should ever feel guilty was beyond her. Breda had not heard her calling, no matter what she said. She did not even remember what she was thinking about as she stepped off the pavement. It was just a moment's lapse of concentration, which she paid for with a lot of pain and broken bones, although the doctors said she was recovering very rapidly.

Her mother said she was never to see the Cholmondesley girls again. She said they were not their type of people and she didn't like them. It made no sense to Breda. But then her mother said that maybe they should move back north, to where they had been when evacuees, so Breda promised she would have nothing more to do with Mattie and Amelia.

Breda felt there was an underlying threat, and acquiescence was easier as she did not want to go and live up north. Before she might not have minded, but now she did. She wanted to see Mattie and Amelia again.

Time hung heavily on her hands. Her mother was out at work and she was alone all day. She was off work until all her plasters and bandages were removed. She thought a lot about Mattie and Amelia and while she was afraid of one of them coming to visit again because of the repercussions from her mother, she also wanted to see them. She supposed she wanted to see what their world was really like.

And so she went to visit and there they were, in this house in North London, living with a man. She could hardly believe the loveliness of the house, the ease with which they moved around each other, and all the space they had.

They wanted for nothing. They seemed to feel there was no end to the possibilities for their lives. Mattie had worn red on each of the occasions Breda had met her. Breda thought about that with admiration. She had never met anyone who went around in different shades of scarlet – always. Mattie drove a motorbike. She had masses of dark curly hair – like her own, she supposed, only Mattie wore hers freely falling over her shoulders, or scooped up in some way or another. Breda always kept hers neatly tied back out of the way. And Amelia was a mirror image of her. The same vibrant eyes, the same dark thick hair, slightly shyer, a little gentler, and rather bookish, in fact. While Mattie was very forceful in her opinions, Amelia was more reserved. Neither of them was terribly talkative.

They had it all: freedom, money, talent, possibilities – all were theirs for the taking, she felt. Their house was lovely. Rather olde-worlde, her mother would have said. But Breda loved it. She loved their old furniture, and the ease with which they moved around each other in their busy kitchen. Their strange friend, Lucas, was preparing dinner when she called that time.

The bus was slow coming and she was aching with tiredness by the time she got on to it. This trip out had been her biggest venture since the accident. She longed to get home and to go to bed, but knew she would have to sit and talk to her mother and pretend that there was nothing wrong. And everything was wrong. Everything was so wrong that she did not know where to begin to clarify her thoughts. She ached to see Mattie and Amelia, and yet she knew there was no place for her in their lives.

It was some three weeks afterwards, subsequent to a hospital visit to have the plaster cast taken off her arm, that she thought she might drop back to see how they were, and to show them how much better she was. She was nervous approaching the house, remembering too well Mattie's animosity and irritation from the previous visit, but she could not keep herself away any longer

As she was walking along their road, a tall leather-clad man pulled up on his motorbike.

He looked at her carefully, before removing his helmet, shaking his blond hair free, and saying, 'Hello, Breda. For a moment I wasn't sure if you were Mattie or not.'

'I'm not,' she said. She tried to make it sound joking, but she was afraid that it sounded brusque. She was delighted that he might think she was Mattie.

'Do you remember me?' he asked, getting off his bike. 'I'm Thomas Kobaldt.'

She looked at him slowly. 'You're the doctor,' she said.

He grinned. 'Well, I pretended to be, because we couldn't see what other way we could get in to visit you. I live here with Lucas, Mattie and Amelia,' he gestured towards the house. She nodded in amazement. There was no end to the surprises attached to Mattie and Amelia Cholmondesley.

'You coming to visit?' he asked, looking at his watch. 'I doubt if there's anyone home yet. It's Tuesday. Amelia doesn't get in until six – she does some extra class on a Tuesday and then goes to the library. And Mattie and Lucas are working on some project in their college. They've managed to combine an art and a chemistry project, for their separate departments. God knows how. Saves on work, Lucas said. Regardless, there's no one here.'

'Oh,' Breda said. She hadn't thought of that possibility. 'What a pity.'

'Come in anyway and have a cup of tea with me,' he said.

She was hoping it was because he wanted her to, and not because she looked so dejected. She certainly felt dejected. All she could think of at that moment was how lovely it would be to sit in their kitchen drinking their tea and maybe pretending she was part of their circle.

But the truth was she was part of no one's circle, and she knew it. But for Jane she did not have any friends – just acquaintances. She got on well enough with the girls at work, but her mother had brought her up in such a reclusive way that she did not mix easily. She had hoped her shyness would pass when she left school and got a job, but it didn't really. She was just awkward in company, and she knew it.

Thomas parked his bike on the road, and while he tucked his helmet under his arm, he handed her the keys to open the front door. He was very at ease with himself, and she liked that because it made her feel that she could just be herself.

He took her coat from her and hung it in a cloakroom off the hall, and they went into the kitchen.

'I hope you don't mind me entertaining you in here,' he said. 'It's the only warm room in the house until someone lights the fire in the drawing room. And that someone is Mattie. She won't let anyone else do it.'

'Oh,' Breda said. She did not understand what he was talking about. But she was delighted to be taken to the kitchen. Her mother never took anyone into theirs, but then it was very small, so it wasn't surprising really. This being her second time in their kitchen made her feel like she was one of them.

Thomas directed her to a press where she found cups and saucers and he put the kettle on. 'Do you know Mattie and Amelia's background?' he asked her suddenly.

She did not. They had never said. They had mentioned something about Malta and she somehow thought that was where their parents lived. She shook her head. 'We've only ever really talked about me and my accident and broken bones. They said something about Malta, though.'

He told her then about how they had been born in Ireland, about the plane crash and how their father had died that night, and how Amelia was born, and their mother had died within days.

'How terribly sad,' she said. She had had no idea.

'Yes. Yes, one more tragedy from the war,' he said to her.

'How do they cope with that?' she wondered.

'The way anyone copes,' he said with a shrug. 'Amelia never knew her parents and is very close to her aunt Lucy. Lucy is now married to my uncle. My uncle Rhino – he took me from an orphanage after the war.' He smiled at her. 'So, you see,' he added, 'all these lost people – finding each other.'

This was so surprising. She had not realised the connections between them all.

'Where does Lucas fit into all of this?' she asked.

'Oh, his mother, Maria, is a friend of my uncle's. My uncle Rhino was involved in the bombing of Malta, and he carries a burden of responsibility – I think that is the best way to put it, so he keeps an eye out for Lucas. He and his friend Friedrich – they look after Lucas's education, that kind of thing.'

He said it so casually, as if this was all normal. She was stunned. She could not help wondering how it had come to pass that all these people were so closely involved, so connected. How did they handle such things? She wanted to ask Thomas, but did not know how. She had thought they were an ordinary happy family – her notion of a happy family being a father and mother and children, and she thought that was what they had.

'And this aunt – Lucy?' she asked. 'Where is she now?'

'Oh, she lives with my uncle although I think their relationship is not so steady at the moment. Her mother, who is Mattie and Amelia's grandmother, lives in Sliema, which is a town in Malta.'

'Do they have children?'

'Rhino and Lucy? Yes, one child. Charlotte.'

It all seemed both sad and yet exciting. The exciting part was the many links between them all and a life she knew nothing about. It made her feel more like them in some way. She had lost her father and didn't remember him at all – so that made her a bit like Amelia, she decided. And she was like Mattie in that she had actually had a father who had once held her, even though she could not remember any of that. Her idea of happy families was based on her friend, Jane Boole, and her parents who doted on her. Jane was now engaged to be married, and Breda supposed she would repeat the pattern that had been set for her in life. She suddenly thought that it did not say much for her chances. She did not want to become like her own mother, whom, she knew, was quite a bitter woman. It showed in her face. And she was so protective of Breda that Breda could not do anything without her knowing about it. And she always disapproved. Breda knew she loved her but there was a sense of dissatisfaction that emanated from her.

'Do they miss their aunt?' she asked. 'Aunt Lucy.' She tried the words to see how they sounded.

'Amelia does,' he said. 'Amelia worships her aunt Lucy. I think that when Lucy married and went to live in Malta, Amelia felt rejected, even though she has never said.'

'And Mattie?'

'Mattie is a law unto herself,' Thomas said with a laugh. 'I shouldn't laugh,' he added. 'It isn't funny. I think Mattie lives with memories of a past that was shattered by that plane crash. She is reckless and careless about things. She breaks all laws, and just does her own thing.'

'Is she happy?'

He seemed to think about that and in the silence that followed she waited for his answer, but the silence stretched into minutes and she wondered if she had said something wrong, if her question had been too intrusive, if she had overstepped the boundaries.

'No,' he eventually replied, both thoughtfully and slowly. 'I think she was happy for a while when she was in Malta, during school holidays. But Mattie is angry. She has been since I first met her. For a while the anger seemed to be gone, but now it's back. I suppose it has always been there.'

Poor Mattie, Breda thought. This was really heartbreaking. Breda had seen their lives as a sort of success story – trivial words, she knew, but that was how it had appeared. They seemed to have what she supposed she aspired to but could never have. Trips abroad to their family and an idyllic life in London now appeared more as fate.

Fate? Was that what she meant? She supposed it was. It was like they were playthings in the hands of fortune. What her mother referred to as 'the Emergency', was truly the tragedy of conflict clearly and actually reflected in their lives.

Thomas eyed her from across the table. 'I can see so clearly why Amelia thought you were Mattie,' he said.

He was smiling at her. She felt slightly awkward, and didn't know what was expected of her. She looked down at her hands resting on the edge of the table and her carefully polished nails caught the light, and suddenly he reached across the table and took one of them in his. 'Even your hands,' he said. 'The same bone structure, the same skin ... extraordinary.'

She liked the feel of his hand on hers, and she thought of him holding Mattie's like that and she wondered if they were lovers. She could not imagine the intimacy that was involved in being a lover. She had had the occasional kiss when she had been out at a dance with Jane, her friend, but she always felt uncomfortable, not sure what was expected when someone kissed her. And they all kissed differently anyway. Jane said she just had not met the right person to kiss. Jane may have been right, as Breda suddenly realised, because she really wanted something from Thomas, and at first she did not know what it was, and then she knew that she wanted him to kiss her. But it didn't seem a very likely thing to happen, because they were sitting at opposite sides of the table, and he had had to stretch right across to take her hand. And, anyway, she did not imagine that he was thinking about kissing her; he just seemed more interested in the strange similarity between Mattie and her.

And then his eyes met hers, and she felt as if something clicked between them, and if the door had not opened at that moment, she did not know what would have happened.

'Hello.' It was Amelia. 'I saw a coat in the hall and wondered whose it was. How are you, Breda?'

Thomas released Breda's hand from his.

'I was just commenting on how like Mattie's hands Breda's are,' he said.

'I'm much better, thank you,' Breda said quickly, her response overlapping with Thomas's in her effort to make it appear that everything was normal. But it didn't feel normal.

'They're like mine too,' Amelia said, looking down at her own hands.

Breda, glancing at Amelia's hands, thought that her own nails were nicer than hers, and as if reading her thoughts Amelia suddenly said, 'I'm going to stop biting my nails.'

'About time too,' Thomas said.

Breda realised she could not stay much longer because she knew it would take ages to get home and she did not want her mother worrying about where she was. A slightly uncomfortable silence descended in the kitchen, and she did not know what to say or how to deal with the sudden awkwardness.

'You look great without the plaster,' Amelia

said, as Breda put on her coat. 'Pity you have to go. Will you come again?'

She seemed so nice. She was quite gentle and for the first time Breda thought that maybe she was not as confident as she had thought on the few occasions she had met her.

'I'd like to,' Breda said.

And she meant it. She wanted to come back, and to sit in their kitchen and to be part of them.

And she did go back, many times, lying to her mother about having tea after work with some of the girls. Which, of course, was true in one sense, just not with the girls her mother thought she was meeting. Sometimes she stayed to supper and she started to feel that there was a tiny niche in their home into which she slotted. Occasionally she felt incredibly uneasy, not sure why she was there with them and not sure if they accepted her. Mattie wanted to give her a red scarf to use as a sling for her arm, which still ached even though the plaster was long gone.

'Please take it,' Mattie said.

'I won't be able to use it,' Breda said, touching the fabric and wanting so much to have the scarf.

A look of both hurt and anger came over Mattie's face.

'Why don't you take it?' Thomas intervened before Mattie could say something hurtful. 'Why don't you say you bought it?'

'I didn't think of that,' Breda said, now holding the scarf in her hands. It was lovely and it smelled of Mattie and she wanted it so badly.

'Look, if you're feeling that you're deceiving

your mother over the scarf ... does it make any difference?' Mattie said. 'You're misleading her by coming here anyway. She doesn't know, does she?'

Breda shook her head. Thomas took the scarf from her and, fitting it, he tied a knot in it so that it hung from her neck and supported her arm.

'That looks a lot nicer than your old sling,' he said.

Mattie picked up the sling and threw it in the bin. 'See,' she said. 'That wasn't so difficult, was it?'

They were sitting in the kitchen a few months later when Lucas said he had applied to study medicine.

'You've what?' Mattie said in disbelief.

'I should have done it to start with,' he said. 'Remember that evening we pretended to be doctors, Thomas – that changed my life. See the effect you have had on me, Breda?'

'For God's sake, Lucas, I don't think medicine is as simple as that,' Mattie said to him, eyeing him from under her dark eyebrows, her head extended and tilting slightly downwards in a pose Breda was getting used to. 'It's not all clean white coats and pretty girls lying in beds, you know.'

Breda liked the fact that Mattie had referred to her as a pretty girl, if indeed that is what she meant. She already knew that one could never be sure with Mattie. Then Mattie looked at Breda and added with a grin, 'Or even awful-looking ones.'

They all laughed and Breda did too. She knew

410

Mattie had not meant it.

Secretly she felt pleased that maybe Lucas's interest in becoming a doctor had been because of her lying in that hospital bed. She was so aware of the impact they had on her life that it thrilled her to think she might have some influence on theirs. She really started to feel like part of them and she looked forward to those visits all week, eking out the days until she felt she could reasonably drop in again.

A few days later it transpired that they were all thinking of going to Malta for the summer once Mattie and Amelia's exams were over. Amelia was doing her A levels and Mattie her third-year exams in her four-year chemistry degree. This holiday in Malta sounded like a reward for when their work was over.

Breda felt her heart miss a beat. The idea of them not being there for her to drop in on was really upsetting.

'I think now is the time to tell you,' Amelia said in her careful way. 'I'm not going with you. I've other plans,' she added.

'Well, what are they?' Mattie asked.

'We never go without you,' Lucas protested.

'We can't leave you here alone,' Thomas said. 'Lucy wouldn't like it. Nor would I,' he added.

He was very protective of them. Breda envied them that, even though his protection seemed sometimes to include her too. She sometimes thought about how he had touched her when he was fitting the sling on her, and how he had lifted her hair, which she now wore loose when she was visiting them, and how his fingers had felt as they had touched the back of her neck. It had almost felt like he was stroking her. He showed interest in her work, such as it was, and always included her in their conversations, even on the awkward days when she felt as if she was sitting on the edge of her chair questioning herself as to why she kept coming back to them.

And when Amelia went in to study after supper, Thomas asked Breda to help clear away and it made her feel even more a part of things, which was what she wanted, and she thought that he knew that.

Mattie and Amelia's exams were approaching. Mattie seemed uninterested and aloof, while Amelia's industry astounded Breda. She had worked hard and also had her mother putting pressure on her. But there was no one to put pressure on Amelia. She just did it herself. She was doing her A levels in both Latin and Greek, neither subject having been available in Breda's school. One more thing to envy her for, Breda thought, as she loved languages, and while English had been her best subject in school, she had done very well in French as well, and would have loved to have done another language, even a dead one, as Lucas called both Latin and Ancient Greek.

'I'm going to Ireland,' Amelia said. 'To Ithaca.'

'Ithaca?' Lucas said. 'I thought that was some mythical place.'

'It's where Odysseus went back to,' Thomas explained.

They were all so erudite, Breda thought. She felt she knew nothing by comparison.

'It's the name of our old family home in Ireland,' Mattie explained. 'Why are you going there?' she asked Amelia.

'I want to see it again,' she explained. 'I've been thinking about it a lot. I just have a need to go back there. I want to see if it is as I remembered.'

More than that she would not say.

Breda sat there looking at her, unable to believe how independent she was. Amelia was going to do what she wanted to, and no one was going to stand in her way. They might try to talk her out of it, but ultimately they would support her.

But the empty weeks lay as dull days and heavy nights as Breda thought of what the absence of the Cholmondesley sisters and their friends would mean. Work would occupy her daytime hours, but the evenings she would pass alone, as Jane was so busy with her forthcoming wedding and was always with her fiancé. A bit of her was aware how dependent she was becoming on her visits to their house and she feared that it was a bad thing, because it would pass. They would go on with their lives and sooner or later she would be left behind and the thought of that was terribly upsetting. The thought of not being a tiny part of them left an emptiness in her that she felt she could never fill. There was no way she could not keep coming back here.

'Pity you can't come with us,' Thomas said to her. 'I'm sure you'd love Malta. Both Mattie and Amelia love it.'

But Breda did not have the money and, anyway,

she knew it was not a real invitation, just one of those things that got said, but that did not go anywhere.

'Will you come out and join us after you've been to Ireland?' Lucas asked, turning to Amelia.

She said that she didn't know.

'Don't know why you are going back there anyway,' Mattie said. 'Have you any reason to think they will even invite you into the house?'

Amelia now looked surprised. 'Why wouldn't they?' she said. 'I'm not planning on staying with them. I just thought I'd drop in.'

She explained to Breda that the house had been bought by a German family after the war and that they had always said she and Mattie were welcome to go back and see it. And that they had even kept the Cholmondesley family paintings on the walls.

'They've probably burned them by now,' Mattie said. 'Anyway, what makes you think they still live there?'

'How are you going to fund this trip?' Lucas interrupted.

'I'm due to get some money from my parents' estate on my birthday,' Amelia said.

'It won't come through immediately,' Mattie told her. 'Mine didn't. It took months.'

'Oh,' Amelia looked downcast. Then she looked hopefully up at Mattie.

Mattie said, 'Don't look at me. I'm not lending you anything.'

'Then I'll ask Lucymem,' Amelia said. 'I'm sure she will loan it to me.'

Breda wanted to say that she would lend it if

414

she had it, but it did not seem the right thing to interject and Mattie might take it amiss. But she would have liked to help Amelia, even if she did not have a penny to give her. She would have liked to go with her, to keep her company and give support.

'Will you go on a holiday?' Thomas asked Breda, drawing her back into the conversation.

She shook her head.

'I went once to Brighton when I was a child,' she said. 'With family friends. It was wonderful.'

Amelia looked at her with interest. 'Brighton?' she said. 'Really? When?'

'I don't know. I suppose I was ten or eleven. I'm not sure.'

'I went there once,' Amelia said to her. 'With my grandfather. Did you ever go there, Mattie?' she asked.

'To Brighton? No. I was either incarcerated in school or locked up in the back garden in Kent. I never went anywhere,' Mattie replied. 'When did you go with Grandfather?'

'It was that summer he died,' Amelia said.

'I never knew that,' Mattie said.

'No,' Amelia replied thoughtfully. 'No...'

'What's puzzling you?' Lucas asked her. 'You look like a lady lost.'

'It's the oddest thing,' Amelia said, 'but I thought I saw Mattie one day in Brighton – all those years ago. I thought she might have run away from school or been taken out for the day. Now ... well, now, I think it was Breda.'

'How interesting,' Lucas said. 'What a coincidence.'

415

'Life is a coincidence,' Thomas added. 'What do you remember about Brighton, Breda?'

'The pier, the rides, the Punch and Judy.'

'I hated the Punch and Judy,' Amelia said.

'So did I,' Breda admitted. They smiled at each other.

But Grandmother took ill later that week, and the moment Amelia's exams were over, she went to Malta with the others. Ireland can wait, she said to Breda.

'It'll be there for another time. Grandmother is very ill, and Lucymem says we really ought to come out.'

Breda was sorry for them when she said goodbye. And she was also sorry for herself. They each had hugged her on her last evening in their home, and then her life returned to its normal mundane routine, and she tried not to think about them all the time, although in their different ways they each had a place in her mind and her imagination. It was Thomas she thought about when she went to bed at night, holding his image in her head and the thought of his hand on hers in their kitchen resting on the kitchen table, or his fingers lifting her hair and touching the nape of her neck. She thought of Mattie giving her the red scarf as a sling, Amelia sitting in the window with a book on her lap, Lucas chopping up food in the kitchen, making witty comments. She thought of her chair in the kitchen – her chair, as she had come to see it – her place in their kitchen. And she missed them all terribly.

The four of them packed their bags, closed up the house for the weeks they would be away, checked with Roger Farrington next door that he would keep an eye on the place, and pushed the two motorbikes into the hall.

'I love this feeling,' Mattie said as they closed the front door. Her eyes were alight and she even jostled Amelia as they went out on to the pavement. 'Remember how I used to be so afraid of flying?' she laughed.

'You even burned down the wing of a school to change the course of events, if I remember rightly,' Thomas said.

'I love that story,' Lucas said. 'It's so Mattie.'

Amelia said nothing. It was not one of her better memories.

Mattie laughed. 'It worked,' she said.

The flight was good, with a clear sky as they came over the Alps, and the pleasure of looking at the various islands in the Mediterranean as they flew southwards.

'I feel like I can smell it,' Amelia said to Mattie. They were sitting beside each other on the plane, just as they had always done. They held hands as the plane came in low over Gozo.

'Look at the cliffs,' Amelia said, as they came along the south side of Malta. 'You know, the very first time I saw them, I thought that Malta had been lifted up on this side. And I was right. An earthquake had lifted it.'

She looked at Mattie. They smiled at each other.

'You are a funny girl,' Mattie said.

Amelia wondered what she meant, but she didn't ask. There was always the possibility that Mattie meant something not very nice, and Amelia did not want to ruin the pleasure of any moment.

They came through Customs together and out into the Arrivals Hall.

'Oh, mother of the gods,' Lucas said. 'If it isn't old Cyclops.'

There stood Friedrich Arnheim, in his beige clothing and his shiny shoes. He greeted them, explaining that Lucy was unable to come to the airport because she didn't want to leave Harriet.

'I'm helping out,' he said.

'Rhino couldn't make it?' Mattie asked.

Lucas said in an aside on the way to the car, 'Maybe the one-horned animal couldn't get it up today.'

Mattie snorted with laughter, and Thomas gave Lucas a shove and told him to lower his voice.

Amelia walked with Friedrich, trying to find out what exactly was happening.

'Lucy moved back in with her mother a while ago,' Friedrich explained smoothly. 'I'm living with Rhino now,' he added. 'I've had problems with the drains in my place and Rhino kindly has given me a bed.'

'I think someone might have told us all of this,' Mattie said. 'I thought we'd be over in the house with you, Thomas. I hate this,' she muttered in the back of the car. 'We never know what is going on. One minute we're living in one house and the next we're in another one. No one ever consults

418

us. We just have to fit into everybody else's life as though we don't count.'

Thomas put his hand on her arm. 'It's OK, Mattie,' he said. 'Don't let them do this to you. And I won't let it affect me either. We'll just take this as it comes. Are you all right?' he asked Amelia.

She nodded. She didn't feel all right at all. There were such mixed emotions at coming back here. It should have been just pure joy, but instead there was the worry of her grandmother being ill, combined with the uncertainty as to what was going on between Lucymem and Rhino, and the fact that they would not be staying where she had thought.

Friedrich dropped Mattie and Amelia in Sliema, at their grandmother's house. Putting their bags on the pavement, he said goodbye and got back into the car. He pulled away quickly as Mattie reached to knock on the door.

'This is awful,' Amelia said.

'Don't worry,' Mattie retorted. 'We'll find out what is going on. I promise.'

Thomas and Lucas went back to the farmhouse where Rhino had just arrived home from work. Having greeted his uncle, Thomas immediately asked if there were plans for a divorce, but Rhino said categorically no.

'I love Lucy,' Rhino said. 'I want her back.'

'I don't think she's likely to come back with Friedrich living here in the house,' Thomas said reasonably.

'She may well come around,' Rhino said. 'Harriet is ill and is unlikely to get better. I think Lucy will come back then.'

Thomas was surprised that Rhino was thinking along those lines. 'I really don't think that's very likely,' he said. 'I mean, well, do you think she would want to come back here with ... well ... with Friedrich here?' He wondered how Rhino could possibly imagine that Lucy would find such a situation acceptable.

'Oh, Fritz is only staying here at the moment,' Rhino said. 'He's having problems with his drains, and while they're being sorted out, I'm just helping him out by giving him a bed.'

But it was Rhino's own bed that was being given and shared, as Thomas quickly discovered. He and Lucas were both bemused that Rhino could see a solution to his marital problems while he actually had Fritz in his bed.

'Is he being serious? This is naïvety brought to a whole new height,' Lucas said to Thomas as the two of them walked together down to the rocks to swim.

'I know,' Thomas said. 'I can't imagine what he is thinking. Maybe he is under the impression that Lucymem isn't aware that Cyclops has taken up residence here.'

'Men, men, men,' Lucas said. 'A breed apart.'

They both laughed.

'Maybe we will be just as simple when we grow up,' Lucas said.

'We are grown up,' Thomas said, and they laughed again.

'Of course Lucymem knows that Friedrich is living with Rhino,' Mattie said later in the day when they met up. 'On an island this small, how could she not know?'

'Rhino is hoping she'll come back,' Thomas said.

'Do you think she still loves him?' Lucas asked the girls.

'Lucy has strong feelings of duty and responsibility – like Grandmother,' Amelia said. 'I don't think it would occur to her to walk away from those feelings. She sticks with things that she sees as duty. It's the way she is.'

'More bloody fool her,' Mattie said. 'Why on earth should she come back to Rhino's place? See? I even think of it as Rhino's place, not as his and Lucy's. That says it all. Why should she come back and be humiliated by his actions and by the one-eyed bugger. Sorry, Lucas,' she said.

Lucas was sitting looking at the sea with a pained expression on his face. 'Why are you saying sorry to me?' he asked.

'Because the way I said that implies I have a problem with homosexuality, and I don't. I don't care what or whom you poke. I do care about Lucymem being humiliated.'

'I couldn't agree more. Life is for living and having fun, but not when you are hurting someone. And yes, you're right, the situation is nothing short of humiliating for Lucy. Her dignity is in walking away from it. And dignity is as much a part of Lucy as is her sense of duty.'

'What do you think, Thomas?' Amelia asked him.

'I think it comes down to both dignity and integrity,' Thomas said. 'I think Rhino is behaving badly, but for some reason he can't see it. I don't know why. He is blinkered in this regard. He is the one who should never have let this happen. I think if he really cared about Lucy he would have made sure this had not occurred. In my opinion if he wants to save his marriage, he should show Friedrich the door, and go down on bended knee to Lucy and grovel in his apologies. But that is not going to happen. He has no idea about integrity. I think he's weak. I hate saying that. He's my only living relative and I don't want to see him as being weak, but that is how it is.'

'He's not your only living relative,' Amelia said. 'You've got us, Mattie and me.'

'I meant blood relative,' Thomas said. 'I meant the person from whom we learn how to behave.'

'We don't just learn from blood relatives,' Amelia said. 'We learn from observing. And if you really think that we only learn from blood relatives, then we can learn from them how not to behave too.'

'Look at me,' Lucas said. 'I've learned everything from my mother. I even fancy men.'

'Oh, shut up, Lucas,' Mattie said. 'Your mother is a perfectly nice person – you're implying that she is man-mad. And she's not. She's just a decent human being.'

'Anyway,' Lucas said, ignoring her, 'if I were Cyclops, and I found a man as attractive as Rhino, but more my own generation, I might well move in on him, regardless of whether or not he has a wife.'

It was typical of Lucas to joke about the situation, but Mattie taking him seriously said, 'You wouldn't.'

'I might.'

'You jolly well would not. Thomas, Amelia and I wouldn't let you,' Mattie said firmly. 'Anyway, you can't joke about something like this. Personally I don't care a jot about Rhino. I think he is a selfish bastard. But I do care about Lucymem.'

Amelia looked lovingly at Mattie. She loved her for voicing those words aloud. It was probably the first time she had ever said anything as direct as that about their aunt.

'She's always been there for us,' Amelia said. 'She may need us to help her now. And she deserves better than this.'

'No one deserves this,' Mattie said. 'No one should be humiliated by a wandering husband, regardless of whether it is a Cyclops he is buggering or a...' She couldn't think of a way to complete the sentence.

'A nymph he is bedding?' Lucas suggested.

'You know what I mean,' Mattie said. 'No one should do this to another human being, especially when they claim to love them.'

'Yes, you're right,' Thomas said.

'There's not much we can do about it,' Lucas said.

'Of course there is,' Mattie informed him. 'Cyclops is supposedly staying with old Rhino because of the drains in his house. So let's go and see about those drains, for starters.'

What it lies in our power to do, it lies in our power not to do.

Aristotle

CHAPTER SEVENTEEN

There was nothing wrong with the drains, as Thomas and Lucas both announced that evening at dinner in Rhino's house.

'We even checked with the neighbours,' Thomas said. If he felt irritation, he hid it well, and kept his voice as impassive as he could.

'I had someone in two weeks ago,' Friedrich said stiffly. 'They cleared them and said I should give it time to be sure that the problem has eased.'

'If you're not there, how can you know if the problem has eased or not?' Lucas asked, looking up from his fish, one eye of which appeared to be glaring at him. 'God, but this one-eyed fish reminds me of someone.'

'How is Harriet Entwhistle?' Friedrich asked, touching his patch and changing the subject while helping himself to potatoes as he spoke.

'She's very weak,' Thomas said. 'Have you been to see her?' he asked Rhino.

'I visited her a week ago,' Rhino said.

'Lucy could do with your support,' Thomas said.

It sounded like a rebuke, and normally Rhino

would have responded with a sharp retort, but he did not. Instead he picked up his glass of wine, and said, 'I know. I'm going to see her tomorrow.'

'I thought you were taking the day off work so that we could go sailing,' Friedrich said.

'I am,' he replied. 'But we can fit both in.'

'Do you want me to come with you?' Friedrich asked, slight surprise in his voice.

'I was not suggesting that you would,' Rhino said. 'I just meant there was time for me to do both and then we can go out in the boat. Maybe Mattie and Amelia would like to come out too. Maybe Lucy will let Charlotte come.' He did not sound very hopeful.

Harriet's heart was very weak and she lay in her bed, her proud face resting on the pillows, her eyes now slightly sunk above her fine cheekbones.

She held Amelia's hand. 'What goes around,' she said to her, 'comes around.'

Amelia was unsure what she meant. 'Grandmother,' she said, 'Mattie and I have the oddest story to tell.'

'Tell me,' her grandmother said.

'It's one of those odd things – and I did think of writing it to you, but it was such an unlikely series of events ... well, I didn't.'

'Good,' her grandmother said. 'I feel like being told a story. Tell me, darling.'

Amelia sat beside her grandmother and, holding her hand, she told her of being on the bus, all about the car accident and how they visited Breda in hospital.

'She's our friend now,' Amelia said. 'She comes and has supper with us – she's sort of become part of the house in an odd way.'

'What a strange story,' her grandmother said. 'Does Breda look like her mother?'

'Well, no, not really. I don't think so. She looks so like Mattie, and me too, although I don't see that so clearly. But the others do.'

'I suppose we can't see our own features or ourselves in others. But you look so like your mother, dear Hilary,' she sighed. 'Both of you do. You and Mattie.'

Amelia reached out and held her grand-mother's hand. 'I was the lucky one, wasn't I?' she said.

'What do you mean, darling?' her grandmother asked.

'Well, I never knew Hilary, so I didn't have to miss her.'

'I don't know,' Harriet said. After a while she added, '"'Tis better to have loved and lost than never to have loved at all." Tennyson.'

'I know,' Amelia replied. 'I love Tennyson.'

'Your grandfather...' She didn't finish the sentence.

She fell asleep then, and Amelia sat a little while longer, watching her and listening to her short breaths.

Looking at her grandmother sleeping, recalling her words, she felt that she loved lots of people and that she did love her mother, or at least the little she knew of her. She wasn't sure if her grandmother was right, though, about loving and losing. She was very uncertain that Mattie could

426

be considered luckier than she. What Mattie had lost did not make her a happier person. Mattie did not give the impression ever of having been enriched by her past. Thomas, on the other hand, was a more content human being and he too had lost his family. And there was Lucas, who had lost his father, and who lived on seemingly unperturbed. Maybe we're all just different, Amelia thought.

Life's rich fabric, Grandfather had said to her once when they were talking about people.

Their grandmother was fading fast, and they knew it.

'Poor Lucymem,' Amelia said to Mattie. She expected Mattie to make her usual response when someone was dying, and that was, 'Well, at least she had her mother all these years.' But Mattie did not say that.

'I know,' she said. 'Poor Lucymem.'

'Grandmother still looks beautiful,' Amelia said. 'I never really thought of her as beautiful when I was a child, but there is something so majestic about her.'

Although the girls were ten days back in Malta, they still had not seen Rhino, despite their visits to his house in Harriet's car, which Mattie had commandeered. Finally Rhino came and visited.

There were a few strange moments as he greeted Mattie and Amelia, neither of whom could think of anything to say to him. They stood awkwardly in front of him and shook his hand by way of greeting. He looked older and sterner.

'Good to see you both,' he said.

Neither said anything.

Charlotte came into the room. She was eight years old now, wispy and sweet, with huge blue eyes and straight blonde hair. Seeing Rhino, she threw herself into his arms.

'Daddy, Daddy,' she said.

He lifted her up and swung her in the air.

'You've grown,' he said when he put her down. 'You're getting bigger every week.'

'When are we coming home?' Charlotte asked him.

He looked at Lucy and said nothing for a moment.

'When your mother is ready,' he then said. 'And now is not a good time, I don't think.'

'I can't leave your grandmother,' Lucy said to Charlotte.

'May I take Charlotte back home even for a day or two?' he asked Lucy.

'It depends on who is there in the house,' Lucy said. 'I'm quite fussy as to Charlotte's company, and I think you can understand that.'

'Thomas is there. He'd love to see her.'

'He can see her here,' Lucy replied. 'As indeed he has. He has been a regular visitor,' she said coldly. She seemed to have regained some of the determination of her youth and it was showing through clearly, even though she was very distracted by Harriet's condition.

Rhino went upstairs to Harriet's room. She opened her eyes and looked at him and then she shook her head.

'You are a foolish man,' she said.

428

He sat on the chair by her bed where the others each took their turn, hour after hour unless Harriet was asleep.

'I'm doing my best,' he said.

'Oh no, you're not.'

'I would roll over and die for Lucy,' he said to her.

'Oh no, you wouldn't,' Harriet replied in a tried voice. 'You just don't see it, Rhino. It's not enough to love someone and then to treat him or her like you treat Lucy. Love is bigger than that. Love is sticking by someone, and making sure that they are not being hurt. You don't see that and you don't do it. When I die, Lucy won't stay here. She'll go back to England. And you will be the lesser for that. You will be the loser. I know you're older than her, and maybe you have more in common with someone your own age and your own ... well, never mind ... but you show a distinct lack of taste.'

She closed her eyes. Despite a few protestations from Rhino, she did not bother to respond.

'What would be the point?' she said later to Amelia. 'He is blind to love. Blind to how you have to treat a woman.'

And Amelia, thinking of the bond between her grandmother and her grandfather, when he had been alive, saw too what Lucy wanted and what Lucy needed, and for the first time she too saw that that love affair between her grandparents was her aspiration for her future. There were things she wanted to do before that, but she knew that the example they had set was where love would lie.

'What is wrong with him?' Amelia asked her grandmother. 'Why does he behave the way he does?'

'He's weak,' Harriet replied. 'He is trying to keep everyone happy, and in fact is making no one happy. Lucy deserves better. When I die–'

'Don't say that, Grandmother,' Amelia said.

'Amelia, listen to me, please. When I die, and I will die – that's what happens at the end of life, and that's all right. I wouldn't want to live on like this, lying in a bed, tired … would you want that for me?'

Amelia bit her lip.

'When I die,' the older woman continued, 'Lucy is going to be lost unless she takes matters into her own hands. I've set her a good enough example about picking up the pieces when things are down. I've taught her stoicism and determination, but I don't want her staying on here alone. She should go back to England and start a new life. She's young enough to do that...'

Downstairs, Rhino asked Lucy again about bringing Charlotte back to the farmhouse.

'In principle I have no problem,' Lucy said. 'But not under the present circumstances.'

'You Entwhistles,' he said. 'A stubborn bunch. And I can see it in Charlotte already.'

Charlotte twirled around in the door and asked if that was a good thing.

He glanced at Lucy before addressing his daughter. 'It will stand you in good stead,' he replied almost reluctantly.

'Lucy *is* weak,' Mattie said to the others later. 'She'll go back to Rhino and the present situation will continue.'

'Well, she won't go back while Friedrich is there,' Amelia said to Lucas. 'Can't we get him out of the house?'

'Do we want to?' Thomas said. 'Do we really think that is the right thing to do?'

Even as Amelia said it, her grandmother's words came to mind and she wondered if Thomas was right and if they should be trying to get Friedrich to go home at all. If her grandmother was right should they not be encouraging Lucy to go back to England?

She told the others about the conversation she had had in the bedroom, and Mattie said with irritation, 'Christ Almighty. It's enough to deal with our own lives without having to take this one on.'

'Come on, Mattie. You don't mean that. We love Lucymem and she gave us everything when we were children.'

'She went and left us as soon as Rhino came along,' Mattie retorted.

'You didn't care, did you?' Amelia said. She certainly had never got the impression that it had bothered Mattie one bit.

'I don't know if I did or not,' Mattie replied. 'I suppose I didn't expect anything else of her.'

'Mattie, you're so bitter,' Lucas said.

'I'm not. I'm a pragmatist. I don't see the point in wasting time on what one can't have.'

'That's a load of rubbish,' Lucas said. 'You

spend all your time regretting the loss of your childhood.'

Tempers were flaring. Amelia was startled as this row erupted.

'No, I don't.'

'Yes, you do.'

'You don't know what you're talking about. Anyway, who are you to talk? You just pretend to fancy men so that Friedrich or Rhino will help you.'

'What do you know about anything?'

'Huh,' Mattie sniffed.

'What was going on there?' Amelia asked Thomas later.

'I think Lucas is feeling bad because he can't get Friedrich to go home. He knows he is not going to leave.'

'But...' Amelia was puzzled, 'first of all, why would it be Lucas's responsibility to get Friedrich out of the house? And also, what did Mattie mean that Lucas is only pretending to be ... you know...'

'I think that Lucas feels that the special link between him and Friedrich makes him in some way responsible.'

'What special link?'

'The fact that Friedrich funds his education, and looks out for him and his mother. Anyway, Friedrich is not going to leave.'

'Then we have to encourage Lucy to leave. If she stays here, she will waste her love and her ... oh, I don't know, her loveliness, I suppose ... she will waste those on nothing and will never be happy.'

Thomas looked at her and he reached out a hand and put it on her shoulder. There was something supportive and kind in his movement, reinforced by the stillness of his hand resting on her. She felt his strength flowing into her.

'What are you thinking?' Amelia asked him.

'I was thinking that you are a very nice person,' he said.

'But don't you feel the same way?' she asked.

'I'm not sure that I do. I suppose that like many people I want the older generation to settle down and be happy so that I can get on with my own life. I don't want to be worrying about them. I just want them safe in their own houses, getting on with their own lives.'

'It's a bit like how Lucas feels,' Amelia said thoughtfully. 'I wonder why I don't feel like that.'

'Probably because you remember Lucy so well from before she married Rhino and you know that she was happy back then.'

'But don't you remember Rhino from before he married Lucy?'

'I do. But I don't think he was particularly happy. I think Rhino has always felt an unclear sense of responsibility – like as though he owes a debt to too many people, and has no real idea that there are some debts you can't pay.'

'Well, he can't be happy now. I wonder why he doesn't do something about it and kick old Cyclops out, if he really wants Lucy back.'

'I don't think he knows how to,' Thomas said. 'I think he feels that he owes everybody something and is just spreading himself around, trying to keep everyone happy.'

'And ending up hurting everyone,' Amelia said.

'Stupid ass,' Mattie said, coming in to the room at the end of this conversation. 'Why would he feel that he owes everyone something anyway?'

'Oh, come on Mattie. Surely you must have guessed that years ago. He bombed Malta.'

'What?'

'I don't mean that he personally is responsible for the total devastation of Malta, but he was one of the bomber pilots – in the Luftwaffe. He was involved in the huge bombing in nineteen forty-two which is when Lucas's father was killed.'

There was silence from Mattie and Amelia as they took this in.

'I see,' Amelia said.

'Well, I don't,' Mattie responded. 'So he feels he owes the Borg Cardonas – so what! He kills her husband and then tries to take his place as Lucas's father. What a load of rubbish. He can't take that responsibility on himself. What's that got to do with old Skullfucker? What does he owe him? And what does Skullfuck owe the Borg Cardonas? They are all too intertwined with each other.'

'Mattie,' Thomas laughed, 'what names! Anyway, I don't think it is as clear-cut as owing something in particular. I think it's more complicated than that. In some way he loves Friedrich – years of mutual support, being there for each other during the war and after, prison camp together, finally coming here and putting down roots. Friedrich is part of the past. Rhino lost everything else – all his family, except for me. I think that like us all, in his own way, he is just

434

doing his best, even though his best is not really good enough.'

'But to deliberately hurt Lucymem...' Mattie said crossly.

'I don't think he has done it consciously. I think that it just evolved,' Thomas said.

Amelia puzzled over Mattie's attitude. It seemed a contradiction of all the things she had always said and thought as she sought to find someone to blame for the destruction of her own family. It was all so personal, all so relative, and she felt sorry for them – for Rhino and Mattie, for the uselessness of guilt and anger, and the waste of love.

Thomas and Amelia were alone a while later when Amelia asked him something else that was on her mind.

'Thomas, what did Mattie mean when she said that Lucas didn't really like men ... you know what I mean.'

'I think she meant that Lucas just doesn't know what he really wants. Lucas is lost in his own way. Just like Mattie is.'

'But if he doesn't ... you know, like men ... what is he doing? Is he pretending?'

'No. No, I don't think he is,' Thomas said thoughtfully. 'I'm not sure. I know that he admires Rhino. Rhino helped both his mother and him. Friedrich too. I think that Lucas is just searching for himself. Isn't that what we all are doing?'

Harriet died peacefully a few days later in her sleep. The last thing she said was to Amelia.

'Go back to the beginning,' were her words.

Amelia, holding her hand, wondered what she meant, if indeed it had any meaning at all. It was different, losing her grandmother from losing her grandfather, Amelia thought. Now there were people around. People supporting each other. Comfort from neighbours, comfort within each other. Although she felt very sad, she also felt that death like this could be handled. There was a sense of inevitability about it, and she had not liked seeing her once-robust grandmother laid low in her bed.

Lucy, although grief-stricken, held herself with the utmost dignity.

'Are you all right, Lucymem?' Amelia asked her. Both she and Mattie had noted that Lucy had not cried.

'Yes,' Lucy said. 'No ... not right now. But I will be. It's difficult to comprehend ... to take on board ... we had become so close, such friends over these last few years, after years of not really knowing her at all. And I liked her. I always loved her, but I discovered that I liked her – really admired her. I feel shocked, I suppose. I've lost a friend as well as a mother.'

Amelia was sitting with Charlotte on her lap, and it was Mattie who put her arm around Lucy and suddenly leaned forward and kissed her aunt on the cheek.

Because of the heat the funeral was being held the following day, and Thomas phoned early in the morning and told Mattie and Amelia that Friedrich was coming too.

'He can't,' Mattie said.

'He is,' Thomas said. 'I can't stop him.'

'Well, I will,' Mattie said.

She took off in the car and returned about an hour later, looking pleased with herself.

In due course Rhino arrived with Friedrich and Thomas in tow.

'What could I do?' Thomas said to the disbelieving Mattie and Amelia. 'He insisted on coming.'

'Why in God's name would he want to come? He hardly knew Grandmother and we all know what he's done to Lucymem,' Amelia said crossly.

'I don't know,' Thomas said.

'It's bloody prurience,' Mattie said. 'No one should come to a funeral if they aren't there to grieve or to support.'

'I really tried to talk him out of it,' Thomas said. 'I even spoke to Rhino about it when Friedrich's intentions were clear. He didn't understand what I meant.'

'That man,' Mattie said angrily. 'That stupid, stupid man. Well, Cyclops is not coming back to the house. I wish ... you know the way at weddings there is a piece where you're asked if you know of a reason for the marriage not to go on? Well, I wish there was a bit like that at funerals where you could be asked if there was anyone there who should not be. And then I could stand up and state why Cyclops shouldn't be there.'

'Well, there isn't. We can't stop him,' Amelia said.

437

'I'm going to stop him from coming back to the house.'

'I'm not sure you're going to be able to,' Thomas said.

'I jolly well will,' Mattie retorted. 'I've got a plan. Already in action,' she added.

'You won't be able to,' he repeated.

'Watch me. Just make sure that he doesn't get near Rhino when it's over,' she said to Amelia.

'How am I supposed to do that?'

'Just do it,' Mattie said.

Rhino, Lucy, Amelia and Charlotte went in one car to the church and cemetery.

Mattie said she would take Thomas and Friedrich in the other car.

Some thirty people gathered at the open plot while Harriet's coffin was lowered in to it. Amelia stood close to her aunt and held Charlotte's hand. Rhino was standing on the other side of Lucy. They stood in silence as the prayers were concluded.

Mattie nodded to the others when it was over, and the people had formed into small groups, talking together, coming up and speaking to Lucy.

Mattie drew Friedrich aside.

'It's so hot,' she said to him.

'No hotter than usual at this time of the year,' came the reply.

'I know,' Mattie said. 'But Rhino said he'd like you to take the boat round to the point and he will join you there as soon as he can get away.'

Friedrich expressed surprise. Thomas looked

across the cemetery to where Amelia was talking to Rhino and in fact had slipped her arm through his. She clearly had him well occupied.

'Why would he want me to bring the boat round when we could both get on it down in the port?' he asked.

'He said that he'd bring the car back to the farmhouse,' Mattie said evenly, 'and he could change and just go down to the point and board there. It would be easier. He said it was so hot and that he could think of nothing nicer.'

Everyone knew how Friedrich was always trying to get him to go out on his boat, and the bone of contention it had been with Harriet as Friedrich had always tried to scupper the Entwhistle plans.

Friedrich smiled. Mattie could see how he liked the idea of spoiling the end of the funeral party by Rhino leaving to go on the boat.

'I'll drop you down to the port,' Mattie said generously. 'Maybe Amelia and I will join you later. It'll probably take you a while to get the boat ready.'

'No, you should stay with Lucy,' Friedrich said. 'And anyway, the boat is ready. I always leave it so that I can just get on board and go.'

'That's very generous of you,' Mattie said sweetly. Thomas turned away to hide his smile. He had not seen guile in Mattie before and he was quite impressed at her skill – she who was usually so forthright and blunt.

'Well,' Mattie said, as Friedrich got out of the car and slammed the door. 'That's got rid of him for

439

a while.' She turned and grinned at Thomas. 'Get into the front,' she said. 'And exorcise him from the car.'

As soon as Thomas got out of the back of the car, Mattie revved up and pulled away, stopping slightly down the road and waiting for Thomas, who was now running after the car.

'Just teasing,' she said.

'You're in good form,' he answered as he got into the passenger seat beside her.

'Always happy when I accomplish what I want.'

Despite the heat of the day and the blueness of the sky, the sea was choppy from a wind the previous evening. As they drove along the seafront to the house in Sliema, Thomas commented on the waves.

'Rough ride for old Cyclops,' Mattie said with a grin.

They both laughed.

Back at the house with food and drinks and Harriet's friends gathering, there was a mixture of sadness and joy.

'She always made me laugh,' was one of the comments most often repeated.

'Not the worst epitaph,' Mattie said.

Friedrich did not come home that night. Thomas phoned Mattie and Amelia the following morning.

'Rhino is really worried,' he told them. 'He's called the police.'

'We'll come over,' Mattie said forthrightly.

'How's Lucy?'

'We'll bring her with us,' Mattie said.

Lucy declined, even when she heard that Friedrich was missing.

'I've enough things to be doing here, enough to be thinking about. If Rhino thinks I'm concerned about Friedrich, well, what can I say?' was her comment. 'I really don't need any of this at the moment.'

They left her and took Charlotte with them in the car.

Charlotte bouncing in the back was gleeful at going back to her home, even if it was only for the afternoon.

The police were at the farmhouse when Mattie, Amelia and Charlotte arrived. Thomas was waiting for them outside in the lane, to fill them in on what was happening.

'Look,' he said, 'they've been to Friedrich's house and there's no sign of him there. And they've checked his boat and it's not moored down in the harbour. It looks like he went out in it and didn't come back.'

'Well, we know he went out in it,' Mattie said.

'Yes, but when he comes back, he's going to be furious and so is Rhino. Friedrich will say that you sent him off on the boat. There'll be trouble then.'

'Do you think I care?' Mattie said.

'Well, I think you ought to,' Thomas said. 'You know what happened last time you crossed Rhino.'

'He can hardly take his belt to me now,' Mattie retorted.

'What if something bad has happened to him?'

441

Amelia said.

'Like what?' Mattie said.

'Well, he went out on the boat and he never comes back, Mattie.'

'What do you want me to do?' Mattie said irritably.

'Come on,' Thomas said. 'I think we ought to go in and tell what happened. We tell the truth. We all agreed it – we agreed that Friedrich shouldn't come back to the house. In fact we felt he shouldn't even have been at the funeral.'

Inside, Rhino and two policemen were sitting at the dining-room table.

'We've remembered something,' Thomas said carefully, interrupting the conversation.

Rhino looked up, nodded at the girls and then, seeing Charlotte, he got up and held out his arms to her.

She ran to him. 'Uncle Fritz is missing?' she said to him.

'Yes.' He held her close. His face looked worried, and then, recalling what Thomas had said, he looked up quizzically at them.

'What have you remembered?' he asked.

Between the three of them, they explained what had happened and how they had sent Friedrich off on the boat to buy Lucy time.

'Buy her time?'

'Grandmother had just died and been buried,' Mattie said impatiently. 'Lucy did not need Friedrich back at the house.'

'Mattie is absolutely right,' Thomas interrupted. 'Friedrich should not have been there. It

442

wasn't fair on Lucy and it wouldn't have been what your grandmother wanted. In fact he should not have been at the church or at the cemetery. It was intrusive – I said it to you at the time, Rhino. We were right to forestall Friedrich from going to the house.'

Rhino looked at Thomas. 'But he wanted to give Lucy support,' he said.

'No, he didn't,' Mattie snapped. 'He had no place at the funeral. He shouldn't have been there. It was simply to distract you from Lucy-mem. So I suggested he took the boat around to the point and maybe we would all go out on it later.'

It was only half a lie and the others backed her up.

The two policemen looked at each other.

'I think we can assume then that Mr Arnheim went out on his boat straight after the burial?' one asked.

'He headed down to the harbour,' Mattie confirmed. 'I brought him part of the way and left him in walking distance.'

'We'll go and inform the appropriate authorities,' the other said. 'We'll be in touch.'

Charlotte stayed with Rhino, while the others went for a walk. They wandered down on to the rocks where they sat, feet in the sea.

'What if he doesn't come back?' Amelia asked in a small voice.

'Then he doesn't come back,' Mattie said firmly.

'But...'

'But what? I don't have any regrets in telling him to take the boat round here. Why should I? We all felt he shouldn't have been there, and I did something about it. I'm not going to have remorse now. I thought he was a better sailor than to disappear in the Mediterranean.'

'Imagine if they never find him,' Amelia said.

'So what?' Mattie said. 'They'll give him seven years and then bury an empty coffin and say it's him.'

'What?'

'You know what I mean. He'll be declared dead after seven years. And they'll have some kind of a service and stick something in the ground and say it's him.'

'What are you talking about, Mattie?' Thomas asked.

'That's what they do,' Mattie replied.

'I never heard such nonsense in my life,' Thomas said.

'It is what they do,' Mattie insisted. 'They buried a coffin for Georgina but they never found any of her.'

'How do you know that?' Thomas asked her.

'I heard Lucymem and Grandmother talking about it once.'

'That was different,' Thomas said. 'That was during the war and there had been a crash.'

Lucas turned up later in the day. His face was worried. They had not seen him since the funeral.

'What's up?' they asked him.

'My mother is missing. I've just been to the police station to report it.'

444

'Your mother? Since when?'

'She wasn't at home when I got back yesterday after the funeral. She didn't come home last night. I've contacted everyone I can think of, but no one knows where she is.'

They told him about Friedrich being missing too.

'A coincidence?' Thomas wondered.

'How could there be a connection?' Amelia asked.

But there was a connection. Maria Borg Cardona had been seen down in the port at around the time Friedrich was going to his boat.

'I bet he gave her a lift round the island,' Thomas said.

'Oh, bugger,' Mattie exclaimed. 'Oh, bugger. I don't care what happens to old Cyclops, but Lucas's mother...'

'They're probably fine,' Thomas said reassuringly.

Mattie's face was pale.

In the house in Sliema they woke in the night to the sound of Mattie screaming. It reminded Amelia of something in her childhood – the nights when she woke and Lucymem was trying to console Mattie, trying to hold her stiff solid body in her arms and not being able to waken her from her nightmares.

Lucy came running to their bedroom where Mattie was howling into the pillow and Amelia was sitting up in bed looking at her.

'She hasn't done this in a long time,' Amelia

said to Lucy. 'There's no point in trying to waken her – you won't be able to.'

But Lucy tried anyway. 'It's all right, Mattie,' she said. 'I'm here. It's over. It's all over.'

Charlotte appeared sleepily in the doorway.

'What's wrong with Mattie?' she asked. 'Why is she crying?'

Tears were pouring down Mattie's face and she was making a whimpering noise like an animal.

'She's very upset,' Lucy said to Charlotte as Amelia got out of bed to comfort the frightened child.

But it was Charlotte who calmed Mattie in her troubled sleep. Charlotte who climbed into bed beside her and said, 'I'm here, Mattie. It's me.'

And Mattie whispered, 'Oh, Georgina. You're here, Georgina,' and the sobbing noises she was making stopped and she settled back down on the pillow.

'I'll stay here,' Charlotte said to Lucymem, and in due course Lucy left the three of them to sleep. Amelia waited until Charlotte drifted off and then she went downstairs and joined Lucy in the kitchen where her aunt had made tea and was sitting at the table, staring out the window at the darkness of the night.

'It's been quite a bad few days,' Amelia said to her aunt. She meant for Lucy and not for Mattie, but Lucy misunderstood her.

'I did my best,' Lucy said. 'But I was never able to repair the damage.'

'For Mattie? No one could,' Amelia said. 'Mattie is Mattie.'

'I know. I know. But I wish that somehow I

446

could have made it better for her.'

'Lucymem, you did everything for us. We both know that. Mattie will always have nightmares about her childhood. There's nothing any of us can do about that. I think that death in any shape just brings the nightmares back and Grandmother dying obviously has brought things to the surface.'

Two days later and a boat was found drifting off the coast of North Africa. Friedrich Arnheim flew back alone from Libya the following week when the paperwork was cleared for him.

'Hell,' Thomas said. 'I don't know what is worse, the thought of burying Friedrich or actually having him back. He is not going to be pleased. Rhino says he was kept in prison for the several days.'

Mattie laughed. 'Just when I thought we'd be off to another funeral. Cyclops and his one-eyed head return from the Med.'

'What about Lucas's mother?' Amelia asked.

Rhino had spoken to Friedrich on the phone but the line was bad and he couldn't hear what Friedrich was saying, other than that he had been released.

'I'm sure she's coming back with Friedrich,' Thomas said. But he wasn't sure. None of them was.

Mattie was distraught every time there was mention of Maria Borg Cardona. Amelia had never seen her like that.

Friedrich came back and he was alone. There were shocking moments in the airport when he explained what had happened. Lucas stood there listening, Thomas and Amelia with their arms around him; Mattie, white-faced, shaking her head in disbelief.

Friedrich had met Maria on his way down to the harbour. He offered her a ride in the boat round to the south side. As they skirted the east of the island, the fuel gauge suddenly showed up empty. He could not remember having filled it the previous time when he had moored, although it was something that he always did. He filled the tank with the spare canister of fuel that he always kept on board. About five minutes later something went wrong with the engine and it chugged and died. They drifted east, then southeast, and there was nothing he could do about it. The storm hit them sometime during the night. He had cast anchor by then, but had to raise it as the boat was being pulled by the strength of the waves.

'We were both up on deck,' he said. 'It wasn't safe below. One minute we were upright, and the next the boat tilted out of control. I lost her in the dark. I lost her...'

Rhino reached out and gripped his arm.

'Lucas, I'm sorry,' Friedrich said. 'I lost her... I couldn't find her. I stayed with the boat. Sometime the following day – four days ago? – I have lost track of time... Sometime later, I was picked up. They towed the boat. They still have it. It was impounded.'

He was almost gabbling. They had never seen him like this before.

'And Lucas's mother?' Thomas said.

'We looked for her. But I'm not sure they believed I was with someone.'

Lucas stood there. There was nothing to be said.

Rhino reached out to him in an embrace. 'Come here, Lucas,' he said. 'You are not alone. Know that ... you are not alone.'

There was a lot of discussion about what would happen next and who would go where for the rest of the long hot summer.

Lucas spoke about selling his family home, but it was Rhino who told him not to do anything in haste.

'Later you may be glad you kept it,' he said. 'Don't let something go when you are in any kind of mental turmoil. You may regret it.'

'Are you saying that from experience?' Lucas asked him.

'Possibly. It's not something I've really thought about,' Rhino replied. 'Once we had a coffee farm in Kenya. It's long gone now, and I had no part in the decision to sell it, nor do I hanker after it. But I know that to have been part of that decision would probably have been easier for me. Now, I mean. Not back then, though – it was much easier to have someone else making those arrangements.'

'Your roots are here,' Thomas said to Lucas. 'You don't have to make any decision about your home now. There are enough people to look after it while you complete your studies in London. You can decide later...'

'If only Friedrich hadn't come to the funeral,' Mattie said.

'If only we hadn't wanted to stop him,' Amelia said, shaking her head.

'If only my mother had not been down at the harbour,' Lucas said ruefully.

'An awful lot of "ifs" there,' Thomas said. 'You could go further back and say if Rhino had never come to live in Malta, or if he had never known Friedrich, or met your mother, then the story would be a different one, and might not have ended like this.'

All the ifs and buts that make up a life, Amelia thought, all the randomness and chaos ... all the disarray and commotion in life. If Lucymem had not been on that ship on that day, would she ever have met Rhino? Would she ever have come to Malta? If her own mother, Hilary, had not met Matthew Cholmondesley ... all the fragments of existence that interweave and bring about destiny. She went back in her mind, back to the beginning as she knew it, and she wondered if that was what Grandmother meant with her last spoken words.

She looked at Mattie, with her lovely cross face staring intently – almost wildly – at Lucas, and she thought how one could not exorcise the past. The most one could do was to learn to live with it.

They sat with Lucymem in their grandmother's courtyard.

'You don't have to make any immediate decisions,' Amelia said to her aunt. She was thinking about Rhino's words, telling Lucas not to sell up while he was in such a state of distress.

'I think I do,' Lucy said to them.

'No you don't,' Mattie said.

'I do. If I don't act now, I will drift back to Rhino...'

'Would that be such a bad thing?'

'Yes, it would. It would be bad for me. The only way I could go back to him now is if Friedrich left the house – no, if he left Malta. That's not going to happen. Where is my dignity in this? No. I need to rebuild myself,' Lucy said. 'And Rhino needs whatever it is he needs. I don't know what that is, but I'm not just going to be available for him, because things have changed. I wouldn't want that for any of you. And I therefore don't want it for me.'

'Are you all right?' Amelia asked Mattie.

'Why?' Mattie's face was tired. She was still not sleeping properly and when she did she was cursed with nightmares that caused her to call out in her sleep and to cry.

'I just wondered,' Amelia said to her. 'I keep thinking about the day of Grandmother's funeral – you went out that morning – you were going to do something. What was it?'

'I don't remember going out,' Mattie said sullenly.

'You don't have to tell me if you don't want to...' Amelia said.

'I don't know what you're talking about.'

451

'By the way,' Mattie said the following day, 'I'm not leaving Malta.' They looked at her in surprise.

'How do you mean?'

'I'm not going back to university,' she said. 'I don't much care for studying and I've got a job here. So I'm staying on.'

'What are you going to do?' Amelia asked.

'I've got work in a petard factory,' she said.

'Petard?'

'Fireworks. That's where the future lies. Well, my future, anyway.'

Amelia looked horrified. The thought of Mattie loose in a fireworks factory was terrifying.

Lucas laughed. 'I think that's brilliant,' he said. 'You'll make bigger and better ones.' And we'll all be waiting for the big bang, Amelia thought, but did not say aloud.

Later she asked Thomas why he did not try to talk Mattie out of her new career.

'Let her go and do it,' he said. 'Maybe it's the right thing. She's not pushed about studying, and at least this way she will be doing something she loves but in a controlled environment.'

Amelia had not seen it that way. She had a vision of Mattie blowing the whole factory up, but she said nothing more about it because she too had her own plans.

So Mattie stayed on with Lucy and Charlotte while they sorted out the contents of Harriet's house and made arrangements for leaving.

Lucy did not tell Rhino her plans until she had the plane tickets bought, and her mother's

452

personal items cleared out. Mattie was going to live there in Harriet's house in Sliema.

Lucy contacted Rhino and asked to meet him.

'Come over this evening,' he said.

'No,' Lucy replied. 'I think it's better we meet on neutral ground.' She did not want to go over and to find Friedrich there.

'I'm sure he won't be there,' Amelia said to her.

'That might be worse,' Lucy replied. She feared the strength of her own resolve, and knew that Rhino could still lure her back. But she also knew that would be her downfall. The magic was long gone, but there was ease in habit. She felt the need to hold on to the strength that had emanated from her mother. She knew that it was now she must leave, or she never would.

Rhino met her in Valletta. He protested at her intentions, begged her to stay, made promises that she knew he could not, would not ever be able to, keep.

'I used to be jealous of Maria,' she told him. 'I thought that was where your affections lay. I found that so difficult. But it is more difficult because it is Friedrich. You see – I can't compete with him. Whatever it is he gives to you, I cannot give you that. Whatever past you both share, whatever friendship and camaraderie, I have never been able to give you that.'

'You don't understand,' he said.

'Only because you never explained it to me.'

'Then let me explain it now.'

Lucy did not know if she cared to hear. It was all too late.

'Please hear me out,' he said. 'I met Friedrich

453

in North Africa before the war. We spent that year together, training, flying, visiting places – what you might call pre-war work. We did our duty. I will defend nothing. I will not protest innocence.'

'I'm not interested anyway,' Lucy said coldly.

'I met Maria Borg Cardona – that was not her name then – I met her in Rome and we had an affair. I left her with Friedrich while I travelled back to Germany. There was a bomb near the embassy, and Friedrich, in saving Maria, lost his eye. I returned to Rome and she stayed with him, she nursed him. We got her back to Malta where she married. We then bombed Malta to pieces and we killed her husband. We are linked – she and Friedrich and I – inextricably. We both felt responsibility to her and I feel responsibility to Friedrich...'

'But you are sleeping with him,' Lucy protested. 'What has that got to do with responsibility?'

'He loves me,' Rhino explained.

'But just because somebody loves you doesn't mean you have to go to bed with them. It doesn't give you the right to betray your wife. To diminish her...'

'But I love you,' he protested.

But she no longer knew what love was, and no longer knew if he ever had.

As she got up to leave, drawing herself to her feet, she turned to him and said, 'By the way, when was it you met Maria Borg Cardona in Rome? Was it on your trip back to Germany just after meeting me?'

He was quiet for a long moment, and she knew he was toying between telling the truth and lying.

'Yes,' he replied. 'It was.'

She looked at him for a long-drawn-out moment, and then she walked away.

Mattie and Amelia went over to his house to pack the rest of Lucy's clothing for her, as Lucy said she could not bear going there now.

'Is she really leaving?' Rhino asked them. He seemed dismayed, stunned, as though he could not understand it. 'I can give her everything,' he said.

'You just don't get it, Rhino,' Mattie replied. 'You could have given her everything but you made choices that have hurt her to the quick. She's right in her decision.'

'You must give her time, Rhino,' Thomas said to his uncle. 'She may come back after she has been to England – after she finds out what she really wants. For now she needs to be left alone.'

While Thomas was confident that he would come back to Malta, both because he loved the island and it was where he saw home, he was not sure that Lucy would. He could not imagine that she would ever return to Rhino. But he said none of this to his uncle.

As he confided later to Amelia, he was glad that Lucas was not around for those discussions, because there was so much that Lucas had to handle anyway, without listening to the problems in the farmhouse.

Amelia left Malta two days later. She had

borrowed against the money her grandmother was leaving her, as her inheritance still had not come through.

'We'll be leaving Malta next week,' Lucy said. 'Why not wait for us? Where are you going?' she asked. 'Why so soon?'

'I'm going back to the beginning,' Amelia said.

Courage is the first of the human qualities because it is the quality which guarantees the others.

Aristotle

CHAPTER EIGHTEEN

Back in London, Amelia thought of contacting Breda, but then changed her mind. It would have taken more time and she did not want to wait any longer. She spent only one night in the London house and then she flew to Dublin. She made her way by train down the east coast, getting out at the nearest station to Ithaca, and spending the night in a small hotel in the town. Climbing into the high old-fashioned bed that night, with its rough white sheets, she asked herself what she was doing. But there was no answer easily found. She felt that she was doing something by instinct, but did not know what it was.

At breakfast the following morning she asked the proprietor of the hotel about hiring a bicycle, and was immediately loaned one that belonged to someone's daughter from down the road. And then she set off on that journey into the past, not knowing what if anything she was looking for, but longing to walk again on the beach where she had spent her childhood. Before she actually knocked on the door of Ithaca, she wanted to feel the grains of sand beneath her bare feet, and look up from the water's edge across the dunes to

457

where their house stood, and to see the upstairs windows and remember what it was like to get out of bed and go and look out across the sea.

She cycled out of the town and down the coast. The sun was shining down and it was going to be a warm late summer's day. She pedalled easily along the road. Fields and hedges separated her from the sea, which she occasionally saw when she rode over the brow of the road. She came upon Ithaca more suddenly than she expected and was surprised at how the stone pillars on the entrance seemed smaller than she recalled. She cycled on to the next bend where there was a laneway that ran down the side of the land and on to the dunes. There she left her bike and, taking off her shoes, she ran down over the golden sand towards the sea.

The tide was on the ebb and she ran across wet sand with her feet slightly sinking into it until she was ankle-deep in the water. Waves splashed up her legs and she tucked her skirt up at her waist and gasped at the coldness of it. She was now so used to the warmth of the Mediterranean and its tideless flow that she pulled up short and stood for a moment thinking about her family over there, and then she pulled herself back into the present and started to walk along the shoreline, letting the waves wash over and over her feet. For some reason words from the Bible came to her: 'My God, my God, why hast thou forsaken me?'

As she walked she let the memories of her childhood flood back in, and she remembered watching Mattie crouching on the beach with her magnifying glass and little bits of paper, and she wondered about Sean and his family and if they were still up there living in the cottage beside the house. She turned and looked up to see what the view looked like from the water's edge, and she recalled the day that Lucy had, as usual, been sitting with her back to the dunes reading, and Grandmother had appeared on the top of the dunes. Then she became aware that there was someone sitting just where Lucy used to sit, and the person, who was holding a book in his hands, was looking down the sand at her. For a moment she was discomfited as she had not realised she was being observed. Indeed, the thought that there might be someone there at all had never occurred to her.

She hesitated briefly, looking up at the top floor of the house, with its sloping roof and chimney pots, and then she started walking again along the shore. She walked briskly, letting the smell of brine envelop her, and the sound of the water beating on the sand, and the occasional screech of a seagull in the distance. She walked as if walking back into the past, but nothing came to her at first except for the sounds of nature and the memory of the thud of croquet mallets on balls. Then she remembered the sandcastles on the beach and digging a tiny channel from the sea so that water would swamp the moat, and Sean and she running up and down the beach, trying to get Mattie to play with them, paddling in the sea...

Turning back she walked more slowly along the water's edge, out of the lapping waves, wondering what she would do next. She looked up to see that the man who had been reading at the bottom of the dunes was now walking somewhat hesitantly down towards her.

Before he got to her a dog came bounding out of the dunes, charged past the man and straight for her. The dog's head was like a bowling ball, with a wide mouth and dark snout. It was propelling itself forwards at the most amazing speed. She tried to sidestep out of the way, but the dog still hit her as it belted past, and she fell sprawling on to the sand.

'Heidi, Heidi,' the man was calling, now running up towards Amelia. 'I'm so sorry.'

Meantime, the dog, having overshot her, had turned back at an equally amazing speed for an animal so solid, and was now holding her down and licking her face.

'Heidi...' The man finally arrived and pulled the dog back by the collar. 'I'm so sorry,' he said again. 'She's just very friendly and enthusiastic.'

Amelia tried to struggle to her feet and he reached out a hand and helped her.

'Are you all right?' he asked.

'I'm fine,' she laughed. 'I really am. What kind of a dog is she?'

He released the dog from its collar and it bounded forwards again but had less impact because it hadn't built up the speed as it had done earlier. It put its paws up on Amelia's chest and tried licking her face.

'She's a Staffordshire bull terrier,' he replied. 'I thought she was inside in the kitchen, which is her favourite place – in the vicinity of food. I really am sorry. I hope you didn't get a fright.'

'No, I'm fine,' she reassured him again, pushing the dog down from her. 'I like dogs.' She bent down and petted the dog's big head with its thick fur and its wide mouth. 'She looks like she's laughing,' Amelia said.

'Oh, yes,' he answered. 'That's her normal expression – one of laughter and mischief.'

She had a chance now to take him in as she petted Heidi. He was tall with fair hair and clear tanned skin, broader at the shoulder than Thomas, and dressed in a pair of cut-off shorts. His face was a mixture of seriousness and kindness, with green eyes and a clear high forehead. Amelia guessed he was roughly her age or a little older.

'We don't get very many people walking on this part of the beach.' He did not sound accusatory, rather just factual. His voice was not quite Irish, but not discernibly anything else.

'I know,' she said. 'This part of the beach was always deserted. I have not been here in a very long time.'

'You were here before?' he asked

'I lived here as a child,' she said, nodding up the dunes towards the house. 'I came back to ... to revisit my childhood, I suppose,' she said hesitantly.

'You lived here?' He seemed truly surprised. 'Are you one of the Cholmondesleys?'

She nodded.

'Then we have met before. Do you remember, when my parents came to view the house – we bought it from your aunt? We met then.'

And she did remember – a little boy and a girl

who were going to move into her home when they were uprooting to live in England.

'That's you?' she said. 'How amazing. I don't know your name. I don't remember.'

'I'm Ulli,' he said. 'It's short for Ulrich, but my sister, Karla, says it's short for Ulysses, and that's why we live at Ithaca.'

Amelia smiled. There was a funny symmetry to this, but she just said, 'I'm Amelia. I don't know if you remember our names.'

'I do remember actually,' Ulli said. 'But then why wouldn't I? You were spoken of so often after you left. Come and sit and talk to me,' he said. 'I'll bring you up to the house afterwards and you can really revisit your past.' He was talking quickly, encouraging her back towards the dunes and she shyly went and sat beside him where they could both see the sea and glance at each other while they spoke. Heidi came and plonked herself down on Amelia's feet, looking up at her with her laughing face and her huge mournful eyes. Her tail thumped a couple of times on the sand before she appeared to settle into a waking doze.

Ulli told her that Cook and Maudge, and Feilim still lived there, that Sean worked in a shop in Wexford, and had got married, but he still came home regularly, that he and Sean had been friends as they grew up.

'You know, he missed you when you left,' he said. 'You more than your sister. Mattie? She is the older?'

Amelia nodded.

'I missed Sean,' she said. 'He and I had been

462

very close growing up. But it was probably worse for him when we left because we had a whole new life to look forward to.'

There was so much to say, so much to catch up on, she felt, even though she had hardly spoken a word to this boy when they were children. She could only remember meeting him the once, and wondering whether he or his sister would have her bedroom.

'Now you have to come up to the house and meet my parents again,' he said. He took her by the arm and helped her to her feet. 'They'll be so pleased, you know. They always said that one day you would come back.'

'Me or Mattie or both of us?' she asked.

'Both of you possibly, but you definitely. Your story – your history – I mean, the history of both you and your sister ... it moved them immeasurably, you know. There are things you don't know...'

He did not finish the sentence, and she wondered what he meant. She wondered if he was talking about changes in the house and if they still had the portraits, or maybe they had stored them away, or indeed sold them.

But they had not. Amelia and Ulli went through the French windows into the drawing room and through to the hall. The portraits were on the walls. They were still there – all those pictures of the Cholmondesleys and the one of Hilary that must have been painted shortly after she moved to Ithaca. And beside the one of her mother there still hung the print of Aristotle looking at Homer's bust. Amelia stood still and looked at the pictures, and then memories came in, memories of running in the hall and looking to see if their eyes were following her and jumping down the stairs, every year trying to leap one stair further, until the day she caught her foot on one of the steps and landed on her face and her nose bled. She breathed in the past as she stood there and he called for his parents.

His mother came down the stairs. Her grey hair was pinned up in a bun. She had a kind if serious face. Her German accent was pronounced but she greeted Amelia with great pleasure.

'How wonderful,' she said, 'to meet you again. After all these years. Where is your father?' she asked Ulli.

Gerhardt Schmitz appeared through the front door, and although he must have been as surprised as his wife at finding Amelia standing in his hall, he expressed the same pleasure and greeted her warmly.

'I always said that you would come back,' he said, shaking her hand. Like his wife, he had a strong German accent and intonation. 'I have always said this to Ulli and Karla. I am so pleased. You will stay with us, no?'

She found herself back in the drawing room, sitting with the morning light coming through from the sea windows, and surrounded by these people whose genuine pleasure in seeing her was encompassing.

'I'm staying in town in a hotel,' she said.

'You have to come and stay here,' Gerhardt said. 'We would really like it, is this not so?' He turned to confirm this with the others and they

464

both agreed.

'I will ask Feilim to fetch your things from the hotel,' he said.

'I borrowed a bicycle,' she said.

'Everything will be sorted. We would like you here. Why did you not tell us you were coming?' he asked.

'I wasn't even sure myself,' Amelia admitted. 'Two days ago I was in Malta and then I flew home to London, and while I have been thinking of coming here for quite some time, in the end it was almost a spur-of-the-moment thing.'

'We are glad either way,' Elsa Schmitz said to her. 'Now, I will get you coffee, or are you like the Irish, and you like your cup of tea?'

Amelia was really moved at the way they were so pleased to see her, and so willing to include her in their home. It almost did not make sense to her, because while her family were always welcoming, it was never as apparent as this. Here was real pleasure at her appearance, and real interest in her. Without the British reserve, she supposed as she looked around at them.

'And your sister?' she said to Ulli. 'Where is she?'

'Karla is up in Dublin. She is starting university in October – she is going to Trinity like me, and she went up to sort out accommodation. She said she would not share my place even if she were paid.'

'Ah, the siblings,' Elsa said with a laugh to Amelia. 'Do you and your sister fight like the cat and the dog?'

Amelia laughed. You wouldn't believe the half

465

of it, she thought. She could not imagine that Karla Schmitz might be as difficult a character as Mattie. 'We have our moments,' she said.

'And what are you doing now?' Gerhardt Schmitz said. 'You too must be finished school. Are you going to study?'

She told them about the house in London where she lived with the others and that she was waiting for her results to come out, but she was confident her exams had gone well. 'Latin and Greek are my subjects,' she said.

'The same as me,' Ulli said. There was even more pleasure and interest expressed. 'You should come to Trinity,' he said. 'It's a great Classics department. You would love it.'

'Oh, I think my application would be a bit late now,' she said.

'I doubt it,' she was told. 'It's not the largest department. I'm sure they would be interested in you.'

Ireland, land of welcomes, she thought to herself when they went outside afterwards. Feilim was not around. She was told he must be up in the fields, and that when he came back they would all go into town with the bicycle in the car, and move her to Ithaca.

'I will get us coffee,' Elsa said. 'Come, Amelia, come with me. Let us surprise Cook and Maudge together.'

Cook and Maudge looked up from their kitchen chores, and stared in amazement.

'My heavens,' said Cook. 'My holy heavens. Which child are you? You look so like your dear mother.'

They both hugged her, their delight apparent, and both kept commenting on her resemblance to Hilary. Their pleasure enveloped her and she began to feel again the security that had been there in those early years, the security and love that had made her who she had become.

'If you think I look like Hilary,' she said, 'then you have to see Mattie. She really is the image of her.' She thought of Breda and was about to say something, but she held back. It made no sense, and what was there to say anyway.'

Heidi was hovering under the kitchen table apparently hopeful for something to fall from it. Amelia bent down and rubbed the big head and she smiled. There was something about a dog that made a place more like home. It made her think of Bruce, old now, but no doubt lying somewhere half in and half out of the sun, maybe listening to music.

'Where would you like to go now?' Ulli asked her, back in the drawing room as they drank their coffee. 'Feilim may not be back until after lunch, I think.'

Amelia said that she would dearly like to visit the cemetery at the village church. They looked at each other, and Gerhardt nodded.

'Of course you would,' he said. 'Would you like to cut flowers from the garden to take with you?' he asked. 'Would you like us all to come with you, or just Ulli, or do you want to go alone?'

They all went, and any fears that Amelia might have had about not being able to find the plot disappeared as soon as they walked through the

467

white-painted iron gates. It too was like coming back to old ground. To her surprise she found there were flowers on the grave.

'Who?' Amelia asked. 'Why? Who put them here?'

'We do,' Gerhardt said. 'Elsa and I, we bring flowers here most weeks.'

'But why?'

He patted her arm but did not explain, and she was really puzzled. She placed her freshly cut flowers beneath the stone and looked at the words on it – the words that Lucy had taught her.

Here lies Matthew Cholmondesley
His beloved wife Hilary
Together for ever with their angel Georgina
Requiescat in Pace

They were all silent as she stood there reading the words. She wondered how Mattie would feel if she were here, and she knew that for Mattie it must have been so much harder, and that it would be so much harder to come back here and stand on this ground. After a few moments she moved away from the grave and looked at the ones around it, and then she caught her breath in amazement.

She had forgotten the names and dates on the other graves. They had disappeared into the darkness and vagueness of many childhood memories. But there it was on the very next grave – little Breda Mangan who died aged two, a mere eight weeks before her own parents and sister.

What an extraordinary coincidence, she

thought. She stood stock-still, staring at the writing.

'Is something wrong?' Ulli asked her. He was standing beside her in front of the grave where Breda Mangan rested with her father, who had died not long before her.

'The oddest thing,' she said. 'This is the oddest thing.'

'Do you want to tell me?' he said.

She looked at him. Her puzzlement was so overpowering that she needed to offload it on to someone.

There was a bench just outside the church and she sat there while she tried to make sense of it.

She told them about Breda Mangan, the Breda she knew in London, who looked just like her and Mattie, whose mother was Irish and who did not like them, and who tried to keep Breda from them.

'It's just a coincidence,' she finished the story. 'It's just so odd. I must have seen that grave a thousand times as a child and I never connected it with Breda when I met her in London. Nor should I. I didn't even remember it. Why would I? It just happens to be someone with the same name. It's just a coincidence.'

The Schmitzes listened in silence to her telling of the tale. They asked her questions about Breda and her life, and how she came to live in London. Many of the answers Amelia did not know, but she told what she could.

'It probably is just a coincidence,' Gerhardt said. 'But I agree it is unusual. Why don't we ask what happened to the baby's mother, and indeed

469

to the baby?'

'It was eighteen years ago,' Amelia said.

'So? It's not that long ago. Yes, I know it is your whole lifetime, but not in a community like this. People will know. The priest, neighbours, doctors – people will know.'

Later in the day, after Amelia had caught up with Feilim, he took her and Ulli back into town with the bicycle and she checked out of the hotel, reassuring everyone that she had thoroughly enjoyed her stay there and was only leaving because she had met old friends.

'We're glad you came back,' the proprietor of the hotel said.

'Back?'

'Yes, Miss Cholmondesley. We're glad you came back to Ireland to visit us. Of course we remember – how could we not? Such a terrible tragedy. Which of the daughters are you? The youngest?'

'Yes, I am the youngest,' Amelia said. She thanked them for their kindness.

'You know, you stayed here before,' she was told.

'Here?' She had no recollection.

'Yes. You and your sister and your aunt. You stayed for a week while your aunt was getting some work done on the house. There had been a small fire around the time you were leaving to go to England. You stayed here while your aunt organised the repair work.'

Amelia shook her head. She did not remember. She recalled the fire and the subsequent trip to England, with Mattie furious and refusing to speak to her. But she had no recollection of where they stayed during that period.

Everything seemed to be coming round full circle. Like pieces in a puzzle, tiny memories were slotting in to each other, and new memories forming.

'People do remember,' Ulli said to her. 'You know, you and your sisters are often talked about. And your parents.'

It was not something that Amelia had considered. It was all so long ago that she had not realised that the tragedy had had ripples outside her family, and that people would remember that night, some with great clarity.

And when they got back to Ithaca there was already news on that front. Everyone remembered Sheila Mangan. She had buried her husband from diphtheria earlier in the year of the plane crash, and then Breda, her two-year-old daughter died from it just weeks later.

'And what happened to Sheila Mangan?' Amelia asked. 'Does she still live here?'

Gerhardt shook his head. 'No, she disappeared. She was reported missing around the time of the plane crash. Her brother and his wife, who still live locally, heard from her once. They got a letter from her in England saying she had gone to start a new life there. They never heard from her again.'

Amelia sat there listening to this and trying to see beyond it. Beyond the fact that a poor woman had lost both her husband and child and had gone abroad. She looked at them, at Gerhardt and at Elsa and then at Ulli.

471

'Is this too big a coincidence?' she asked. 'Is there a possibility...?'

'There is more,' Gerhardt said. His voice was quiet and calm and Amelia tried to take in the words he was saying. 'I don't know if you know that no trace of your sister Georgina was ever found. Nothing at all.'

'But the coffin...?' Then she remembered Mattie saying that the coffin was empty.

'It was for show, I suppose. It was thought – it was believed that she had been in your father's arms and that she had ... disintegrated. You can imagine the way things were – the plane, the bits of debris, the pilot, your father ... unidentifiable, you see. And your aunt insisted that there would be a coffin for Georgina – two coffins. One for your father and one for Georgina, even though there was nothing left...'

'My God,' Amelia said. 'Oh, my God.'

Ulli came over and kneeled on one knee on the ground beside her. He held her hand.

'Papa,' he said over his shoulder to his parent, 'what are you saying?'

'I don't know what I'm saying,' Gerhardt replied. 'Amelia, do you know Breda's mother's name?'

'Yes,' Amelia said quietly. 'Yes. It is Sheila. But ... I've even seen Breda's birth certificate. She brought it once to the house. She showed it to us.'

'Her mother would have kept it. Why not? If she found Georgina that night or the following day – and it is not impossible... I've been told that Mattie was not found until two days later. If

472

Breda's mother found Georgina and took her away...'

'And reared her as her own,' Amelia finished the sentence. 'My father ... he had been carrying Georgina, and then he put her down. Mattie held her hand ... she told me once that she let it go. And she ran. Oh God. If Sheila Mangan found Georgina ... if she took her ... reared her ... what a terrible thing to do – if that is what happened. Could that be what happened? Oh, what a terrible thing to do.'

She could see it clearly on the one hand, but on the other it seemed beyond her comprehension. To have taken one of the children as her own daughter, to have fled the country claiming her as her own ... to have left grief behind her while she replaced her own child with one of the Cholmondesleys...

'Is there any way of proving this?' Ulli asked.

'Asking her mother is probably the only way. Or asking Sheila's brother to meet her and to identify her as his sister and confirm that her child had died of diphtheria. There probably are other ways,' Gerhardt said. 'But that's as far as I have worked it out at the moment.'

In the evening Amelia and Ulli walked back down to the cemetery.

'If they are right,' Amelia said, 'it seems such an evil thing to do.'

'I said that to my mother as well, and she said that if Breda's mother was grief-stricken – and why would she not have been, to lose her child – my mother said that in grief we do things that we would not otherwise consider.'

'It would explain Breda's mother not wanting us near Breda. It would explain everything,' Amelia said. 'She is so like Mattie – and so like me. But how could someone do something like that? It is beyond my imagination. If she is Georgina, she was deprived of everything that was her due, of everything that she was born for. Her fate or destiny was changed by that night.'

'As was yours,' Ulli said. 'As was mine.'

'But then,' Amelia said thoughtfully, 'she got something I never got – she got a mother's love.'

'Do you know forgiveness, Amelia?' he asked her suddenly.

'Forgiveness?' she said, puzzled. 'I've never really had anything that I needed to forgive.'

'Don't you feel anger over the plane crash? Over the war and how it affected you in particular? How it deprived you of what you call your due?'

Amelia pondered that as they stood in front of the Cholmondesley plot.

'I never thought about it like that. I never knew what might have been. I've never gone down that road,' she said. 'I had a grandfather – he viewed life differently, and I suppose between him and my aunt – Lucymem – I saw life and the war as they saw it. It was something we survived and other people did not.'

'It's not such a bad philosophy on life,' Ulli said.

They walked back up the lane and somewhere along the way, Amelia realised they were holding hands. She had no idea when that had started.

She thought that maybe it was while they were at the grave, or perhaps as they came out the gate. There were clumps of grass down the centre of the lane and they walked evenly on either side. Amelia glanced over at Ulli and he at her. Neither changed the expressions on his or her faces but there was something in the look they shared, something intense and very real. His grip tightened a little on her hand. She returned his pressure and they walked on. Neither said anything.

Back in the house, dinner was almost ready and Gerhardt and Elsa were waiting for them in the drawing room. Gerhardt got to his feet when they came in.

'We're opening a bottle of champagne,' he said. 'It has been a momentous day for you, Amelia.'

She was pleased by their understanding of the enormity of the day, by its discoveries and the unfolding of events from the past. They drank to loved ones before going in to dinner.

'How are you feeling, my dear?' Elsa asked Amelia.

'I have such mixed feelings,' she replied. 'On the one hand I know in my heart that Breda is Georgina. I think Mattie knew it too. From the beginning. As if we knew it on one level, but could not understand it. There was no evidence that Breda could be one of us – nothing, other than the fact that she looks like us. I mean ... all the evidence was that she was Mrs Mangan's daughter. But...'

'Please go on. Please tell us what you are

thinking,' Elsa persisted.

'I keep thinking about Breda – about how she was drawn to us and wanted to be with us. I wonder how she will handle this.'

'You will tell her,' Gerhardt said.

It could have been a question or a statement, Amelia was unsure.

'I don't know. I can't imagine living with this and not telling her. And yet, telling her is going to throw her life upside down. What will she feel towards her mother – I mean towards Sheila Mangan? What will it mean to her? How will it make her feel? If I feel like I'm feeling – and there are not words to describe how I am feeling – then how will she feel?'

And Mattie, she thought. How would Mattie take this? What would it do to her? And yet, how could she live with this secret? How could she not tell them? They had a right to know.

She drank her champagne. She longed for the silence of her room and the quietness of her bed where she could go over the emotions in her heart and the thoughts in her head. Her usual stability was disturbed beyond anything she had ever been able to imagine. And leaving Breda out of the equations in her brain, there was the added feelings to do with sitting in this room, with these people and knowing that if that terrible accident had never happened, she might still be sitting in this room, but with her own parents and her sisters. The comfort of the room brought back the happiness she felt as a child living there, when the only real problem that lurked for her was what Mattie might do next.

476

'We are glad you are here,' Elsa said to her. 'For us it is good to know that you have had a good life.'

Amelia smiled at her as they got up to go into dinner. 'You are so generous in your thoughts about Mattie and me – thank you.' She couldn't imagine why it would matter to these people what kind of a life she had had, and yet it seemed to. These comments did not appear to be superficial. They were not superficial people.

'Karla is coming down tomorrow to meet you,' Elsa said. 'She is delighted that you have turned up. It was only recently that she spoke about you.'

'Elsa and I have always believed that you would come back,' Gerhardt said to Amelia as he pulled her chair out for her at the table.

'You seem to have placed some kind of faith in us,' Amelia said. 'I don't know why. Even though I only remember that childhood meeting vaguely, and knowing that Lucymem – my aunt – was pleased that you were buying the house. I suppose that as a child if you know that the adults are happy it gives you a sense of security. And Lucymem was happy – until Mattie tried to set fire to the place,' she said. As she said it, she wondered if they knew about that day of departure, or if Lucy had got everything repaired before they arrived with their furniture. She couldn't remember the sequence of events.

Gerhardt smiled at her wryly. 'It was quite a dramatic thing to do,' he said. 'We wondered if it was because we were Germans – specifically us, I mean – or if she would have done it regardless of

477

who was buying the house.'

'I know Lucymem was concerned you wouldn't want to buy it after that,' Amelia said.

'There was symmetry in our buying Ithaca,' Gerhardt said.

'Symmetry? How do you mean?' Amelia asked. 'Why did you come to live in Ireland?' she added. She hoped that her curiosity was not too plain, and that she had covered the inquisitive question in politeness.

In the momentary pause that followed, she saw Elsa give Gerhardt a tiny nod of her head, and he put down his knife and fork. She was aware that Ulli was watching her intently and she smiled across the table at him. She looked at Gerhardt, who appeared to be puzzling over how to answer. Under the table she was aware of Heidi's great head resting beside her feet, and she could hear the occasional thump of her tail. Gerhardt dabbed at his mouth with his napkin.

'May I answer by asking you a question?' he said. 'Why did you come back here to Ithaca?'

'To revisit the past,' she said evenly. 'To lay some ghosts.'

'Yes,' he said. 'To lay a ghost – that is why we came too.'

The Gods too are fond of a joke.
Aristotle

CHAPTER NINETEEN

Amelia thought of saying, what ghosts could they have to lay in a place like this, but she said nothing, as she did not want to break the moment of Gerhardt's thoughts.

'I had a twin brother,' Gerhardt said. 'Ulrich. Another Ulrich. This Ulli's father,' he gestured towards his adopted son. 'Ulrich was my identical twin, Amelia.'

She was aware of the silence from Elsa and Ulli, they too listening to the words, though they already knew this story and that he was telling it to her, for her, and that it was of great importance to him.

'Yes,' she said gently. She remembered him mentioning a twin long ago when she had stood across the room watching him and his family, when the house was still the Cholmondesley family home.

'We were both in the Luftwaffe,' he continued. 'Fighter pilots – bombers, I suppose. We did our duty as good Germans. We fought in the Battle of Britain. We fought for the Fatherland. Our duty...' he repeated.

'That's war,' Amelia said. She was thinking of her grandfather.

479

'My brother – Ulrich – he was coming up from the south,' Gerhardt continued. 'I was not on duty that night. Sometimes we both were sent out on the same missions, but sometimes not. On that night the weather turned. That is what they said. A storm brewed somewhere behind them and caught up with them. And somehow he lost his direction and came further west. He crashed in the mountains over there.' He gestured towards the window and out into the evening.

In the distance, as the light faded, Amelia could see the hills rising in the darkness and thought of how on a night like the one Gerhardt was describing, her parents and her sisters had got into the car and headed up into the gloom on her father's mission to give support to the people across the water.

'I see,' she said. 'I see.'

'I don't think that you do see,' Ulli interjected. 'My father, Ulrich, was the pilot on the plane that crashed the night your father died.'

Amelia looked from one to the other as the meaning of his words sank in.

'You mean...? she caught her breath. 'That night? Your father, Ulli...' she glanced at Gerhardt, 'your brother...' she said. 'That is so sad. He was your family. All Mattie's grief, that was your grief too... I sometimes wondered about him – the pilot, I mean.'

'He was buried locally,' Gerhardt said. 'Although more recently a cemetery for our war dead in Ireland has been opened up in Glencree and his body was moved there, so he is among his own.'

'So you came here to visit his grave?'

'Yes. And then we stayed. It was chance that we came to buy your house, and after your sister tried to burn it down and when we realised that there was this strange connection – well, any doubts we might have had because of the fire, they disappeared. It was as if we knew we must buy it, regardless.'

Amelia knew that their telling her this series of events was of great importance to them. She felt that they were waiting for something from her, but she could not think what it was, or what they expected of her. These were events that were remote from her, and nothing like the discovery she had made earlier in the day. She saw their story as being surprising, coincidental, but not really connected with her, even though that pilot's error had changed her life before she was even born.

But she also saw, much clearer, that his error had changed their lives and their families, and, though removed from her by the fact that it was prior to her birth, she could see that their concern was because she had lost so much – the mother and father she had never known, and the sister whom they all had thought had died that night. She wondered if they were expecting blame from her, but she could not imagine how or why. There was no blame on them. They too were victims of the war. They too had lost so much.

'I don't know what you expect of me,' she said suddenly. 'All I feel is gratitude that I am here, that my family's home is full of joy, with good

481

people living in it. I am pleased to be sitting here with you, drinking your wine and eating your food. I don't feel like a stranger.'

She knew these were odd things to say, but she could think of nothing else. They were the words that sprang to her mouth. She raised her glass.

'It's true,' Elsa said. 'You are not like a stranger. Welcome home, Amelia.' She too raised her glass and then the others did as well.

It was later that night in bed with the curtains open that Amelia went over and over the day's events and the discoveries she had made. She wondered if her grandmother had realised what she was saying when she told her to go back to the beginning. She wondered if her grandmother had somehow remembered the name Breda Mangan on the neighbouring stone and if that was why she had said to go back, or if the words were just the meanderings of someone close to death. Grandmother would have loved knowing that Georgina had survived. Amelia was sure of that, just as she was now sure that that was whom Breda was.

But for now, she thought, I don't have to think about that. She got out of bed and looked through the window. The moon was rising in the east and a glow of rippled light spread out across the sea, as if lighting a path for her down to the shore. She slipped on some clothes and quietly left the bedroom. Barefoot, she was silent on the staircase. She felt her way easily through the house and out the back through the French windows, and down the grass where they had

482

once played croquet, and down the slope to the dunes.

Words from 'Ulysses' came to mind.

The lights begin to twinkle from the rocks;
The long day wanes; the slow moon climbs; the deep
Moans round with many voices.

Once on the beach she began to run towards the water's edge. She thought of taking off her clothes and jumping in, but knew that it would be too cold for her now, not like the warm sea of Malta, which even in the middle of the night was comforting.

I am free, she thought. Just as I have always been. Nothing that has happened changes who I am right at this moment. I am the youngest of the Cholmondesley sisters. I have been given back one who was lost. I am blessed.

She felt almost ecstatic – wild with excitement and a sense of liberation that she did not understand. She loved this house, loved being back there on the beach, and loved every memory it evoked. She turned to look back up at it and there was Ulli standing on top of the dunes where her grandmother had once stood, looking down towards her. The moonlight caught his face and, as if in a trance, she made her way back up the strand towards him. Somewhere there at the bottom of the dunes they met and he put his arms around her. He kissed her slowly and deliberately.

'Welcome home, Amelia,' he said.

They did not make love that night on the beach – they kept that for the following day in his bed when his parents went up to Dublin to collect Karla. Instead they cuddled together in the dark at the foot of the dunes and they talked. She told him every memory she had of living there. She told him of the happiness she felt and how it really did feel like she had come home.

She lay in his arms and he kissed her until the moon was well risen and had disappeared behind the house. She thought of words like symmetry and balance, and knew what they meant.

'Who knows what tomorrow will bring?' he said to her.

'It doesn't matter,' she replied. 'We live for now. There is nothing else.'

We cannot learn without pain.
Aristotle

CHAPTER TWENTY

Amelia stayed a week at Ithaca – a week of drifting through gentle days, allowing herself to be cared for by Gerhardt and Elsa, walking barefoot on the beach with Karla, smiling across rooms at Ulli, and at night finding him down among the dunes, waiting for her.

'Don't leave,' he said.

'I have to go back to London,' she said sadly.

'Come to Trinity and study with me. Don't leave. Now that we have found you and you have found us, do you want to go?'

She shook her head. No, she did not want to go. Here was where she wanted to be. Here in the place that she felt she had searched for all her life.

'Then don't. We'll go to Dublin tomorrow and see if you can come to Trinity too. There is a home for you here for as long as you want it. My parents love you.'

'Your parents are special,' she said.

'Do you think so? I suppose you are right. I always thought that it was just Karla and I who felt that. You know, when they found me in the orphanage in Dresden, and Karla too, she was too little to speak, and I ... I couldn't remember how. Not at first, I mean. I had forgotten how to talk. And they took us in and reared us as theirs. We owe them everything, and yet they expect nothing. They love us, just as we are.'

'They are special,' Amelia repeated.

'But you have special people in your life too, don't you?' he asked.

'Oh, yes,' she said. '"Old age hath yet his honour and his toil",' she quoted.

'What is that?'

'It is Tennyson,' she replied. 'From "Ulysses". It always makes me think of my grandfather. He was special too. So many special people... That quote continues...

"Death closes all; but something ere the end,
Some work of noble note, may yet be done,
Not unbecoming men that strove with Gods."'

'Yes,' Ulli said. 'They strove with Gods. My father, your grandfather...'

'And others,' she said.

'Yes, and others.'

Karla too encouraged her. They walked on the beach together, companionably and with ease. The tide was out, the sand ridged beneath their bare feet, the late summer water warm around their ankles

'We want you to stay,' Karla said. 'You were spoken of all our lives – ever since we came to Ithaca. You are part of our home and our history. Our history is shared. We have all lost so much, so many people, so many memories ... stay.'

Karla was tall, blonde-haired, eyes of blue and grey, with an easy gait and a gentle intelligent face. She was going to study English at Trinity.

'You know,' she said thoughtfully, 'there are so many stories, so intertwined, so entangled. Each is unique and yet each is caught up in other people's lives. We were trapped and then we were taken from one set of circumstances and placed in another ... all the people you have spoken of, and all of us here. You know I am adopted? I was in the same orphanage as Ulli. He was kind to me. I think I had an older brother who must have died, because Ulli meant something to me from the beginning. My first memories are of clinging on to him. I needed his love. I craved it. I have no idea what my real surname is. I was never identified. All I could say was my name – Karla. Or maybe Klara, they were not sure. So they called me Karla. And

"I am a part of all that I have met;
Yet all experience is an arch wherethro'
Gleams that untravell'd world, whose margin
 fades
For ever and for ever when I move."'

Amelia smiled at her. '"Ulysses",' she said. 'That poem means so much to me, you know. My grandfather read it ... I remember it so clearly. It's a coincidence that you know it too.'

'Not really,' Karla said. 'After all, we live in Ithaca – it is not that unusual to read about the place you live.'

Trinity College accepted her late application, and Amelia went back to the house in North London, arriving a day after Lucymem, Charlotte, Thomas and Lucas, who had all flown back from Malta together. The house seemed very crowded with the five of them there, and yet it seemed empty too with Mattie's absence.

It took Amelia a full two days before she could sit them all down and tell them about her discovery in Ireland in the village cemetery.

Charlotte was in bed and they were sitting in the dining room lingering over a late dinner.

Lucas, somewhat quieter now, had been busy enrolling in medical college.

'I was wondering if I should find somewhere else to live,' he said tentatively. 'It's quite crowded here and I am the one who isn't family.'

'I won't be staying here,' Amelia told them. 'So I think there is plenty of room for you, Lucas, if that's what you all want.'

She told them then about her academic plans, and slowly she got around to telling them about what she had found at Ithaca – the extraordinary tale of Gerhardt Schmitz's twin brother, and also the discovery of the tombstone that said 'Breda Mangan'.

They sat in stunned silence, trying to take it all in. It was Lucy who broke the disbelieving stillness by slamming her hand down on the table.

'No,' she shouted. 'No. This cannot have happened. It cannot.'

Thomas and Lucas sat there while Amelia tried to comfort Lucymem.

'At first I couldn't believe it either,' she said.

'And, of course, I'm still not sure – but somehow, I think ... I believe ... I'm almost sure that Breda is Georgina.'

'She has to be,' Thomas said.

Lucas nodded. 'She must be.'

Sharing this again, as she had uncovered and shared it with the Schmitz family in Ireland, brought it deeper into her understanding, closer to her being able to accept it as fact. Lucy's anguish disturbed her greatly, not just for Lucy's sake but also for what this was going to mean to Mattie. As long as no one else believed the story, there was no need to tell Mattie. She thought of Mattie following up on Breda after Breda had left the hospital and how she had visited the Mangans' home. And she knew then that in some way, Mattie had known – maybe just instinctively – quite some time ago.

'What do I do now?' she asked Lucymem, Thomas and Lucas.

'We have to talk to Breda and her mother,' Thomas said.

Amelia was grateful for his saying 'we', his kindness in always taking care of her, his generosity towards her.

'I don't know how to,' Amelia said.

'I think you have to go to them,' Thomas said. 'Maybe you and Lucy. Or you and me. I don't mind. If you need me to come with you, I will.'

'There are terrible implications,' Lucy said slowly. 'You do realise that. What this is going to mean for Breda – for Georgina. If she is Georgina... How is she going to cope?'

'Maybe we should tell her we are back first.

Maybe you should meet her before we confront her mother,' Thomas suggested.

'Do you know how to contact her?' Lucy asked.

Amelia pulled out her notebook from her bag. 'I got her address before we left. No phone, though. I will write her a letter and post it tomorrow, telling her that we are back, and invite her over.'

Roger Farrington, from next door, rang the bell the following day.

'I gave you some time to settle in before coming round,' he said. 'The house was very empty without you all. It's been a long summer. I've got so used to having you as neighbours.'

Lucy came into the hall where Amelia was talking to him. They greeted each other with pleasure.

'You know,' he said, 'I thought I saw you from the window two days ago – with a little girl. You've been gone a long time.'

He and Lucy kissed each other on the cheek. She took him into the drawing room, and Amelia retired upstairs.

In her room, Amelia could hear their voices downstairs and wanted to go down to listen, but instead she sat and wrote a note to Breda and then went to the post box.

Coming back into the house, she could still hear them talking. Rhino's name featured in the conversation, and she knew that Lucy was telling Mr Farrington at least some of what had happened. She was glad Lucy was talking – that was good. It might help her aunt as it was difficult to know how Lucy was feeling or what she was really planning on doing. Lucy had just been so busy since arriving back in London, but Amelia thought that maybe she was doing that deliberately so that she would not have the time to think.

Amelia went upstairs and tapped on Lucas's door. He was spending a lot of time by himself. He didn't answer. She opened the door and put her head around it.

'May I come in?' she asked.

He was lying on the bed with a book on anatomy open beside him. 'Of course you can.' He closed the book and moved over on the bed, and Amelia came and lay down beside him.

'I'm going to miss you,' she said.

He looked carefully into her face.

'I see,' he said finally. 'Yes, I think I see.'

She said nothing more, and he wrapped his arms around her.

'I bet it's not as much fun as when we were children,' he teased her.

She changed the subject. 'Are you really going to be a doctor?'

'Yes,' he said. 'I am. The best.'

'You will be the best.'

Breda came over a few days later. She arrived after work, smartly dressed, with her dark curly hair loose on her shoulders, and Mattie's red scarf tied to her bag.

Amelia and she embraced in the hallway, and all the time Amelia was having to contain herself and not burst out with words like, 'You are Georgina. You are my sister.'

491

Lucy and Charlotte came down the stairs, both stopping in disbelief as they saw her in the hall.

'Lucymem,' Amelia said quickly, 'this is Breda Mangan.'

It was Charlotte who broke the silence. 'You look like Mattie and Amelia. Doesn't she, Mummy?' she asked.

Speechless, Lucy nodded her head.

'I missed you all,' Breda told them. 'Where is Mattie?'

'Mattie has stayed on in Malta. She was not enjoying her studying,' Lucy said. 'So she has stayed there. She's got herself a nice job too.'

'She's making fireworks,' Charlotte said happily. 'And when she comes to visit, she's going to bring lots and lots of them with her. She said she will show us a display that we won't ever forget.'

'That sounds like fun,' Breda said. 'May I come too?'

'I'm sure you can,' Charlotte replied. 'Anyone who looks so like my cousins has to be there.'

'Then I'll definitely come,' Breda smiled at her.

Thomas, coming into the room, stopped when he saw her. 'I love your hair loose,' he said by way of greeting.

She smiled shyly at him. He came round the table and gave her a hug.

'It's lovely to be back here,' she said, smiling at them all.

'How is your mother?' Amelia asked.

Breda looked slightly uneasy before replying, 'Fine, thank you.'

After supper Amelia and she went into the drawing room and Amelia asked her again about her mother.

'Is everything all right really?' she said.

'My mother is talking again about moving up north,' Breda admitted. 'We've argued about it. I really don't want to go.'

'Then don't go,' Amelia said firmly.

'I don't have your independence,' Breda said. 'I've always done what my mother told me to do. I don't know any other way.'

'I think you ought to stand up for yourself,' Amelia said. She said it in a gentler way than Mattie would have, but she could hear overtones of Mattie in her voice. She was aware of all the differences between herself and Mattie. Their looks were so similar, but the strengths and weaknesses of their characters so diverse. Breda and Mattie were like two extremes with her, Amelia, somewhere in the middle.

Later, when Breda was gone, it was Thomas who pointed out that confronting her mother with Breda present could be terribly difficult for Breda, and that surely she had to be at the top of their agenda.

'I think you should tell her yourself, Amelia. And then let her know that we are all here to support her.'

'How do I tell her?' Amelia said. 'When she arrived this evening and I kissed her, all I wanted to do was to blurt out the truth.'

'You tell her just like you told us. And then we are all here to support you.'

Amelia looked to Lucy for reassurance. Lucy nodded.

'I have no doubt,' she said. 'None. No doubt whatsoever that Breda is Georgina. Oh, I know all the differences, but they are ones of upbringing. This girl – this lovely girl – is a Cholmondesley, my lost niece ... I hardly knew how to contain myself. We're going to have to tell Mattie, and then we're going to have to go to the police.'

'The police?' Amelia was startled.

'One step at a time,' Lucy said. 'But a crime was committed that night. Something so much greater than the war. I think of all the lost children – not just those who died but those who were really lost. Like Thomas's sister Klara, Mattie, Ulrich, Thomas himself...'

'Lost?' he asked.

'Yes. If Rhino had not looked for you, you would have been one of the lost children. All of you were lucky in the sense that you were found or adopted. But Georgina? No. No. That makes me truly angry. All the war crimes committed against all of you make me angry – the bombing of Dresden; of Malta; the Blitz; the crash in the mountains in Ireland. All war is criminal, but Georgina ... to deliberately steal a child – our child, one of us...' she stopped in anguish.

'What do we do?' Amelia said. She was upset at seeing Lucy so disturbed. She had never seen Lucy like this before.

They waited until Breda came again, waited until she was sitting in the kitchen. Roger Farrington had taken Charlotte in next door for her tea to give them the space to talk with Breda. Lucy had talked with him, told him what had happened, enlisted his support.

'Come in to me afterwards,' he said. 'Please come in. I'm here for you. I will always be here for you.'

It was Thomas who held Breda's hand when she stared uncomprehendingly at them, as Amelia told about the grave of Breda Mangan and the disappearance of her mother, Sheila.

'I don't know what you're saying,' Breda said, looking blankly from one to the other. 'I have pictures of me and my father and my mother. I have a birth certificate. I'm Breda Mangan.'

'You have pictures of a little girl called Breda Mangan,' Lucy said to her.

Thomas stroked her hand. Breda looked at him in terror as the pieces of her life as she had known it fell away, crumbling like dust into the past, to a moment she did not remember, lost on a mountain in a roar of fire.

'Nightmares,' she said suddenly. 'Terrible nightmares as a child. Fire. A ball of fire... I thought later when I was growing up that these were vague memories of the Blitz... I thought...' She began to cry. Large silent tears rolled down her cheeks, and it was Thomas who took her in his arms, forestalling the others as they started to come around the table.

'You are safe now,' he said. She leaned into him as if all her energy had disappeared.

'You are home,' Amelia said.

'We won't let you go again,' Lucy said.

'Maybe Hilary wouldn't have died if she had

known one of her children was still alive,' Lucy said.

'But she knew I was born, didn't she?' Amelia objected. 'And she died anyway.'

'That's true,' Lucy said. 'That is true. I wasn't thinking properly. I forgot. It is so difficult to see anything clearly right now. Everything is in turmoil. It's almost like a repetition of the chaos that happened at the time of the crash.'

'Do you think Breda – Georgina – can handle this?' Amelia asked.

'I don't know,' Lucy said. 'I really don't know. I don't know how we can handle it, so I've no idea if she can.'

Breda had gone to the bathroom to wash her face, and to try to get rid of the redness around her eyes, to put cold water on the back of her neck, to be in silence for a few moments as she tried to take in what had been told to her.

'We need to go back to her home with her,' Thomas said. 'Lucy, Amelia – one of you if not both. But I'd like to come too.'

It was the following day when Thomas contacted Rhino and told him what had unfolded, and asked him if he could get Mattie over to the farmhouse, as Amelia needed to talk to her on the phone, but wanted an adult there to support her just in case.

An hour and a half later, Mattie was on the phone from Rhino's place.

'Hello there,' she said to Amelia. She sounded very cheerful. 'Is everyone well? Settling in? Comfortable? Who's in my bedroom? What's that

496

little scallywag Charlotte up to?'

And before Amelia had the chance to say anything, Mattie continued. 'Do you know something? I've been spending time with old Cyclops, and he isn't half bad, but don't say that to Lucymem. I can understand her crossness, but by himself, when Rhino is at work, Cyclops is a bit of a laugh. My car broke down the other day, and he came and picked me up. Now he's driving me to work in the morning and collecting me in the evening. You wouldn't believe it. He suggested we went out on his boat – he got a new one. But I'm not going to. Work is great. I've got big plans.'

'Mattie,' Amelia finally managed to interrupt her. She had never heard Mattie so enthusiastic or so happy. 'I have to talk to you. Could you just listen? Please...'

So Mattie listened. She listened in complete silence as Amelia told her what had happened.

'Have you spoken to Sheila Mangan?' Mattie finally asked.

'Yes. We went back with Georgina last night – Lucymem, Thomas and me.'

'And...?'

'She admitted it. Straight away. She said she knew it was going to come out – ever since we had appeared in the hospital she knew there was no way we would go away.'

There was a long silence on the phone.

'Mattie, talk to me,' Amelia said. 'I need to know what you are thinking.'

'I'm not sure I'm thinking anything,' Mattie said. 'I don't know what to think.'

'That's how I felt at first. I couldn't take it in.

But I'm beginning to. It gets easier to understand each day.'

'I'm supposed to understand this?' Mattie asked, her voice now angry.

'Maybe that's the wrong word,' Amelia said. 'Would you like to talk to Georgina? She's here, you know.'

'No, can I talk to Lucymem?' Mattie said.

Amelia put Lucy on the phone.

'Yes, it's true,' she heard Lucy say. 'Georgina needs time too you know... No, she's not sure what she wants to do. She's obviously very upset... Do you want to come over for a bit?... No, of course I understand you have just started work... Well, maybe as soon as you can take some time off...'

'We need to be strong for each other,' Thomas said. 'Rhino will look out for Mattie. Whatever bad blood has been between them, the irony is that he will help someone who is in a weak position, regardless of who they are. That's what he does best. He will be there for Mattie.'

Amelia was aware that it was Thomas who was holding them together over that first week.

'When we are all ready, especially when Georgina is ready, we can report this to the authorities. It should all be fairly straightforward now that Sheila Mangan is prepared to admit it.'

Georgina did not want her mother prosecuted.

'I love her,' she said. 'She is my mother – the only one I remember. I can't find any way around this in my head, but I don't want her going to prison. I don't think I ever want to see her again.

I feel such emotions, but I don't know what they are.'

'You will stay here,' Lucy said. 'There will be time to see it all clearly, and time for us to get to know you.'

It was Charlotte who made things easier. She had such a loving nature and was so excited that she had a new cousin. She went and sat on Georgina's knee at every opportunity.

'I'm feeling quite deprived, Charlie,' Thomas said to her. 'I never get hugged by you these days.'

'Come and sit with us,' Charlotte said, beckoning to the place on the sofa beside her, and when he came over, she slipped off Georgina's lap and went to Amelia, as if linking them all in her childlike way. And they connected. The bonds that had come into existence on the evening Breda had been hit by the car tightened and strengthened as Georgina moved into their London home.

EPILOGUE

It was ten years later and Amelia, pregnant with her third child, was sitting in the garden of Ithaca. She remembered her father picking a wasp from his gin and tonic, believing it had drowned. It had not.

It was merely drunk on the fermented juniper berries, unable to believe its luck, rescued by a lemon on which it momentarily rested until her father's long fingers plucked it from his glass and placed it on the palm of his hand for her sister Mattie to admire.

She had been resting with her eyes closed, and she opened them now to see her husband picking a wasp from his gin and tonic with long careful fingers.

'Ulli, it's not dead,' she said suddenly, and he immediately shook it from his hand on to the grass.

'Thank you,' he said. 'It certainly looked dead. I was going to show it to Harriet.' Harriet looked from one parent to the other and then at the wasp, which was now crawling on the grass.

Ulrich stepped on it. 'Just putting it out of its misery,' he explained to his eldest daughter.

She looked up at him with her large eyes, but she said nothing.

'It was the kindest thing to do,' he said to her. 'Come, let's play croquet. It's time I taught you.'

He fetched two mallets, one of a normal length and the tiny one that Amelia had played with as a child, and which her father had shortened for Mattie.

'The top of that is very rough,' Amelia said to him.

He went back to the tool shed and got a piece of sandpaper and he polished it smooth. 'I meant to do that long ago,' he said, handing the tiny mallet to the four-year-old Harriet. 'Now, Harriet, how is that?'

Harriet was dressed in white shorts and T-shirt with white runners on her feet. Her white sun hat was lying on the table.

The lawn was the brightest green, carefully tended by the now aged Feilim the gardener. The croquet hoops were arranged on the slope at the end where they had always been when Amelia was a child.

Harriet followed her father down the grass and, in trying to take a swing at the ball, she nearly fell over from the weight of the head of the mallet.

'Champion,' Ulrich said.

Amelia, watching them, had a sense of déjà vu, and she picked up her glass of lemonade and sipped it. She swivelled her wedding ring round on her finger and stared at it with vacant eyes. She was finding the summer long and hot and difficult to deal with. The final weeks of pregnancy lay heavy on her, but none the less she looked down the garden and smiled at Ulrich and her eldest daughter at the edge of the dunes engrossed in their play.

There was something exceptional about that

day. It was not merely hot, it was sweltering, and there was a dull heaviness in the air making any kind of movement difficult. Heidi lay at her feet. She too seemed overcome by lethargy.

It was Amelia's birthday.

On the table in front of her lay a pile of papers weighed down with a book. There was something strangely haunting about the day and she put her hand on her heavily gravid stomach and smiled as she felt tiny feet kicking inside her.

'Are you all right?' Ulrich called to her, seeing her movement and how she placed her hands across her swollen abdomen.

'Never better,' she replied. She removed the book from the pile of papers and went back to what she had been doing, which was amalgamating Lucas's line drawings into the book of legends that she had written, and which had been accepted for publication. Lucas, now a doctor, still drew as a hobby, and she loved his work. She was absorbed in her activity, only partially aware of the thud of ball and mallet and the occasional squeak from Harriet.

'Should I waken Athena?' Ulrich called.

'We could leave her another half-hour or so,' Amelia replied, looking up to see Harriet giving her mallet an extremely hard swing. The mallet flew from her hand and landed some distance away.

'Did you see that?' Ulrich called. 'It's cricket I should be teaching you, Harriet. You'll be a fast bowler if that throw is anything to go by.'

Amelia, listening to his words, suddenly shivered. There was something wrong but she could not put her finger on it.

She picked up a letter from the table, and slid the folded sheet of paper from it and began to read again.

Dear Amelia,

How strange to think that I am about to return after all these years to find my Ithaca. I know it's been arranged so many times, and I know that I must have annoyed you by my consistent change of plan. But it never seemed right. I don't know why – of course that isn't true. I do know why and so do you. I have envied you your ease with life, your accepting nature, your ability to handle what others – well, what I at least – could not cope with.

I did two things in my life that I have never been able to forgive myself for – I let go Georgina's hand, but you know that. The other you don't know. I put diesel in the spare canister on Cyclops' boat. In case you didn't know, his was a petrol engine. I did tell Lucas recently – he took me out to dinner a month ago. He is well, thriving in fact. He was forgiving. I did not seek forgiveness, though. The burden of guilt ... and there is no atonement.

I never said to you, although you asked, I am at peace with Thomas being married to Georgina. More than 'at peace' – I am glad. It is rather like Lucymem marrying Roger Farrington – maybe it was just supposed to happen that way.

My plan is to fly to France where I have to visit a petard factory, and I will bring with me sufficient fireworks to give Charlotte that display

I always promised her. I will be there in time for your birthday dinner.

Please give my love to everyone, those I know and those I don't... I thought of Grandfather the other day. I came across a book of Tennyson's poetry in a shop and I remembered him reading to us in the evenings. Do you remember that? It's not like me to wax poetical but I am going to.

Life piled on life
Were all too little, and of one to me
Little remains; but every hour is saved
From that eternal silence, something more,
A bringer of new things;

I'm sure you follow.

I always meant to tell you, you have been a good sister.

Amelia had read and reread the letter many times over the previous few days. While its content disturbed her, it also thrilled her. She felt love and acceptance in it, and was sure that this time Mattie was going to come. She had always known that Mattie had done something to the boat. There had been no surprise when she had read that line. It was in the past. There was no point in dwelling on it. It was over, and at least Lucas knew.

'I'm so excited,' Amelia called to Ulli. 'It's actually going to happen. Mattie this afternoon, and Georgina arriving this evening.'

'And Uncle Thomas?' Harriet said.

'And Uncle Thomas,' Amelia replied. 'He's coming with Georgina.'

'I was thinking,' Ulrich said, 'that we could drive up into the mountains this afternoon and maybe we will see Mattie coming in.'

Mattie had finally learned to fly a plane in North Africa. Friedrich had gone with her and helped her put in the hours she needed to get her licence. This was to be her first solo flight from somewhere in the north of France to Ireland, to celebrate Amelia's birthday. Now the owner of her own petard factory in Malta, she was a highly successful businesswoman.

'I can't wait for them both to be here,' Amelia said. 'You know they have never come here ... never returned ... and each has always thought she was the only one to pull out, not knowing that the other had done the same. We are actually going to be all together – the three of us.'

'I know,' Ulrich said gently, coming and putting an arm around her shoulders. 'This is special. I know that. I'm sorry my parents aren't here to see this reunion. They would never have taken off for Austria if they had thought there was the remotest chance of this finally happening.'

Amelia nodded. She knew that. She rather wished they were here because their presence always comforted her. She had never imagined what it would be like being a daughter-in-law and having parents-in-law involved in her life. But the love the Schmitzes felt for her had pulled her up short and filled the aching holes that had always been there. Each time Mattie and Georgina were due to come, each pulled out at the last moment, using work as an excuse. Six or seven times it had happened and each time was followed by silence from Malta until Mattie was able to make contact again, and a corresponding silence from Georgina.

Thomas always telephoned, always asked forbearance, always explaining that Georgina was still not ready. And every time Amelia kept the links going, made the right noises, reassured them all, told them when they were ready... It seemed almost impossible to believe that it was about to happen, and that the three sisters would finally meet again – this time as sisters.

On one level, being a pragmatist, Amelia doubted it. But Mattie had phoned from the north of France the previous evening and it looked as if she really was coming – in her own dramatic way, of course, solo-flying a plane. Her phone call reinforced the content of the letter and affirmed Amelia's belief that they would meet again at last.

'Should we waken Athena?' Ulli called again to Amelia.

Looking up, Amelia saw her cousin Charlotte coming out through the French windows carrying Athena.

'No need,' she replied.

Charlotte was now eighteen, a slip of a girl with her mother Lucy's fine-boned features and the same straight blonde hair. Athena, in her arms, was clinging on to her and making gurgling sounds.

'Charlie,' Harriet called, dropping her little mallet and running up the grass. 'Carry me too. Carry me too.'

Obligingly Charlotte passed Athena to Ulrich and lifted Harriet off the ground. 'You're getting bigger and bigger,' she said to her, tickling her under her arms.

Harriet giggled and squirmed but did not try to escape.

Amelia laughed.

'We're going to go up the mountains,' Ulrich said to Charlotte, 'and we're going to wave Mattie in. I think she should be flying over them at about four o'clock.'

'Will we see her flying?' Harriet asked.

'We might do. I hope so, anyway. She's flying on to Dublin and then your Aunt Karla is going to fetch her and bring her back here. They'll be here in time for dinner,' Ulrich replied.

'I've never met Aunt Karla,' Harriet said, a question in her voice.

'No, you haven't,' her father affirmed. 'Your Aunt Karla has been living in South America for years now. This is her first visit home in a long time.'

'And Karla has never met Mattie, Thomas or Georgina,' Amelia said. 'Oh, I'm so looking forward to us all being together. It's such a pity Lucymem couldn't come too,' Amelia said.

'I think she and Roger assumed it would fall through like it always has in the past,' Charlotte explained.

They had a late lunch in the garden – salad and ham, and bread that Amelia had baked. As Charlotte cut the bread on the garden table, Amelia thought of something – something that linked this moment with some other one somewhere, maybe long ago, but she could not think what it was.

'Did you bake this?' Ulrich asked her.

'Yes,' she said slowly. 'I did.'

'It's wonderful.'

She smiled at him, pleased at his approbation, pleased with the bread she had baked, and she basked in the moment, so aware of his love.

'Are you all right, my darling?' he asked.

She nodded, but she was unsure. The heat of the day had become oppressive, and the baby inside her became still. Amelia could not eat. She drank water and sat back in her chair under the parasol and watched the others. Heidi, still lying close to her, seemed for once, more interested in her than in food. Her large inquisitive eyes watched Amelia closely. Normally they followed the progress of food from cooker to plate, from plate to mouth – now they did not stray from Amelia's pale face.

Charlotte cut Athena's ham into tiny pieces, and Harriet insisted on cutting her own. Both used their fingers to eat, and Amelia smiled, watching their individual dependence balanced against their independence. It was how it should be, she thought.

At a quarter-past three, Ulrich lifted the girls into the car, Harriet bemoaning the fact that she was being put in the back, Athena laughing in glee at something undetermined.

Charlotte said she would stay behind. 'I'll hold the fort,' she said.

Amelia kissed her before getting into the front seat.

'Are you sure you don't want to come with us?' she asked.

508

'I'll clean up here,' Charlotte said. 'It's too hot for me to come in the car with you.'

On the drive at the foot of the mountains they passed a woman walking alone.

'Careful,' Amelia said.

'Careful of what?' Ulrich asked.

'Didn't you see her?' Amelia said. 'There was a woman – back there. You nearly hit her.'

'I didn't see anyone,' he said.

They drove on, uphill towards the place where Amelia had been born.

'Ulli,' she said in a small voice.

'Yes?' He glanced at her. 'What's wrong?'

'Ulli, I think we should go back home,' Amelia replied.

The wind whipped up and there were storm clouds gathering in the south. Heavy and gloomy, the sky appeared to change above them, with cloud rolling in and filling the heavens with an ominous darkness.

'Please, Ulli,' she said, her voice sounding almost childlike. 'I want to go home.'

He stopped the car and looked at her carefully, his green eyes taking in her pallor. He twisted in his seat and brought a finger up to her cheek, caressing the curve of her face.

'Talk to me,' he said. 'I don't know what's wrong. We can leave you here in the car, you know, and I'll take the girls up higher and maybe we'll see Mattie. It would be fun.'

Amelia twisted her fingers round and round each other. 'I think we should go back home,' she repeated.

'All right, my darling,' he said to her. 'We'll turn round and go back home.'

They were almost back at Ithaca when the thunder started, roll after roll of it with forked lightning splitting the skies in the distance. Ulrich pulled into the driveway and parked in front of the house. Helping Amelia from the car, he stopped and looked towards the mountains. They were barely visible in the darkened sky with its menacing clouds, and it was only in the flashes of lightning that they were clearly to be seen.

Charlotte and Heidi came out on to the front steps.

Amelia, holding Ulli's hand as she got out of the car, turned to see what he was looking at. Claps of thunder echoed round and round them. She leaned against him momentarily as they stared across the fields.

Suddenly there was an almighty noise, louder than the thunder, and a ball of fire rose in billowing waves through the dark sky in the distance. It was followed by hundreds of shooting sparks in a firework display of proportions never seen in the mountains before.

And then there was peace.

The publishers hope that this book has given you enjoyable reading. Large Print Books are especially designed to be as easy to see and hold as possible. If you wish a complete list of our books please ask at your local library or write directly to:

Magna Large Print Books
Magna House, Long Preston,
Skipton, North Yorkshire.
BD23 4ND

This Large Print Book for the partially sighted, who cannot read normal print, is published under the auspices of

THE ULVERSCROFT FOUNDATION